Heat[...] [...]ough-Walden was born in California and started writi[...] [...]e age of five. She has written more than a dozen nove[...] [...]t stories and poems. Her award-winning paranormal roma[...] [...]illers have achieved huge online success and record-breal[...] [...]les of over half a million copies. Heather loves to travel and l[...] [...]n all over the world. She currently lives in Texas with her h[...] [...]d and daughter.

*Deat[...] [...]gel* is the third novel in Heather's *The Lost Angels* series. The [...] wo novels, *Avenger's Angel* and *Messenger's Angel*, were high[...] [...]sed:

'Wit[...] [...]aunch of her new *Lost Angels* series, Killough-Walden offer[...] [...]ers a sizzling novel populated with highly intriguing char[...] [...] not the least of which is the "villain." Good story pacin[...] [...]evable characters and sizzling sex add up to an author and [...] [...]to watch!' Jill M. Smith, *Romantic Times Book Reviews*

'*Ave[...] Angel* is a fantastic addition to the paranormal romance genr[...] [...]h sexy Archangels and a strong, beautiful heroine. The worl[...] [...]triguing and the action is fast-paced. I for one can't wait to re[...] [...]ure instalments. Fans of paranormal romance will lap this [...] [...]great start to a new paranormal romance series' Book Chic[...] [...]

'HK[...] [...]ost Angels* series is going to create an entire new para[...] [...] on the subject of Angels and in particular one specific fallen angel we all know well. Over the course of the book each and every one of the characters managed to worm their way into my affections, and I am eagerly looking forward to the next books in the series so that I can spend more time with them' Sugar & Spice

'An enjoya[...] [...]develop human syr[...] [...]e blurred' Book Savv[...]

D0273791

Titles in Heather Killough-Walden's *The Lost Angels* series:

Always Angel (an ebook novella)
Avenger's Angel
Messenger's Angel
Death's Angel

THE LOST ANGELS

# DEATH'S ANGEL

## HEATHER KILLOUGH-WALDEN

First published in 2012 by
HEADLINE PUBLISHING GROUP

1

Cataloguing in Publication Data is available from the British Library

ISBN 978 0 7553 8045 9

Typeset in Fournier by Avon DataSet Ltd, Bidford-on-Avon, Warwickshire

Printed and bound by CPI Group (UK) Ltd, Croydon, CR0 4YY

Headline's policy is to use papers that are natural, renewable and recyclable
products and made from wood grown in sustainable forests. The logging and
manufacturing processes are expected to conform to the environmental
regulations of the country of origin.

HEADLINE PUBLISHING GROUP
An Hachette UK Company
338 Euston Road
London NW1 3BH

www.headline.co.uk
www.hachette.co.uk

# Dedication

I would like to dedicate this book and all of the dark, sexy magic within it to the people in my life who encourage me, inspire me, and believe in me the most when it comes to creating something so incredibly hot that the entire world begins to sweat.

Cherie Brewster, Brittany Weidenfeller, Lauren Duarte, Aspen Arnold, Amanda Sue, Aleah Flowers, Crystal Shannon and Maria Lakhouili, this is for your loyalty, your kindness, and for helping to spread the word about my work by creating swag, doing street team work, and being there for other readers. You're the irrefutable proof that I have the world's most wonderful fans.

Mary, Susan S, Susan L, Tricia, Kelly, Meagan, Jeannine, and Christy, this is for your friendship. You have no idea how precious it is to me.

Mom and Dad, sister and brothers, this is for the strength that comes in family, the loyalty that comes in blood, and because you always ask me how I'm doing.

Eric, this is for everything. You are my archangel.

And you, little girl, my tiniest angel, my Bella Lucia. This book is dedicated most of all to you. Because you love vampires.

# Acknowledgments

*Death's Angel* is a book that encompasses some of the things my heart holds *most* dear, not the least of which is the city in which it takes place. For this reason, I would like to begin my acknowledgments page by thanking the city of San Francisco. Thank you, Bay City, for your pizzazz, your dimension, your mysteries and thrills, and your unbelievable majesties. Thank you, Golden Gate Park, for your four-leaf clovers. Thank you, Ocean Beach, for your sand-dollar angels. Thank you, Pier 39, for your sights and sounds and ever welcoming presence. Thank you, Susan at South Beach Marina Apartments, for your enormous smile and tremendous warmth. And thank you, Golden Gate Bridge. For obvious reasons.

I would like to thank my agent and Trident Media for believing in me and helping to make this print series a possibility. I would also like to thank my publishers for the same. ☺

As always — and forever — thanks to the people I love and who love me for doing all of the necessary, priceless things that make it possible for me to write my books.

That means you, my readers, who stand staunchly beside me, steadfastly support me, and provide me with the emotional sustenance every author needs.

That means you, my guardian muses, who stimulate and motivate, guide and kindle, reviving my artist's soul and provoking the faithful flourish of my pen.

That means you, my family and blood, the boomerangs of life's roller-coaster ride who always come back to take my hand, no matter how hard you've been thrown.

And most of all, that means *you*, husband, my unflagging Gibraltar, my port in every storm. I love you. Thank you.

# Introduction

Long ago, the Old Man gathered together his four favoured archangels, Michael, Gabriel, Uriel, and Azrael. He pointed to four stars in the sky that shone brighter than the others. He told the archangels that he wished to reward them for their loyalty and had created for them soul mates. Four perfect female beings – archesses.

However, before the archangels could claim their mates, the four archesses were lost to them and scattered to the wind, beyond their realm and reach. The archangels made the choice to leave their world, journey to Earth, and seek out their mates.

For thousands of years, the archangels have searched. But they have not searched alone. For they are not the only entities to leave their realm and come to Earth to hunt for the archesses. They were followed by another . . .

# Prologue

*Two thousand years ago . . .*

Michael gripped the rock in his right hand so hard that his fingers left imprints in the stone. Azrael heard it crack. Michael's jaw was clenched tight, his eyes shut fast against the pain Az knew to be coursing through his veins.

Azraél could feel that pain as if it were his own. It was there because of him.

The woods were sparse this far north and Az knew that the ground beneath his brother grew colder and harder for him as the strength was sapped from his inhuman body. Azrael's fangs were embedded deep in the side of Michael's throat, and with each pull and swallow, Michael experienced a new and deeper agony.

'Az . . . that's enough,' Michael ground out, hissing the words through gritted teeth.

*I'm sorry*, thought Az. He didn't speak the words, but whispered them into his brother's mind. They were laced with genuine regret. Az had yet to pull out and stop drinking Michael down. He *couldn't* stop.

For not the first time in the two weeks since they'd come to Earth, Az felt his brother's mounting fear and knew that

Michael would soon have to use force against him. It was an inevitable tragedy.

Az watched through eyes that glowed bright gold beneath half-closed lids as Michael raised the rock he tightly clutched, and after another grimace and wince of pain, slammed the stone into the side of Azrael's head. Az knew it was coming; he'd registered his brother's thought long seconds before the deed had been done. But he still hadn't been able to pull away. He needed the blood so badly.

At the impact, Az was knocked to the side and his teeth were ripped from Michael's throat, tearing long gashes in his brother's flesh. Az toppled sideways, catching himself on strong but shaking arms.

Across from him, Michael dropped the rock to cup his hand to the side of his neck. 'Az,' he gasped, 'I'm sorry.' He slowly rolled over, propping himself on one elbow as he attempted to heal the damage Az had done. That was Michael's gift – the ability to heal.

Azrael's gift? The ability to harm. It seemed that was all he would ever be able to do.

Light and warmth grew beneath Michael's palm, sending curative energy into his wound. Az watched him in silence, his head lowered, his long sable hair concealing his features from Michael's sight.

'Az?' Michael let his hand drop from his neck, his wound obviously healed.

'Stop, Michael,' said Az. 'I can't bear it.'

The blond archangel closed his eyes as the other-worldly sound of Azrael's voice infiltrated his mind and body. Az scraped his brother's mind, reading his surface thoughts. He was desperate for some fleeting word or phrase that might distract him from the endless torture his existence had become.

Michael was thinking that Azrael had a beautiful voice.

It almost made Az laugh. He had always had an incredible voice. But now, in this bizarre and horrible form he had taken on Earth, it was more powerful than it had ever been. This much Azrael had to admit. He had become a monster – but a monster with a voice like no other.

Michael was also thinking that he could hear the despair in that voice.

Of course he could. It was plainly evident. How could it not be? Az was desperate. He despaired as no living creature ever had.

Michael opened his eyes again and looked upon his brother's bent form. 'This pain you're going through can't last much longer,' he said softly.

'A single moment longer is too long,' Az whispered. Slowly, and with great effort, he straightened. He raised his head so that his brother could see his stark, unnatural gaze, and Michael stilled beneath the weight of it. 'Kill me,' Azrael said.

Michael steeled himself and shook his head. 'Never.'

Az didn't know why he'd bothered asking. If any one of the four archangel brothers could have summoned the will to kill the other, it would not have been Michael or even Azrael, but rather Uriel. He was the Angel of Vengeance. Only Uriel would be capable of comprehending what it would take to smother reason long enough to deal the final blow Azrael begged for.

But Uriel was not with them. He and their other brother, Gabriel, had been lost in their plummet to Earth. The four archangels had been separated and scattered, like dried and dead leaves on a hurricane wind. Azrael had no idea where the others were, much less what they might be going through. He didn't care.

He only knew that he had gone through a transformation as he'd taken on this human form. Both he and Michael had, and he assumed the other two had as well – wherever they were.

Michael was not as powerful as he'd been before their descent. The nature of his supernatural powers was the same, more or less. He was still the most accomplished fighter Azrael had ever known – and, most likely, the most accomplished that had ever been created. He was also still capable of healing. But the *scope* of his powers had diminished greatly. He was able to affect only what was immediately around him, and only for a relatively short period of time. His body grew weary. He knew hunger. He often felt weak. He had changed drastically.

But not as much as Azrael.

As the former Angel of Death, Azrael experienced a change that was different from Michael's. It was darker. It was painful. It was as if this new form were steeped in the negative energy he had collected during his endless prior existence. As the reaper in the field of mortal spirits, Azrael had ushered away so very many lives. There was a weight to that many souls, and they carried him down with them now. His altered form bore the fangs of a monster, a sensitivity to sunlight that forced him to hide in the shadows of night, and worst of all, a demand for blood.

Always blood.

'Please, Michael.' Azrael's broad shoulders shook slightly

as he curled his hands into fists and the powerful muscles in his upper body drew taut and pronounced. He glanced down at his hands, slim-fingered and perfect, and marveled at his pale skin. He knew what it looked like against the midnight color of his hair. He was a study in contradiction. Even his eyes were wrong. The sun was caustic to him – and yet his irises glowed like the very same star.

He was a living joke, cruel and merciless. Vicious anger now joined the pain-induced adrenaline flooding his inhuman blood. He gritted his teeth, baring his blood-soaked fangs. '*Don't make me beg.*'

Michael got his legs beneath him and stood. He backed up against one of the few trees in the area and opened his mouth to once more refuse his brother's request . . . when Azrael suddenly blurred into motion.

Michael's body slammed hard against the tree's trunk and the living wood splintered behind him. He was weaker than he'd been several minutes before; Azrael had seen to that. Blood loss drained precious momentum from the former Warrior Archangel's reflexes. Though Michael was still able to heal his wounds on Earth, for some reason he was not able to replace missing blood. It was a new weakness, especially in the face of Azrael's bloodthirsty new form.

Az and his brother had been here before, locked in combat as they now were. They had been here every night for weeks.

Azrael didn't know how long Michael would be able to engage in this nightly battle with him. Az was very strong. Even half-crazed with pain, he was most likely the strongest of the four of them. The monster that he had become was eating him up inside. It was devouring the core of his being, leaving him an empty shell.

Life was different on Earth. There had been no discomfort before this. No hunger. No thirst. These sensations were novel to them both, but whatever discomfort Michael might be suffering in his human form, Azrael was suffering a thousandfold.

Az knew now that pain had not existed before this. Not in any form. Not for anyone. As far as he was concerned, *suffering*, in and of itself, had been conceived the moment his soul had touched down and solidified into the tall, dark shape it was now.

But he knew that despite what he was putting his brother through, Michael wouldn't give up on him. Not now – not ever. The foolish archangel would probably die first.

With great effort, Michael shoved Azrael off of him, and Az managed to hold himself back long enough to allow his brother to prepare for another senseless fight. Somewhere, Uriel and Gabriel were most likely struggling as well; either with themselves, or with each other. If Az and his brother survived this – if Azrael didn't simply walk into the sun the following morning – they had to find them.

They were on Earth for a reason, though it was nearly impossible for Azrael to contemplate that reason while under the spell of the tormenting affliction of his transformation. The Four Favored archangels had come in order to find their other halves. They'd come for the soul mates that the Old Man had created for them. They'd come to Earth to find their archesses.

If the lacerating chaos that now engulfed him was any indication of how their quest would play out from here, Azrael was certain they didn't stand a chance of finding their archesses until they found one another first. If even then.

And at the moment he couldn't have cared less.

Michael gritted his teeth, narrowed his gaze, and rolled up his sleeves. Azrael came at him like lightning, and like thunder, Michael met him halfway.

## *Eleven years ago . . .*

Sophie gritted her teeth, grimaced at the sharp pain that shot through her knee, and hurriedly pushed herself back up. When she did, the wildflowers she carried in her right hand were once more crushed. She'd lost several petals the last time she'd fallen, but this fall was what really did the damage. The sweat from her palm was wilting the stems of the buttercups, sweet dame's rockets, and star-of-Bethlehems. The second fall had almost entirely mulched the highly delicate sweet white violets.

But she didn't have time to pick more. With a worried glance over her shoulder, Sophie pushed off once again. At fourteen years of age, she had legs that were suddenly longer than they should be. Normally that made her look like a doll on stilts, but this afternoon she was incredibly grateful for the added height. Her stilts carried her on a mad dash through Greenwood Cemetery, toward the headstone and empty flower vase she knew waited just over the next hill.

He was close behind. She could hear him grunting. He couldn't move fast without grunting. He made noises when he ran, just like he made noises doing everything else. He snored when he slept and wheezed when he ate and seemed to be enveloped in a permanent whistling, which was caused by the extra thickness around his neck and nasal passages.

Sophie heard those sounds in her nightmares. But right now, they served as a warning. She could hear him clearly over the fog-dampened hills. Each sloppy crunch of his tennis shoes and each subsequent *humph, humph, humph* was an alarm bell warning of his pending arrival.

She had a hundred yards to go. She felt it like a magnet on her blood. Her heart raced and her eyes watered and the grass's unevenness jarred her joints, but she pushed harder. Faster. Seventy yards to go. She could almost see it now. Mom would be there, waiting. She would be wearing an orange zip-up hoodie, like she always did. Dad would be sitting on the stone, gesturing animatedly as he talked to his wife – who wouldn't be listening because she was looking for her daughter. She was always looking out for Sophie, waiting for her to come over that last rise.

Fifty yards to go—

'Sophie! Get back here, you fucking little cunt!' Her pursuer's voice cut through the fog, slicing through her reveries like a chain saw through flesh. It was brutish and out of breath and utterly cruel. He was mad now. Madder than she'd ever heard him. 'I swear to God I'm gonna kill you, you little bitch!' he hissed. She heard him slip and slide on a wet spot at the bottom of the hill and she pushed harder.

Faster.

Thirty yards to go, and there it was, its rounded top peeking through the swirling mists like a lighthouse in a fog. It had several small stones atop it – left there from Sophie's previous visits.

'Stop!' he bellowed, each extra foot he was forced to run making him that much angrier. But Sophie didn't stop.

Her mother was waiting.

There she was, in her favorite color, smiling warmly at Sophie as Sophie ran from the monster, tears streaming down her cheeks, her jeans torn, her knees bloodied. There she was, waving in welcome, her caramel-colored hair shining in sunlight that came from nowhere.

Sophie called out to her. She wanted her mother to hear her. She wanted her to know that Sophie had tried. The rim of the metal vase at her mother's feet peeked out of the mist, beckoning.

But the beast was gaining and her mother didn't seem to hear. The crunching was too close now. *Humph, humph, humph—*

*No!*

The back of Sophie's shirt ripped, nearly choking her into instant unconsciousness as her foster father grabbed her by the garment and jerked her to a violent stop, spinning her around with the momentum. The two of them went down hard, Sophie landing on her arm and destroying what remained of the wildflowers she had picked for her mother's birthday. She wanted to cry out with the pain of the impact, but she had learned long ago not to appear hurt in front of the predator.

Never let them smell your blood.

'What the fuck do you think you're doing? I'll teach you—' He was up and pulling her with him before Sophie could see past the stars that swam in front of her eyes. 'Disgusting little troublemaking whore. You aren't worth a shit.'

His fingers bruised the flesh of her arm as he began to make his way back across the cemetery, dragging Sophie with him. She ignored the pain and looked back at the waiting headstone. Her mother was gone. For the first time in eight years, there was no shot of orange above the stone. It stood empty and alone. Even the pebbles Sophie had left seemed smaller than before.

The graveyard mists turned red, shrouding the cemetery in scarlet contrasts. 'No!' Sophie screamed. She didn't even realize she was the one yelling. Before either of them knew what she was doing, Sophie had jerked out of her foster father's grip. His grubby fingernails dug furrows in her upper arm as she pulled free and stumbled backward. 'No!' she cried out again, fury boiling her blood and painting the landscape crimson. 'Get away from me!' She took a shaky step back, rage causing her to tremble uncontrollably.

Her mom was gone. She'd lost her flowers. And the grave marker stood empty on her mother's birthday.

Alan Harvey stared at Sophie with wide eyes. Something strange flickered across his unshaven features. Maybe it was surprise – maybe something else. His gaze shot to her neck and then to her shoulder, exposed and white where he had ripped her shirt free of her body. 'Why, you little tramp,' he hissed, his voice different now, too. It had lowered and was gravelly with an emotion that sent nausea roiling through Sophie's belly. 'You wanna fight me?'

Sophie's legs flooded with numbness. Her stomach cramped and her heart began to beat between her ears. It was the *whoosh-whoosh-whoosh* of utter terror and it threatened to overwhelm her. She was alone with him. This part of the cemetery was deserted.

She'd pushed him too far.

Her vision tunneled as Harvey took a threatening step

toward her. This was it. He was going to rape and kill her out here. He wouldn't have to travel far in order to bury her body.

*I'm gonna die*, she thought. *This is it.*

When he lunged at her, she was too numb, too heavy with fear to move out of his way in time. Her world became a thump and a whir of pain and motion. Something crunched beneath her as she went down again. She felt the corner of a burial plaque bruise her spine and hip.

Harvey's fingers curled into the waistband of her jeans – and suddenly, Sophie's fourteen-year-old body was moving of its own accord. Her leg came up as if controlled by someone else. Her bloodied, bruised knee connected with his groin, digging hard and fast and deep.

But it wasn't enough to dislodge his body from hers. Harvey grunted as he continued to paw at her. He always grunted. He was so heavy. Her wrists twisted and her fingers went numb as she dug her fingernails into his skin, trying to claw him off of her. Her hands slapped and pulled and punched. Harvey's palm found the side of her face, but she felt no pain. She heard the impact and her head moved a little and there was warm metal in her mouth running rivers over her tongue. But there was no pain.

She just kept fighting. Finally, her right knuckle banged something hard and cold. Metal. She knew instantly what it was. It was Harvey's gun – he owned a gun. She didn't know where he'd gotten it, but he loved to take it out and clean it and load it and unload it and wear it tucked into his pants. Like it was now. It formed an indentation in the pudge of his belly where it separated flab from denim. Sophie wrapped her numb fingers around it, forcing them to grip it tight.

She yanked and knew that the hammer sliced into him as she pulled it out.

She didn't get it far before he realized what she was doing and tried to grab it out of her hands. So she took a chance. Anything was better than this. If the barrel was pointed at her, so be it.

Sophie pulled the trigger.

# Chapter 1

*Present day*

*H*e's an archangel, Sophie told herself sternly as she tried with all her might not to fidget. She stared up the long aisle of decorated chairs to the altar before Slains Castle in Scotland. Azrael stood there beside the groom, and to her, he was the epitome of everything desirable in a man. His incredibly tall, imposing form was draped in the color of night and it was tailored to fit his extraordinary physique with absolute perfection. His sable hair fell in gentle waves to his shoulders and made Sophie's fingertips itch with the need to touch it. His skin was so fair it was nearly translucent. He looked like a vampire lord in his expensive tux, his gold eyes nearly glowing in their intensity, and it was making her a little nuts inside.

Juliette Anderson, Sophie's best friend, was getting married. Sophie was the maid of honor. It was her job to stand there and be supportive, to take the bouquet and carry the train and all of that business. But as the vicar gave his Gaelic blessing to the gathered members of the wedding party and the pipers poured their bittersweet music across the castle grounds, Sophie could concentrate on nothing but Azrael.

Azrael, the archangel.

Juliette had told Sophie all about him. He and his three brothers were the Four Favored, the Old Man's favorite archangels. Jules had hammered Soph with the news about them mere hours after Sophie had stepped off the plane in Edinburgh. Sophie had had her own news that she'd been wanting to share with Juliette for the last three weeks, but when she'd seen the look on Juliette's face and caught the frantically anxious tone in her voice, Sophie's affairs had instantly taken a backseat to Juliette's and they'd remained there ever since.

Gabriel and his brothers were none other than the four most famous archangels in existence: Michael the Warrior Angel, Uriel the Angel of Vengeance, Gabriel the Messenger Angel, and Azrael – the Angel of Death.

*He looks the part*, Sophie thought now as she again stole a surreptitious glance at the beautiful man. He was too handsome. It was the kind of handsome that was difficult to look at. He had a Dorian Gray appearance about him that made her wonder whether he'd sold his soul so that he could look the way he did.

According to Juliette, the Four Favored had come to Earth two thousand years ago in order to find something very precious to them: their mates. It sounded like something out of a werewolf romance, but there it was. Apparently the brother archangels had been given gifts by the Old Man in the form of four perfect *female* archangels. These, he called archesses. Before the archangels could claim them, however, the Old Man sent the archesses to Earth, and there they were scattered – lost to their mates for centuries. Lost, until now.

For some reason, archesses seemed to be popping up all at once. *Well, maybe not all at once*, Sophie reasoned as she dutifully lifted the train of her best friend's gorgeous wedding gown and followed her down the aisle toward the altar. After all, Juliette was only the second archess to be found of the four that had been created. Maybe it was only coincidence that she and the first archess had both made their appearances within months of each other. Still . . . two thousand years without anything, and then in the course of a few months, two archesses appear?

Sophie glanced furtively toward Uriel, the first archangel of the four brothers to have met his archess. He also looked unbelievably handsome in his fitted tux, with his piercing green eyes and wavy dark hair. Uriel had been surprising enough for Sophie to take in because he was also Christopher Daniels, the famous actor who played Jonathan Brakes, the 'good' vampire in the hit movie *Comeuppance*.

Azrael was harder for Sophie to come to grips with. Not only was he literally the most handsome man she had ever laid eyes on, but he was supposedly the lead singer for Valley of Shadow, which was at that moment the most popular rock band in the world.

Once she'd processed the information, she'd realized it made a lot of sense. *Yea, though I walk through the valley of the shadow of death . . . How fitting*, she thought.

As the enigmatic lead singer of Valley, Azrael always took the stage wearing a black mask that hid half of his face from his fans. His voice crooned and hypnotized, pouring out over his audience with immense influence. His identity remained hidden.

Sophie had been a breathless, swooning fan of Valley of

Shadow since its inception. She'd been as mesmerized by the Masked One's physique, charisma, presence, and otherworldly voice as every other woman in the world. When she downloaded his songs to her iPod, she was able to close her eyes and pretend that he was singing to her – and her alone. Hell, she even dreamed of him.

*Oh jeez*, she thought as she flushed with both embarrassment and baffled anticipation at the memory. The bride took her place at the front of the altar and Sophie held her bouquet as the ceremony began. Sophie couldn't believe she was actually standing there a few feet away from the Masked One. To say nothing of the fact that he was also an archangel. The Angel of Death, no less! Her mind spun with the implications.

*He's looking at me*. She could feel the archangel's golden gaze searing into her from where he stood opposite her. She forced herself not to meet his gaze. She couldn't do it again. Every time she glanced up at him, she felt that he was staring right through to her soul, reading her from the inside out, absorbing her very spirit with those piercing orbs of his. It was too much. And yet, even as she knew she shouldn't because of the way it made her feel – she wanted to for the same reason.

She was a moth to the flame.

The vicar called for the rings and Sophie actually felt Azrael's gaze lift. He gracefully pulled the set of heavy gold bands from the inside pocket of his black tux and handed them to the handsome groom. Gabriel took the rings with a very real smile and turned to face his bride.

Sophie found herself transfixed by the image of Gabriel sliding the band onto Juliette's slim finger. The knotted gold Celtic design winked in the moon- and candlelight. The ring fit Juliette perfectly, resting on her hand like a brand, final and complete, and Sophie imagined the tall and enigmatic Azrael sliding a ring on her own finger in the same fashion.

And then she blinked. Her heart thudded hard behind her rib cage. She could almost feel the physical weight of the metal on her finger – and the heat of Azrael's touch on her hand. Where the hell had that image come from? It had appeared out of nowhere, clear as day, and now it was refusing to fade away.

Sophie felt her face flush with embarrassment at the thought. If he only knew what she was fantasizing about in that moment!

With a start, she realized that the ceremony was over. The piper began to play 'Amazing Grace,' and Juliette and Gabriel kissed. The vicar said a few more words in Gaelic – which Juliette seemed to understand – and then she and Gabriel turned to head back down the makeshift aisle.

It was the last night of the full moon. Its blue-white light cast the decorated castle and its grounds in stark, beautiful contrast. Streamers and ribbons of lace and satin had been strung between stone columns and draped over the battlements of Slains Castle so high above them. The waves of the waning tide crashed against the rocks far below, and seagulls sang the last piercing notes of their nightly lullabies.

Roses and lavender scented the air, which was unnaturally warm for this time of year. While the rest of the people who had gathered to see the wedding – namely members of Gabriel's clan – were unaware of the reason behind the unseasonable pleasantness, Sophie knew that the warm weather was due to Eleanore Granger, the first archess found by the Four Favored.

Eleanore was Uriel's archess and possessed powers much like Juliette's — which Sophie was still trying to wrap her head around. Ellie and Jules could both control the weather to some extent, throw things around with telekinesis, manipulate fire where it already existed, and most importantly, they could heal.

It was this power to heal wounds and sicknesses with no more than a touch that really set the archesses apart from every other supernatural creature in the world. And that was another thing Sophie had been forced to take in rather quickly. Apparently, archangels and archesses were not the only ones to inhabit the planet alongside unsuspecting humans. There were others out there — other beings with powers.

Still, none of the other paranormals possessed the ability to mend injuries and pain. That power belonged to the archesses and to Michael and seemed to be limited solely to them.

Juliette had sprung a lot on Sophie, to be sure. But luckily for Jules, Soph could handle it. She didn't have a lot of memories from her early childhood. But what she did have from those precious days, she held on to with unequaled fierceness. She'd had six treasured years with her parents. They'd died in a car accident a week before her sixth birthday. Until that day, Sophie had been in paradise.

Her mother had been an assistant curator at the American Museum of Natural History in New York. Her father had been a pilot. When he was out of town on a job, Sophie's mother would take her to the museum after hours and the two of them would explore ancient Egyptian tombs and tell ghost stories in what Sophie called the Whale Room.

Sophie's mom, Genevieve Bryce, had been a unique woman possessed of an open mind. Nothing was impossible to her. 'There are more things in heaven and earth, Horatio,' she would quote from Shakespeare to Sophie. It was one of the few things she could remember her mother saying. Such things as magic and miracles were not pipe dreams upon which to fantasize, but very real possibilities to Genevieve. This respect for a world greater than human knowledge was passed on to Sophie, even in the six short years she had been with her parents.

Luckily, it was enough; otherwise what Jules had told her over the last few days would have sent Sophie to the loony bin. Or convinced her that *Jules* belonged in one, anyway. If Sophie hadn't been the person she was, Juliette would have had a much more difficult time bringing her best friend into the circle of archangel knowledge.

Now that she was here, witnessing the archangels' immense physical presences and intensely vivid gazes first-hand, she was definitely convinced that magic could exist. To say nothing of what Ellie was doing with her powers.

There was also the small fact that Juliette had actually shown Sophie her wings. Real, honest-to-God wings. Apparently Juliette could control when they appeared and when they didn't, which was fortunate, because the wings were massive, stretching to a good seven or eight feet on either side. Most impressive of all, perhaps, was the fact that the wings were actually *functional*.

That one hurt a little. Sophie was happy for Juliette and all that she'd found in the last few weeks. Jules deserved the best. She was a kind soul and always had been. She was empathetic, understanding and giving, and Sophie was lucky to have her as a best friend. They'd met while in high school and during Sophie's stay with her fifth set of foster parents. As luck would have it, and like so many people who became fast friends, they'd been given lockers right next to each other. Juliette noticed the Jack the Pumpkin King poster in Sophie's locker and mentioned that she was going solo to a Reel Classics replay of *The Nightmare Before Christmas* that Friday night. There was almost no hesitation before she went on to ask Sophie whether she wanted to tag along. And that was it. Their friendship was almost magical, it happened so fast and formed so strong. That Juliette never judged Soph for her past or her lack of a 'real' family or, when they got older, a 'proper' education, was like a gift from the fates to Sophie. She didn't know what she would do without Jules.

And yet, when Juliette spread those magnificent wings of hers and beat the air with them and rose from the cliffside where they'd been standing, Sophie had experienced a pang of something she'd never before felt toward her friend. Jealousy. Envy.

It was a sour, bitter kind of feeling that left a bad taste on her tongue and coiled tightly in the pit of her stomach. She couldn't help it. She would give anything for the ability to leave Earth's bonds and escape all that was trapped below. To rise above it all. She would give *anything*.

Gabriel and Juliette reached the end of the aisle and Gabriel's Scottish friends began tossing flower petals upon the couple. Hundreds of white rose petals cascaded down upon the bride and groom amid shouts of congratulations. It was a heartwarming scene, especially combined with the gorgeous music pouring forth from the pipers who stood like sentinels along the castle walls.

'My best friend's getting married,' she whispered to herself, in awe as the enormity of the event finally hit her. Juliette laughingly pulled rose petals out of her mass of beautiful hair. And then Sophie watched as Juliette's new husband leaned over and kissed her tenderly on the cheek. He closed his eyes, seemingly lost in the wonder that was his new bride.

And Sophie smiled. 'Congrats, Jules. You deserve him.'

Azrael stood still in the men's restroom of the portable guest- and bathhouse that had been erected outside of Slains Castle for his brother's wedding. He was alone, and the air was filled with the hollow sound of foreboding. There was a storm brewing. It was a hurricane, hot and windy and destructive, and it was ripping through Azrael's insides, begging to be released. He exhaled a shaky breath and pressed his forehead to the mirror in front of him, glancing up at his reflection as he did so.

Another human myth gone horribly awry. Vampires did indeed have reflections. It was the wraiths that didn't. Azrael bared his teeth and laughed a cold, hard laugh at the thought. The most asinine things were going through his head at that moment. The thoughts were like fireflies on a pitch-black night, chaotic and useless and utterly distracting.

Sophie's whispered thoughts echoed through his mind, taunting him. *I would do anything*. She'd been thinking about Juliette's wings and wishing she could fly. If she'd had any idea how dangerously tempting her thoughts were . . . To say nothing of her reaction to the image he had so carelessly planted in her mind of the wedding ring sliding onto her finger. He hadn't even meant to do it; he'd simply imagined it. However, he'd been in her head at the time, thoroughly rapt in all that she was, and she'd caught the impression clear as a bell.

Her heart had skipped, her cheeks had flushed, and her lips had actually grown fuller as blood rushed into them. Her eyes had become glassy and unfocused. Her breath had hitched. And Azrael lost a little of his sanity then and there at his brother's wedding.

He'd never felt like this before. Not in his two thousand years on Earth – nor in the thousands upon thousands of years before that in the realm of angels. Never had he lost focus in this manner. He felt like he had the flu. But vampires didn't get the flu. Archangels didn't get the flu. The Angel of Death most certainly did not get the flu.

Azrael swore under his breath – and the mirror in front of him cracked beneath his palm, slicing into the skin of his hand. He blinked and slowly pulled away, straightening as he turned his hand over and gazed down at the welling red line across his palm. Even as he watched, it began to heal.

Azrael looked back up at the mirror and glared at the evidence of his rage. Lightning had indeed carved itself across the glass, a reflection of the storm that raged within him and was now breaking free. *Get control*, he told himself sternly. He was the most powerful vampire on Earth. If he couldn't control his emotions, they would leak out in an incredibly destructive manner. Broken mirrors would be only the beginning.

He needed to think. He needed to plan. But Sophie Bryce was two hundred yards away, a walking, talking piece of the sun, and Azrael was losing it.

The lights in the men's restroom began to flicker, and the shadows in the corners grew longer. The temperature in the room seemed to drop. Thunder rolled in the distance. Again Azrael swore. He was fighting a losing battle. The image in the broken mirror reflected a tall, broad-shouldered man draped in stygian black, his sable hair framing a strikingly handsome face that was entirely too pale. Eyes that were entirely too bright.

And fangs that were entirely too long.

With a great amount of effort, Azrael forced his fangs to recede. He couldn't get rid of them completely; his incisors would always be noticeably sharp and a touch longer than human canines. But with a good deal of concentration, he was able to make them look passable. This was a learned vampire ability; new vampires had to practice at it, and it could sometimes take years.

Azrael would know. When he had left his realm and traveled to Earth with his brothers two thousand years ago, something had happened to him. Michael's theory was that what Azrael had done up until then as the Angel of Death somehow negatively influenced his material form on Earth. Unlike his brothers, Az had been transformed into some kind of supernatural monster.

At the time there was no name for what he was. The fangs, the nearly unquenchable hunger for blood, the new and horrid deadly aversion to the sun – these symptoms had never existed in a being until Azrael came along. He was the first vampire. He gave himself the name because it sounded right.

It took him months to learn to control the hunger inside. It had been a very painful period of time, and in the years since then, he had never forgotten the way it tore him up inside, shredding his soul like tissue paper. Now, every night as he awoke with the stars, he thanked fate that he no longer suffered. He still had to feed. It was necessary for the survival of a vampire that he ingest human blood every night. But his need had become a simple understanding of his physiology – and an acceptance of the same. He considered himself immensely fortunate and never took for granted the fact that he no longer craved and hungered the way he had in those horrid moments of vampiric inception.

But tonight . . .

Now, as Azrael stood in the men's restroom outside of the castle, he was gripped by acidic, mind-numbing fear. Because he felt it again. It was the same driving kind of need – one that shoved every other thought or desire or inclination ruthlessly out of the way and threatened absolute subjugation. Only this time, it was focused. Directed.

He hungered. He craved like a madman. But what he craved and hungered for was Sophie Bryce.

His archess.

# Chapter 2

'Hey, Az? You in here?'

Azrael looked up from where he bent over the sink, his head down, his hands gripping the porcelain with dangerous strength. Michael slowed as he came through the restroom door and caught sight of him. The blond archangel took in Azrael's bent form, saw the reddish glow to his gold eyes, and his expression became wary. 'You okay?' he asked.

For the first time in what seemed like ages, Azrael didn't know what to say. He wasn't sure how to respond to his brother. Was he okay?

Not by a long shot.

He straightened and ran his tongue over his teeth. They were in check. 'I'm fine.'

'You look hungry.'

Azrael went with it. 'I am.' It certainly wasn't a lie.

'You haven't fed tonight?' Michael asked, his brow furrowed. If Azrael had bothered to read his brother's mind at that point, he surely would have heard Michael thinking that it was Gabriel's wedding – it was a big event – and that Az should have taken his meal before attending. Michael was right. And Az *had* fed before coming. He just hadn't planned on the maid of honor being his archess.

27

'I guess it wasn't enough,' he stated simply. His voice was as melodic as ever, but now it had a sharp edge to it.

Michael studied him closely and Azrael kept his features neutral. Michael had always more or less acted as the 'leader' of the four brothers, and for good reason. He was good at leading because he was good at reading others. He didn't need to be able to read Azrael's mind to know that he was lying.

'What aren't you telling me?' Michael asked calmly.

Azrael took a slow, deep breath and turned away from his brother to once more glance at his reflection in the mirror. He could have come clean in that moment. He could have told Michael about Sophie. But he didn't, and there were a thousand reasons why.

Michael was the Old Man's favorite. It was the main bone of contention between the brothers and Samael, the archangel they were consistently at odds with – Michael unwittingly usurping that particular throne. And yet, against all logic, Michael would be the last to find his archess. Why was that? If Az told him about Sophie, Michael would wonder if he'd done something wrong. How had he fallen out of the Old Man's favor?

He would ask, and he would get no answers. The four of them had been involuntarily out of touch with the Old Man since their arrival on Earth. Michael would be left to speculate, and the notion would drive him nuts. That was bad enough. Az didn't want his brother to suffer in such a manner.

To make things worse, Michael would grow antsy and distracted. At the moment, the former Warrior Archangel was a cop for the NYPD. He was understandably their best officer. He was an archangel, after all. Michael alone prevented more homicides and beatings and rapes than all the other members of the precinct combined. It wouldn't be good for him to suddenly become distracted. How many humans would suffer for it?

Then again . . . the archesses were the reason the Four Favored were on Earth to begin with. It was for their mates – and not for the good of the human race – that Azrael and his brothers currently resided on the planet. Where did they draw the line between circumstance and responsibility?

Still, Michael's current lack of an archess wasn't Azrael's only reason for remaining silent about Sophie.

While Az had been standing across from Sophie beside Gabriel and Juliette at the altar, he had dipped into his archess's mind. He hadn't been able to help himself. She was three feet away – and he'd needed to be closer. He couldn't touch her. He couldn't kiss her. He couldn't step forward, wrap her in his dark embrace, and take her to the skies.

So he'd settled for allowing his mind to touch hers instead. At once, the difference between her mind and those of other humans was staggeringly clear. The spirit of an archess was almost painfully complex and bright; like ninety trillion fiberglass lights woven in and out and over and through in a labyrinth of thought and possibility. Unlike sweeping up the dust-mote thoughts of humans, reading an archess or archangel mind took concentration.

Sophie's was even more complex than the others. At first, Azrael hadn't understood why. He'd simply been silently astounded by the impossibly intricate networking of her brain. But as he stood there and tuned the vicar out and concentrated on Sophie, he'd become more clear as to why she posed such a puzzle.

Her surface thoughts made his body come alive with something he'd never felt before. During his existence, he'd experienced pain, yes. He'd felt hunger and sadness, hopelessness and despair. He'd even felt the serenity of resignation that came with the knowledge that these things were a part of life – and, in his case would go on forever.

Then he heard Sophie's words to herself. *He has an archess out there, Soph. You can't have him, no matter how freaking hot he and his long black hair and gold eyes and insanely gorgeous voice are.* At the sound of those softly whispered mental words, Azrael had felt something entirely new. It was a tingly sensation combined with a horrid restlessness that bordered on severe anxiety. It was anticipation. It was happiness. It was hope.

Sophie Bryce was *into* him. He had almost laughed aloud at the realization. It was an incredibly modern endearment and it was such an understatement of a sentiment when compared with the astounding importance of the situation. But that was what had gone through his head nonetheless. And it was something.

However, once Azrael finished relishing the magic of her surface thoughts and began delving deeper, his tingly jubilation was smothered in a blanket of confusion. She was light and warmth on top – and shadows underneath. Sophie hadn't led the easiest life. Her parents had been killed in a car accident when she was six years old. She went from foster home to foster home, each worse than the one before.

It was as if the archess were cursed. She was surrounded by abuse and death, and with each passing year under these circumstances, her mind had woven more mazes for her to get lost in. Ways for her to forget.

There were bits of her past, in fact, that even *he* couldn't reach. Not easily, anyway. He was the Angel of Death and the oldest, most powerful vampire in the world. He could have ripped the memories from her if he'd chosen to, but she would know he was doing it and she would experience them again herself. She would remember things that her mind had obviously wanted her to forget. Azrael wouldn't do such a thing to a normal human being. There was no way in hell he would do it to his archess.

He had taken a mental step back and reined himself in. If she had secrets, he would let her keep them – for now. He'd gleaned enough anyway. He knew now that she had been through so much suffering in her young life, she was officially afraid of the human race, no matter how tough she pretended to be.

Sophie was unnaturally attractive, and that attractiveness had earned her various unpleasant attacks from foster fathers and a few strangers. As a result, Sophie didn't date much. She wasn't physically 'innocent,' but she was as spiritually innocent as they came.

She currently worked as a maid in a hotel due to a lack of higher education, but she longed to one day open her own dance studio where she could teach children.

Children, she trusted. It was an inherent need of hers to surround herself with the happy childhoods that she herself had not been granted.

She had been wounded, and moving too quickly with her would only reopen those wounds.

If Azrael told Michael that Sophie was Az's archess, Michael might intervene. He might do something that made Sophie aware of the situation. Michael didn't like lies. He didn't like secrets. He would come clean with Sophie – about everything – in an attempt to draw her immediately into the fold. He would tell her, point-blank, what she was and he would tell her what Az was; vampire and all.

Az didn't want that. Not yet. He didn't want to do anything that might scare her away.

Watching Uriel and Gabriel with their mates had been an educational experience. An archess had to grow to love her archangel unconditionally. She had to learn to trust him and had to give herself over to him completely. Sophie would never do that with Azrael if she was pushed. She was a rare bird, and just as delicate as one. She needed time.

This wasn't going to be easy, and Azrael didn't need anyone making it harder on him. For now, Michael didn't have to know.

'It's nothing,' he finally lied.

Michael stood there, a few feet away, in the men's restroom and simply watched Azrael. Az reached out and brushed his brother's mind. Michael was well aware that Az was lying. The good news was that Michael had his own ideas as to what was wrong. The blond archangel thought that Az might simply be jealous. He was wondering whether watching two of his brothers find their archesses was putting pressure on the former Angel of Death.

*Fine*, Az thought. *Let him believe it.*

Several more beats of quiet followed before Michael broke the silence by clearing his throat. 'I have a favor to ask,' he said, changing the subject and letting the issue drop with practiced grace.

'Ask it,' Azrael replied.

'I want to bring McFarlan in on something that is going

on in New York. It's a rape case, but I think something non-human is involved. Randall's expertise and talents would really come in handy.'

Randall McFarlan was one of the vampires Azrael had created over the last two thousand years. He was a wise man, an ex-cop, and had helped Michael on occasion in the past.

Azrael nodded, just once. It was a simple response, but his brother knew it well and was satisfied with it. 'Thanks,' Michael said. 'I know this isn't really the right time or place, but it's been on my mind and you've been out of reach.'

That was true. Az had been returning to the mansion only to sleep lately. His job as the Masked One was keeping him busy. And this case *had* been bothering Michael. Az had caught a few of his brother's surface thoughts of late, and many of them were troubled by a serial rapist case that hinted at something supernatural.

Michael straightened, taking a quick breath. 'Why don't you go get something to eat and I'll let Gabe know,' he said, changing the subject once again. He dropped his head a little and his gaze slipped to the floor. 'And be careful,' he added. 'The Adarians are still out there.'

Azrael considered that for a moment. The Adarians were a separate race of archangels who had caused nothing but trouble for them over the last few months due to the fact that their leader was hell-bent on getting his hands on an archess of his own. Michael was right. They were still out there and no one knew when or where they would strike next.

Az didn't strictly need to feed again that night, but doing so might not only help him prepare in case the Adarians did attack, it would also strengthen his resolve and fortify his will where Sophie was concerned. He was going to have to take things one step at a time with her, and every little bit of strength he could come by would help him see this to fruition.

He turned to step past his brother, but Michael's hand on his chest stopped him. Azrael was taller than Michael by an inch or so. He was taller than everyone. He looked down into Michael's blue, blue eyes and waited.

'I'm here for you,' Michael told him. 'You know that.'

Again, Azrael brushed his brother's mind. Flashes of memories were assaulting the Warrior Archangel. He was remembering their first few horrible days on Earth. The pain he had endured on Azrael's behalf had been much more immense than Az had been capable of appreciating. Michael had been there for him in those hellish moments. He always would be.

'I know,' Az admitted softly. Michael dropped his hand and Azrael waited a few more seconds before moving past him and through the door.

'Soph, there you are.'

Sophie turned from the view she had been lost in as Juliette stepped through the open archway of the castle ruins. 'Wow, girl,' Sophie whispered. 'Have I told you how awesome you look in that dress?'

'Only about a thousand times.' Juliette laughed.

'You're gorgeous, Mrs Archangel,' Sophie said, smiling broadly. She'd never seen Juliette so radiant. So happy. It made her already beautiful features glow with impossible perfection.

Juliette smiled and shrugged her shoulders shyly. 'Thanks.' She bent, lifted the mass of her white wedding gown, and joined Sophie on the cliff's edge. The wedding ceremony had taken place at night and the reception, also at Slains Castle, had gone on long into the evening hours. It was now very early morning and the threat of dawn lightened the smooth, eternal edge of the North Sea. The seagulls were already hard at work hunting for their food; their cries pierced the morning air along with the crashing of the waves against the black rocks below.

'I heard that Gabriel's brothers actually bought Slains Castle for you,' Sophie said, unable to take her eyes off the view once more.

Juliette sighed happily beside her. 'Can you believe it?' she asked softly. 'I'm pretty sure this is the most beautiful place in the world. This – right here. And I get to wake up to it every morning.'

Sophie turned to face her best friend. 'You deserve it, Jules. And as long as you invite me for a visit every summer, I'll forgive you for moving out of the country.'

Once she said it, Sophie realized that the truth of the statement had been bothering her. It had been there, in the back of her mind, niggling at her. Ever since she'd heard that the castle was now Juliette's, she'd known that it could mean only one thing. Juliette would leave the States and move to Scotland permanently. She loved the land of the thistle too much to do otherwise. Scotland was in Juliette's blood.

Juliette gave Sophie a sidelong glance and then nodded. 'I knew you would figure it out even before I did,' she said. 'And you're right. This is where I want to live.'

Sophie waited a few seconds and then said, 'I guess it's okay if I tell you, then.'

Juliette turned to fully face her. 'Tell me what?'

Soph smiled what felt to her like an awkward smile. It was half happy and half extremely nervous. She'd been wanting to share this particular news with Juliette for weeks now, but Jules had been in Scotland and more or less incommunicado. And then she'd met an archangel — and things had gotten complicated, to say the least.

Now, just after the wedding and while Jules was still wearing her gown, was probably not the best time to share it either. Juliette was about to embark on her honeymoon and Sophie was still reeling from the twenty minutes she'd spent standing a few very short feet from the lead singer of Valley of Shadow.

The mere thought of the man made Sophie's insides heat up almost painfully.

But the subject of moving had brought Sophie's secret rushing back to her, and now she simply had to get it out. There was no reason for her to stay in Pennsylvania, especially now that Jules wouldn't be there any longer. There was also no reason why Jules wouldn't be happy for her.

'I got a scholarship to Berkeley,' she said quietly, feeling a rush of elation even as she admitted it. It was the first time she'd said it out loud. It was like she'd been afraid she would jinx it.

Over the years, Sophie had acted in countless plays and musicals. It was one of the ways she had made money while working various minimum-wage jobs. The roles didn't pay much, but they reminded her of her mother, who had been a big fan of Shakespeare and of the arts in general.

On Halloween, Sophie almost always managed to dress up in three different costumes for the chance to act out the roles of three different people or monsters. She liked losing herself in a role and escaping from her own life for a while. But what she *really* loved to do was dance. She'd wanted to be a dancer since she was a child and she and her mother had spontaneously begun dancing in the aisle at the grocery store. Sophie's mother had loved music, and it was one of the genetic, bone-deep, instinctive things that she and her mother had in common. There was something about slipping into the lyrics and letting them take over that had always appealed to both of them. It was like acting without having to speak.

When Sophie lost her parents, music carried her past the pain and fear and loneliness. At the orphanage, she wore her earbuds day and night. And when she was alone? She *moved* to that music. And she was *good* at it. Not that anyone but her closest friends knew this.

As it was for so many little girls, getting a degree in dance and somehow earning a living through it was a dream. For Sophie, it was an especially impossible one. She was an orphan, after all. Money was tight or nonexistent, and she lacked the essential support of proud, advocating parents.

So she shelved the idea of dancing professionally. Then, a year ago, she'd realized that she was twenty-five and wasn't getting any younger. Most of her friends were pursuing advanced studies. Like Juliette. For a dancer, she was *especially* old. Dancers became prima ballerinas at age fifteen. At twenty? They were nearly finished with their careers.

At this point Sophie was no longer interested in being in the spotlight onstage. She would always love dance, but her priorities had changed with age. Now she was far more interested in learning whatever it took to teach dance to others. In particular, she wanted to teach children.

Regardless, time wasn't waiting for her.

And with that realization came the nerve Sophie needed to finally give it a try. She took the necessary exams and filled out applications. Berkeley was a shot in the dark; she only applied there because if she could get in, then she could rest easy knowing that the money her parents had left her was going toward an education at one of the best schools in the world.

She'd never expected to actually get in, much less to receive a scholarship. But being an orphan had helped on that front, since considerable financial assistance was often available for such prospective students. And now here she was. If she wanted to, she could begin classes in the fall.

San Francisco was outrageously expensive, but luckily for Sophie, her parents had left her a bit of money when they'd died. It wasn't much, but it was enough to help pay for a place to live. Sophie had been granted access to the account when she'd turned twenty-one, but she'd never touched it. To her, it felt like all that was left of her parents' legacy. She didn't want to squander it on something perishable. And everything seemed that way to her – perishable.

But not this. This was knowledge. It was a solid foundation upon which she could stand. She could live with spending her inheritance on an education. It was perhaps the one thing in the world worthy of its cost to Sophie.

She had also saved most of the money she'd made working as a housekeeper at various hotels in Pittsburgh. She loved the job. She just put on her iPod, let AC/DC or Leonard Cohen or Valley of Shadow seep into her bones, and danced her way through the rooms, making each one as welcoming as possible. She was good at her job, and though it didn't pay much – just enough for rent, food, and clothes – she almost never failed to receive a tip when her clients left. More often than not, there would be a twenty sitting on the bedside table with a note of thanks. Or a ten-dollar bill and a hand-drawn picture from a five-year-old. These tips she put into the same savings account that held her parents' money.

She'd received the acceptance letter from Berkeley almost four weeks ago, and the fact that it was in a ginormous envelope filled with a folder and course catalogs had given the acceptance away even before Sophie had read the words on the front page. The acceptance and scholarship constituted a change in her luck that she was completely unprepared for. She hadn't known how to react to it. She was afraid that if she was too happy, the fates would take it away from her. If she celebrated, she would ruin it. She was afraid to brag, afraid to even smile.

Now, finally speaking the words out loud had a dual effect on her. It was liberating. And it was also terrifying.

For a moment, Juliette just stared at her and blinked. Sophie was sure that a number of questions were most likely going through her best friend's head: *Berkeley? Sophie applied to school? When did this happen? A full scholarship?*

And then a smile spread across Juliette's face and her green-brown eyes glittered with understanding. 'So *that's* why you were talking about going back to school the other day,' she said, referring to the afternoon that she and Sophie had spent walking through the Hogsmeade-style streets of Edinburgh. The subject had turned to school and aging and now Juliette obviously put two and two together and figured out why. Sophie had been thinking of her own situation, her own acceptance, and the fact that she would be a twenty-five-year-old freshman working on her undergrad degree at one of the most famous universities in the world.

Sophie mirrored Juliette's smile and nodded. 'Yeah, I guess it was.'

Juliette turned to fully face her and took Sophie's hands in her own. Her smile was so genuine, it melted Sophie's heart. Again, she was struck by how lucky she was to have a friend like Juliette. It was what Sophie imagined having a sister would be like.

'I'm sorry I can't act surprised,' Juliette said with a laugh. ''Cause I'm not. I knew you would break down and apply one day, and I knew they would beg you to come once you did.' And then Juliette's eyes were shiny with what looked like tears. 'You're a dancer, Soph. I bet your audition tape knocked 'em dead.' They hugged. A wealth of unspoken congratulations for each other passed between them in that moment. They both had a lot to be grateful for.

'Can I get in on this?' came a deep brogue.

Sophie pulled away enough to see Gabriel Black, Juliette's new husband, standing on the stone steps of the castle behind them. His silver eyes were shining and his smile was stunning. He looked like a model in a tuxedo catalog, too good to be real. And then Michael and Uriel joined him on the top step. The three of them together in their respective finery was a breathtaking sight. Sophie blushed and Juliette laughed.

But under the blush, Sophie realized she felt something else. Azrael wasn't with his brothers. *Where is he?* she wondered. It was incredibly disconcerting to find that she felt immense disappointment.

*Oh no*, she thought. *I'm crushing on him bad.* No, it was worse than a crush. Sophie actually felt an ache in her chest as she stood there and scanned the faces of the men before her. She just wanted them to be Azrael. She would have traded them all for his tall frame and golden eyes.

*My God*, she thought as she swallowed hard. *I just met him! One night – a few short hours – and I'm obsessed. I need to get out of here.* She could feel her smile slipping, and just as she knew her friend would, Jules noticed. Out of the corner of her eye, Sophie could see Jules do a double take.

'Soph?' Jules asked, her tone concerned. 'You okay?'

'I'm fine,' Sophie swore, feeling at once guilty for the lie. *I need to get back to the States and move to San Fran before I start stalking him*, she told herself. She glanced up from Juliette to find Michael's impossibly blue eyes pinning her to the rock upon which she stood. He seemed to be looking right through her. She remembered that he was a cop. It fit him because she felt as if he were reading her for clues.

'I just forgot to eat, that's all,' she insisted.

'Well, we can't have that,' said Michael. He came forward, as did Uriel, and the two men hooked their arms in Sophie's. She could have inhaled her tongue right then and there. It was an immensely strange feeling to be touched in such a friendly manner by two men of their stature. Not only were they gorgeous – they were archangels.

And yet . . . they weren't Az.

Still, she couldn't help the deepening of her blush as they pulled her away from Juliette, whom Sophie could hear laughing and softly speaking with her new husband where they left them overlooking the North Sea.

# Chapter 3

Azrael watched the exchange in silence. He went unnoticed where he waited in the shadows above Slains Castle's highest crumbling turrets. He crouched low and still as a gargoyle and allowed his power to surround him like a shroud. It protected his presence from his brothers' detection. And from Sophie's.

He listened to the news about her scholarship, which he was already aware of, having pulled the information from her surface thoughts as she'd stood opposite him at Gabriel and Juliette's altar. He made a mental promise to himself then and there that at some point in the very near future, Sophie Bryce would dance for him. He would make sure of it.

And then he entered her mind once more, stepping onto the complicated grid of her consciousness as if he couldn't stay away. He couldn't. She was a drug to him already.

And it was there that he tasted her desire for him – and heard her self-deprecating guilt over those emotions. He listened as she vowed to flee to California in order to get him out of her head, and he tried not to laugh. As if there were any location on the planet to which she could flee to escape him.

But that was beside the point. The fact of the matter was, she didn't *want* to escape him. She just had no idea that her feelings were completely natural. She was his archess. He was her archangel. There was no fighting that kind of fate.

'Okay, Sunshine,' he whispered to himself from where he remained hidden atop the castle walls, his black trench coat flapping about him like a cloak in the cold wind coming off of the sea. 'If you want to go to Frisco, then to Frisco we will go.'

He watched as his brothers led her off toward the reception hall, and for the first time in his existence he met the green-eyed monster of very real, very possessive jealousy. This he tamped down with a steadfast resolution. He wasn't going to lose control. Somehow, he'd managed to hold it together all night. He wasn't about to let go now, just when he was starting to get a handle on the situation.

He waited until Sophie and his brothers disappeared over the rise and Juliette and Gabriel wandered away from the castle wall. Then Az leapt down from his hiding place and landed on the black rock of Cruden Bay's cliffs with unnaturally perfect grace. He turned to face the dark waves of the North Sea, pondered his destination, and blurred into vampire motion.

Within seconds, he reached the doorway of an ancient kirk.

Shortly after their arrival on Earth thousands of years ago, Azrael and his brothers had been blessed with the use of a massive and very magical mansion. That mansion existed in so many dimensions and so many times, it defied all logic and physical law. It also imbued the archangels with the magical ability to open a portal through any doorway in the world – then through said mansion – and out the other side again, so long as there was a door to exit through at their destination.

Using this magic now, Azrael opened a portal through the old church's doorway and stepped through. By the time he closed the swirling vortex behind him, he was in California's Bay City. There, he again blurred into motion and took to the skies.

He could feel the heartbeat of San Francisco beneath him as he soared above its glimmering skyline. It was the pulsing culmination of a kaleidoscope of emotions. Several people he passed over were crying. More were laughing. A few were fighting. Firetruck sirens called out in the night while waves crashed onto a shore and slowly receded again. Sailboat rigging clinked rhythmically against boat masts, sea lions barked, and gulls cried to one another through the fog. Squealing brakes on cable cars synchronized with warning bells, and San Francisco weekenders gathered in squares and coffee shops to make the most of what remained of their time off.

Azrael knew exactly where he was going.

It was a fault of human reasoning that people automatically assumed those who were older would prefer older things. While this was often the case, there were exceptions. Age sometimes had little bearing on the novelty of a mind. And a novel mind thoroughly enjoyed new experiences and unexpected sights, sounds, or feelings.

Fisherman's Wharf had been around for hundreds of years in one form or another. Fishermen had sailed out and thrown their nets from the wharves for as long as there had been settlers on the West Coast. Immigrants from China and Italy had each at one time called it home. San Francisco was the gateway to those seeking fortunes during the gold rush, and Angel Island in the bay was the Ellis Island of the West, having seen countless of the hungry, tired, and hopeful.

Pier 39 had not always been what it was today. It had been moved, destroyed, built up again, burned down, and restored. In 1978 one man decided to do what had previously been thought impossible: create a breakwater pier where families could go to shop, dine, and relax. He fought for the legislation and funding to make it possible – and against all odds, Pier 39 was completed in just one year.

Azrael was not a young man and he most certainly wasn't a tourist, but because Pier 39 had bucked the system and proven naysayers wrong, it was Azrael's favorite place in San Francisco. It was also quite lovely at night. It was quiet in a hollow, echo-like way. It was there that he headed now.

The Pier became overcrowded on the weekends, but at ten o'clock on Sunday evening, six hours earlier than it had been in Scotland, the weekend revelers were beginning to put the finishing touches on their short escapes from reality. Street performers were packing up, musicians were putting away their instruments and counting their change, and the beggars were gathering on the sidewalks to share or exchange the day's winnings.

As the stragglers drifted away, restaurants shut off their lights and wharf maintenance crews broke out the brooms and dust pails. Garbage and recycling bins clanked as they were emptied. Azrael's boots echoed loudly on the wooden planks of the pier as he landed in a shadowed recess behind a shop that had string puppets dangling in its window.

Pier 39 was empty. There was no reason for people to remain once the shops had closed down. The calls of the sea lions just off the south side of the pier were harsh in an otherwise eerie silence.

Azrael strode slowly out of the shadows and approached

the empty stage upon which performers plied their trade during the day. Beyond that was a massive, beautiful carousel. Az could imagine that during operating hours it whirred in a blur of color and sound as children lined up to ride dragons and sea creatures for three dollars a pop. Now the complex structure was covered in a plastic tarp, unmoving and silent.

Az took it all in with the same quiet sense of awe that he always felt when gazing upon the echoes of the world. Nighttime held afterimages of people coming and going, buying and selling, smiling and waving goodbye. And by the time Az's boots followed the footsteps left hours before, only memories remained. They smelled like cotton candy and sea salt and waffle cones. And they felt like the caress of ghosts – there . . . but gone.

Azrael moved gracefully down the pier toward the sailboats anchored off the north side. He made his way past a handful of seagulls fighting over the remains of a corn dog and stopped at the wooden barrier, allowing the wind to whip through his hair. Then he closed his eyes and sent out a mental call.

At the moment, Valley of Shadow was on tour across the United States. With the help of the archangels' mansion, Az and his band mates always showed up in time for each of their appearances. In fact, they were scheduled to play in San Francisco in two weeks. Azrael knew that Sophie planned to be in California by that time. He also knew that she would most likely jump at the chance to see the show. That is, if she wasn't allowed to psych herself out when he invited her. Azrael could easily make certain of that.

In the meantime, he had two weeks to charm his way past her defenses and win her trust. That was the difficult part, and it wasn't something he could use his powers for. No matter how strong supernatural creatures were, one thing they could never master was the ability to make someone love them. There were drugs that made women pass out, there were spells that made them sexually aroused, and vampiric powers could force submission with no more than a passing will. But true love was evasive and unattainable by any means other than one: it had to be earned.

And the truth was, Azrael wouldn't have wanted it any other way. From the moment he'd laid eyes on Sophie as she'd helped Juliette down that aisle, Az had known that he was gazing upon a piece of his soul. The sunny piece; the opposite of his dark, dark moon.

But she didn't love him. She lusted after him and dreamed of him and fantasized about him – or, at least about the Masked One – but she didn't love him. Why would she? She had absolutely no reason to. She didn't know him. Not yet, anyway.

Sophie was planning to leave Scotland the following day. He'd caught that thought skating through her mind. There was no point to her remaining there; her best friend would be honeymooning, and knowing Gabriel, there would be no interrupting that. Sophie didn't want to feel like a third wheel, so she'd booked the trip home for sunrise.

And that was where things got complicated for Az. His brothers would most likely insist that she allow them to simply open a portal in the mansion for her and send her home the easy way, but that would fix only part of the problem. She might get home faster, but she would still be traveling by day.

Az might be the former Angel of Death and the king of all

vampires, but his weaknesses were as strong as they came. He wouldn't be able to watch over her once the sun came up. She might've been oblivious to it, but she needed watching. Sophie was an archess, and the Adarians were still at large. Their leader, Abraxos, was more dangerous – and more determined – than ever.

There was also Samael and his enigmatic plan to contend with. Neither Az nor his brothers or their guardian Max could determine what the hell was motivating the Fallen One to behave as he did. He'd gone after Eleanore Granger in the devious, underhanded manner for which he was infamous. And then he had gone out of his way to help Juliette Anderson escape the Adarians and wind up safely with Gabriel. Some days, Samael was blatantly opposed to the Four Favored. Other days, he appeared to aid them. He was a riddle. But whatever he was up to, Sophie wasn't safe on her own.

Az waited only a few moments after summoning his subjects before he felt the air around him stir in a way both enticing and unnatural. He opened his eyes and stepped back. Three male figures dressed in varying degrees of black and gray landed gracefully on the pier's wooden planks in front of him. All three of them bowed their heads with extreme deference, and it was only after several long moments of respectful silence that any of them spoke.

'Az.' One of the men greeted him in a deep, somewhat gravelly voice. He spoke the name tenderly, as a friend would, and his blue eyes glinted with something akin to love. He was quite tall, though not as tall as the Four Favored and certainly not as tall as Azrael. His reddish brown hair was thin on top, his blue eyes were intelligent, and his mustache gave him a friendly appearance. He looked a bit like a seasoned cop.

This was Randall McFarlan. His fangs were not as pronounced as those of the other two men; he was older than they were by centuries and had learned how to retract his teeth a good deal so that they were less noticeable. He looked to be somewhere in his late forties or early fifties and had the easygoing air of a man who had been very handsome in his youth but had probably not noticed it because he'd been concerned with other things. He seemed wise and gentle, and in this case, what he seemed to be was exactly what he was.

'Randall, I need your help and the help of your servants,' said Az. 'You have humans who work for you. I need them to work for me now.'

Randall's brow furrowed with concern. 'Of course,' he said. 'What's goin' on?' His words drawled, easy and slow, but the worry that laced them was evident.

Beside him, a younger-looking, thinner man cocked his head to one side and asked, 'It's something big, isn't it?' He had short-cropped brown hair, blue eyes nearly the same color as Randall's, and a disposition that was the antithesis of the older man's. His face was open and youthful, and his tall, slim body seemed to radiate a hyperactive energy. 'I knew it. I've had a feeling all week,' he went on matter-of-factly, nodding at his own words and clasping his hands behind his back as if he were pleased with his premonition. 'It's go time, isn't it?'

Randall turned toward the younger vampire and frowned. 'Terry, what the hell are you talkin' about, "go time"?' he asked, shaking his head. 'What is "go time"? "Go time" for what?'

Terry blinked, looked from Randall to Az, and then shrugged. 'I don't know, I mean – just *go* time. You know. Something big is about to go down. Right? I can feel it in my bones.'

Randall rolled his eyes and took a deep breath. 'Your bones, Terry?' he asked incredulously, managing to appear infinitely patient by the fact that he had yet to raise his voice. 'Seriously?'

'Well . . . I *am* pretty old, you know. Don't old people start feeling things in their bones?'

'Old *humans* do, Terry,' said the third man. He hadn't spoken until now, but at the sound of his very soft voice, both Randall and Terry glanced at him. 'Old vampires – not so much.' He shook his head a little, shrugged as if to make nothing of what he'd said, and focused on smoothing an invisible wrinkle from his sport coat. He was a middle-aged Hispanic gentleman, impeccably dressed in a crisp white button-down, brown slacks, a brown sport coat, and shiny brown dress shoes. His name was Casper MonteVega, but his companions had called him Monte for decades.

Azrael had created each of the three vampires before him for different and carefully considered reasons. Randall McFarlan had been in Ireland during the Elizabethan wars and was fatally wounded in 1584 when Az happened upon him. He was not the first vampire Azrael had ever created, and he hadn't been the last, but he was one of Azrael's most trusted. He worked under the radar on cases with Michael on occasion and had grown closer to the four brothers than many of the others that Azrael had created. At the moment, he happened to live in San Francisco. And right now, he was just coming off of his second ten-year stint as a night-shift police officer in Marin County. He had to space out the services he chose, in both time and location, to lessen the chance of being recognized, but one way or another he always found a way to serve on the force.

Terrence Colby, or Terry, had been born in Tennessee in 1850 and joined the Texas Rangers in 1875. There, he worked under Randall, who took a strong liking to him and thought of him as the son he'd never had. However, a mere three months into his service, Terry was fatally shot by the outlaw John Wesley Hardin. That was when Randall had called on Azrael for help.

As a vampire himself, Randy inherently possessed the ability to create a new vampire on his own, but he had never done so, and he wasn't certain how to do it now. Azrael answered the call and helped Randall turn Terry before the young man's heart beat its final time.

Randy and Terry had remained in each other's company ever since, and their behavior toward one another was today as it always had been. Terry's youthful energy kept Randall young. Randy's wisdom kept Terry out of trouble.

Casper MonteVega, the third vampire to answer Azrael's call, was the youngest among them, though his behavior would never reveal it. Monte had been a very successful author living in New York when he'd climbed out on the icy ledge of his thirty-second-story apartment on the morning of February 22, 1959.

Monte had suffered from severe obsessive-compulsive disorder since he was a child. He was an incredibly sensitive individual who noticed things that others did not. However, he was unable to block out the stimuli all around him and, though it helped him to write bestselling novels and earn a lot of money, it also made him miserable. He'd reached a breaking point.

In a move that Monte would never forget for as long as he lived, Azrael proceeded to land on the ledge beside him, scaring him so badly that he nearly slipped off anyway. Of course, Az would have caught him if he had.

Azrael knew the man didn't want to die, but could no longer bear the pain of life. He told Casper there was another way. Vampires did not suffer from psychological disorders. It was, perhaps, the silver lining in the thunderhead of their strange existence. A few softly spoken words between two troubled figures on the ledge of an apartment building in the midst of a New York winter – and moments later Casper MonteVega became a vampire.

He met Randall McFarlan and Terrence Colby a few years later in San Francisco, and the three of them had become fast friends.

Now Randall turned away from Terry and faced Az with a serious expression. 'Terry's right in a way, though, isn't he? I've felt something strange in the air lately.'

Azrael nodded. The Adarians were shaking things up, changing the rules. But there was something else. It was odd to Az that the archesses seemed to be coming to light all at once. Why now? After two thousand years? And wasn't it a little too much of a coincidence that two of them not only knew each other but were best friends?

What did it mean?

'I have an edict to deliver,' Azrael announced, looking them each in the eye and allowing them to feel the urgent, stark command behind his words. The reaction was strong and instantaneous. The air around them thickened, the three men straightened, and Terry stopped fidgeting. Azrael had no idea what was happening on a global scale, but Randall was right. There was a new sensation in the air. Whatever it was, Sophie Bryce was sure to wind up at the middle of it all – just as the previous archesses had. So he was going to send out a message – to every vampire on the planet, and every human servant they depended upon.

'Sophie Bryce is to be protected as if she were your queen,' he told them softly. *Because she soon will be*, he thought. Against all odds and no matter what it took – she would be.

The three vampires before him nodded once, their serious expressions indicating that they understood.

'And Randall,' Az added, almost as an afterthought, 'Michael needs your help with a case.'

Abraxos, also known as General Kevin Trenton among his fellow Adarians, was a patient man by nature. You couldn't live as long as he had and not develop some kind of resistance to the frustrating idiosyncrasies of time. However, time seemed to have sped up around him of late, and he had the sensation that if he didn't hurry up and start running along with it, he was going to miss the train.

Kevin had lived on Earth with his Adarian brethren for thousands of years. The Adarians had been created by the Old Man long, long ago – and subsequently disposed of here, on this trash heap of a planet, along with a plethora of other beings, both supernatural and *non*. In those thousands of years, he had suffered a lot. His men had suffered a lot. The one ability their powerful bodies lacked was the one that could make their existences less painful. None of the Adarians possessed the power to heal.

For this reason, Kevin had been searching for such a power for millennia. He'd found it in young Eleanore Granger – and for fifteen years, he'd hunted the girl, who became a woman and was eventually revealed as an archess.

Several months ago, Kevin had located the archess and tried to apprehend her so that he and his men could determine some way to absorb her ability to heal. Of course, it didn't hurt that Ellie was a beautiful woman. She always had been lovely, even as a teenager. Kevin could think of no sweeter victory than to finally have her in his possession.

However, he lost her in a battle with the Four Favored and she was consequently claimed by her mate, the former Angel of Vengeance, Uriel.

In that battle, Kevin had lost several of his men. He'd lost more in the fights that followed when a second archess, Juliette Anderson, made her appearance. Of the twelve original Adarians, only seven remained. And Kevin was no closer to achieving his goal than he had been before their deaths.

Now there was another archess – the third. They were cropping up like weeds all of a sudden, after thousands of years. Something was happening, and he was running out of time. Despite his age and the calm that comes with the millennia, he was running out of patience.

Kevin now stood still on the rocky outcropping of Alcatraz Island, a solitary figure who gazed out over the dark, deep bay at the San Francisco skyline a mile away. It was quiet out here at night, cold and lonely and perfect. The bustle of the city was far enough away that its sounds could be heard only on the occasional breeze. He'd been in the Bay Area because of the third archess. He knew now that this was where she lived, and so this was where he lurked, planning and plotting and biding his time.

But in this infamous, lonely place, Kevin felt a kindred spirit. It was a rock, famed for housing the wicked and the wrong . . . an island from which no goodness escaped.

At his right, an information booth with a map of Alcatraz swayed gently in the strong wind coming off the ocean. It drew Kevin's attention and offered his reflection on the surface of its smooth, polished plastic.

Kevin smiled at the reflection, flashing sharp white fangs in an uncommonly handsome face with sapphire blue eyes and hair the color of a raven's wings. He chuckled softly. *Another vampire myth shot to hell.*

There was one favorable circumstance that had come out of his continual confrontations with the archangels and their archesses over the last few months.

During his initial battle with Uriel and his brothers after Kevin's attempt to abduct Eleanore Granger, Uriel had been inexplicably trapped in the form of a vampire. Kevin still wasn't certain what had caused this, and no intel on the sudden change – not to mention the switch back to his normal self – was forthcoming. However, while he was briefly in this form, Uriel had attacked two of Kevin's men and taken some of their blood.

In so doing, Uriel managed to temporarily absorb the powers of the men he drank from. This had given Kevin pause. If Uriel was able to take on the abilities of those he attacked, then perhaps another archangel, or more specifically, an *Adarian*, could do the same.

Kevin had made the hard decision to sacrifice one of his own men in order to determine once and for all whether this was possible, not just temporarily but on a permanent basis. After all, if it was possible, then it meant that Kevin had solved the problem of how to absorb the archess's powers as well when the time came.

The outcome, however, had been worth it. Kevin was able to permanently absorb his victim's powers along with his blood. The downside was that this dark act came with a dark consequence.

Kevin was no longer just an Adarian. He was now also a vampire.

It had been a week since their last battle with the Four Favored. Kevin and his men had spent the time resting, planning, and learning valuable life-changing lessons. The fact that Kevin had become a vampire after draining another being to the point of death and ingesting that blood made him wonder about the effect it would have on his Adarian brethren. It also made him wonder whether the effect would occur only after draining an Adarian, or would also happen with the killing of a mortal.

He decided to put it to the test. After all, he knew that Azrael, the 'king' of the vampires, had been turning men into vampires for centuries. Clearly, it was possible to do so without killing a being. However, Kevin had no idea how this was done, and he had no internal, natural, *instinctive* knowledge burgeoning to life within him. He was guessing that Azrael taught his subjects how to do it – and that the Angel of Death wouldn't be teaching Kevin anytime soon.

On the other hand, if it were possible to turn an Adarian into a vampire with the killing and drinking of a mortal's blood . . . well, becoming vampires could only increase an Adarian's power tenfold. The possibilities were enormous.

Ely was the first to attempt the transition. He seemed to have the best constitution for the task of them all. The enormous black man managed to down nearly every last drop of his human victim's blood without once appearing as if he wanted to vomit. Kevin was impressed – and hopeful.

As fortune would have it, the grisly task had not been completed in vain. As Ely ingested the human's blood, it became easier for him to do so. By the time he was finished, he appeared nearly hungry for the thick red liquid. And within twenty-four hours, a transformation had begun to take place.

Now when Ely smiled, he did so through wicked, sharp fangs and from behind eyes that could glow a hellish red.

Kevin selected Mitchell and Luke to follow suit, but once they had become vampires he stopped the others from doing the same. Kevin was very aware of a vampire's one incredibly strong weakness – the sun – and he wanted the remaining three Adarians to be able to stand guard during daylight hours.

The Adarian family was now composed of four very powerful and dangerous archangel-vampires and three non-vampire Adarians. Kevin liked those odds. And that wasn't all he had going for him. The ability to absorb *powers* through blood opened up new doors for the Adarians. Each of the men possessed his own unique abilities, and it had occurred to Kevin that it might be possible to join certain abilities together, through the ingesting of blood, in order to produce *new* powers. He was right.

One of his Chosen, Mitchell, had the Adarian ability to read minds. Another, Luke, was able to invade a person's dreams from anywhere in the world and determine that person's location in this way. Because people often dreamed of what they had experienced during the day, Luke was able to recognize certain places in the backgrounds of those dreams, thus learning their current whereabouts. Out of curiosity, Kevin combined the two powers by mixing his men's blood and ingesting it. As a result, he gained the temporary ability to scry a person's whereabouts. It was how he and his men had located Juliette Anderson several days ago.

It was also how Kevin located the third archess now.

In the last week, he had experimented with many different powers, acquiring supernatural skills that he and his men had dreamed of for centuries. The Adarians now had a handful of high cards and aces up their sleeves. They had regrouped and were stronger than before. Kevin had a few surprises in store for Michael, Gabriel, Uriel, and Azrael.

Unfortunately, the ability to heal was still beyond their capacity. But no matter. As a vampire, Kevin was certain that he would now require assisted healing much less often than he'd needed it before his transformation. There were far fewer supernatural creatures who could do real harm to a vampire than to an Adarian. They still existed, and the ability to heal would still be a tremendous boon, but it wasn't as urgent now as it had been. And it didn't matter, because Kevin was going to possess it soon anyhow. Thanks to Sophie Bryce.

Randall McFarlan stood as still as the death that had created him, waiting and watching in the shadows of Angel Island. When the intruder he'd been following finally left the bay, Randall nodded once to himself, stepped back into the receding darkness behind him, and disappeared.

# Chapter 4

The teenage girl on the bed tossed and turned, her sleep clearly interrupted. Her covers had been wrapped tightly around her in her restlessness and hugged the curves of her body, hinting vaguely at the form beneath them.

The man beside the bed watched her with hungry eyes. His tall form was a tower of hard darkness in the quietly disturbed room. With slow determination, he reached down and grasped the top of the covers. Inch by inch, he pulled them off of her body. She wore the same clothes she'd worn the day before, from her thin gray sweatshirt to her painted-on jeans.

Marcus shook his head. Teenagers lived so hard these days. She hadn't removed her makeup, and her mascara was darkening her bottom lid as she slept.

But despite her carelessness, it was clear she was pretty. Her hair was dark, her skin fine, and her formfitting jeans and top were stretched taut across her curvy legs and ample bosom.

As he watched, the girl shivered, curled in on herself, emitted a soft moan, and rolled over again. Her dreams were troubled; he made sure of that.

His kind had been invading the nighttime thoughts of mortal women for countless centuries. Of course, they'd never done so in the manner that he was using right now. Their king would never have allowed it.

His kind lived by a strict and simple code: harm no woman. Their supernatural gift, in fact, was of the opposite ilk. He and others like him were capable of imbuing their partners with pleasure so complete and intense that it was often considered unequaled in the supernatural world.

The reason for this was as simple as their code. They could see into a woman's soul, well past the thoughts her mind harbored and the subconscious fears she kept hidden inside. Deep down – in the core of who and what she really was.

Here, at a woman's absolute center, could be found her deepest and truest desires. Her needs. And it was those desires and needs that his kind both fed – and fed *from*.

If he had been living by their code, he would have given the young woman pleasure, taken his own, and left her in the morning with no recollection of what had transpired the night before. That was the way it was *supposed* to happen.

But there was a fury inside of Marcus that couldn't be quelled by the rules that their king had set forth thousands of years ago. It burned in his veins and consumed his mind, and now here he was, standing in the bedroom of yet another unsuspecting victim.

Marcus wondered how many women it would take. How long would it be before King Hesperos understood what Marcus was doing? Before the others figured out it was him and came after him?

With a strange, sick feeling in his chest, he glanced at his reflection in the mirror above the girl's dresser. He was uncommonly tall. But all of his kind were: tall, handsome, built. It felt like a brand – a bad joke. It was worthless, and he'd finally realized it.

He turned from his reflection and dropped the covers at the foot of the girl's bed, his once hazel eyes now glowing gold and green. He watched her for a moment and then smiled to himself. He raised his hand, palm down, to wave it over the girl's body. As he did, she awoke.

Her eyes came open fast, and her breath hitched. He could hear her heart pounding. He knew what she'd been thinking, what had been going on behind those pretty blue eyes. She was so young. The dream he'd given her had caused her nipples to harden against the fabric of her top and had moistened her panties between her legs. He knew damn well that she'd never experienced anything quite so . . . *delicious*.

Slowly, the girl blinked against the darkness in her room, trying to adjust her vision. He sensed her disappointment at having awakened. It was natural; she'd been so *close*. But then she noticed the tall shadow beside the bed. Her vision adjusted a little more and she noticed it breathing. Then she stared up into his glowing eyes.

In a split second they were both moving. Her back arched as she tried to sit up in the bed, her lips parting as she inhaled a scream.

But his hand was over her mouth and his body was pressing hers to the bed before she could make a single sound. And then he was in her head again – and she went still beneath him, her eyes lost in his.

'That's it, little one,' he whispered, his words caressing her lips. 'Remember what I did to you in your dream?' He smiled, and he knew that in the dim light of the room, it was a wicked smile. 'Would you like me to do it again?'

The air around him shifted a split second before the voice came from behind him. He had no time to prepare for the intrusion.

'You're finished here, Marcus,' said the voice. 'Get off the bed and face us.'

Marcus froze where he was positioned over what would have been his fifty-seventh victim. His muscles flexed, his mind quieted, and he felt a strange sense of completion. It was over. He'd been caught – and he had his answer as to how long it was going to take Hesperos to find him.

With deliberation, he removed his hand from the girl's mouth and moved off the bed to stand beside it. The girl watched him, her mind trapped between his control and hers, her body caught in a confused state of arousal and fear.

Marcus gave her an enigmatic smile and turned, just as slowly, to face his would-be executioners.

The two men who stood before him were dressed in street clothes. Nothing in the manner of their attire would have given them away as being from the higher echelons of Hesperos's army. But Marcus knew better.

'You'll have to kill me, Aarix,' he said to the first of the two – a very tall man with jet-black hair and deep, dark eyes. 'I'm done with you and our king. I'm done with our kind.'

They would be able to keep him there. As soldiers in Hesperos's army, they possessed the power to anchor him in place, preventing him from transporting away. There was no escape this time.

Aarix watched him for a moment in silence. The man beside him cocked his head to one side, watching him just as intently. His name was Darion. His thick brown hair and seafoam eyes had fulfilled the dreams of countless women for eons. There was a time when Marcus had been proud to be among the ranks of some of the most beautiful creatures in any realm. Now it left him cold.

'Hesperos would rather hear your case than kill you outright,' said Aarix. 'But I have no problem with the latter if that's the way it has to be.'

Behind Marcus, the girl stirred on the bed. At once, he felt Aarix's influence slip past him as the soldier quickly infiltrated her mind and sent her spinning into another deep – this time *peaceful* – sleep.

Marcus gave a bitter smile. 'Your heart is too soft, Aarix. You are the perfect tool.'

Aarix's dark eyes glittered. 'I'll take that as a compliment,' he said. And then he and his companion extended their well-muscled arms. The air shimmered. As the unnatural glow receded, swords that shone with a magical light remained in their grips. The blades of the swords were decorated with ornate etchings, their hilts wrapped in what appeared to be leather that sparkled like stardust.

'Arm yourself,' Aarix warned.

Marcus shook his head. 'Like I said, Aarix,' he repeated. 'You'll have to kill me.' His smile broadened as he extended his empty hands out at his sides. 'I don't intend to let you feel good about it.'

Darion's gaze narrowed, his sea-colored eyes taking on a brighter cast. 'I have no issues with striking down an unarmed man,' he told him, 'especially if it means saving even a single innocent from your depravity.'

'My *depravity*?' Marcus asked, raising a brow. 'Honestly, Darion?' He shook his head in stark disappointment. 'Are you so blind that you can't see what is happening around you? For thousands of years, we've used women as nothing more than sustenance, choosing one every now and then to bear our child before we move on and never know that woman again. Another man raises our offspring. Another man knows his childhood, his first word, his first step.' Again he shook his head, feeling bewildered by the words he was finally giving voice to. 'Someone *else* is there to see it the first time he ties his shoes or rides his bicycle. The first time he kisses a girl!'

'It's not our place to judge why things are the way they are, Marcus,' said Aarix. But his voice sounded tired, and his dark eyes seemed sad. Marcus wondered whether he had possibly reached the ancient soldier with anything he'd just said.

Beside Aarix, Darion had lowered his weapon, just a little. His expression was mercurial. He said nothing.

'That you're unhappy is one thing,' Aarix went on. 'But what you've chosen to do about it is another. What were you trying to accomplish?' he asked, shaking his head. 'What could *possibly* have been your plan? To impregnate as many women as possible in as little time? Were you trying to prove a point?' Aarix asked, his eyes narrowed, his look one of disgust.

'Yes!' replied Marcus. His head began to ache and his heart pounded in his chest. 'Yes, Aarix! If it is our sole purpose in life to leave behind children we can't raise ourselves, then so be it! I'll leave a thousand!'

'No, you won't,' Aarix told him simply. He straightened, raising his sword arm once more. The darkness in his eyes had hardened, though they still seemed sad. When he spoke next, it was with an edge that brooked no argument. 'Your freedom ends here,' he said. 'Tonight.'

Once more the air warped, shifting with supernatural influence. And once more, it happened so fast that Marcus could not trace it or act before a fourth voice rang out through the room.

'Wrong,' it said calmly. 'As luck would have it, this is only the beginning for Marcus.'

There were several flashes of light so bright that Marcus was forced to shield his eyes from the blinding pain they caused. Something solid hit him squarely in the chest, knocking him violently back into the wall. He hit it hard and slid to the floor, trying to clear his head. Stars swam before his closed lids.

On the other side of those lids, there were more flashes – and the sounds of a horrible struggle. Growls and grunts of pain filled the small space, terrible, nightmarish sounds that would have haunted a mortal soul.

Marcus forced his eyes open. But just as he did, the air shifted a final time. He blinked and lowered his arm. Aarix and Darion were prone, their bodies spread across the floor, both severely wounded. Their blood covered the walls and the beige carpet of the girl's bedroom. The smell of acid and smoke filled Marcus's nostrils. The fallen soldiers of Hesperos's army were there on the floor one moment, and then, with what was most likely the last of their strength, they transported away. Their bodies wavered and warped for a second – and were gone.

Marcus swallowed hard. A lump filled his throat. It was a lump of cold, hard fear. Beside the spaces where Aarix and Darion had once been stood two other men. They wore jeans and leather jackets, but their boots and the leather of their coats were encrusted with what Marcus knew were very real gems. The stones glittered in the moonlight coming through the girl's blinds.

'My employer is a fan of your work,' came a calm voice beside Marcus. He blinked and looked up. Beside him stood an average-looking man with thinning hair and wire-rimmed glasses. He wore a suit. 'He would like a word with you,' the man continued. 'He may have use for your particular talents.'

Marcus forced himself to focus. He pressed his palms to the wall behind him and pushed himself to his feet. At his height, he was a good seven inches taller than the man who spoke to him. But the man seemed completely unbothered by this.

'In the meantime,' the man continued, stepping past Marcus to make his way to the bed, where the teenage girl still lay in her enchanted sleep. 'We will be taking this one along with us as well.' He stopped and stared down at the girl, taking in her peaceful form with not a single show of emotion.

'Who are you?' Marcus asked. Concern for the girl niggled at him. But confusion was winning out. 'Who the hell is your employer?' It would take someone very dangerous and very powerful indeed to control the men who stood behind Marcus. He knew what they were. Marcus glanced nervously over his shoulder at the leather-and-gem-clad men. His skin broke out in goose bumps.

'You'll see soon enough,' came the enigmatic reply. And then the man turned and nodded toward the two behind Marcus. 'Bring her,' he instructed. The men didn't speak, but instead moved to stand beside the bed. One of them bent and lifted the girl easily into his arms.

Marcus's breath caught. His concern for the young woman blossomed into real fear.

'Don't worry,' the bespectacled man said, noting the agitation in Marcus's expression. He smiled a strange, tight smile and pushed his glasses farther up his nose. 'In all probability, she'll live to see the morning.'

# Chapter 5

Sophie sat back in the metal folding chair at her desk in her apartment and popped open her laptop. In a way, it felt good to get back to a sense of normalcy after traveling. Though she had to admit that this time it was easier than it usually was, since she'd been granted the use of the archangels' mansion to get back to Pittsburgh. Talk about taking a few hours off of your travel time. Still, there were some things she needed to take care of, and the sooner the better.

She soon had the computer up and running and had established a connection. The first thing she did was open her e-mail account and look to see who was logged in. When she saw who she was looking for, she opened a chat box and began typing.

> S: Angel! I'm so glad you're on. You won't believe where I just got back from! Scotland!

There was a brief pause as Angel, a long-distance friend whom both she and Juliette chatted with a lot online, was no doubt noticing the message and getting ready to write back.

> A: Hey girl! What's up? Do tell! What the heck were you doing in Scotland?

S: Okay, drumroll . . . Juliette got married!

There was another brief pause.

A: *shaking head* You've got to be kidding me!
Everyone I know is getting married! And you're
saying she got married in Scotland? To who?
Connor MacLeod?

Sophie's brows rose and her lips pursed. As a matter of fact, Angel wasn't all that far off. Gabriel was, after all, immortal. He just didn't have to go around taking people's heads off in order to stay that way.

S: The wedding was a few days ago. His name is
Gabriel Black and he's gorgeous. What's more
is that he has the most beautiful brothers. One of
them—

She broke off, suddenly not certain what she'd been going to say about Azrael. She was covering for Gabriel well enough, using the name he went by among humans. But she needed to be just as careful on Az's behalf. Surely she hadn't been about to give away any of his secrets. He had so many of them. He was the Masked One. He was an archangel. He had been on Earth for two thousand years, searching for his destined mate – his archess.

But she desperately wanted to talk about him. Even now, thousands of miles away from him, his gold eyes haunted her and her fingers tingled with the need to shove them through the sable silk of his hair.

A: Yeah? His brother?
S: Sorry. LOL.
S: His brother is drop-dead perfect, girl. You have
no idea. I want him bad.

She decided to be honest at least as far as that much was concerned. There was a pause before Angel replied this time. It seemed longer than normal. But then her words at last appeared on the screen and captured Sophie's attention.

A: So, go for him, Soph. You're an incredible catch
– smart as a whip, imaginative, talented. And
don't forget that I've seen your picture. You could
have any man you wanted, and you deserve the
best.

*Not this one*, Sophie thought. *He's out of my league.*

S: He's back in Scotland and I'm here in Pitt again.
But speaking of travel – guess what?
A: You're getting married?
S: LOL, no.

She chuckled softly and shook her head.

S: I'm starting classes at Berkeley in September. I
applied and got a scholarship. I can't believe I'm
headed to San Francisco!

She stopped typing and slowly sat back in her chair. Her fingers and toes tingled and her chest grew tight at the same time. It was happening again. She was happy-scared. It was hitting her that she would be packing up the few things she owned and traveling across the country within the week.

She'd met Juliette here in Pittsburgh. But now Jules was in Scotland, and Berkeley was thousands of miles away. There was nothing left for her here in Pittsburgh. She needed to get her feet under her in San Fran – get the lay of the land, get an apartment, and get a job. She might have a scholarship that paid for classes, books, and housing, but she would still need money to live on.

> A: Holy shit. I bet you're freaking out right about now, aren't you, College?

Sophie smiled, breathing a laugh despite herself. Angel always knew what was really going down. The woman must be psychic. She seemed to be able to read Soph and Jules from the inside out, and they'd never even met in person. They'd come across each other when Sophie and Juliette were commenting on a romance author's blog a few years ago. Angel had commented on the same blog and the three began meeting in chat rooms. Angel was a wonderful friend – never demanding, yet always there. Her advice was never unsolicited, and when it came it was never bossy and always brilliant.

> S: You know me too well.
> A: Don't freak, girl. This is what you want – it's what you need. I'm SO not surprised you got the scholarship. And it's about time this happened,

too. Jules and I have been trying to get you to
apply forever. When do you leave? And speaking
of leaving, does this marriage thing mean that
Juliette is staying in Scotland?
S: I leave this weekend. A friend is taking me to a
go-away Pens game. They're playing Tampa Bay. I
have to see Geno on the ice one last time before I
head out. And yes – Juliette's staying there. So . . .
this is it.

There was a pause and Sophie could imagine Angel
smiling and nodding sagely. She had no idea what Angel
looked like, though Jules and Soph had sent *her* a drunk
Halloween costume picture once just for fun. However, she
couldn't imagine Angel as being anything but gorgeous. It
was just the way she seemed.

A: Very good, my friend. Very, very good. Throw a
hat for me if anyone gets a trick. See you on the
flip side. xoxo
S: Bye sweetie. xoxo

Sophie closed the chat box and then shut down her
computer without checking her e-mail. The truth was, she'd
been up all night at Juliette's reception and she was going on
nearly forty hours with no sleep now. It was time for a shower
and a nap.

As she closed the door to the bathroom and slipped into
the shower, she didn't notice the man in the apartment across
the street close his own laptop and dial his cell phone. It rang
once, was picked up, and the man glanced at the windows

from which he had been watching the young woman with golden hair.

'I have some information for Lord Azrael,' he said.

Sophie had a hard time wiping the grin off her face as her friends Taylor and Emily led her through the massive crowd at the entrance to the Consol Energy Center. It was seven thirty on Thursday night, and as it was on most Thursday nights during hockey season, the downtown Pittsburgh area was wall to wall with fans.

The Consol Energy Center was a new building, and when Taylor handed over their tickets and Sophie stepped inside, she was met with the brightly shining, vast, sweeping architecture of the new home of the Pittsburgh Penguins.

'Wow,' she whispered. She'd been to a few games at the old Mellon Arena and she'd always loved them, but this was already topping them. 'They did a wonderful job,' she said as she took in the hockey jerseys behind glass, the sculptures and plaques, the gift shop and the multi-tiered walkways. 'It's gorgeous.'

'Wait until you actually see the ice,' Taylor said, gesturing down one of the halls that bustled with people in jerseys and Penguins sweaters. 'Our section is down that way. Section one-oh-two, row H.'

Sophie's eyes opened wide and her jaw dropped. 'Holy shit,' she muttered, taking the tickets from Taylor's fingers. 'Seriously? You have that much clout?'

Taylor worked for Consol Energy and it was through work that she'd come by the tickets. These were prime seats. Sophie had never been up so close at a hockey game before.

Emily gave her a baby-faced smile and shrugged. 'What

can I say? I got people. Now let's go before we miss the puck drop!'

After the three of them took their seats, Sophie immediately began taking pictures with her cell phone. The boys were already out on the ice practicing. She couldn't believe how close she was. Number Seventy-one skated by and Sophie felt as if she could jump up, reach out, and grab the back of his jersey. She wondered what Evgeni Malkin, lovingly known as 'Geno' to his fans, would do if she ran down there, slip-slided on the ice, and placed a big wet one on his cheek. She smiled at the thought and clicked a few more pics.

Emily got up and bought them refreshments, returning with a drink and a bag of peanut M&M's for Sophie.

The players took the ice and the lights dimmed. Sophie's heart began to hammer as the three of them jumped to their feet and cheered like madwomen. This was the part of the game she loved the most: the streaming lights of red, white, and blue, the national anthem, the sudden and strong camaraderie that thrummed through fifteen thousand people. She loved how the massive cube-shaped screen that hovered above the ice like a digital god sported a slide show of billowing flags, soldiers, and hockey players of yesteryear. She loved glancing at her fellow fans and catching sight of unshed tears in grown men's eyes. This was the magic spark that lit the flame for the rest of a fiery game.

The anthem began and Sophie placed her hand over her heart. Taylor had been right. The ice glowed in red, white, and blue, and the wall of fans lit up with projected stars. It was stunning.

A few minutes later, the puck dropped and Sidney Crosby slammed it into the Lightning's zone. Sophie didn't have a jersey like the others did; all of her extra cash went toward savings. But she cheered just as loudly and she'd brought a cap with her just in case a single Penguins player scored three goals for a hat trick.

Five minutes into the game, one of the group of boys seated behind Sophie and her friends began attempting to flirt with her. She had to admit that it was flattering, and the guy was nice enough. But she'd never been good at flirting. Guys made her nervous. She felt like she could never tell what they were really thinking – what they really wanted. Were they lying to her? Could they be trusted? She knew she was paranoid in the worst way, but she couldn't help it. Her past came back to haunt her over and over again.

To make matters worse, like a horribly obsessive fan, Sophie still couldn't get the Masked One out of her head. Especially now that she'd seen him in person – without the mask. Every time she tried to smile back at Mr Flirt, she saw Az's gold eyes and heard his otherworldly voice and the wind was knocked out of her sails. The smile slipped from her lips at the thought and she quickly looked back to the game.

Once she realized that she wasn't going to be able to carry through with any kind of meaningful conversation with Mr Flirt, Sophie gave up and pretended to be really involved with the game. She loved hockey and it would have been easy if it hadn't been for her preoccupation with a certain archangel who she knew was touring the country with his band, Valley of Shadow, right now. The former Angel of Death was turning Sophie inside out. For the last three nights, which was every night since she'd met him, she'd done nothing but toss and turn in bed and fantasize about him.

She'd tried reading and she'd tried watching television.

*Monk* was her favorite. It was supposed to take place in San Francisco, and though she knew it was actually mostly filmed in Toronto, she loved the ambience of the thing. And San Fran had been her mother's favorite city. Genevieve Bryce may have lived and worked in New York, but it was a city on the opposite coast that held her heart captive. Sophie had been so young at the time – only five – but she'd gone to San Francisco on vacation with her parents the year before they'd died. She remembered so much of it so clearly, it was as if no time had passed.

The water had been Genevieve's favorite. She'd enrolled in sailing lessons while there. Sophie remembered her mother smiling coyly and telling her it was her reward to herself. Together, they'd also taken a cruise under the Golden Gate Bridge . . . And every time Sophie saw that bridge featured on *Monk*, she half smiled – and half cried.

It usually did the trick. It usually took her mind off everything else.

But not this time. The archangel Azrael had all but consumed Sophie, and she hated herself for it. She must be a nut job. She was so embarrassed about her new obsession, she'd stopped listening to his music. Whatever it was going to take to get over him, she was going to do.

Now, as she gradually ignored Mr Flirt more and more, Taylor gladly took up the slack and Mr Flirt didn't seem to mind. Taylor was cute with her shoulder-length black hair, hazel eyes, and generous breasts. Her perky disposition didn't hurt.

By the end of the first period, Emily had taken to flirting as well and was having a lively discussion with Mr Flirt's friend. Sophie had begun to feel like a third wheel – or, rather, a *fifth* wheel. Despite the wonder of the arena and the thrill of the game, she felt distinctly uncomfortable with the semi-romantic chitchat going on around her and was toying with the idea of leaving.

Jordan Staal had scored two goals and there were still two periods to go, so there was that looming chance of a third. If it happened, she really wanted to see it. She owed it to Angel to throw her cap down on the ice. But now that Sophie was surrounded by people flirting, she not only wanted to be by herself and give the couples around her privacy; she frankly also wanted to be by herself in her *bed* so she could masturbate to thoughts of the Masked One.

At that thought, Sophie squeezed her eyes shut and covered her face with her hand.

'What's wrong?' Taylor asked, gently placing her hand on Sophie's arm. Sophie looked up and met her gaze, truly not knowing what to say.

'Sophie?'

Sophie froze at the sound of the deep voice. It seemed *everyone* froze at the sound of the voice. It had that kind of power. Taylor went still beside her, her hazel eyes transfixed by something over Sophie's head. Emily and the boy she'd been chatting with stopped talking. The guys behind them straightened in their seats and turned toward the voice.

The air around Sophie felt strange. It buzzed – or maybe that was just a ringing in her ears as the blood began to rush through them and her stomach leapt into her throat and her heart began hammering painfully against the inside of her rib cage. It actually hurt.

Sophie slowly turned toward the owner of the voice she knew far too well. Azrael stood on the stone steps of the aisle at the end of the row, two seats away. His immensely tall, broad form effectively blocked out the rest of the world. Sophie's breath caught, her lips parted, and though her mind was screaming, not a single sound escaped her lips.

# Chapter 6

Azrael smiled, flashing perfect white teeth that sported incisors slightly longer than the norm. Some people naturally looked like that, he knew, but on him it looked different enough that he didn't smile often. On him, it seemed to fit too perfectly and served only to reinforce the other-worldly impressions people often had when looking at him.

He was a starkly charismatic individual. He was taller than anyone he knew, save perhaps Samael. His voice could literally mesmerize. He was also uncommonly, almost painfully handsome. He wasn't certain why the Old Man had seen fit to bother with such a thing while simultaneously making him a vampire. It was like the curse of Beethoven, who created the most beautiful music in the world and couldn't hear it. What good was a beautiful face when placed on a monster?

But Sophie didn't seem to mind the hint of fang he exposed. In fact, as he brushed her mind, unable to keep himself from drawing nearer to her in any way possible, he was surprised to find that she found it attractive. *My God*, she thought, *he really does look like a vampire*.

This was the second time she had thought such a thing. If he'd been capable of choking, he would have done so the first time her mind had muttered the impression. Hearing it now had nearly as strong an effect on him. Sophie wasn't repulsed by vampires. And the idea that he resembled one was appealing to her.

Of course, Azrael was no fool. A lot of girls believed they would enjoy the company of a vampire – if vampires existed. In reality, he knew they would cower or scream or run, or most likely all three. Still . . . he found himself hoping.

'Sophie Bryce, right? The maid of honor?' he asked, his smile utterly disarming. He'd had millennia to practice it.

Sophie blinked and he read her thoughts. She was desperately trying to find her head in the wake of his sudden presence. She'd been torturing herself over the last few days, and he knew it. He'd watched her every night. Listened to her. He knew damn well that she was drawn to him – and that she hated herself for it.

He sensed it when a slight pain twinged up her arm and Sophie realized that her friend was holding her tight. Taylor's fingers curled into Sophie's forearm in utter distraction, her hazel eyes glued to Azrael. He knew she couldn't help it and wasn't aware of what she was doing, but the fact that she'd brought his archess even the slightest discomfort was difficult for Az to ignore. It upset him.

And with practiced control, he tamped down the anger.

Sophie, on the other hand, appeared to be glad for the pain. It shot through the dazed fog that Az's appearance had caused. It also cleared her senses enough to allow her to pull her arm out of Taylor's grip, clear her throat, and say, 'Yes.' He tried not to smile when her voice cracked halfway through the single syllable. She cleared her throat some more and forced a smile to her lips. 'That's me.' She was so fucking cute with half of her glorious golden locks tucked up underneath that Penguins cap. Wisps of hair fell about her face, framing it and caressing it the way he wanted to.

He chuckled softly, watching her carefully to gauge the effect his laugh had on her. Sophie's gold eyes brightened, her lips parted, and her cheeks flushed ever so slightly. Az's monster reared its head and he felt his vision begin to heat up. If he wasn't careful, his eyes would begin to glow. 'We never got the chance to actually meet the other night,' he told her, forcing himself to continue with the charade.

'No,' she agreed, relieved that she was finally finding her voice. 'We didn't.'

He tilted his head to one side and slid his gaze from hers to regard her friends. He needed to look away – just for a moment. Long enough to get himself under control once more. He slowly scanned the faces of her companions – and then stopped on the pair of men who sat behind them.

A quick scan of their minds told him they were recent graduates of Carnegie Mellon University. The one on the right was the son of a wealthy factory owner here in the city. His name was Richard. And he'd been thinking all sorts of biblical things about Sophie that night.

Azrael grew very still and something dark flickered across his face. He knew it was there; he knew he was failing to hide his sudden fury. But he barely cared.

Richard fell back into the curve of his seat and swallowed hard as the blood drained from his face. Below him, Sophie cleared her throat, at once drawing Azrael's attention. She slowly stood and turned to face him. 'Az, these are my friends, Taylor and Emily.' She gestured toward them and they smiled nervously but politely, nodding in his direction.

Emily's and Taylor's eyes were still a little glazed at his

presence, so Az allowed some of his vampiric influence to snake around and through the girls, easing them into a more comfortable state of relaxation.

It worked like a charm. Within seconds, Taylor was smiling easily and standing to greet him properly. 'It's a pleasure to meet you,' she said, extending her hand.

'Likewise,' Az agreed, and with a slight bow, accepted the offered hand of Taylor and then Emily, who quickly followed suit.

While he shook hands, Sophie's thoughts echoed through Az's mind.

She couldn't believe that her friends weren't guessing he was the Masked One. It seemed so obvious to her now that she knew his secret. Everything about him screamed the kind of rock star charisma that it took to hold millions of fans rapt.

Meanwhile, Sophie's gaze traveled over Azrael's form, and he tried not to visibly crow with the triumph he felt when she shamelessly took in the way the black button-up shirt under his sport coat and trench coat stretched taut across the muscles of his chest. She was particularly fond of the curve of his neck where it met his shoulder.

Azrael released Emily's hand, straightened again, and heard Sophie's heart rate speed up.

He looked up to see that her sunshine eyes were glassy with unabashed desire. And, as if it would hide the way her mouth watered for him, she had pressed her bottom lip between two perfect white teeth. Azrael's gaze locked on the plump lip. He quickly slipped his hands into the pockets of his trench coat as they tightened into fists at his sides, and his nails began to cut into his palms. He imagined her pressing hard enough with her teeth to draw blood.

If she did . . . it would all be over.

'Juliette mentioned you live in Pittsburgh,' he said, trying to break through not only his tension but hers. 'I'd forgotten.' His tone was gentle, personal. He knew that to her, it was as if they were the only two in the arena.

'For now,' she told him. She didn't want to bore him with the fact that she would be there for only two more days, but he was well aware.

'But what are you doing here?' she asked, honestly curious. It seemed quite a coincidence that she had never seen him before in her life – and then, suddenly, she'd seen him twice, on two different continents, and within the space of a week. She wasn't stupid; she was wary.

That was okay with him. He had a story and he would use it, but even it was too much of a secret for him to share with her friends. Az glanced at Taylor and Emily and smiled an easy, even somewhat shy smile. 'It's a personal matter, actually,' he said. 'However . . .' He paused, turned, and glanced up toward the private suites above them. His band awaited him in one of them; they had a bird's-eye view of the entire arena from their vantage point. He knew because he'd been watching Sophie from it all night.

He also knew that Sophie had never been in one of those suites herself, and he was hoping she'd be tempted enough by what he was about to offer that he could pull her away from her companions, at least for a little while. 'Second period will begin in a few minutes,' he said, looking back down at her and scorching her once more with a smoldering look. 'And there's plenty of room in our suite for another guest.' He chanced another glance at the men seated behind Sophie – especially Richard – and was smugly satisfied when the young man looked as though he wanted to piss himself. 'Perhaps you would care to join me?' he asked, turning his gaze back on his archess.

He could hear her blood rushing through her veins. He was scaring her and thrilling her at the same time. She was finding it hard to think.

He wasn't opposed to working with that; he had no desire to stand here and play the good guy much longer, anyway.

A gentle push of his power, and it surrounded Sophie. In a few moments, she not only found it difficult to think, she found it impossible. Seconds ago, she'd had a thousand reasons why she should stay away from Azrael. But just then, all of those reasons – and in fact, reason *itself* – fled from her consciousness and she found herself saying, 'Yes.' She'd barely whispered it, but it was enough.

Azrael's smile broadened.

Taylor, still under Azrael's calming influence, turned to Sophie with her own beaming smile. 'Way to go, Soph! You get to watch your last game at this arena from a *suite*! There's no better view of the ice, girl!' She got up at once and stepped out into the aisle beside Azrael so that Sophie could get out.

Sophie stood slowly, nervously, and stepped into the aisle beside him. Az closed in on her, barely managing to rein in his power so that it didn't instantly overwhelm her. If he'd wanted to, he could have made everyone but the vampires in the arena pass out with it. It was roiling beneath his surface, begging to be released. He could have subjugated Sophie's mind. With effort, that is. She was an archess and therefore would be more difficult to control than a human. But if he'd really wanted to, he could have done it. And then he could have taken her into his arms and shot through the roof of the arena. He could have used a door in the arena to transport them to any other location on Earth. Or he could have simply forced her to pull back her hair and expose her throat to him so that he could sink his fangs into her and drink her in once and for all.

He could have done a thousand powerful things with the supernatural forces that raged through him in that moment, but they would all be overkill, and by some fortuitous twist of fate, he managed not to do any of them.

Instead, he calmly gestured to the stairs that led back into the communal part of the arena and the elevators that would take them to the suites. 'Shall we?'

Sophie nodded and made her way up the aisle ahead of him. He followed so close behind her that he knew she could still feel him there, eating up her personal space with his big, bad darkness. Again, he brushed her mind. She was confused by him, and he wasn't sure he didn't like that. It was a delicious feeling to be wreaking havoc on a mind like hers. A body like hers.

It was also frightening, because he realized that he wanted to do it more. She was awakening a dangerous part of him. It was an aspect he didn't recognize. It was a touch cruel. Decidedly wicked. Wholly selfish and hungry.

As he followed her through the archway that led to the elevators beyond, Azrael nodded almost imperceptibly to a vampire who was dressed in the uniform of an usher and politely helping a couple with children to their seats. The vampire nodded back, just as imperceptibly, his starkly colored eyes flashing a respectful glow for a fraction of an instant. The vampire had acknowledged his king.

There were several more like him spaced throughout the arena. They were there by order of Lord Azrael – to protect one very special woman.

Azrael came up beside Sophie then and gently took her by the arm to lead her toward the elevators. She wouldn't know the way from here on in, and he longed for any excuse to touch her. 'This way,' he said as they approached the elevator and the doors automatically opened.

Two floors up, his fellow band members were enjoying the hockey game from suite one, which provided what was possibly the best view of the arena in the entire house. Sophie wouldn't be expecting to walk into a room with all of Valley of Shadow present. It was sure to throw her and probably overwhelm her if he didn't warn her first.

He had to smile at that thought because it might be a shocking revelation, but it was nothing compared to the fact that each member of Valley of Shadow was a vampire. Not that he planned to tell Sophie that. At least, not anytime soon.

Az had turned all of his band mates at one time or another, and again, each for their own special reason. They hadn't been his band mates at the time, of course. Uro, the guitarist, was from Egypt. Az had met him there only a few years after Azrael had first arrived on the planet. Uro had been a prince among his people, chosen for his incredible height and beauty. He was Azrael's first and oldest turned vampire. Mikhail, the keyboardist, was turned in Russia in the year 1570. Rurik, the bass guitarist, was of Viking descent and Az had pulled him from the jaws of mortality at the turn of the millennium, in the year 918. The drummer, Devran, was Turkish. He'd become a vampire in 1687, during one of many Russo-Turkish wars that took place over the centuries.

Az had never positioned himself as their king. Rather it was something about a created vampire's makeup that demanded he give his respect to the one who had turned him. And because all vampire blood in existence could be traced back to Azrael, they thought of him as their sovereign and treated him accordingly. They were all well aware of who Sophie Bryce was and what she meant, not only to Azrael, but to them, too.

A king needed a queen. As far as most of them were concerned, it was about time.

They also knew that Azrael was the Angel of Death – and that Sophie was his archess. This made her more precious than any human could possibly comprehend. As a vampire, each member of Azrael's undead empire was forced to live in darkness and hide a very big secret. Should any of them ever be lucky enough to be presented with a being capable of both lifting the weight of that secret off their shoulders and figuratively bringing them out of that eternal darkness, they would fight to the death to keep that being. They understood all too well.

'So why are you here?' she asked, just as he'd been about to warn her about his band mates. It gave him just the opening he needed.

'Taking in a game with the guys. Max is out with the sound crew getting a round one look at Heinz Field,' he told her, lying through his fangs. 'We're scheduled to play here in a few weeks, and given that Valley's crowds tend to be . . .'

'Ridiculously large scale?' Sophie provided with a half smile.

Az chuckled, letting out a breath. 'Exactly. We need a venue large enough to house them all.'

'Wow,' Sophie whispered. Heinz Field was an enormous football stadium capable of seating sixty thousand people. He could see that it was hard for her to even imagine a concert being held in such a place, though some of the biggest bands in history had played there. And where those other bands might not have filled the venue to the rafters, so to speak, Valley of Shadow most certainly would.

Suddenly Sophie froze. 'Wait, does that mean your entire band is up there in that suite?' Her voice shook a little as the surprise sank in, just like he'd known it would.

He didn't have to answer her, because the elevator came to a stop then and the doors opened into the communal hall behind the suites, revealing the open door of suite one.

# Chapter 7

Sophie had to fight not to step back into the elevator. She'd been trying so hard to escape this burgeoning obsession she had with the rock star archangel – and then he had to appear out of nowhere, thousands of miles from where she'd left him, and cause her to throw all of that effort out the window. Now he was presenting her with not only his own gorgeous self but every member of his impossibly perfect band.

She literally couldn't breathe as they stood up, one by one, and turned to face her and Azrael. He was behind her, nudging her into the room as if he knew she couldn't walk on her own. Her feet scuffed the carpet as she inched forward, but she somehow managed.

*Good grief*, she thought numbly. Even her internal voice sounded too high-pitched and scratchy. *They feel the way they look* . . . It was a strange thought, but it's the one that went through her mind because, as she drew nearer, the air began to feel stranger. It was as if it were magnetized. It felt electrically charged and pricked at her skin in a way that was both uncomfortable and tantalizing.

Valley of Shadow was a five-member living, breathing, singing *seduction*. Every member of the band was beautiful. Their eyes were those rare eyes that stood out, their hair looked glossy and healthy, their complexions were clear and luminous. Their bone structure was strong, their frames were tall and built, and there was an edge to them – an indescribable *something* – that made them appear both dangerous and delicious. It was one of the things about Valley that had propelled it to the top of the charts.

Its members were as different as night and day but for one nearly painful fact: they were drop-dead sexy. And Sophie couldn't believe her luck. In truth, although she felt stupid for crushing on the lead singer the way she was, she had to admit that she was more than a touch elated. *Wait till I tell Angel*, she thought.

'Gentlemen, this is Sophie Bryce, a friend of mine,' came Azrael's deep, melodic voice. It sliced through her starstruck reveries like a shark's fin through water. She experienced the quick bump in heart rate that she always did when he spoke with her, but she was pretty sure she was getting used to it. 'Sophie, I'd like to introduce you to the other members of Valley of Shadow.'

Sophie turned to look up at him.

*Shit*. Azrael's gold eyes scorched her in her Doc Martens. He looked like he was seeing through her – *into* her. He didn't even look away as he gestured toward the nearest member of his band. 'This is Rurik, our bass guitarist,' he said.

Sophie somehow managed to pull her gaze from his so that she could turn toward the blond, blue-eyed bass guitarist. He stood about six feet tall. His hair was cropped short and there was a scar above his left eyebrow. It would have made him look mean if he hadn't been so young. She would place him at around twenty to twenty-five.

He was wearing blue jeans and a light blue T-shirt under what looked like a designer army jacket replete with medals, buttons, stripes, and pins. On his feet were combat boots.

Rurik gave her a friendly smile and bowed low as if she were royalty. She blinked, caught a bit off guard. She'd expected a simple nod and a 'hi,' maybe. But the bow was beautiful. And somehow it fit the rock star image even more. 'It's a pleasure to meet you,' Rurik said. His voice, too, was smooth and beautiful and she detected a hint of accent, though she couldn't place it.

'This is our drummer, Devran,' Az said, introducing the next member.

Sophie turned to face the drummer, who was also quite tall, though maybe an inch or two shorter than Rurik. He had swarthy skin, short and straight layered pitch-black hair, and amber eyes. They stood out in the darker complexion of his face, giving him a mesmerizing appearance. He wore red and white layered T-shirts under a red zip-up hoodie embellished with metal detailing, and faded black jeans. Devran copied his band mate's greeting nearly to the letter, bowing low and smiling what felt like one of the warmest, most welcoming smiles Sophie had ever been on the receiving end of. His teeth were so incredibly white. 'It is a great pleasure, Miss Bryce,' he said.

'This is Mikhail, our keyboardist,' Az said, gesturing to the third member of the group. Mikhail was dressed in dark blue jeans, a black T-shirt, and a black leather sport coat that made the light blond hue of his hair pop. He stood at about the same height as Rurik, maybe a tad shorter. Though he also had blond hair, it was longer than Rurik's and stick-straight. It fell in expertly cut layers to his broad shoulders, framing a face with a strong jaw, a five o'clock shadow, and glacier green eyes. They reminded Sophie of Uriel's eyes, though she doubted that they glowed like Uriel's did. Because he wasn't an archangel.

Mikhail's smile broadened as if he could read her thoughts and found them amusing. His green eyes twinkled as he, too, bowed low. 'It is an honor,' he said. She couldn't believe how much he sounded like he actually meant it.

But how could he? How could these men really care about meeting her? She was just another girl and she didn't understand how they could see her as any different from the millions of girls who would drop everything, including their pants, for the chance to be in the same room with any member of Valley of Shadow.

'And this is Uro,' Azrael said, again pulling her out of her thoughts with a voice that wrapped around her like silk ropes. 'Our very talented lead guitarist.'

Sophie turned to the last member of the group and felt the air around her grow warmer. At least, that's what it seemed like as she met Uro's dark, dark eyes. They were bottomless, absent of color. She remembered seeing them on music videos here and there. Despite their lack of vibrancy, she recalled thinking that except for the Masked One's piercing gold gaze, the guitarist had the starkest, most stunning stare.

She'd been right.

Uro looked as though he were peering into her soul. It felt a little like being looked at by Azrael. She found her throat going dry as Uro stepped around his seat and came forward. She had no idea how tall he was; she didn't check. She had no idea what he was wearing – she couldn't look. She was trapped in that gaze until he pulled it away himself and bowed low. 'Sophie,' he said softly, nearly whispering her name with tender respect. 'It is wonderful to meet you.' He was the only one of the four who had spoken her first name. It sounded like a prayer on his tongue.

Now that he wasn't looking at her, Sophie was able to take in the rest of his appearance. He was tall, just as everyone she met lately seemed to be. She'd place him at about Uriel's height, somewhere in the range of six feet two or three. He wore dark jeans, black boots, and a crisp white button-up shirt with the sleeves rolled up at the wrists. Around those wrists were several leather bracelets, some bearing what looked like silver beads carved with intricate designs. Around his neck was a gold pendant on a leather string. Sophie recognized the design: an ankh – the Egyptian symbol of life.

Uro straightened slowly, gracefully, and Sophie found herself watching him with a sense of fascination. His skin was the color of honey or melted caramel and seemed to glow under the suite's lights. His hair was black, like Devran's, and it fell to his shoulders in very gentle waves that he now ran a hand through to push it back from his beautiful face.

Sophie felt devastatingly sorry for the women of the world in that moment. They had men like this to fall in love with. But so many of them actually wound up with short, fat, balding men. And some of those threw beer bottles at the television during football games and then went after their foster daughters in a drunken rage . . .

Sophie blinked when Azrael suddenly moved around her, his arm sliding along her shoulders. His closeness was at once all-encompassing. Instinct demanded that she step back, give herself room to breathe, to think. But his arm around her prevented the retreat, and when she looked up, she was caught in the pull of a pair of eyes so powerful, she felt as if she were staring into the sun. She would go blind.

'Sophie,' he whispered, his voice thrumming through her like magic. She shivered once violently. Her breath caught when his forefinger curled beneath her chin to hold her in place as he peered down at her, something like concern etched in his painfully perfect features. All thoughts of foster fathers melted away.

'Are you all right?' he asked.

*No*, she thought. *You're killing me*. But it was a pleasant death, and one she would suffer a thousand times. *And how fitting*, she thought next, *considering what you used to be*.

'I'm fine,' she croaked.

Azrael smiled. Again, she caught sight of the tiny hint of fangs that tantalized her imagination. 'Why don't you come and sit down with us?' he asked. 'There are plenty of seats.'

Sophie stared up at him for several more long moments and then, realizing that she was staring, she blinked and yanked her gaze away. It actually hurt. It was like the sun had stopped shining on her world. She shook the feeling off, steadying her breath. 'Okay,' she said. 'That sounds nice.' She was proud of the fact that her voice shook only a little.

*You're being an utter idiot*, she told herself. *What the hell? Cut it out. Grow up and get over it. They're just people.*

With that punishing thought, she squared her shoulders and pulled out of Azrael's comforting embrace. He let her go, but instead of allowing her to pull completely away, he gently caught her hand – and Sophie sucked her lip between her teeth for the second time that night. It was better than gasping out loud.

Thankfully, no one seemed to notice. He felt good. Very,

*very* good. For half a second, she forgot that he was an archangel searching for his lost soul mate. It was a beautiful half a second.

Az turned to lead her toward the rows of seats overlooking the balcony of the impressive suite.

'May I get you a drink, Sophie?' Uro asked. She glanced at him, was caught in his dark gaze, and nodded. 'Yes, please.' He smiled and nodded back, moving toward the other side of the large room, which included an entire kitchenette complete with microwave oven, sink and faucet, and full-size refrigerator. There was a long table set up with platters of dessert foods and drinks, and there was a wine cooler that appeared to be fully stocked.

The room had that brand-new paint and furniture smell that Sophie loved. She'd so rarely smelled it in her life. In fact, the only time she really had was when she'd gone to work for a hotel in Pittsburgh that had just been constructed. It was such a pleasure to clean a brand-new room. Not that she particularly loved cleaning, in and of itself, but it was easy, steady work and it gave her a lot of time to think.

Beside her, Azrael gestured to one of the seats. 'So I guess this was why you couldn't tell me about your reasons for being here when I was with my friends,' she said, trying her best to carry on a normal, human conversation with a man who was obviously so much more than that.

Azrael nodded, taking the seat beside her. 'I'm not sure a Penguins game would be a great place for the Masked One's secret identity to get out,' he said, smiling mischievously. 'I'd hate to steal any of Sid's glory.' He chuckled and she joined him. She couldn't help it; his laugh was contagious.

Over her shoulder appeared a A&W Diet Root Beer,

which happened to be one of her all-time favorite drinks. And it was in a bottle that actually had ice on the outside. 'Wow,' she said, taking the bottle from him with grateful hands. 'This is my favorite drink.'

'Really?' Az asked. 'It's Dev's, too, which is why we have to keep a dozen of them stocked everywhere we go.' He nodded toward the drummer, who grinned guiltily and held up his own half-empty bottle of A&W. Sophie smiled and took a sip. She loved that first ice-cold taste that seemed to quench the worst thirst.

She could feel Az watching her carefully as she swallowed, and she chanced a glance at him. There was a strange, secret smile on his lips. She lowered her drink, but before she could ask him what he was smiling about, the atmosphere in the arena changed.

Sophie scooted forward in her seat and peered over the railing. Cheers erupted throughout the building as the players returned to the ice. Second period was beginning.

# Chapter 8

It turned out that the Valley of Shadow band members were excellent company during a hockey game. Each of them seemed to know exactly what was happening at all times. They were able to follow the puck as well as, if not better than, the announcers, and anytime Sophie missed something, they happily told her all about it. They joined her in cheering, and when Staal made three goals, getting his hat trick after all, and Sophie was stricken because there was no way she could throw her cap from the suite room, Azrael gently took the hat from her, winked, and sent it sailing across the arena. It landed at center ice, a few feet from Staal's skates.

Sometimes, it really paid to have an archangel for a friend.

*He's a friend?* She gave him a sidelong, surreptitious glance and sipped at her second A&W. He was laughing about something one of his mates had said. The five of them seemed very close. They were amazing together, and they'd been amazing to her as well.

She had to wonder why. Was he including her like this just because she was Juliette's closest friend? Is this how tight-knit the archangels were? Any friend of a friend?

*Or* . . . She blushed and looked down, hiding her face behind her root beer bottle and a lock of her hair. *Could it possibly be something more?* She pretended to watch the game as a shred of guilty hope rushed through her. She knew damn well it was impossible. He was immortal. He was destined to be with someone else. She was a human. It didn't get much more impossible than that.

But he was So. Fucking. Hot. It was making her insane. She felt like she was trapped in a dream there with Azrael and his band. She never wanted to wake up.

Second period came to a close and the Pens were up by two with a score of five to three. Whether they won or lost this game, they were seeded for the play-offs, which would begin in a week and a half. Sophie was lost in her thoughts about hockey – and about Az – when she felt him go still beside her.

She looked over to see him straighten in his chair, a broad grin spreading across his gorgeous face. 'Sophie, look,' he said softly.

She loved it when he said her name. It never failed to flush her with warmth. She looked in the direction he was pointing and found herself staring at the four-screen digital monitor that hung above the ice. The crowd began to coo in unison, a vast chorus of 'awww' and giddy whispers.

Somewhere in the locker room, a video camera was focused on Sidney Crosby – who was holding up a big white sign with black lettering on it. The sign read, VALERIE, WILL YOU MARRY ME? LOVE, DONOVAN.

Sidney had the most perfect smile on his face. He was loving this. He cared about his fans – and this was good press. Plus, it was probably just plain fun for him.

'Oh my God,' Sophie breathed, covering her mouth as if that could hide her own mile-wide grin. Someone was popping the question – and they'd managed to get Sidney Crosby, arguably the most valuable player in hockey today, to do the proposing.

At last, the camera flicked off Sidney Crosby and reappeared on a man kneeling in front of a woman in the narrow space of their row. Everyone around them was flushed with excitement. They were right there with the action! A few of them waved at the cameras.

Sophie held her breath and stopped moving. And then the woman nodded, and the arena erupted in a cacophony of cheers. Sophie felt elated. She felt giddy. She felt happy for people she didn't know and hopeful for their futures and jealous.

She stilled, her heart thumping hard.

*Jealous?*

She frowned, still staring down at the couple hugging and laughing on the screen, and slowly sat down. They seemed to be the same age as her. But they would soon be getting married. Just like Juliette. Soon, they would be buying a huge house in the suburbs and having tons of kids.

Sophie was a housekeeper at a local hotel and was just now going to college. She wasn't even dating anyone. They were at completely different stages of life, despite their relative age similarities. Sophie had the sudden sensation that she'd missed the boat. And now she was standing alone on the pier, looking out at a sea she had no hope of swimming.

'Sophie.'

A rush of pleasure rolled through her, jolting her from her unhappy thoughts. Sophie turned in her chair to find the indomitable archangel watching her carefully. Every time she met his gaze like this, she wondered how long she would be able to do it.

'Juliette tells me you'll be moving to San Francisco,' he said, smiling. 'I didn't realize that Pittsburgh is the place you'll be moving from.'

Sophie nodded, again trying hard to appear easygoing and calm. 'I leave the day after tomorrow,' she admitted.

'Starting at Berkeley, if I'm not mistaken,' he said.

Sophie blinked. Juliette sure had been talking a lot. 'Yeah,' she said, pulling her eyes away to peer out over the crowd again. *Wow*, she thought, *you lasted a whole ten seconds that time*. 'I start required courses in the fall.'

'What will you be majoring in?' he asked.

Sophie chewed on the inside of her cheek for a moment and considered whether or not she should tell him. It was one thing to say 'molecular biology' or 'law,' and it was quite another to blurt out 'dance.'

But he saved her the trouble by sitting back in his chair and cracking another beautiful grin. His gaze slipped from her face to her neck – and farther down. 'Let me see if I can hazard a guess,' he said thoughtfully. Then his eyes shot back up to hers and his expression became wicked. 'Dance.'

Sophie's gaze narrowed. 'My friend has a big mouth.'

Azrael threw back his head and laughed, the sound so sinfully delicious that Sophie actually felt a dampness between her legs.

'Okay, you got me,' Az admitted. 'But I could have guessed. You look like a dancer.'

'And that has to be the oldest pick-up line on the planet,' Sophie said, smiling right back at him.

Azrael's gold eyes twinkled merrily. He cocked his head

to one side and regarded her carefully. He seemed to settle down a bit. 'Well, I'm one of the oldest men on the planet,' he whispered. Then he leaned forward a bit and his expression became a touch more serious. 'If I was trying to pick you up, Sophie, would it have worked?'

Sophie felt the blood drain from her face – and then climb right back up her neck and into her cheeks. She felt dizzy, and there was a roaring in her ears. Was Azrael, the former Angel of Death and lead singer of Valley of Shadow, asking her out? Was he flirting with her?

'Um . . .' Her mouth closed. Then opened again. *Jesus, say something, girl!* her mind screamed at her. 'Yes?' she finally croaked, her face on fire.

Azrael grinned widely and then chuckled. He leaned closer, at once filling up her world. 'Good,' he said. 'Because I was.'

Az listened as Sophie's heart tap-danced and the scent of her blood filled his senses. Her long golden hair shimmered beneath the suite lights, setting off the sunshine spark in her eyes and begging him to touch it. She couldn't believe what he'd just said.

She was thinking that Azrael was toying with her. That he couldn't be serious because he was Azrael, the archangel, and she wasn't meant to be his.

As if.

He was beginning to grow irritated with the way she continued to belittle herself. Over the last few nights, he'd listened in on so many of her thoughts, and far too many of them were punishing. She was the single most precious woman in the world and she treated herself like the lowliest of creatures. In all fairness, she had no idea she was an archess. But even if she hadn't been, she was still beautiful, inside and out. How could she not see and appreciate these qualities?

Every human male they'd passed on their way from her seat to the elevators had noticed and appreciated her. There was grace in her every step, a glow to her skin, a brightness to her beautiful, sunshine-filled eyes that was captivating. She was walking charisma – and she had no fucking clue.

He was tempted time and again to subjugate her mind, bend her will to his, and simply pound it into her brain. But that wasn't what he wanted. Not really. If a slave was what he had wanted in an archess, he would have broken her to begin with. No. One of the most beautiful things about Sophie Bryce was the inherent strength that radiated from her tall, slender form. He knew she had been through hell. There were parts of her memory so dark and twisted, they were knotted woods that even he couldn't get through. Not without hurting her.

And yet she'd come through it all to be what she was now. A good person – a *gorgeous* person, in spirit and mind. An angel.

He wanted Sophie to realize her worth on her own. He wanted her to learn to love herself . . . so that she could then learn to love him.

In that moment, he was so tempted to tell her everything. He wanted to tell her that she was his archess – and that he was a vampire. If she freaked and ran, she wouldn't get far. Not now. Not from him. Especially not while he was surrounded by some of the oldest vampires he had ever turned. The five of them knew each other so well at this point, had been together so long, they worked as one. Onstage, each of them was so in tune with what the others were going to do that the end result was a cohesive synchronicity unlike any the human race had ever known. It was part of the reason they were at the top of the charts and poor Max was inundated with requests from interviewers across the globe who wanted a chance at the Masked One.

Right here, right now, if Sophie turned rabbit, the moment she even considered bolting, Uro and the others would be mobile and she wouldn't get far.

Not that he couldn't have handled her on his own. The point was, she wasn't going anywhere. But that wasn't what he was afraid of. He wasn't afraid of losing her physically. He was scared that he would lose her mentally – *spiritually*.

He couldn't tell her. Not after the way she'd just recalled one of her foster fathers and his abuse. She was hurting too much inside. These thoughts sprang up in her head at the slightest provocation. She'd simply been through too much. In fact, he knew this was the basis for her lack of self-esteem. It happened to the most beautiful people; they eventually believed what humanity, in its inhumanity, told them. Especially the lies.

Sophie wasn't ready. If he sprang the truth on her before she learned to trust him, he would lose her for good. With that thought, Azrael pulled himself out of her mind and asked, 'Sophie, will you join me for dinner tonight after the game?'

Sophie pinched her lip between her white teeth again, as seemed to be her habit when she was feeling really nervous or shy, and Azrael found his gaze once more locked on the plump, pink object of her torture. Every muscle in his body tensed up as he waited for her to either answer him or break the skin. *Answer me*, he thought, but forced himself not to put the command into her head. He was leaving her to her own free will for the moment. He had to know that her agreeing to go out with him was through genuine desire. *Answer me before I kiss you and pierce you myself.*

'Az, I . . .' She trailed off, obviously unsure. He didn't have to read her mind then to know what was going through it. She was unsure because she thought she wasn't his archess.

'Say yes,' he demanded out loud. It was old school. But effective.

Sophie's breath hitched, her lips parted, and then she smiled. 'Okay,' she said. 'Yes.'

Azrael was completely helpless to stop the broad smile that spread across his face.

'But I get to pick the restaurant,' she said. 'I'm not a big fan of garlic.'

Az wanted to laugh. He wasn't going to tell her why he agreed. 'Fair enough,' he said. 'I'm not either.'

'Okay, then, how about Panera? I love the soup in a bread bowl, though I can't wait to get to San Francisco and try Boudin's. I hear it's to die for.'

Azrael's gaze flashed with something dark. It happened sometimes – when people mentioned dying without giving it any thought. But it was gone as soon as it had come, and though Sophie in her sensitivity noticed the darkness reflected for a moment in his eyes, she didn't mention it. He was glad.

'Panera it is,' he said.

A few minutes later, after Uro had gotten her another drink and Sophie had shamelessly downed her third A&W in less than an hour, the third period opened and the Penguins won. Azrael watched in proud fascination as Sophie jumped up and hollered and cheered with more vigor than most of the men in the arena. When she shouted, 'I love you, Geno!' at the top of her lungs, he didn't even feel any jealousy.

Well, he felt a little. But it was fleeting.

And when she belched loudly, and then blushed and hid her beautiful face behind her sleeve, he actually found himself laughing. Sophie Bryce was definitely full of life. And soda, it would seem. She truly did brighten his night.

Like sunshine.

Uro and the others said their goodbyes to Sophie and headed out of the arena ahead of her and Azrael. For the sake of keeping up appearances, the others pretended to have to take an exit route that would bypass the crowds so they wouldn't risk being recognized and mobbed by fans of Valley of Shadow. Azrael led her out after them.

At once, upon leaving the confines of the arena, Az could feel the presence of the vampire minds of his band mates. They were nearby and would remain so unless directed otherwise. If Az hadn't been with Sophie himself tonight, the edict he'd charged Randall with would have seen several other vampires as her guardians.

But for now, she was with their king.

A black Lincoln Town Car limousine pulled up to the curb as Azrael and Sophie neared it. He stopped and waited while the driver got out and opened the rear door for them.

'Whoa,' Sophie whispered beside him. 'This is our ride?'

Azrael turned to regard her. She was obviously impressed – but he didn't want to make her uncomfortable. 'I'm sorry,' he said. 'We can walk if you'd prefer. I believe there's a Panera just around the corner.'

She let out a breath and laughed softly. 'No way,' she said. 'I'm riding in the limo.'

Azrael smiled again. He couldn't remember the last time he had smiled so much. Or at all, really. Yet Sophie managed to land the expression on his face with amazing ease.

Sunshine, indeed.

# Chapter 9

'What is her name?' Samael repeated, his tone still undeniably calm, despite the agitated scene before him.

'I don't know!' Daniel cried, his hands curled into fists at his sides, his body bent under the agony it was enduring. 'I told you,' he almost sobbed, 'I don't know. I can only see her face.'

'He's in pain.' A soft female voice spoke from near the doorway. Sam looked up to find Lilith standing beside the open door to his sixty sixth floor office. The door had been shut moments ago. Lilith was not invited.

'Yes, I know,' he replied, shoving his hands into the pockets of his charcoal gray suit pants and turning toward the floor-to-ceiling windows that lined his office in the former Sears Tower. The view of Chicago and the lake beyond was breathtaking. When the sun reflected off the water, it almost never failed to calm Sam's nerves. However, right now, his reflection gazed back at him instead, unsettling him. 'It happens when he attempts to divine something,' the tall, imposing reflection said. His dark gray eyes looked like pending storms, his ash blond hair brushed the collar of his impossibly expensive suit, and his strong jaw was set with determination, despite his controlled tone.

'If he were an archess, you would take the pain away from him,' Lilith calmly accused.

'Would I?' Sam asked, glancing at her over his broad shoulder.

'You know you would.'

Sam chuckled and shook his head, turning back to face the petite dark-haired woman and the man who knelt on the office rug, his forehead covered in sweat. 'I think we can both plainly see that he isn't an archess.'

Lilith shot him a dirty look and started toward Daniel. Daniel's real name was Xathaniel, and at one time he had been an Adarian. However, two weeks ago Daniel had been tricked into signing a contract that locked him in eternal servitude to Sam. And now he was paying the price.

'I know what you're up to, Sam,' Lilith said as she knelt beside Daniel and placed her hand on his back. 'You think that he can find Michael's archess for you before Michael does.'

Sam stilled. He was impressed. Of course, Lilith was a very smart woman. She was so much more than her small frame, librarian-style clothing, and porcelain skin led the world to believe. Lilith was ancient. She was the oldest being Sam knew. And her secret was darker than most. She had eons under her size twenty-two belt to back up her inherent wisdom and intelligence.

Lilith straightened and went on, pinning Sam now with her big, dark eyes. 'Do you really hate Michael that much?' she asked. Her tone was barely more than a whisper.

That was a good question. Sam's knee-jerk reply would have been *yes*. Thousands of years ago, Samael had been the Old Man's favorite archangel. It was widely known and universally accepted. And then the Old Man created Michael and his three brothers . . . and Michael quickly and smoothly usurped Sam's place at the Old Man's side.

The Warrior Archangel never would have admitted it, of course. The winged bastard may not have even been aware of it. Michael was good. He was the *epitome* of good. Even now, the archangel worked as a police officer for the NYPD, and Sam was sure that the department had never seen a better cop. Samael had never hated a being more.

So, in short – *yes*. He did hate Michael that much. He wanted to cause the former archangel as much pain as possible, and he could think of no better way to do it than to take Michael's archess as his own.

The idea had first occurred to him when a report on Abraxos and his Adarians had come in through one of Sam's many channels. Samael now went by the name Samuel Lambent. Lambent was a billionaire media mogul who controlled the airwaves with puppet master expertise. Sam's fingers were in everything these days. Not much went on that he didn't hear about before anyone else did.

He had people working for him all over the world. Some were human and knew him only as Mr Lambent. Others were more.

Samael glanced up at the man in the dark blue suit who stood against the bookcases at one end of the office. Jason watched the proceedings with a detached air, careful blue eyes, and a silent tongue. He was Sam's assistant – handsome, efficient, impeccably dressed, quick-witted, fast to obey, loyal to the end. He was also an incubus, a creation of the Old Man's that had gone horribly awry and ended up on Earth with the rest of his faulty or frightening creations.

Speaking of Michael and frightening creations . . . 'The serial rapist loose in Manhattan,' Sam said to Jason, abruptly changing the subject and more or less ignoring Lilith's question. 'The one our archangel in blue is fighting so hard to find – he's one of yours, isn't he?'

Jason's blue eyes glittered like crushed sapphires. He nodded once.

Sam considered this. Michael had been tracking a serial rapist through New York City for months now. It was unlike the former Warrior Archangel to let a criminal slip through his fingers. Sam didn't like rapists. Any creature so weak that it had to prey on the physically weakest beings ever created was a worthless abomination in his book. But what *Jason* was – what he had once been – was different.

Humans referred to them by many different names. In Germany, they were known as *alps* – perhaps giving rise to the famous mountain range's name. In Chile, they were known as *trauco*. In Hungary, they were *liderc*. In Ecuador, they were *tintin*. They were called *boto* and *tokolosh*. And in the United States they were known as incubi. However, among themselves and those old enough to be aware of their true origins, they were simply referred to as Nightmares.

These male demons fed off lust and sex in the same manner that vampires fed off blood. There was no physical force involved when they attacked. It was a subjugation of the mind, a bending of the will, and a toss in the sack. And then the woman was left behind, often pregnant, and the Nightmares continued to feed – and to spawn.

Nightmares were normally careful enough to go after women who had had intercourse with other men so as to hide any resulting and otherwise unexplained pregnancies. They were also smart enough to imbue in their children a genetic likeness to their human 'fathers,' further protecting the mother from scrutiny.

The serial rapist in New York wasn't leaving a bloody trail behind him like most rapists did. He wasn't killing his victims. There were simply more than fifty women with a vague but slightly disturbing recollection of a strange, handsome man in their beds. And they were all pregnant. It was driving the NYPD crazy because blood tests on the fetuses all showed that the babies belonged to the women's sexual partners, even though they swore under oath and lie detector tests that they had been impregnated by strangers.

'He is beginning to figure it out,' Jason said, interrupting Sam's thoughts. 'Michael, that is.'

Sam nodded. 'I imagine he is.' It was only a matter of time before the archangel would put two and two together and come up with supernatural. What troubled Sam was that a Nightmare was on the rampage in the first place. Those particular demons hadn't shown their handsome faces for centuries. Like most supernaturally aligned creations of the Old Man, such as dragons, wraiths, and phantoms, they had more or less gone into hiding long ago in order to prevent themselves from fighting with one another and ending up extinct.

It seemed to Sam that the world was coming to a boil just now. Someone or something had turned up the heat. The hidden had been gradually coming out of hiding for the last two decades or so, and the archesses were appearing one after another. Now. After two thousand years. It was for this reason that Samael had been confident Daniel would be able to determine the location of the fourth archess.

'Sam,' Lilith said, her soft tone laced with disappointment and impatience. He glanced at her as she rose from where she'd been kneeling beside Daniel. Samael hadn't given the Adarian permission to come out of the divination yet, and so he hadn't. He was truly at Sam's mercy, body and soul.

Samael strolled slowly toward the kneeling man and considered him for a moment. Daniel hadn't been able to give him the name of the fourth archess. But knowing which archangel she belonged to had been enough for the man to at least call up an image of her face.

'What does she look like?' Sam asked calmly.

Daniel swallowed hard, clearly in agony. 'Beautiful, of course,' he hissed. 'Red hair . . . brown eyes. She looks . . .' Daniel trailed off and Samael felt his patience beginning to slide.

'She looks what?'

'Angry,' Daniel said at last. 'She's fighting someone.'

Sam's brows rose. An archess? Fighting? *Interesting*.

'Give me more,' he commanded, never raising his tone. Across from him, Lilith inhaled deeply and stiffened. He could feel her dark gaze cutting into him, but he chose not to address her anger, instead focusing on the archess in Daniel's mind.

'She's in an alley,' Daniel said. 'Skyscrapers above her. She's moving fast. That's all I can see.'

'Very well,' Sam said with finality. 'You're finished here. For now.'

Daniel fell forward onto the rug, curling his hands beneath his forehead as he obviously attempted to get his body back under control. Sam watched him for a few seconds and then looked up to catch Lilith's gaze.

'Jason, help our friend to his quarters,' Sam instructed, not looking at his assistant. He felt Jason moving behind him and then watched as the assistant offered his hand to Daniel. Daniel refused the help, just as Sam had known he would, and got his feet under him on his own. He was a strong man, Xathaniel, and Samael had been abusing him horribly. The truth was, he felt a touch guilty for his treatment of the Adarian. But there was something he desperately wanted and only Daniel could give it to him.

He waited until the two men had left his office, closing his door behind them, before he again turned his attention to Lilith. 'Whatever fire is waiting on your tongue, Lily, have out with it. Before it burns you.'

'You're wrong about him,' Lilith said, not bothering with pretense.

'Who?' Sam asked, making his way to the liquor cabinet against one wall and popping the heavy cork out of a crystal decanter. 'Daniel?' he asked, though he knew damn well that Lilith wasn't talking about Daniel.

'Michael.'

'Oh?' he asked, raising a brow and shooting her an inquiring glance.

'You're more wrong about him and the Old Man than you can imagine,' she said, her tone so soft now that it sounded laced with guilt. This was more interesting to Samael than what she was actually saying. He put the decanter back on the marble top of the bar and straightened, regarding her carefully.

She looked pale, and when he tried to capture her gaze with his – she looked away.

'What aren't you telling me, Lily?'

But Lilith didn't answer this time. Instead, she crossed the room and opened the door, giving him one last enigmatic glance before she stepped out and closed it behind her, leaving him alone with his thoughts.

*Her favorite music is classic rock, her favorite color is orange, her favorite movie is Tim Burton's* Alice in Wonderland, *her favorite chocolate bar is the Violet Crumble, her favorite food is Thai spring rolls, her favorite place in the world is . . .*

Azrael blinked. Sophie was shyly downing her tomato soup in the booth seat across from him. He'd managed to convince her that he was eating his as well by using an ability that inherently came with vampirism. He was able to make his food vanish without consuming it, and as ridiculous as it sounded, that particular power actually turned out to be quite handy on many occasions.

As they 'ate,' Azrael stared fixedly at his archess, unabashedly absorbing everything he could about her. As usual, he'd had to steer clear of the deeper, darker memories that were blocked off, not only to him but to herself as well. He told himself that in time he would know them. When she decided to let him in.

He'd been drilling her with questions about her plans for school, for the dance program, for the future. Randall McFarlan had come to him several nights ago to tell him that the Adarians had been poking around in San Francisco. The former archangels had free rein of the entire world, of course, and could go where they pleased, but Azrael wasn't foolish enough to consider their sudden renewed presence in Frisco a mere coincidence. He had no idea how they'd come upon the knowledge, but however they had, they were there because they knew that Sophie soon would be. Now Azrael wanted to know every single detail about his archess's planned move. Knowledge was power.

She'd been telling him about Berkeley and the campus, when her spoon stilled in her hand, her expression changed, and her eyes took on a far-off cast.

'Sophie?'

She blinked and looked back up at him.

'Are you okay?' he asked.

But she smiled and shook her head. 'Yeah, it's nothing.'

The reply was obviously either an outright lie or a half-truth and completely unacceptable to Azrael, whose protective instinct was perhaps stronger than that of any other creature on Earth at that moment. Without hesitation, he slipped once more into the warm, comforting embrace of her mind to see what she was seeing.

Sophie had returned to eating, but her inner eye was suddenly focused on a single, very vivid memory. She was standing on the pier at Fisherman's Wharf. It was a quiet Tuesday night and the bay was shrouded in fog. There were a few stragglers, street performers folding up for the night, weekday tourists making their way lazily back to their hotels. But for the most part, it was just Sophie . . . and her parents. She was five years old and leaning heavily on the wooden barrier overlooking the rising tide. Seagulls cried out and the occasional bell sounded from somewhere in the thick mist. The Alcatraz lighthouse sliced through the gray soup, flashing for an instant before it once more disappeared.

There was a stillness to the wharf in that moment that was rare and precious and true. Little Sophie closed her eyes and inhaled the salt and the sea, smiling at the way a few strands of her hair clung to her cheeks in the wet air. She was cold, just a little. And she loved it.

It was her fondest memory. Her parents used to take her to Fisherman's Wharf every few months. Her mother loved San Francisco; the city by the bay was her favorite city.

Azrael suddenly understood. Sophie wasn't necessarily driven to become a dancer or even to teach dance. She wasn't going to school out of pride or guilt or fear. Going to Berkeley was simply a way to revisit the one place on Earth where she could be close to the spirit of her parents; and a higher education – especially at a prestigious school like Berkeley – was, to her mind, the only thing worthy of her parents' inheritance.

It was a moving realization, but it wasn't what stunned Azrael at that moment and blew a disrupting breeze across the desk of his thoughts. Rather, what amazed him at that moment was the realization that Pier 39 in San Francisco was Sophie's favorite place in the world. And it was his as well.

Just as Azrael was realizing that he shouldn't have been surprised by this commonality, his senses pricked and were shoved into hunter mode by the sudden static in the air.

*They're here*, he thought, sending the notice out on strong mental waves. His band mates would hear it immediately, but it would also surpass them, reach far and fast, and the vampires closest to his location would rush to answer the call.

Without hesitation, he shoved his will upon his archess, subjugating her mind and sending her into a state of compliance. It was much more difficult than he'd expected; her mind was unusually complex. Taking it over was like stationing guards at the billions of crossroads that made up the map of her consciousness.

116

But he accomplished it in seconds, and when she set down her spoon beside her bread bowl and stared straight ahead, Azrael stood, moved around the table, took her by the elbow, and led her from the restaurant.

As he stepped out into the night, he felt the weight of his band members' attention, as well as that of the others of his kind who had heeded his call and were there to protect their future queen.

Azrael was struck with a cocktail of hard emotions as he led Sophie into the nearest alleyway and called Uro to him. He hated that the Adarians were ruining this night. He was furious that Abraxos would dare to interfere. He was filled with wrath that Sophie should be subjected to any more danger at all in her youthful life. But most of all, he was regretful that he had been forced to impose his will upon his precious archess in this manner.

She deserved better than this.

Abraxos was a dead man.

# Chapter 10

Azrael had flown Sophie back to her apartment, surrounded by vampires on every side, and as soon as he'd reached the relative safety of her rented home, he'd gone to work transforming everything inside to solid gold. Whether gold was still caustic to the Adarians now that they were turning to vampires remained to be seen, but Az wasn't taking any chances. Whatever she'd been paying for rent would now no longer amount to even the daily interest on what the apartment's interior was worth. He would change it all back before Sophie moved; leaving it would cause quite a stir.

As he worked, he sensed the ebb of the Adarians' presence. Apparently the general and his men had noted the vampires – and decided to fall back in the name of living to fight another day.

Azrael let them go. It was one of the hardest things he'd ever had to force himself to do. The monster, the predator, the Angel of Death within him wanted to track the Adarian general down and turn him inside out. He wanted to take off his head, chain his remains to a gold block in the desert twilight, and suffer the scarring effects of the sun just to watch what was left of the dangerous man turn to ash.

But he wasn't about to leave Sophie alone. Not tonight.

He'd used a little of his vampiric power to usher her into sleep. She wouldn't wake until the sun rose, and by that time Azrael would be underground, hiding from daylight, and Sophie would be under the protective watch of a dozen human vampire servants.

The logical thing to do would be to come clean with his brothers about Sophie and demand that she remain at the mansion under their care. It was the safe thing to do and it was the sane thing to do, but it was also the wrong thing to do as far as Sophie was concerned. He would be able to keep her physically safe and make sure that no Adarian ever came near her, but he would lose her spirit and be forever shut out from her heart. It was a consequence Az wasn't willing to incur.

Azrael sat on the edge of Sophie's bed in her room, which was now devoid of decoration and held almost nothing but moving boxes, and stared down at the woman of his dreams.

He hadn't fed tonight. Despite being the king among vampires, Azrael was bound by the same laws of vampirism as the youngest of his creations. The sun weakened, scarred, and killed. Fire was all-consuming. Decapitation brought a swift end to existence. And if he did not feed every night, he would become gravely ill. Most younger vampires would die from the rapid and painful onset of this hunger-like disease. Azrael simply became ravenous, maddened, and unpredictable after a night with no blood. This effect was slow to heal; it took a week or more of steady meals to recover from the sickness.

It was not something that Azrael wanted to experience while around his archess.

He had intended to find a meal after his date with Sophie. He hadn't planned on the Adarian general and his men putting in such a brazen appearance. They'd been halfway across the country only a few nights ago. It was as if they were closing in . . . *stalking*.

Az needed to feed. But Abraxos was out there somewhere. They had pulled back significantly, but they hadn't gone far. The Adarians had a vibration all their own and it was easy enough to detect their presence, even on a normal night. However, these nights were no longer normal – and Abraxos was no longer just an Adarian. The former angel had willingly infected himself with the very sickness that Azrael had fought tooth and nail when he'd first come to Earth. Abraxos had become a vampire, and the man's signature was all the stronger because of it.

No other vampire on Earth had come about the curse the way Abraxos had. Every other vampire in existence shared a line of blood with Azrael. Abraxos was a rogue, a wild card . . . another king.

Az wasn't sure what this would mean. But he was betting that it was going to make going up against the Adarian that much more interesting. It changed everything.

At first, the Adarians had hunted the archesses because each archess possessed the ability to heal – and Abraxos desperately wanted that ability for himself and for his men. Now that Abraxos was a vampire himself, he possessed the inherent ability to heal his own wounds. However, when fighting against other paranormal creatures, injuries could be sustained that did not heal at the same rate as those inflicted by humans.

Azrael had never tested any of the archesses to this end.

The precious women were capable of healing the arch-angels; this had been determined time and again. Juliette and Eleanore had both done their fair share of paranormal healing when Michael, Gabriel, and Uriel had taken damage from the shard guns the Adarians wielded. The weapons' blasts were unusual and cruel, capable of petrifying flesh on contact. Ellie and Jules had healed these petrified wounds, bringing their archangel mates back from the brink of painful death.

However, Azrael was unsure of what would happen should either of them attempt to heal *him*, a vampire. Not that he'd ever given them need to; he didn't take damage as often as his brothers did. Almost never, in fact. And neither the archesses nor Michael were capable of replacing lost blood, which was essential to a vampire.

Come to think of it, Azrael wondered whether this had occurred to Abraxos. Or whether he even knew about this specific archess weakness.

Not that it would matter as far as Abraxos and Eleanore were concerned. Azrael had been in Abraxos's head. The two vampires had fought hand to hand, mind to mind, on more than one occasion. Of late, the general's thought processes were more disturbing than normal. Not only had he gone through an abrupt and decidedly dark *physical* transformation, but his true feelings toward Eleanore had become decidedly clear.

He was still after the archesses, Ellie in particular. But he could no longer pretend to be hunting them for their healing abilities alone. He felt too deeply for the first archess. He was obsessed with Ellie. But it was clear that to the general's reasoning, if he could get his hands on Sophie, he would be that much closer to obtaining Eleanore.

*Not gonna happen*, Az thought now as he gently brushed a lock of Sophie's golden hair from her forehead. In sleep, she was the very image of an angel. Her long lashes brushed the tops of her slightly pink cheeks, her lips were flushed and full, her skin was unblemished and perfect. There was a glow about her that reminded Azrael of the sun he hadn't seen in two thousand years.

*My sunshine*, he thought.

Sophie stirred and turned in her sleep. As she did, her sweater slipped over her shoulder, her hair slid to the mattress, and the side of her throat was exposed. Azrael's focus suddenly zeroed in on the pulse gently beating in the blue vein that graced her neck. His senses were at once filled with the scents of her – the shampoo in her hair, the soap on her skin, the root beer on her tongue, and the blood in her body.

Azrael turned away from the bed as his fangs erupted in his mouth, lengthening to their full predatory length, wicked and sharp. He closed his eyes as blood roared through his ears like the rapids of a raging river.

Behind him, Sophie moaned in her sleep, moved by some gentle emotion that stirred her slumber. Azrael's heart slammed painfully in his chest. An ache awoke within him, blossoming to life somewhere in his gut and spiraling out through his body like the symptoms of a fever. He gritted his teeth and curled his hands into fists, focusing on the quick, sharp pain his nails elicited as they sliced into the flesh of his palms.

He had a choice. Either he left Sophie with Uro, who was currently outside along with the others standing guard around the apartment complex, or he stayed where he was and fed from his archess here and now. A more tempting thought had never crossed the vampire king's mind.

But that wasn't how he wanted to do this. It wasn't what he wanted to show her. A vampire's bite could be given in anger and deliver exceptional cruelty. It could hurt in a way that little else in life could. But it also had the power to become the most sensual, sexually satisfying act a human being ever experienced. Azrael possessed the ability to take Sophie soaring through bliss and never let her down again. The first time he sank himself into her, he wanted it to be complete, heart and soul, body and mind.

Not like this.

Azrael made an anguished, desperate sound, and almost at once, Uro was inside his mind.

*Are you well, my lord?* came his query. Even in thought, the Egyptian prince was regal and composed.

*Watch over her, Uro*, Az returned, trying with all his might to keep his mental tone under control. Anguish was pouring itself into his bloodstream now, and his vision was shifting into the red. Azrael remembered the pain he'd felt all those years ago when he'd first taken on the form he now possessed. It had seemed to last forever, an extended period of sheer hell that nearly broke everything he was. Once it subsided enough that he was able to regain some semblance of his sanity, he honestly thought he would never suffer such torture again.

But that horrid hunger was returning after all. Only now it was focused solely on the supple, sultry form of his innocent archess.

There was a slight stirring in the air, a breeze that picked up from nowhere, and then Uro was standing in the doorway to Sophie's bedroom, his pitch-black gaze taking in every detail of Azrael's sudden transformation.

'Go,' he said simply, nodding to emphasize his understanding of what was happening to his king. 'Sophie will be safe with me so long as I draw breath.'

Azrael didn't waste time replying. With no effort at all, he allowed his form to mist and then sent it into the shadows. In this form, pain did not assault him as badly; he was transitory and incorporeal and unburdened by the nerve endings that plagued his physical body. However, he didn't like to remain incorporeal for long and certainly not when he needed to be alert. Just as his physical body was scattered and insubstantial, so were the senses that came with that body. He couldn't protect Sophie in this form, but with Uro watching over her, he was willing to slip into it now.

A boon that came with being one of the oldest vampires on the planet was the power to move through the shadows. That he knew of this ability was the gift of only one other kind of creature – a black dragon. But black dragons had been rare when they'd roamed Earth; now that they'd been in hiding for thousands of years, Azrael wondered whether they even existed any longer.

The ability to traverse the shadow realm was incredibly useful. Just as the archangels were able to use their mansion to pass from a doorway in one location to a doorway in any other location in the world, Azrael was capable of entering the deepest, darkest recesses of shade in one stretch of night – and exiting through the same somewhere else. He did so now, leaving the confines of Sophie's room and apartment building to transport to an alley in downtown Pittsburgh.

It took him only seconds to home in on a tainted soul.

Another few seconds and Azrael was sinking his fangs into his victim's neck and drinking deep.

As the vampire flies, it takes very little time to get from point A to point B. Kevin did not have the benefit of the archangel mansion to transport around the globe, but he possessed an Adarian soul. He was a very old being – and a very powerful one.

This ancient magic lent its essence to his vampirism, fueling his unnatural speed so that he moved not only as a vampire would, but even faster. It took him only a few hours to make it from Pennsylvania to the West Coast. A 747 had nothing on him.

Kevin landed on the black rock outcropping that clung to the side of the cliffs overlooking the Pacific and looked down. White water crashed a hundred feet below. It echoed his own inner voice and mirrored his emotions. He was filled with turmoil.

Checking up on the new archess in Pittsburgh hadn't been strictly necessary. He and his men had been able to divine Sophie Bryce's plans well enough; she would be in San Francisco by the end of the week, and they could very well have just waited for her there.

But Kevin wasn't feeling like himself lately. He was agitated and restless. He'd gone to Pittsburgh alone, not bothering to endanger his men on the wings of a whim. Especially one as meaningless and dangerous as the one he'd exercised tonight.

This behavior was not normal for him. Kevin was known to be a careful man. Granted, his transformation into a vampire had come with many unexpected 'side effects' that were more than a little difficult to get used to. The hunger alone could be maddening, and drove him and his three Chosen to feed more than once a night. He wondered if it would get easier to manage with time.

It seemed to be that way for 'Lord Azrael.' Kevin had done some studying up on the enigmatic vampire archangel who was also the former Angel of Death. According to rumor running through the paranormal grapevine, Azrael's initial transformation had been an incredibly difficult one.

Kevin and his transformed men weren't really suffering *that* badly, and as far as he knew, other turned vampires didn't suffer that horribly either. It was something about Azrael in particular that had forced the archangel to endure the torture he'd been subjected to. Kevin had his theories. He supposed you couldn't do what Azrael had done for as many years as he'd done it and not retain some sort of negative energy. He was guessing that negative energy helped mold him into what he'd become – and made the agonizing bed of nails he'd been forced to lie on.

Still, Azrael appeared to have risen above that initially painful transformation and had his undead life under control now. In fact, Kevin would be hard-pressed to come up with a man who had more control over himself and his surroundings.

Kevin ran a frustrated hand through his thick black hair and gritted his teeth against a new, gnawing hunger that was once more growing within him. He would need to feed again soon. Before the sun came up.

At the moment, the very thought of the sun made Kevin break out in a cold sweat. It was perhaps his solitary regret in making this vampiric change. He'd had no real warning that something so integral, something so natural as to be necessarily taken for granted, would be missed so badly when it vanished from his life for good. Ely, Luke, and Mitchell had known what they were getting into; they'd had Kevin's warnings to mull over before deciding to follow his example. But Mitchell had never been much of a fan of the sun to begin with; he'd always been a creature of the night in his habits. Luke was able to find beauty in *all* things, day or night. And Ely was interested only in becoming more powerful. In the end, Kevin seemed to be the only one who missed the sun at all.

However, that said, there was a chance – slight but there – that his deadly sensitivity to the sun could be reversed, at least for a little while. One of his men, Asteraoth, or Adam, as he was called now, possessed the ability to both create and control fire. Kevin had been mixing and ingesting the blood of his fellow Adarians in order to absorb different powers and combinations of powers for weeks now. The new abilities he inherited were temporary, but strong and effective. If Kevin could successfully concentrate and ingest Adam's power through his blood, he would gain the ability to withstand the damage that fire caused to his flesh for some small but essential amount of time.

And what was the sun but a giant ball of fire?

Kevin didn't know enough yet about vampirism to guarantee that this endeavor would prove fruitful. But it was certainly worth a try.

In the meantime, Kevin had learned a lesson tonight. In Pittsburgh, Azrael and his vampires reacted to Kevin's presence with such incredible speed and efficiency to protect young Miss Bryce, it was mind-boggling. Azrael was not an opponent to take lightly.

When Sophie did finally make her move to the City by the Bay, she wouldn't come alone. Kevin knew that Azrael would be shadowing her, along with probably half of the vampires he had ever spawned. Kevin's only hope was to strike fast, without warning. His best bet for this was to do so during the day. And for this reason, he hoped against hope that his little experiment worked.

# Chapter 11

Michael pushed away from his desk and ran a hand through his thick blond hair. He was tired. Archangels weren't supposed to get tired. He was working too hard, had too much on his mind. And the call that had just come in had a strange feel to it, just as the serial rapist case did.

It was a missing teenage girl, possibly a kidnapping – probably a murder. The crime scene was covered in blood, or at least that was how the girl's parents had described it to the 911 operator.

Forensics would meet him at the site. 'Pool, I'm heading out. Get me the file on Alexandra Thames, would you?' He turned to a sergeant who happened to be walking behind Michael's desk.

The sergeant nodded. 'Right away, sir,' he replied and turned on his heel to head back the way he'd come. Michael watched him go and then glanced toward the windows of the precinct. Darkness and a New York City night waited beyond.

Alexandra Thames was the last woman to have been victimized by New York's newest and most enigmatic serial rapist. It was just a gut feeling, but Michael had an instinctive inkling that this missing-person case was related somehow. That was why he wanted her file. Maybe he'd overlooked something . . .

His gaze dropped from the windows as Sergeant Pool returned, handing him the file. 'Thanks,' he said. He moved around his desk and headed for the front door of the precinct, picking up his car keys with one hand while he flipped the folder open with the other. So far, none of the victims seemed to be linked to each other in any way but one – they were all women, all good people, and now they were all pregnant.

But that inkling of a feeling niggled at the back of Michael's mind. Was this possibly the end of the serial rapist's trail? Was this missing teenage girl the straw that broke the camel's back? Was she a twist in the plot of this strange story?

Michael made his way out of the precinct building and to his issued car, tossing the file in the passenger seat. Thanks to Max and his ability to control human minds, Michael had never had to work with a partner, and no one questioned it.

Michael stood in the open door of the car and pulled out his personal cell phone. He dialed a number, and wasn't at all surprised when the line was picked up before the first ring was half through.

'Michael,' said the gravelly voice on the other end. It belonged to Randall McFarlan, the cop who was one of Az's created vampires. 'Azrael told me you'd be calling.'

'I need your advice on something, Randy. You think you could get Az to let you use the mansion to get to New York?'

'I could do that,' came the easy reply.

'Good. I need you to meet me somewhere. Here's the address.'

Thirty minutes later, Michael parked his flashing vehicle

beside a host of other police cars and got out. Randall was already there, and thanks to his vampire powers, none of the other cops or crime scene investigators on the premises were bugging him in any manner.

Randall made his way gracefully through the crowd and met Michael at the crime scene tape. 'There's a lot of blood inside,' he told Michael without the preamble of a greeting.

Michael grimaced inwardly. Of course Randall would know; he'd be able to smell it.

'You wanna fill me in?' Randall asked as they both turned toward the two-story row house that was seeing a steady stream of officials in and out of its front door. They ducked beneath the crime scene tape and approached the building side by side.

'It started in February,' Michael began. 'On Valentine's Day.' He filled Randall in as quickly as he could as he nodded to men he knew and flashed his badge at the appropriate people.

Over the last few months, a serial rapist had been leaving a trail of victims across New York City. On the upside, the victims were neither physically harmed nor murdered. On the downside, there were more than fifty of them at this point, and each woman was pregnant.

To make matters worse, the women all came to the police with the same unbelievable story. Their husbands or boy-friends had been out of town. A very handsome man had entered their bedroom at night uninvited. The women had been overcome with desire, and – several hours later, the strange man disappeared, leaving a confused and pregnant woman in his wake.

They claimed that as the hours of the night wore on, they became more aware of what had happened to them and felt increasingly violated. Some of them had managed to procure 'morning-after' pills. Others had not. But it didn't matter; the pills never worked.

Now these rape victims were expecting children that they knew did not belong to their spouses or partners, and they were faced with a very, very difficult choice: give birth to a rapist's child or have an abortion. Several of them had been having marital problems since the attacks. Two were filing for divorce. Another was separated.

Whoever this man was, he was carving a path of misery across the city and its surrounding areas.

The mortals Michael worked with as a police officer all had their theories about the perpetrator. Maybe he was using some sort of gas on the women to cloud their perception and judgment. The man was sometimes described as having blue eyes, other times green or brown. But because he was uniformly referred to as exceptionally handsome, several cops figured he was probably a performer of some sort, perhaps a model or a stage magician, and was using wigs and contacts to change his appearance. Others went the athlete route; the rapist was apparently very built as well. So far, talent agencies and sports teams alike had been questioned.

Michael had a much different theory.

The physical description of the rapist, as well as the account of what actually transpired within the bedroom, all reminded Michael of something he had dealt with before. Long ago.

It had been many, many centuries since the Warrior Archangel had come across a Nightmare. They were notorious for using human women as their breeders. It was how the incubi of the world continued to populate the planet; human women were the means to their species' survival. However, Nightmares were not necessarily evil creatures. As far as Michael's dealings with them were concerned, he'd never known them to be overtly selfish or cruel.

When an incubus, or Nightmare, impregnated a woman, he usually chose a woman who wanted children anyway. He made certain she would be a loving, caring mother. And when he had finished leaving his seed deep within her womb, he never, *ever* allowed her to remember the Nightmare's visit.

It was essential to the woman's happiness that her memory of the night of her child's conception be wiped. The Nightmare child was then magically given physical traits of the woman's significant other in order to further protect her in the months and years to come.

The little boy  it was always a boy – would be born happy and healthy. Approximately twenty to twenty-five years later, he would come to know what he was. His Nightmare powers would kick in and along with these powers, he would gain a profound understanding of the incubus culture and expectations. And the cycle would continue.

Michael would have been willing to bet all the gold he could create in a day that the rapist now leaving pregnant women in his wake was a Nightmare. The problem with that, however, was twofold. First, the Nightmares had disappeared long ago with the majority of Earth's other paranormal creatures, and no one had heard anything from them for more than a thousand years. If this was an incubus, then the creatures had come out of hiding. Why?

And second, Michael knew the Nightmare king on a personal level, and there was no way in hell that Hesperos would have allowed one of his subjects to behave the way the rapist had been behaving. Which meant that the culprit had gone rogue and was no longer interested in playing nice.

'So you want me to sniff out the crime scene and let you know whether Nightmares were involved.'

'Yes,' Michael said as he gestured for Randall to precede him up the stairs of the victim's house to the second level. 'But I also want you to tell me whether any of this blood you smell belongs to the missing girl.'

'It doesn't,' Randall said without hesitation. 'And you're right about the Nightmares,' he added, glancing over his shoulder at Michael. 'Good instincts. But you're falling short, my friend.'

Michael frowned as they reached the landing and turned down the hall toward the girl's bedroom. Here the scene became more somber and the flash of an investigator's bulb lit up the dim atmosphere. 'How so?' he muttered, well aware that he needed to keep his voice down now that they were in close company and the din of the others had hushed.

Eyes watched them as they moved down the hall, and Michael's gut clenched. They were warning him, those eyes. It was a cop's way of saying, 'Get ready. Try to keep your lunch down.'

'There are Nightmares involved, to be sure,' Randy drawled in his deep voice. They came to the girl's bedroom door and peered in. 'But Nightmares aren't the only supernatural creatures with their hands in the pot.'

The room beyond was awash in red. The walls had been painted in streams of blood. The carpet was sticky with it. The curtains clung to the window, the red liquid acting as a magnet for the fabric.

'What the fuck . . .' Michael's whisper drifted off. The blood didn't affect him. His fellow police officers wouldn't know it, of course, but as the Warrior Archangel, Michael was more than used to the consequences of battle. Blood was par for the course. What bothered him was the idea of a young mortal girl being caught in the midst of it.

'No human did this,' he said next.

'Nope,' agreed Randall.

'But no Nightmare did it, either,' Michael said. Nightmares were not violent like this. Not even the serial rapist had been violent with his victims. This kind of bloodshed simply wasn't in their makeup.

'Nope,' said Randall again.

Michael turned toward him. 'Then what the hell did?'

Randall took a deep breath and let it out in a heavy sigh. 'Well, I've got good news and bad news for you,' he said. 'Which do you want first?'

'Randy, just give it to me straight.'

'Okay,' said Randall, his blue eyes pinning Michael with their knowledge. 'The good news is, this is Nightmare blood, but the incubi are alive. You know as well as I do that it takes a hell of a lot more than blood loss to kill a Nightmare.'

Michael could agree to that. If this was Nightmare blood, then the incubi had probably transported away once they were injured enough to scare them into flight.

'What's the bad news?'

'That's the interesting bit,' said the vampire. 'When was the last time you came across a dragon?'

Michael's heart hammered a little more solidly against the inside of his rib cage. 'A dragon?' It had been centuries. Longer, even.

'Been a while, huh?'

Michael nodded.

'Well, I guess it's about time, then. I'm fairly sure that the dragons I smell here were the ones doing the fighting,' Randall said as he gestured to the blood on the walls and floor. 'But there's another scent here as well; something that I don't even recognize. And whatever they are, they took the girl with them.'

Michael's head was spinning. Nightmares were one thing. Dragons were quite another. And from what Randall was telling him, it didn't end there.

The supernaturals of the world were coming out of hiding.

The Adarians were out there scheming to do God only knew what. Samael was sitting in his tower in Chicago plotting something that was sure to be painful, at the very least. Nightmares and dragons were out in the open and fighting with one another, and now they'd waved their existence in humanity's face by kidnapping a mortal. And somewhere in the world, two archesses remained to be found.

There was so much going on all at once, it made Michael dizzy. He glanced at the blood on the floor, the rumpled sheets, and the night beyond the windows. That night held a lot more danger than it used to.

Michael thought of his brothers, most importantly Azrael. He hadn't spoken with the vampire archangel since he'd walked in on Az during Gabe's wedding almost two weeks ago. Azrael was in San Francisco at the moment, preparing for a concert he would be giving over the next few days.

But Michael couldn't get the image of the archangel bent over the sink out of his head. The mirror had been cracked, and the air in the room had been thick with the feel of Azrael's power. There was so much more to Az than there seemed to be to the others, not only because of what he was now, but because of what he had once been. Michael knew that even after all this time, there was a lot about Az he and his other brothers did not understand.

Michael's instincts in battle were legendary. Those instincts didn't go away when he wasn't fighting, and right now his intuition was telling him that as far as Azrael was concerned, something was *wrong*.

He wasn't as worried about the others. Gabriel and Juliette were busy building a new home in Cruden Bay right beside the remains of Slains Castle, which they now had the rights to protect with utmost care. Uriel and Eleanore were with them. The brothers had agreed it would be a good idea to remain relatively close to one another at least until they figured out what was brewing out there.

The crime scene around Michael right now told him quite a *lot* was brewing out there. More than any of them had imagined.

Michael frowned as he considered this. Randall hadn't said anything about the Adarians taking part in this mess, but Abraxos and his posse were a threat nonetheless. So far, the four brothers and the two archesses they'd managed to find had played on the defensive. They'd simply existed – and then when the Adarians struck, they'd fought back.

Michael didn't like that. It wasn't a good strategy. As far as he was concerned, the adage about the best defense being a good offense was true. If it were up to him, they would go after the Adarians instead of waiting around for the insane general and his men to strike.

But it wasn't up to him. Michael's hands curled tightly at his sides as tension rode its way through his tall, strong body. He realized what he was doing when Randall leaned over and nudged him.

'Not a good idea to go all Champion of the Winged Warriors in here, my friend,' he whispered, pointing at his own eyes. Michael blinked. He realized that his eyes felt hot in his face and that they were most likely beginning to glow.

He closed his eyes. With a deep breath, he forced his shoulders to relax.

In the realm he'd come from two thousand years ago, he'd possessed an army of angels to lead into battle. Now if he wanted to charge headlong into a fight, he would have to drag his brothers into danger along with him, to say nothing of their soul mates. So he held back. He had no right to put their lives on the line simply because he felt impatient, especially now that they had so much more to live for.

'So what do I do now, Randy?' he asked, talking to the ex-cop-turned-vampire as he would a close friend. He needed to find the human girl who had been taken. But where did he start?

'That's a good question,' said Randall. 'But on the upside, I have a feeling you won't have to answer it.'

Michael opened his eyes, no longer burning in his face, and fixed them on Randall.

'You're not going to have to track down whoever did this,' Randall continued.

Michael realized he was right. Something in his gut was telling him that whoever was responsible for this incident wouldn't need to be found.

Because he would find Michael first.

# Chapter 12

The night was calm, the fog hadn't yet rolled in, and because it was Tuesday, the normally thriving tourist attraction that was Pier 39 was quickly winding down.

The street performers, beggars, and tourists were all packing it in and heading home or to their hotels. Though the fog remained nestled just beyond the Golden Gate Bridge, the air was already thick with the scent of it; it muffled the clanging of mast and rigging. The tide was rising. The seagulls were quieting down, making room for one another on crow's nests and the wooden beams of the pier.

Out on Alcatraz Island, the lighthouse winked its eternal message, its light temporarily piercing the graying darkness in unhurried rhythm. Somewhere in the distance, a cargo ship sounded its horn. The sea lions, from where they vied for space on the wooden rafts that had been left for them long ago, replied.

Alone on the lookout point beside one of the many pay telescopes that lined the north side of the pier stood a woman with beautiful hair. It curled more than usual in the damp air, a waist-long mass of thick waves and spirals that shimmered like gold beneath the pier lights. She leaned casually against the wooden railing before her and peered out into the bay. Her mind had been spinning until now; he could hear it grow steadily calmer as she took a deep breath, pulling in the salt air. She closed her eyes as she let it go.

Azrael noticed the drops of moisture on her long, full lashes as they rested on the tops of her cheeks. He'd been watching her since sundown – he and his band mates, who were stationed, unseen, at intervals across the wharf and the piers.

When she opened her eyes again, she did so with a smile. That smile was like a sunbeam and brought to mind an image of the fiery orb that he hadn't seen in two thousand years.

Azrael's body flexed beneath its dark garb, his hunger spiking once again. He'd had to feed more than normal lately. Sophie Bryce had awakened the monster within him, and that monster was voracious.

'You okay?' came a gravelly voice beside him. Azrael tore his gaze from the object of his desire and glanced at his old friend. Not much escaped Randall McFarlan. Not much escaped a vampire in any case, but Randall's skills of perception were especially fine-tuned.

Az could have lied. But it would have done no good, and in all honesty he wanted to tell someone how he was feeling. He wanted to get it off his chest. So he didn't say anything at all, knowing that his silence would be more telling for Randall than a lengthy confession.

Randall nodded once in understanding and his stark vampire gaze returned to the profile of the young woman standing alone on the boardwalk. 'A funny thing about young Miss Bryce,' Randall said. 'She doesn't seem to be opposed to the night.' He smiled slowly, glancing back at Az before he continued. 'In fact, I would say she seems quite fond of it.'

Azrael turned his attention back to Sophie. She straightened from where she had been leaning against the wood railing and sighed. Then she tucked a curly lock of hair behind one ear and began digging into the large leather messenger bag she had slung across her body.

It had been a few weeks since he'd seen her last. Their brief 'date' had ended so quickly and on such a sour note for him – he'd never been more furious with the Adarians. As Sophie slept that night, Azrael entered her dreams and manipulated her memory of their date so that she would assume Az had simply brought her home after dinner and said good night.

The next day, Sophie awoke to a single bloodred rose on her pillow and a handwritten note: *Sweetest Sophie*, it read. *I thoroughly enjoyed getting to know you a little better tonight. I hope you will allow me to do it again very soon. Always, Azrael.*

According to her watchers, Sophie had smiled winsomely, inhaled the rose's heady scent, and then set herself to the task of packing up her meager belongings and preparing for her flight to San Francisco. The apartment she was leaving behind was furnished, and almost nothing of what she'd been using for comfort actually belonged to her. The rest – the blankets, the clothes, the shoes, and the books – she'd managed to fit into two large suitcases and a carry-on for the one-way trip.

As Sophie left her key with the building manager and caught her flight, the human vampire servants entrusted with her safety continued their task of watching over the future vampire queen. Randall had called in the big guns for Sophie. She was being watched twenty-four/seven.

A part of Az felt decidedly strange about all of this. He felt uneasy, jealous even. But the bigger part of him was well aware that it was necessary. She was too precious and far too vulnerable during the day. And he'd been careful. He had made certain to scour the minds of the men who guarded her, searching for any signs of unwanted emotion or duplicity. They were clean.

The network of human servants who were loyal to the vampire nation spanned the globe like a massive spiderweb. These people were more carefully chosen than the vampires themselves. They had to be. It was because of them that many of the vampires who roamed the night now were alive to do so.

Randall was the man in charge when it came to the humans. He, Monte, and Terry led the network of day walkers with perfect efficiency. Randall's wisdom and patience made him the ideal head of the operation. Monte's attention to detail made certain that nothing ever slipped through the cracks and that no human servant ever went rogue. Terry's easy nature and people skills made communication with the humans painless and reassuring.

It was fortuitous to a supernatural degree that Randall, Terry, and Monte currently resided in San Francisco, where the third archess now lived. Azrael had never been more convinced that something greater than him was at work of late. Everything was too interconnected for him to think otherwise.

Out on the pier, Sophie pulled a chunk of leftover sourdough out of her messenger bag. It was still wrapped in the paper bag from the Boudin Bakery, and Azrael could smell it even from where he watched, on the garage roof across the street.

He knew she was about to toss it to the birds. According

to the day walkers on her guard, she was always giving away what she had. Whether to the homeless who dwelled on the streets of San Francisco or to the pigeons, Sophie was a sharing soul.

'All right, boys,' she said softly. No other humans were around. She was alone where she stood on the damp planks of the boardwalk. 'Here's your supper, but I'm not supposed to be feeding you, so this is our little secret.'

She tore off several small chunks and tossed them to the seagulls nearby. There was a brief white flutter, several more seagulls joined the first group, and they commenced to fighting over the pieces of bread.

Sophie's smile broadened as she fed the birds what remained of the day's lunch.

'Think she was talking to you?' Randall's gravelly voice cut through the silence beside Az. Azrael shot him a dark look and Randall chuckled, ignoring him. The smug look on his face said everything.

Azrael turned back to Sophie. She began to move away from the birds, allowing them their privacy. As she did, she shoved her hands into the pockets of her vintage military-style jacket and her look became distant. At once, he wondered what she was thinking, and without the slightest restraint, he entered her mind to find out.

As usual, her thoughts were more difficult to infiltrate than those of a normal human mind. However, Az managed to breach her outer walls without allowing her to suspect that he was there, and as she made her way down the boardwalk toward Pier 41, he listened in on her inner musings.

She was thinking about Alcatraz. She kept glancing at it across the water. Not much of the dark island was visible through the black and gray of the slightly misty night, but the lighthouse sliced through the dimness faithfully, marking its location. Sophie was wondering what it would feel like to go sailing through a dense fog out on the bay. She imagined herself on a boat, surrounded by the mists, somewhere between Alcatraz and the Golden Gate Bridge. Her inner thoughts listened, picking up the sound of nothing but the silence and the lapping of the waves upon the hull of her imaginary vessel. She felt at peace as she imagined this, and because a part of him was with her in that moment, he felt it as well.

It was something he had never experienced before. Being inside someone's mind while that person so clearly pictured something that was felt so deeply was a little like taking a really deep breath while underwater and getting nothing but clean air. Azrael watched his archess with a mixture of pride and burgeoning impatience. Over and over again, she took an existence that he thought he knew everything about and introduced it to something new.

He was falling in love with her.

At that thought, Azrael closed his eyes. But he remained comfortably sequestered within the warmth of Sophie's mind as she let her reverie go in order to replace it with a new one. She now wondered what it would feel like to fly out over the bay like Superman and land on the island of Alcatraz when it was quiet and dark, as it was now. She was thinking that if she had wings, the way she sometimes did in her dreams, she could wait until it was so late that there was no one around. Then she would stand on one of the wooden beams surrounding the pier – and jump. And then . . . she was wondering what it would be like to have Az, the archangel, catch her while she was in the air, and kiss her.

Azrael straightened and opened his eyes, his lips parting. Beside him, Randall stood straighter as well, his instincts no doubt going on alert at the sudden change in his sire. Azrael's senses focused. His heart beat a little faster. He couldn't believe the images that were floating before Sophie's mind at that very moment.

In her head, Azrael took her to Alcatraz Island . . . where his band mates were waiting. And in her head, they were vampires.

Az could feel his gaze begin to heat up. His blood hummed to life; his gums ached where his fangs threatened to lengthen. Sophie was imagining him seducing her, toying with her. In her daydream, she ran from him, willingly playing the prey to him and his men. Uro easily blocked her path. Then Azrael was behind her once more.

Down below, Sophie suddenly stopped on the boardwalk, reached out to steady herself on the chain-link fence beside her, and closed her eyes as she imagined Azrael sinking his teeth into her neck.

Azrael's fangs exploded in his mouth, his vision went red, and he swore softly, turning away from the sight of his archess on the boardwalk. Beside him, Randall came forward, at once concerned. But before the other vampire could speak, Azrael held up his hand to indicate that he wanted silence. He shut his eyes tight against his impending transformation, ruthlessly willing his body back under control.

*Sophie* . . . He'd already known that she thought he looked like a vampire, but she also *daydreamed* of him being a vampire. Of him coming after her! His mind spun with the implications, the biggest of which was probably that Sophie not only didn't mind his resemblance to the monster – she *liked* it. She spent time conceiving what she thought to be impossible scenarios involving him and his big, bad teeth . . . because they brought her pleasure.

Again he swore, but this time internally.

He'd planned to take this slowly. In fact, as far as Sophie knew, he'd stayed completely away from her for the last week. He'd given her space and time to get acquainted with the school and her new apartment and the big city. There had been no sign of the Adarians, making his apparent distance possible. He wasn't sure what Abraxos was up to, but whatever it was, it didn't seem to be taking place in San Francisco, at least for now.

In the meantime, Az was never far from Sophie, and his men and their servants watched her twenty-four hours a day. But as far as she was concerned, she'd been on her own. He didn't want to crowd her. He knew some of what she'd been through at the hands of men and he didn't want to scare her off.

But now her presence, only a split second away from him as the vampire flies, was calling to him like an amplified siren song. Knowing what she wanted – what she *truly* wanted, deep down inside – was killing him.

Down below, Sophie laughed to herself, no doubt chastising herself for her wicked thoughts as she was so wont to do. Azrael's gut clenched. He tasted blood in his mouth and realized he'd pierced his lower lip with his fangs. The taste surprised him. It had been forever since he'd done that.

'No offense, Az, but you're a mess.'

Azrael spun to face Randall, who was watching him with an inherent wisdom glinting in his blue, blue eyes. The other vampire pulled a gold pocket watch out of his tan trench coat and flipped it open. It was vintage, having belonged to Randall's father hundreds of years ago. It didn't keep time as accurately as modern timepieces, and for a vampire, that was gutsy. But Randall was sentimental – and every soul deserved a vice.

'According to what she's done every other night this week, in roughly seven minutes she's going to leave that pier entirely and head for the cable cars at Ghirardelli,' Randall said in his rough but gentle voice. 'If you ask me—'

'I didn't ask you,' Azrael cut in curtly.

Randall continued as if he hadn't been rudely interrupted. 'It seems the perfect time for a few members of Valley of Shadow to hit the town and relax.' He nodded a little to himself and slipped the watch back into his pocket. His gaze traveled over the streets and buildings around them. 'Middle of the week, middle of the night, not as many people around. It would be a believable coincidence should your paths happen to cross that of one Sophie Bryce.'

A beat of silence passed between them. And then Azrael almost laughed. Randall was cutting to the heart of the matter and simultaneously offering up a solution. It was his way. It was part of the reason Azrael had brought him over all those years ago. McFarlan was a very, *very* smart man.

He was also right. Azrael had waited long enough. He'd been planning to send Valley of Shadow tickets to her new apartment and meet up with her at the concert, but this taking-it-slow thing was turning into a jaunt through Tartarus.

He turned away from Randall and took the few steps necessary for him to be flush with the ledge of the garage's roof. He gazed down at Sophie as the wind caught her lustrous hair and blew it around her perfect face. He caught the scent of her shampoo and swallowed hard.

So . . . she liked vampires.

The dark part of him – the slowly rumbling, glowing-eyed monster part of him – smiled cruelly and inhaled deeply, absorbing her scent until he knew that he no longer appeared even remotely human. His little archess fantasized about being taken by him, pierced by him. She imagined having an orgasm beneath his fanged ministrations. She wondered what it would feel like, even as she 'knew' it wasn't possible. Such things as vampires didn't exist.

Azrael understood that it was a fantasy and was meant only to be such. Humans often imagined things that were pleasant in a make-believe world. However, to believe that vampires didn't exist was a shortsighted assumption on Sophie's part. She, in particular, should have known better. She already believed in the supernatural; Juliette had introduced her thoroughly to their world.

Sophie thought him an angel.

'Little fool,' he whispered. There was more than one kind of angel.

# Chapter 13

Sophie shook her head and pushed the images out of her mind. Her body was uncomfortably flushed now. It was a cool night, as it almost always was in San Francisco, but she was warm. All over.

She sighed heavily and shoved a mass of golden locks out of her face with an impatient hand. She'd thought that moving to the coast and not having any contact with the rock star archangel would get Azrael out of her head, but it appeared that wasn't the case. She had to admit to herself now that she had it bad for him. Which was just pathetic. She'd never imagined that she would become obsessed with someone, but that seemed to be the case.

She was even taking liberties with her little obsession. She'd imagined Azrael doing so many different things to her in so many different ways, it was becoming crowded in her head. Now she'd turned him into a vampire and was including his band mates? She made a frustrated sound, stopped in her tracks, and pinched the bridge of her nose. She couldn't help it! They were so *hot*! And she knew damn well that she wasn't the only woman in the world to harbor such thoughts about certain men. It was natural – it was what imaginations were *for*!

She dropped her hand and turned to peer out over the

dark, bottomless bay once more. *I'm just daydreaming*, she told herself soothingly. Wasn't a girl allowed to day-dream?

Alcatraz Island winked at her, flashing its signal and then going black once more. Sophie blinked. She pushed up the sleeve of her jacket and glanced at the oversized watch that dangled from her left wrist. The cable car would be leaving any minute now. She'd been caught up in her reveries and moving a little slower than she'd thought.

Sophie turned and sprinted down the Embarcadero toward Ghirardelli Square. She'd been blessed with long legs that now came in handy, helping her to eat up the ground at a quick pace. She was also lucky that there was almost no one else on the piers at that hour, so no one got in her way to slow her down.

She made it to the cable-car stop with several seconds to spare and slipped onto one of the outside benches. There were about half a dozen other riders at this time of night, as opposed to how it was in the middle of the day, when every available inch of the transportation device was occupied and ten people stood clinging to the poles on either side of the car.

Sophie was about to pull the monthly public transportation pass she'd purchased out of her messenger bag when the cable-car operator boarded the car and saw her sitting on the end.

'Well, hey, girl,' he said, smiling. 'I don't need to see your card again; it hasn't changed, right?' He cocked his head to one side, teasing her.

She smiled, shook her head, and closed the bag.

'I was wondering if you were gonna catch this last run,' he

told her as he looked around to make certain everyone who wanted to ride was on.

'Am I that predictable?'

'You *are* making kind of a habit of this,' he said, chuckling. He was a big guy; it took a lot of muscle to work the deadweight of the cable car. Sophie watched him pop the massive clutch-like brake out of its locked position, and the cable car started to roll forward. 'But I'm glad to have you aboard,' he added once they'd cleared the exit. He winked at her, his middle-aged, dark-skinned face wrinkling merrily under the expression.

Sophie hid her blush by looking away and focusing her attention on the row houses and streets as they passed by. San Francisco was all hills and coastline; every intersection they reached went up sharply one way and down just as sharply the other. But despite the attention-grabbing inclines, one distinctive detail remained easily visible, appearing in shop windows and taped to the walls outside of apartment complexes.

Valley of Shadow was coming to San Francisco. The band's posters were enormous Gothic-inspired black-on-black works of art that featured the group in agonizingly tempting detail. Five pairs of piercing eyes stared out at the world with dark promise. Sophie could barely bring herself to look at them.

The band would be playing this weekend – and the concert had been sold out for months. Sophie knew because she'd actually looked into acquiring tickets. She didn't normally spend money on anything that could be considered 'frivolous.' She purchased her clothes at second-hand and vintage stores; she *loved* the shops along Haight-Ashbury. She never went to a professional hairstylist, instead choosing to trim her own ends. She slept on a futon, and bought her table and chairs at Goodwill.

But she loved music. She always had. Valley of Shadow was up there at the top of her list.

For so many reasons.

Sophie thought about her 'date' with Azrael and the note he'd left on her bed before apparently leaving town. On the one hand, it hurt that she hadn't seen him since then. She hated that she felt a little like a one-night stand, despite the fact that there had been no sex involved.

On the other hand, she felt awkward enough as it was. Forget the third-wheel thing. Sophie felt more like a *ninth* wheel. There were four archangel brothers and each one had an archess. She might be Juliette's best friend, but Jules really had made a new life for herself and it included being a part of a family that contained four very definite, fated-in-the-stars couples. She wasn't a part of that.

She and Jules had spoken over the phone a lot since the wedding, but even during those conversations, Sophie couldn't shake the feeling of being an outcast. It would be strange when she visited Juliette. *If* she visited Juliette.

Sophie closed her eyes just then and swallowed back the swell of sadness that rose in her throat. She didn't like that thought. So she shoved it away and opened her eyes to stare out once more at the up-and-down streets and the bay that stretched dark and misty beyond.

As the car started up Hyde, a street that was decidedly non-horizontal, Sophie held on to the bar beside her to keep from sliding across the bench and smashing into the couple seated a few feet away. It was fun; it cleared her mind of her previously unpleasant thoughts. She loved the cable cars; they were a carnival ride, a nostalgic history lesson, and reliable transportation all rolled into one.

As always, once they reached Washington, Sophie had the choice of getting off and walking the seven blocks to her apartment on Hemlock – or staying on and taking the cable cars out of her way so that she could catch another on California and get a little closer to Hemlock without walking through alleyways. It took longer to stay on the cars, but it was safer and she certainly didn't mind the ride. She was never tired at this time of night. If she had her way, she would wake up at ten or eleven in the morning and not go to sleep until four a.m.

In fact, she'd been presented with that choice of late. She would begin classes in the fall, but that meant that she had the whole summer in San Francisco. Her parents' inheritance money, combined with what she'd saved from working over the last ten years, was enough that for once, if she chose to, she could go without working for a summer or two. She could kick back, sleep in, roam the streets of Frisco – er, *San Francisco* – without having to worry about getting to work on time.

No alarm clocks. No curfews. Just life to live, time to live it, and a beautiful place to live it in. It was somewhat stunning to realize that she suddenly had this freedom.

Where had it come from? Had it always been there, waiting for her to take it? Or had she earned it herself?

Sophie smiled and shook her head. She felt scared – but all in all, pretty happy with life at that moment.

She stayed on the cable car until they reached California, and then she waved to the operator and hopped off. It was a little after one a.m. and a few minutes before the second cable car would come along, but there were other people waiting at the junction as well, so despite the late hour, she never felt that she was in any danger.

She was sitting on the steps in front of the Caffe Cento and more or less staring off into space when the sound of footfalls beside her drew her out of her reverie. She looked up . . . and up. Shock hit her system and her adrenal glands began pumping like mad. Her heart thudded hard, almost painfully, and she shot to her feet.

'Az!' she exclaimed, not knowing what else to say. At once, she shoved her hair out of her face again and wondered if she looked as much like a rag doll as she felt in that moment.

Azrael was standing just a few feet away, gazing down at her through those amber eyes that scorched her to her core. His perfect lips were turned up in an enigmatic, absolutely beautiful smile. As always, he was dressed in dark hues and, as always, they flattered his tall, strong figure in a way that made her chest ache and her stomach coil with warmth.

To make matters worse, he wasn't alone. Uro was with him, and the gorgeous guitarist was watching her with the same mysterious and oddly flattering expression that graced Azrael's perfect features.

She could barely stand it. Hell, she could barely breathe.

'Sophie,' Az said, allowing her name to roll off of his tongue with such deep, delicious clarity that Sophie could have melted. He bowed his head in a respectful nod, his eyes never leaving hers. The sound of his voice instantly brought to mind the images she had been entertaining only minutes ago on the pier, and her blush was back, but this time it was furious.

*Pull yourself together.*

Her inner voice had grown stern, managing to override the chattering of nervous twitters echoing through the remaining chambers of her brain. She rolled back her shoulders and offered Az a lopsided smile. 'What are you doing here?' she asked, truly curious. How the hell did they keep managing to meet up?

Azrael hadn't stopped watching her. His eyes glittered with untold emotion. His smile broadened before he gestured to his band mate beside him and said, 'It's rather difficult for us to get out during the day.' He looked beyond Sophie to the few people remaining on the streets. 'But right now, we're more free to relax,' he explained.

'We needed a break,' Uro added. Sophie glanced at him and felt her blush deepen. He'd featured rather prominently in her last little daydream. And with the way he was looking at her right now, she could almost swear that he *knew* that.

'You're setting up for the concert this weekend,' she supplied, figuring it out despite the befuddled feel of her brain. Anyone who knew Valley of Shadow would recognize Uro on sight. And if they spotted Uro with a tall, handsome man with long black hair and an angelic voice, they would put two and two together and figure out that Az was the Masked One. His cover would be blown.

'Indeed,' Uro said in reference to the concert.

'I understand,' said Sophie, as if she weren't at all affected by their sudden presence. 'You're playing at the stadium.'

'There's quite a bit of work to do to get it ready,' said Uro.

'I can imagine,' Sophie said. The AT&T Giants baseball stadium was an enormous venue capable of seating more than forty thousand people. Once again, Valley of Shadow was following in the footsteps of some very notable greats such as Metallica and AC/DC. And she expected that, unlike shows by other bands who more often than not encountered acoustical problems as they tried to find ways to make themselves heard across that many seats, Valley concerts were always perfect, always mind-blowing. Nothing ever went wrong. Sophie figured she probably had the inside scoop as to why Valley of Shadow always succeeded in impressing its enormous crowds. Azrael was an archangel. He could do anything.

She wondered if his band mates knew. She realized just then that she would feel so much better if they did. It would mean she wasn't really a ninth wheel after all. She would simply be part of a circle of trust.

'Sophie.'

Sophie's head snapped up to meet Azrael's gaze. He never failed to yank her attention back to him, as if she were a puppet on a cord.

'It's fortunate that we should meet tonight,' he said softly. 'I'd been hoping you would attend Saturday's concert.' He had either the audacity or the raw talent – or both – to look genuinely coy in that moment as he shoved his hands into the pockets of his trench coat and offered up a slightly crooked smile. 'In fact, I'd planned to have an invitation and a backstage pass dropped off at your new place, but since we're both here right now . . .' His voice trailed off and his eyes filled the silence. 'Perhaps you'd consider joining Uro and me for the evening?'

If she could have pulled her gaze from his, Sophie would have checked to see whether the earth had slipped out from beneath her feet. Azrael the archangel was asking her out again?

*Don't get ahead of yourself, Soph.* After all, he wasn't alone. It couldn't really be considered a date if she was with both of them, could it?

She opened her mouth to answer, and in a dry voice said, 'I'm sure you guys have your own thing planned for tonight. You don't need me tagging along.'

Azrael's smile broadened.

'Nonsense,' Uro said.

'Absolutely not,' Az agreed. The two came forward at once, moving to either side of Sophie. She froze as they effectively caged her in; it was rather discomfiting being surrounded by their incredibly strong presences. But then they turned and deftly wove their arms through hers, hooking them at the elbows. It was a friendly gesture, done gently and intimately.

Sophie was too surprised to say anything when they began walking back down the street the way they'd come, taking her right along with them.

# Chapter 14

Her name was the *Calliope*. And she was stunning.

Every inch of her was pristine, perfect white. She was a cutter ketch, with two masts and four sails, and the symbol painted in white relief on the back and sides was a pair of angel wings that matched the shape of the sails themselves.

The *Calliope* was Azrael's boat. It surprised Sophie for some reason. Maybe it was the fact that he always wore black and leather. He just didn't seem the sailing type. And not only did he own a boat; he docked it at Pier 39, the most famous dock in the nation.

When he and Uro had walked her from the cable-car stop, they'd put her in a limousine and driven her right back to the wharf she'd just left. From there, they walked her down to the C dock and through the gate that led to the slightly unsteady walkway and the scores of vessels lined up beyond.

She knew she'd stared with wide eyes and an open mouth when Azrael gestured to the *Calliope* and welcomed her aboard. She couldn't help it. It was just too much – too perfect. If she'd woken up and recalled everything clearly, she would have considered herself one lucky girl for having such an incredible and unrealistic dream.

But she wasn't dreaming. This was all real.

Sophie looked up once again from her seat on the deck where Az had placed her. Uro was in the cockpit of the boat, an indentation at the ship's center where the steering wheel, radar readout, and engine control were located. Azrael was at the forward end of the boat, doing something with the ropes that Sophie vaguely remembered her mother talking about.

The bay was Sophie's favorite part of the city. It was the reason she insisted on living in San Fran instead of Berkeley, despite the fact that she would have to take the Richmond train under the water every Monday, Wednesday, and Friday for classes. She needed to have an excuse to be near the sea as often as possible. Maybe it was the bay's connection to her mother . . . maybe it was simply that the ocean was free.

Whatever the reason, as she had been walked out onto the pier and introduced to Azrael's secret hobby, Sophie had found herself feeling genuinely happy. Happier than she'd been in a very long time.

She had no idea how she'd gotten to be so lucky. She figured she must have done something good in a past life — who knew? But she'd come to a decision as he had helped her up onto the pristine deck of his boat. If Azrael the archangel didn't mind hanging out with her while he waited for his perfect archess to come along, then she wasn't going to mind either. Granted, he was bound to ruin her for all other men, but it was worth it.

A part of her had been initially uneasy about the idea of going out onto the dark water at night with two very obviously strong men, no matter how handsome they were. No one knew where she was. A lot of bad things could go down.

But her fear dissipated with the first reassuring, heart-wrenchingly warm and inviting smile Azrael had cast her way. *Poof.* It was gone. And she found herself smiling back – almost laughing out loud – with the gleeful anticipation of what was to come.

Once they'd lifted the ropes off the dock and Uro motored the boat out into the open waters of the bay, Azrael hoisted the sails. Sophie's throat felt tight as she watched the sails rise and pop loudly when the wind filled them with its Pacific breath. There wasn't much wind, of course, but at their height, it was enough for the sails to catch and hold.

It was a relatively calm night for April and the more dangerous thick fog had yet to ride in from the west. Sophie wasn't a sailor, but she knew enough about boats and fog to understand that the two didn't mix. The bank of white low-lying clouds seemed stationary, at least for the moment, and she knew in her heart that even if it did decide to roll in full-swing, Azrael could handle it.

Sophie watched the archangel leave his place at the fore end of the boat and make his way once more to her side. There, he shrugged off his trench coat and Sophie went still as he settled it over her shoulders. He knelt before her and his gaze leveled with hers. Sophie found herself holding her breath.

'Is that better?' he asked with a killer smile.

Sophie blinked. She hadn't been cold. It made no sense; the San Francisco nights were cursed with wet air that cut to the bone, especially out on the sea. But Azrael's nearness and the very fact that she was on a sailboat had honestly chased away her discomfort. She'd barely noticed it. But she didn't want him to know that.

'Yes,' she breathed, smiling back. The coat was heavy and made of some rich material that smelled like Azrael – like sandalwood soap and the very night that he seemed so much a part of. *I'm in heaven.*

As if he could hear her thoughts, Azrael chuckled softly, again sending a warm shiver rolling through Sophie's body. And then he stood and turned his attentions back to the boat and the water around them.

The gorgeous, streamlined hull of the *Calliope* sliced through the deep, dark water with quiet precision, parting the thin streams of mist ahead of it without fear or hesitation.

Every once in a while, Az left her side on the deck and moved to the front of the boat, where he was right now.

*Trimming and easing*, she told herself, recalling the terms for what Az was doing with the ropes. In the cockpit, Uro took the ropes that Az loosened or tightened and wrapped them around a wench and then cranked the wench on his end. They were making the sails more taut or relaxed, based on how much wind they wanted them to catch. It determined direction and speed to a certain extent.

Sophie smiled, proud of herself for recalling so much. Although her mother had taken sailing lessons, Sophie actually knew very little about it herself. Still, it seemed she had more in her subconscious than she'd thought.

Azrael finished adjusting the sail and looked back at her and smiled. Sophie's breath caught. In those moments, when he smiled at her like that, she felt as if she were the only woman in the world.

She was so wrapped up in how the rock star archangel was making her feel, it took a while for her to realize that the fog had indeed decided to roll in. With a bit of a start, she straightened and looked around. A wall of white had almost entirely surrounded the *Calliope* and was moving closer by the second. Sophie had been watching the low, rolling waves that gave the boat gentle shoves and were mesmerizing in their constant ebb and flow. Now she looked up and over the bay to find that visibility around the yacht had been diminished to a mere fifty feet or so.

The night was calm; what wind there was would never cut through the dense pea soup that was subjugating the bay around them. Sophie watched it approach, and as it came nearer, she recalled the reverie she'd entertained earlier that night. She'd stood on the pier and looked out over the water and wondered what it would be like to sail the sea in the fog, surrounded by only the quiet and the lapping of the waves on the hull.

And now . . . here she was. By some fortuitous twist, she'd dreamed something and in the next hour that dream had come true. Sophie's gaze became lost as she stared into the mist around them. They were in another realm on the *Calliope*, a trio of landlubbers hoping for a one-night stand with wayward waters.

Suddenly, both Azrael and Uro were standing back and letting go of the rigging and the controls. They became still, straightening where they stood, their expressions at once as calm as the sea, as if a reflection of the water upon which they sailed. But they also appeared to be watching the mists around them.

It was as if they were waiting for something.

Sophie frowned. She turned to Azrael as he made his way over to her with wholly unnatural grace. Only an archangel could move the way he did. Nearly everything he did was a reminder that he was something more than human.

Azrael stopped in front of her and offered her his hand.

'What's going on?' she whispered. It was so quiet, she felt that to speak any louder would be sacrilege.

'You'll see,' he replied, with an enigmatic smile. She placed her hand in his and he helped her stand, maintaining his gentle but firm grip on her hand once she had her legs beneath her. The boat gently swayed with the motion of the slow, rolling waves.

As always, Azrael's touch was electric, sending a buzzing warmth up through her arm and into her chest. She felt her cheeks redden as she looked about them, trying to make out any kind of shape or form at all beyond the wall of thick white that had formed around them.

Sophie's hair was now damp with moisture from the low-lying clouds, and strands of her long, golden locks had formed corkscrew curls to frame her face. She could feel their wet kisses upon her cheeks.

Azrael's grip on her tightened just a little and she looked up at him. His smile was predatory and perfect, and a glint of something mischievous touched his sunbeam eyes. He turned away to look up at an angle. She watched as he raised his free hand toward the sky.

Sophie felt her jaw drop and her lips part as the wind picked up and the fog around them began to recoil from the area around the boat. Tendrils of white spun backward, as if someone had waved a massive turbine blade through their midst. The fog roiled and ebbed, clearing a path of fog-free air from the boat upward.

The clear path climbed and climbed, spreading high above the *Calliope* until finally it lifted outward and revealed the rust-orange beams of a massive, glorious, world-famous structure.

The Golden Gate Bridge soared above the sailboat, revealing itself to Sophie and her companions with a graceful, silent glory. Its tremendous support columns and cables rose to majestic, mind-blowing heights, claiming the night sky as if it were its queen and the stars above were its diamond-laden throne.

'Oh my God,' Sophie whispered. Her chest felt at once tight and wide open. She felt choked with emotion and also wanted to laugh – to shout and dance and cry. It was probably the most beautiful thing she had ever seen, and she was seeing it from a vantage point that few were ever lucky enough to witness.

High above, late night travelers continued in their routes across one of the only two bridges that connected San Francisco to the rest of California. She watched their tiny headlights spear through the darkness. She watched the sea-gulls weave in and out of the cables. She listened as the foghorns sounded somewhere in the distance and the bridge above remained stoically proud, a gateway to the promised land draped in royal red garb, strong and true.

She must have been staring for five minutes or more when she was finally struck with something so important she couldn't believe it hadn't occurred to her right away.

She blinked and lowered her head, ignoring the twinge of pain that came from her neck as she finally changed positions. Despite the view above, Azrael wasn't watching the bridge. He was watching her. Being the object of his attention was like being in an intense spotlight, and for a moment, she almost forgot to ask him what she needed to ask.

'Az,' she finally managed, chancing a glance at Uro, who was staring up at the bridge. 'Does this mean . . . I mean . . .' She ducked her head a little and turned her back to the guitarist so that he wouldn't hear. 'Does he know . . .' She trailed off. The fact that Azrael had cleared the fog away from the boat and opened a view to the bridge above meant that he'd used some kind of magic, not only in front of her, but in front of Uro as well. She wasn't perfectly clear on what an archangel could and couldn't do; Juliette had bombarded her with too much information on the subject all at once. But she was pretty clear that humans possessed no such powers.

Azrael wasn't so stupid that he would use his archangel abilities in front of anyone who didn't already know what he was unless he was planning to let them in on the secret. There had been no untoward reaction from his band mate. Which meant that Uro knew – and *that* meant that she wasn't alone in knowing the truth about Azrael. She wasn't a ninth wheel after all. But she was afraid to ask for the confirmation out loud – just in case.

Azrael's smile was warm. He nodded. 'He's known for some time, Sophie.' The sound of his deep, throaty chuckle was so enticing, it was a veritable music of its own, and the way he said her name made her legs go weak beneath her. 'They all have.' He glanced at Uro and then back down at her, and Sophie understood that he was referring to the other members of Valley of Shadow.

Sophie tried not to let her very physical response to him show, instead turning away to once more gaze up at the bridge.

'Does it please you?' he asked, releasing her hand so that he could gently tuck a stray strand of her golden hair behind her ear. She shivered and, just for a moment, closed her eyes. It was involuntary.

*Yes*, she thought helplessly. *Oh yes* . . .

'We used to come out here when I was little,' she told him. 'The bay was my mother's favorite place in the world.' She looked from the bridge to the man beside her. He was watching her so carefully, appearing to listen so intently, she couldn't help but go on. 'She took sailing lessons in San Francisco and promised that when she was good enough, she would bring us out here herself.'

For half a second, Sophie saw the gravestone that bore her mother's name. For the tiniest fraction of a moment, she felt the all too familiar sadness that came when recalling that her mother had never been given that opportunity. She'd never sailed them out to the bridge herself. Death had taken her before she'd had the chance.

*Death.*

But then the thought was gone and her sadness was lifted and all she could do was stare up into the glowing golden gaze of the archangel beside her.

*Glowing?*

Again, her uncertainty was there one split second and gone in the next, lifted away just as easily and quickly as the fog had lifted from the hull and sails of the *Calliope*.

'Sophie,' Azrael said as he turned to face her fully. Sophie felt mesmerized by him, trapped in space and time. She was happy and numb and filled with breathless anticipation all at once. 'Sweet, sweet Sophie.' With both hands this time, he tucked the hair once more behind her ears and then very gently cupped her face. His fingertips brushed the back of her neck and his thumbs touched lovingly upon her cheekbones.

He used this intimate, tender grip to hold her fast as he took the final step that closed the distance between them.

Sophie could barely breathe. She couldn't blink, couldn't look away. Azrael lowered his head, closing the two of them off from the rest of the world as everything she knew in that moment became only what she could see in his eyes.

'I'm so sorry, my love,' he told her. 'If it had been me . . .' He paused and shook his head just a little. Sophie could only wait and listen. 'I never would have hurt you.' His words whispered across her lips, he was so close. '*Never*, Sophie. I wouldn't have allowed you that pain.'

There was no boat and no bridge and no sea and no bay as Azrael the archangel brushed his right thumb across her plump bottom lip. Sophie was no longer processing coherent thought. His words floated through her and away, and it was merely the sound of his beautiful voice that occupied the deepest recesses of her mind. She shivered once more beneath the incredible influence of his touch.

And then he was closing in and his power was all around her, inside of her, encompassing her. He bent, graceful and certain, and just before his lips found hers, she closed her eyes again, at once lost in a sensation so heavenly blissful she was sure that she would die.

# Chapter 15

He couldn't help himself. It might have been wrong. She might have needed more time. But he'd been in her head all night, taking away her fear, using his vampire powers to put her at ease and erase her worries. He'd surrounded her with the calm and happiness he so badly wanted her to experience. And in doing so, he had left himself open and exposed to everything sweet and pure and beautiful that was Sophie Bryce.

It was a mistake. Regardless of what Randall had said, Azrael couldn't trust himself around Sophie. Any other woman, yes. He'd existed for countless generations; he'd seen more, heard more, and felt more than most humans could fathom in their most altered of states. He'd been everywhere, and through it all, temptation had been on the back burner, always waiting, always potential, but never demanding his full attention.

Not since his transformation. Not until now.

It was her innocence that intoxicated him the most. She knew so little; all of humanity knew so little. But Sophie accepted it, was aware of it, and would never try to hide it. She watched him part the fog as Moses was said to have parted the sea, and she assumed it was simply an archangel power that she was unaware of. In truth, archangels could not control the weather; that was a talent reserved for the archesses alone. And for Samael, who was an enigma in so many ways.

However, Azrael was a vampire and vampires exerted a certain amount of control over the very air around them. It was this influence that allowed them to fly. If a fog existed, he could bring it in closer. He could also send it away. The older the vampire, the farther his reach. It was hardly a task at all for Az to clear a way to the bridge above and light up the fire in Sophie's eyes.

That something so simple could make her so happy – this woman who had been through so much in her short life – was nearly beyond his ability to comprehend. She turned her smile on him and he felt the warmth of the sun . . . after all this time. He was instantly lost in that light.

And then she had opened up to him, so innocent and truthful. She'd shared with him something that she hadn't shared with anyone else, ever. It meant she trusted him.

It was his undoing.

Now, as he took her head in his hands and held her beneath him, he caught the clean scent of her simple shampoo and the soap she'd used on her perfect flesh. On her breath he could smell the chocolate and caramel from the Ghirardelli shop on Pier 39. Above it all, he caught the sweet, sweet scent of her blood. It was all around him, teasing him, urging him on.

The monster within him awoke and came to attention, its head rearing, its eyes glowing. With a body that nearly trembled with need and breath that was painfully bated, Azrael leaned in and claimed Sophie's lips in a kiss.

He felt the shudder move through her body, an instant wave of pleasure that he was helpless to keep from releasing into her. The archangel in him was slipping into the shadows; he was mostly vampire now, hungry and determined. She tasted like candy. She was warm and soft beneath his fingertips. He knew his fangs were lengthening; he didn't care. He could feel them press threateningly against her plump lips as he parted them and took what he wanted.

Would they pierce her?

*Yes*, he thought desperately. He wanted them to. His body was aching; he was painfully hard now; it had taken mere seconds for him to lose so much control. He wanted to let the rest of it go. He could rip the jackets from her body – or simply wave them away with archangel magic. He wanted to see her . . . her long, lithe form, the sweet tenderness of her milky flesh. She would shiver and melt into him and he could take her here and now.

Would Uro attempt to stop him? Try to save her?

*No*, he thought. When a vampire took a female victim, the act was pure eroticism. Other vampires became entranced at the sight, instantly aroused. It was why Az had never fed from a female, not in two thousand years. He could not bring himself to get that close to anyone who wasn't his archess.

But now here she was, caught in his embrace, and his teeth were showing. If anything, Azrael could have invited Uro to join him.

Azrael almost chuckled at the thought. It was Sophie's fantasy, was it not? The archangel within him was nearly dead as he smiled against her lips and felt the tip of one of his fangs prick at her tender flesh. He was all vampire now, wicked and sinful. Any thoughts of waiting, of taking it slow for Sophie's sake, were faint whispers and distant memories.

*Give in to me*. It was an unnecessary command; physically,

Sophie had all but surrendered. She was an archess, but her powers were as yet undiscovered and without them, she was for all intents and purposes a mortal. She was no match for him. Not here – not now.

Even if she had been, Azrael no longer felt like playing fair.

The softest moan escaped Sophie's lips, vibrating gently against Azrael and then rushing through his system like gasoline on a fire. The flames of his desire roared to leaping life and before he knew fully what he was doing, his hand was fisting in her flaxen hair.

He broke the kiss as gently as he could, and the night was filled with the sound of harsh, ragged breaths. Whether they were hers or his or both, he could no longer tell. He was composed of want in that moment, dictated by need.

He opened his eyes to find the world colored in stark contrasts. His eyes were no doubt glowing like double suns. His fangs were pronounced, and his skin was probably just a touch too pale against the raven black of his long hair. The king of the vampires pulled his mate's hair to the side and leaned in. There was no going back now. The song of her pulse called to him, rapid and inescapable. His grip on her tightened, his lips parted – and then he smelled it: the acrid stench of impending death.

He would never have noticed it if not for the heightened state of his senses. If Sophie hadn't been so devastatingly tempting, he wouldn't have been in full vampire mode and never would have caught the wafting note of a supernatural assassin on the misty winds of San Francisco Bay.

With a start, he straightened and fought the urge to slip into the nearest shadow with Sophie in order to keep her safe.

At once he was communicating his findings to the vampires who waited and watched in San Francisco and beyond. He called them to his location; there was safety in numbers.

However, it made no sense. It had been *ages* since the particular creatures he sensed had shown their presence in any capacity. In fact, Azrael and his brothers had often wondered whether the very dangerous, very deadly monsters had all but become extinct.

But there it was, as icy and telling as a cold breath on the back of the neck. There was a phantom out there somewhere. And there was only one reason phantoms were *ever* found *anywhere*. They were the assassins of the supernatural world.

Azrael wanted to rip through the universe at that moment; it was conspiring against him. He felt his eyes flash to bright, boiling red and glanced at Uro to find that his first created vampire had already slipped into the same hyper-aware and fight-ready state.

As if to confirm his suspicions, a horrid screeching sound came from the bridge above them. Az looked up in time to see one of the massive cables on the side of the bridge vibrate dangerously. And then, before his eyes, a Mack truck jackknifed impossibly through the small opening between two of the strong cables and was airborne.

The enormous vehicle seemed to remain suspended for half a second, its trailer caught on one of the cables before it broke free and began its rapid descent toward the water, heading straight for the *Calliope*.

Az immediately wrapped his arms around Sophie, flooded her mind with his power to black it out, and took to the skies. He sensed Uro doing the same somewhere nearby.

Seconds after they were airborne, the truck went sailing

past him and Azrael watched in furious fascination as the massive vehicle collided with his boat, splintering the vessel in an earsplitting display.

Shreds of white-painted wood and steel shot into the air in a bloom of destruction. The water heaved, metal groaned both above on the bridge and below on the sea, and almost at once the bay began to swallow the remains of the crash.

Azrael knew that someone was inside that truck. If the driver was still alive, time was running out for him. He would need to be pulled from the wreckage and healed, and for that, Az needed either Michael or one of the two archesses who had realized their powers.

Az looked up toward the bridge and sailed higher, making sure to shroud his form in darkness so that no one would inadvertently see him. Somewhere, the phantom lurked. His presence could be felt more strongly up here, and Azrael's skin was starting to crawl.

The mess on the bridge was substantial. At least a dozen cars had piled up. No doubt many passengers were either dead or seriously injured. There was no question that the phantom had caused the wreck. The fact that a vehicle the size of an eighteen-wheeler was able to make it over the railings of the bridge and into open water at all was testament to that. Such a feat would have been nearly impossible under normal circumstances; the bridge had been built with the intention of avoiding exactly such a catastrophe. A car would have to jump one railing only to surpass the pedestrian walkway and jump yet another railing before finally pushing past the impossibly thick mass of giant cables that helped to suspend the bridge.

Az turned to find Uro hovering in the air close by. His

normally black eyes were now glowing a hot, angry red.

*I'm getting her out of here. I will summon Max and the others to clean up the mess*, Az told him.

Uro nodded once and shot farther up into the sky so quickly that if Azrael had not been the vampire he was, he would not have been able to trace the movement. Az watched the mists swirl in a mini-vortex through the hole in the fog that Uro had left behind. A split second later, the vampire returned, only inches from where he'd gone up, and dove into the water like a blurred rocket. His streamlined dive barely made a splash.

Uro would be able to break the truck open and get the driver out. If the driver was alive, Uro could then direct Michael to heal him, and Max could wipe the man's memory clean.

Az glanced up as he sensed the vampires he'd contacted begin to arrive. Quickly, he transferred the information they would need to monitor the situation, watch their backs, and make sure as few people as possible died that night.

When he was finished, he tightened his grip on his archess and shot across the night sky. When he got to the pier, he landed and turned toward the nearest shadow, formed by the moon and the building's east wall. Holding Sophie close to him, Azrael stepped into the shadow and allowed the world to shift around him. Shadow transportation magic allowed a being to step into a space of inky blackness in one location and exit the darkness through a shadow miles away.

Their surroundings grew insubstantial and murky, and then Az was stepping through a shadow on the other side and coming out into a massive man-made cavern.

The interior of the cave was lit by the crackling flames of

torches in sconces along the carved stone walls. It was one of Azrael's many underground chambers around the world. This particular one existed not too far from San Francisco. He'd chosen it without giving it much thought; it had been instinctive. However, later he would realize he'd done so because it would protect Sophie from jet lag, since here she could stay on the same hourly schedule as far as day and night were concerned.

It would be strange enough for her as it was, having her mind messed with as much as he'd been forced to mess with it. She wouldn't remember how she'd gotten from point A to point B unless he planted the false information in her head.

Azrael gently laid Sophie down on his black satin-dressed bed and stood back. Then he swore softly, ran a rough hand through his long black hair, and turned away from her. Everything was falling apart.

*You have to do it, Az. You have to tell her, whether she's ready or not.*

He listened to his inner voice with reluctant acceptance. He knew it was time. Something had either tried to kill Sophie tonight or gone to a lot of trouble in order to scare Azrael. There was no way the phantom had caused the pileup on the bridge in order to kill Az; everyone knew Az was a vampire and could avoid such an attack. A phantom would know that for sure.

Either the Adarians were at some sort of plan that Azrael couldn't figure, or there was another player on the field. If phantoms and Nightmares were roaming Earth again, it was entirely possible that other creatures were as well – perhaps wraiths, or even dragons. In fact, Az had a feeling that this vibration of change he'd been sensing in the air of late was the result of something more important and on a much larger scale than he'd originally thought.

Something big was either already going down – or was about to.

Azrael waved a hand dismissively toward the stone fireplace that had been carved into one wall. It immediately leapt to life with warm, crackling flame. Then he took a deep, slow breath and shrugged off his leather jacket to lay it over one of two nearby plush leather chairs. His trench coat had been draped over Sophie and was lost in the flight from the boat. He rolled up the sleeves of his button-down black shirt and then slowly sank into the empty chair. Both love seats were black. Everything in the room was. He liked black.

On the bed, Sophie stirred and her golden caramel hair spilled across the ebony satin like a honey-colored waterfall. It shimmered in the flickering torchlight that painted the walls in red and yellow, and Azrael's fingertips itched.

Slowly, gracefully, he stood up and approached the bed. With the dexterous determination of a prowling predator, he leaned over the bed, braced his strong arms on either side of Sophie's unconscious form, and leaned in.

Once more the scent of her shampoo, soap, and blood assaulted his hyper-aware senses. His vision shifted, his fangs erupted again in his mouth, and his body tensed. He knew he was torturing himself, but he couldn't help it. He was a moth to the flame. Only it wasn't the moth who could get hurt this time, but the flame – the beautiful, sleeping, unaware, and innocent flame.

And then Sophie moved again, this time turning her head and opening her eyes. She looked right at him, her golden gaze unfocused at first. Azrael froze, disbelieving what he was seeing. He had her under his control – how was she coming out of the sleep he had forced on her?

It wasn't possible.

'Az?' she asked groggily, her brow furrowing in confusion as he no doubt came into focus.

Az shoved his fangs back into his gums and hurriedly closed his eyes, not wanting her to see what was most likely a red glow at the center of his pitch-black pupils.

'What . . .'

He felt her move under him and chanced opening his eyes. His vision had returned to normal. Sophie was looking around, taking in the massive bed, stone walls, and flickering torches.

'What happened? Where are we?' she asked. Then she was looking at him again, and the confusion in her face made his heart ache. 'What happened to the boat?'

Azrael thought fast. 'You fell asleep on the deck, so I let you sleep and brought you here.'

Sophie started to sit up and Azrael moved back out of the way, allowing her room.

'No,' she said, shaking her head and holding her hand to her temple. She frowned, blinked, and stared unseeing at the black comforter beneath her. 'No, that's not right,' she insisted. 'I saw it destroyed.'

Shock buzz-sawed through Azrael. *Impossible*, he thought. He'd asserted his influence on her mind the moment he'd heard the sound of the crash up on the bridge. How could she be aware of what had happened to the *Calliope*?

And worse – if she recalled that, did she recall everything else? Like . . . him taking to the skies with her, for instance?

'Someone was hurt,' she went on. And as she said it, she

climbed further up, coming to her knees beside him. She seemed panicked suddenly. 'We have to help them. Did we help them? Did we heal them?' She looked at Azrael, her gold eyes catching his in their sunshine warmth. 'Az, what happened? And . . . oh my God,' she whispered, her hand dropping to the mattress beside her. 'You . . . can fly?' Her expression was one of awe. 'Without your wings?'

# Chapter 16

The events of the last hour were a blur to Sophie, but she recalled them clearly enough to know that something bad had happened. She'd been standing on the deck of the *Calliope* – kissing Azrael. And then there'd been a noise. It was distant, but jarring. She remembered looking up in time to see something fall.

Then there'd been a blur and another horrible crashing sound, this one much louder than the first. She had looked down to see Azrael's boat in ruins, its fragments sinking along with the thing that had destroyed it – a truck. At least, she thought it was a truck. This was where the blur became thicker, like a fog obscuring the picture of her past.

But through the mists, she was hyper-aware of one vital fact: People had been hurt and they needed to be healed.

*Healed.*

That was the thought that had gone through her head. She'd known they needed *healing*. Not necessarily a doctor or an ambulance or a hospital. Just healing. And the most confounding thing about it was that she'd known – she'd absolutely *known* – that she could provide this healing herself. With her own two hands.

She remembered wanting to dive into the water after whoever it was that was undoubtedly sinking to the bottom of the bay. But something was stopping her. It was solid and yet insubstantial. It was strong but intangible. She felt pulled along in some kind of tide she couldn't fight. Her body wouldn't listen. Her mind didn't comprehend.

Her hands felt warm and her heart was hammering and she so desperately wanted to get to the injured parties, she would have traded her left pinky to be able to do so. But she couldn't *find* the injured people. She couldn't touch them. She could barely even see.

And then she was slip-sliding into blackness and as she did, she knew any hope she had of helping anyone was slip-sliding inexorably along with her.

Now clarity was returning and a cold numbness was setting in. She felt slightly sick, slightly edgy. She didn't recognize her surroundings and what she was recalling made no sense.

Either she was going nuts or she had just seen a horrible accident and Azrael had wrapped her in his arms – and taken to the sky with her.

She'd felt the deck of the boat leave her shoes; the solidness of it beneath her was gone. The wind in her hair felt different, as if the air was cocooned around her, supporting her weight. She'd been flying. It was impossible, but it was as insistent a memory as was the rest of the night.

Az told her she'd fallen asleep. If he was right, then she'd dreamed the things she'd seen and felt. But in her heart of hearts, deep down where she knew things really mattered – she knew that she hadn't. The boat was destroyed. Something bad had happened, and someone was hurt. And she would bet everything she had, what little it was, that Az had taken her flying.

The archangel sitting beside her had fallen oddly silent, and he was gazing at her now with an enigmatic expression on his face. She had no idea what he might be thinking. 'Az, what happened? Please tell me the truth. What's going on? And . . .' She paused as she looked around at the bed she was sitting on and the torch-lit cave it furnished. 'Where are we?'

It was a long, painful while before he said anything. She could see the light dance across his eyes, some of it a reflection of the flames on the torches along the walls, some of it his own internal fire. And then, finally, he sighed heavily.

He looked pained as he said, 'Sophie, God knows I didn't want to tell you like this. I just wanted to protect you.' He paused, looked away, and then stood. She watched as he moved around the bed toward the fireplace. A massive framed mirror rested above it, its edges seemingly gilded in gold.

A bazillion thoughts were racing through Sophie's mind at that moment, but despite them she couldn't help but admire the perfect proportions of Az's tall body. His shoulders were so broad and his waist so narrow, he looked like an impossible dream draped in black. The sleeves of his shirt had been rolled up and she could see the veins in his sculpted forearms from his elbows to the watch on his left wrist.

Slowly, gracefully, Az leaned against the stone mantel of the fireplace. She could see his face in the mirror, as always almost painfully beautiful. And then he closed his eyes and bowed his head and his silken black hair cascaded over his face.

'Soph, clearly you're coming into your powers now, and though I had hoped I would be able to ease you into this gently, it would appear I'm out of time.'

*Powers?* Sophie thought, feeling her fingers and toes

tingle. Her heart was hammering. It was as if her body and mind were preparing themselves for something all-encompassing.

Azrael lifted his head and opened his eyes. Sophie stifled a gasp. They were glowing.

'What's even more clear is that there is a force out there setting things in motion, and I have no idea who or what it is – or why it seems to be centered on you,' he continued.

Sophie watched, wide-eyed and silent, as he turned from the mirror then and pinned her with the full weight of that glowing gaze.

'You are an archess, Sophie Bryce.' He moved away from the mantel and took a slow, striding step toward her and the bed. 'You were created two thousand years ago by an entity neither I nor my brothers have heard from in all of that time. You were created . . .' Here he paused, stopped in his tracks, and something strange flickered across his eyes. 'You were created for me. And then you were lost, sent to Earth with the other archesses, and I have been searching for you for twenty centuries.'

He took another step, but Sophie could no longer hear the sound of his boots against the stone. The roar of her blood through her ears was deafening. Her chest felt odd and her head felt too light and there were stars dancing in her tunneling vision.

'You didn't know,' he told her, shaking his head once and coming flush with the bed. 'You didn't realize how precious you are for so many reasons. Most importantly, your abilities have remained hidden from you until . . .' He stopped, shook his head helplessly, and then shrugged. 'Well, until tonight.'

He closed his eyes and let out a shaky breath. 'I have no idea why.'

When he opened them again, they seemed dimmer than before. They weren't glowing as hotly. But then, his entire face seemed dimmer to Sophie. In fact, the strange cavernous room and its torches looked farther away. Darker.

*I'm fainting*, she realized. *Breathe, Sophie. Breathe!*

Whatever was happening, whatever the truth was, whatever dream she may or may not be stuck in, the last thing Sophie wanted to do in that moment was become unconscious in front of this man. He was an archangel. She knew that much to be true. But he was also the former Angel of Death. And that was proof enough to her that being an angel did not necessarily mean you were good.

*Breathe.*

With a concerted effort, Sophie shut her eyes tight and drew breath in through her nose. She held it for a second and expelled it through her mouth. And then she did it again. Her head began to feel weighted once more, and the roaring in her ears lessened. Her fingers, which had been numb seconds ago, were now hurting.

Sophie opened her eyes to find that Az hadn't moved. He still stood at the edge of the bed, and he still watched her. His eyes still glowed.

Soph looked down to see her hands curled into tight fists in the satin comforter of the bed – so tight that her fingernails nearly sliced through the fabric. That was why they were hurting her.

Her head was beginning to ache as well.

'Sophie,' said Az. His voice was soft, his tone gentle. He was calling her attention to him, nothing more.

Sophie looked up from the bed to peer into his eyes. 'I believe you,' she said. Her voice sounded so very far away. 'Why do I believe you?' She spoke without forethought. Her words seemed to come from somewhere deep inside. She had no control over them. And as she said them aloud, she was baffled by them because she realized they were true.

She believed him. She believed that she was an archess. She believed that she was *Azrael's* archess. She even believed that he was sorry.

Very slowly, as if Sophie were some frightened animal and he was afraid he would scare her off, Azrael sat down on the edge of the bed. 'Sophie, I am so sorry.'

'Why did you lie to me?' As she spoke, she realized that she didn't think she was crazy for believing him. Maybe that was the first sign of real insanity. Or maybe it was because she was an archess.

'You've known all along? Since you met me? But all this time . . . you let me believe I was human – *mortal.*' She swallowed hard as a spike of anger pierced her chest and found its way to her words. 'You led me on. *Christ . . .*' Suddenly she felt bewildered by what had happened over the last few weeks. 'At the wedding? The hockey game? Oh my God,' she said, her voice rising. 'All that time, you knew what I was and I was *killing* myself with guilt, thinking I was messing with some precious archess's archangel! That I was dabbling in something that I was *unworthy* of!'

She rose from the bed, all fury and fire now. She could feel it burning in her chest, sparking in her own gold eyes.

Thunder rumbled outside; the air felt thick with the moisture of an oncoming storm.

'Sophie, no,' Azrael said firmly, coming to his feet as well.

'That wasn't my intention at all. I was trying to protect you. You've suffered so much in your life.' He shook his head, his look beseeching. 'You've endured so many atrocities at the hands of men. How could I add to that with news that you were *made* for a specific man?'

'So you were going to use me, get close to me, draw me into your world without telling me why I was there, and have your cake and eat it too?' she demanded.

'No, Sophie—'

'I *hated* myself for falling for you, Azrael! I felt like a groupie, a trespasser! Do you have any idea how much I've beat myself up over the fact that I've been obsessing over you?' She was yelling now, unable to hold back her anger or keep it from the sharp, frantic edges of her voice.

'*Yes*, Sophie, I do,' he said as he came around the bed and took a step toward her. Sophie took a step back, knowing that it was pointless but feeling as though she needed the space between them.

Az stopped in his tracks once more and his jaw tensed. She could see a muscle twitch as he said, 'I *do* know, Sophie,' he went on, clearly determined to keep this exchange remotely civil. 'In fact, I *hated* that you blamed yourself the way you did. I couldn't stand your guilt; it tainted every wonderful moment I was with you.'

Sophie opened her mouth to offer another heated retort, but it just sat there waiting on her tongue as something struck a strange, uncomfortable chord inside her.

'What did you just say?' she asked, still at the mercy of words that had no filter.

Azrael went still. Something dark flashed across his eyes. Thunder echoed along the cavern walls once more, this time closer and louder than before. Azrael straightened, his expression hardening into some unreadable, unbreachable mask of stark, handsome coldness.

'Did you just tell me that you know about my past? My foster fathers?' Her tone lowered into icy accusation. 'Did you just tell me that you hated my guilt?'

Azrael didn't respond.

'Azrael,' Sophie ventured, her teeth gritted in a fury so strong she didn't recognize it, 'can you read my mind?'

# Chapter 17

It was a good question. Sophie Bryce was a very intelligent young woman. And Azrael was a complete idiot. He couldn't believe he'd let slip what he'd just revealed. He never made mistakes. He never took a misstep. Everything he did was thought out and careful.

He'd been that way forever. His brothers sometimes second-guessed themselves. They overreacted, knee-jerked, and paid for their carelessness time and again. But Azrael stood apart from them and always had. It was a double-edged sword because it made his word golden and his trustworthiness absolute. It also made him lonely.

No being could ever truly feel close to someone who did not possess the means to empathize with them. Not even brothers.

But Sophie Bryce was throwing him for a loop. She was bringing out in him a messy side. An unpredictable, rash, sloppy side. She was making him act human.

And now he'd opened a can of worms he had seriously hoped to keep shut up tight. In fact, it was a subject so detrimental to their relationship that he'd inadvertently shoved it into the farthest reaches of his mind and steadfastly ignored it. He had no clue as to when he'd been planning to bring it up. To come clean. Maybe a part of him half hoped he would *never* have to be honest about this particular thing.

Because though he knew a part of her loved to fantasize and dream about the big bad vampire, when it came down to it and the cards were on the table, a man with real live fangs possessed the potential to be absolutely terrifying. Especially when he could read her mind.

'I asked you a question,' Sophie ground out. She was speaking through her teeth and her body was trembling. No doubt she was on information overload. He wasn't even certain she was fully digesting what he'd told her so far. To say nothing of what he was *about* to tell her.

'I was,' he admitted finally. He realized, as he said it, that his own heart was pounding furiously. He was terrified – *terrified* – of what she would do or say. He'd never been afraid like this in his life. 'I'm not now.'

'You *were*,' she repeated, her gaze narrowing into beautiful but cruel slits of gold. 'But you're not now.' She paused and cocked her head to one side. 'I didn't realize reading minds was an archangel ability,' she said, her tone like ice. They stood just two feet apart, and yet the space felt charged with bad possibilities. He wanted to reach across it and grab her. The space felt like his enemy; it gave her room to be angry.

'It's not,' he said, knowing it was his eulogy.

Outside, lightning struck on the beach above their massive cavern. The walls of the cave shuddered under the attack and somewhere tiny pebbles cascaded to the stone floor.

It struck Azrael that this was not a normal storm. It had come on suddenly – and its fury reflected that of the archess before him.

Her powers were coming to fruition. A moment ago, she had asked him whether they'd healed the people in the accident on the bay. She'd used the term 'heal,' not 'rescue.'

*She* was causing the storm. Just as they had for Juliette and Eleanore, Sophie's emotions were leaking into the atmosphere around her, bringing on the fury of nature's gale. She was becoming what she was born to be. It would explain a lot – such as why his influence over her had slipped earlier. If he'd been in control, she shouldn't have been able to remember the accident or the quick flight afterward. But she did.

Sophie the archess was turning out to be a hell of a lot more powerful than Sophie the Berkeley student.

'What do you mean, "It's not"?' she demanded.

'It's not an archangel power, Sophie. My brothers do not possess the power of telepathy. Only I do.'

*And what makes you so special?* her eyes asked. He could almost read the question on her face; he didn't have to delve into her mind to hear it.

But she surprised him by remaining silent. And instead of asking that question, or one like it, Sophie straightened and took another tentative step back. Her expression changed, just a little. Now accompanying the rage on her beautiful features was the beginning of something resembling fear. Recognition.

Her gaze flicked from his eyes to his mouth, where his fangs remained hidden and, at the moment, much shorter than they were capable of becoming.

Comprehension dawned on her face so fast, so suddenly, it sent a cold, hard chill down Azrael's spine. This was it. It was time to pay the piper.

Her lips parted and he heard her heart beat once very hard against her rib cage. 'You're a vampire,' she whispered, the realization obviously having taken much of the breath from her lungs.

Thunder shook the cave, a mighty boom that for a split second caused Azrael to wonder whether the cave was actually stable enough to withstand the attack. But his gaze never left Sophie's and she stared at him so steadily, it was clear she had no idea what she was doing with the weather.

He watched as she swayed just a bit, literally overwhelmed with the emotions raging inside her. Her eyes reflected a pain that tore at his gut. It was a sensation utterly new to him; he had never hurt this way for someone else's sake.

The vampire in him wanted to enter her mind in that moment; it wanted to push through her unnaturally strong defenses and wipe the knowledge of what he was from her thoughts to make this easier for her. He could imagine what was going through her head – the fantasies she'd had about him, the way she had been attracted to him and he'd *known* it – the fact that all this time, he'd been inches away from her, a veritable monster capable of draining her dry – and she'd *trusted* him.

It was what any woman in her position would think. And a part of him really wanted to verify her fears by acting every bit like the vampire he was and asserting his control over her body and mind.

But he didn't. He wouldn't.

Not with her.

'Yes,' he said. 'I am.'

Something banged on the door of Sophie's memory. It rapped, tapped, and waited, a big bad wolf waiting to huff and puff. Thunder rumbled and her head felt light again. But her eyes were glued to Azrael's. It was all she could see, all she could concentrate on; it monopolized her every breath, her every firing neuron.

Azrael, the vampire.

It made so much sense. The almost-fangs, the perfect grace, the voice that mesmerized millions. *Billions*.

In the Dr Seuss illustration of what life had become over the course of the last hour, it made *perfect* sense. He had been at the hockey game – what a coincidence. It was as though he'd known she loved hockey. Because he *had* known. Because he'd been reading her mind.

She'd only ever seen him at night.

He'd parted the fog because he'd known she wanted to see the Golden Gate Bridge.

Thunder rolled somewhere overhead; it was close. There was electricity in the air. It ran along her skin like liquid static. She frowned – and in her mind's eye, she saw the gun that had discharged to cause the thunder. It was shaking; the hand that held it trembled furiously. The blued metal was slick with sweat. It smelled like fear and brimstone.

Sophie's vision receded, as if the image before her were strapped to a tide and the tide was ebbing away.

'Yes,' said Azrael, but his voice was distant. 'I am.'

*I know*, she thought numbly. She already knew he was a vampire. In the fevered shifting of her mind, it was no longer even a question. Everything she'd once thought make-believe was real. Time was moving differently inside her now. In one place, she was confronting Azrael, coming to grips with his secret, accepting it and moving on. In another, she was living a waking memory. It was unfolding before her and holding her captive as sense and reason fled and her world fractured.

Her knee hurt and she remembered skinning it. In her mind, she looked down to see it bleeding, the jeans torn open and caked with mud and wet grass. Her hip hurt, her back felt bruised. She tasted metal in her mouth.

'*Sophie?*'

She heard his deep voice; its vampire-angel resonance had somehow made it through the wall of her reverie and into this other world. But Azrael was no longer standing before her. There was no fireplace or wall with torches or big black bed with its black sheets that were so very 'vampire' she was surprised she hadn't figured it out sooner.

In their place was a cemetery shrouded in mists. It rolled into the distance, a green and gray rise and fall of headstones, tended grass, and fog. She felt the pain of a grave marker digging into her back.

Her foster father took the waistband of her jeans in his hand and threatened to yank them painfully off of her. She screamed, a voiceless, soundless cry that had been swallowed up by the mists more than a decade ago.

She fought, she lashed out, and she felt herself frozen inside, petrified in the quicksand of this horrific memory. Her hand shook; she'd found something to save her. Her eyes saw red.

She yanked the gun from under his waistband. It hurt; he was pressing her into the ground. She thought she aimed — she tried so hard beneath his horrible, sweaty weight.

Lightning crashed; she felt the trigger give beneath her finger. It jerked violently and her foster father went limp above her. Madness swept over Sophie, a harsh, tangy hysteria that clung to the top of her mouth like a cold spoon. Sophie barely registered what she was doing as she shoved her foster father's deadweight off of her own small body and stood. Lightning crashed again, white light blotted out the world, and Sophie saw no more.

'Sophie?'

There was something wrong. The lightning above them was constant now, parading down upon the outside of the cave with incredible fury. Pebbles rolled off the walls to the stone floor like miniature waterfalls and the ground shook as if from the effects of an earthquake.

Sophie's eyes were no longer seeing him. They were looking at him, she was still standing, but her gaze had shifted somehow – as if she were looking *through* him. The color had drained from her face, and her teeth were no longer clenched. Her lips parted, her jaw went slightly slack, and her fists unclenched at her sides.

Azrael frowned, taking the final step that closed the distance between them. She didn't step back; it was his first alarm bell. 'Sophie?' he said as he curled his finger beneath her chin and tilted her face so that she looked up at him.

She swayed again, and he steadied her with a hand on her arm. Her gaze became unfocused and Azrael realized she was no longer in the room with him. And then the unmistakable darkness of terror flickered in her beautiful eyes and she made the tiniest, most telling sound. A whimper.

Azrael swore internally and rushed her with his dark, penetrating magic, delving into the complexity of her mind with fast and furious intent. The effort was immediately draining. She'd grown stronger in spades. The labyrinth of her memory had complicated itself exponentially.

She was trapped somewhere within it, and wherever that place was, it was horrible. It was the deepest and darkest of her memories, the place that had been shut off not only from him but from her conscious mind as well – blocked out and hidden from her for the sake of sanity. He could feel the inky blackness of it clinging to his being as he traversed her neural pathways and dove into the well of her subconscious.

In the real world, Azrael scooped Sophie into his arms and sat down on the bed to cradle her against him. His eyes glowed brightly, his body radiating magic. The fire in the hearth and the torches along the wall reflected this magic in the way their flames climbed and danced, leaping to enormous, unnatural life. Outside, the lightning played, an electrical storm the likes of which no one had ever seen.

In the realm of Sophie's mind, Azrael stood amid head-stones, and a mist curled around his legs, hiding his boots from view.

*No*, he thought. *Not here. Not again.*

A premonition thrummed through him. The souls of the dead recognized him, a sovereign who had occupied the throne long ago. At one time, their ancestors had looked into his eyes and crossed out of this world and into another. They'd left as children, as mothers, as sons, and they'd gone unwillingly. Almost always, there was a strand of a being that was unwilling at death. Almost always. And that strand remained behind – and remembered.

Azrael never entered cemeteries, for that very reason. Chances were, he would be able to move through them undetected while spirits rested. But sometimes, something tipped them off and his identity was made clear.

Samael had known about Azrael's weakness months ago; he'd used it against the former Angel of Death when Sam and Uriel were fighting over Eleanore. In a cemetery, Samael had called the spirits forth and revealed to them Azrael's presence. The battle had taken a turn for the worse.

The dead were more powerful in the realm between here and there, between the past and nonexistence. It was as if they knew that the end was coming, that time would blot them out for good, and they were desperate. If they awoke now and saw him for what he was, the results could be devastating.

Az was already weak. Sophie's mind had taken too much energy for him to traverse. She seemed to fight him, even unconsciously.

And now his fears were coming to fruition. He felt a multitude of presences tug at him. The wills of the dead were weighing on him, their angry little fists yanking on the cloak of his spirit, trying to pull him under.

Azrael's fangs lengthened in his mouth and he felt the heat of his glowing gaze as he stood in the shrouded graveyard and turned a full circle. Sophie was here somewhere; he could feel her presence like a spot of warmth in all this cold. He just had to find her. And soon.

A scream pierced his reverie, somewhat muffled by the clinging fog. Az zeroed in on the direction it came from and blurred into motion.

Despite his speed, his progress through the cemetery was hard. Fingers of yesterday clung to him, trying their damnedest to slow him down. Memories were a strange thing to move through; they were as real as the everyday world, sometimes more so. But attached to them were emotions: happiness, sadness, fear, regret. Those emotions painted the world in light and sound and dictated how easy it was for Azrael to traverse them.

He had always been able to do this. As the Angel of Death, he had looked into people's hearts and known their deeds – both good and bad. For him, the past was as much a living, breathing thing as the present.

And Sophie's past was a veritable snarling beast.

As he grew closer to her, the warmth she shed grew, but the atmosphere tore at him more. It was trying to rip him to shreds, trying to drain him dry – it even felt as though it were trying to kill him.

*How ironic.*

Azrael shoved through the boiling fury of her memory, concentrating harder than he'd ever had to in his incredibly long life. And then he felt it . . .

*Here?* he thought, bewildered. But just as he had out on the bay beneath the bridge, he recognized the scent, the feel, the sensation of pure, emotionless evil.

A phantom was in the cemetery. Since phantoms could not enter a person's mind, much less view a person's past as Azrael could, the fact that Az sensed one now meant that a phantom had been present on this day in Sophie's past.

The improbability of such a coincidence paled in comparison to the foreboding he felt creeping across the gravestones. It was too real to ignore. It nearly brought him to a halt.

Azrael had heard humans talk about the strange, slow-motion run they often got trapped in while dreaming at night. That sensation of trying as hard as they could – and still not getting anywhere – haunted many mortals. Yet he had never fully understood how frustrating and dire the sensation was until tonight.

Now he struggled, fighting tooth and nail to cross the valley of the dead amid screaming souls that only he could hear and the terrible nearness of a heartless assassin. Until finally, he came over a rise in time to hear the unmistakable sound of a gun going off.

Azrael stopped short and scanned the mists. They parted on a hill fifty yards away. There, a young Sophie Bryce, perhaps thirteen or fourteen years old, lay beneath the bulky, immobile body of a middle-aged man.

Azrael's senses were pricked by the sharp smell of gunpowder, fear, and freshly spilled blood. Sophie's sobs were dimmed by the fog, but still echoed across the small valley between them. Az tried to move forward, to reach her as Sophie frantically heaved the large, heavy body off her, but he was frozen in place, locked in the static importance of this particular moment in Sophie's past.

*Who is that?* he wondered, wishing he had power over the strands of time. He closed his eyes and backtracked through the channels of Sophie's mind. There. The man's name was Alan Harvey. He was her foster father. One of many.

Here, in this cemetery eleven years ago, Harvey had tried to rape and murder Sophie Bryce. But before he could do either, she'd killed him instead.

Azrael's eyes opened as Sophie unsteadily got to her feet. She was covered in blood, none of it hers. The stench wafted across the graveyard, assaulting Azrael in its profuse abundance. He watched, in stunned silence, as Sophie looked down at the gun in her hand.

All around Az, the sense of wrongness, of evil and danger, was nearly overwhelming.

The mists parted behind Sophie. A phantom stepped into the clearing.

It had been so long since Azrael had seen one, to look upon its form now was mesmerizing in the same manner as was an accident scene on the freeway. The phantom smiled at Sophie's back through teeth that were black, in sharp contrast to the milky white of its long, skinny body. It stood more than seven feet tall, and its skin writhed and swirled as if it were coated with the same fog that blanketed the cemetery.

Azrael's lips parted, his instinct to yell at Sophie to look behind her – to turn around – to run. Not that it would have done her any good. He knew that any attempt he made to interrupt the flow of her memory would prove fruitless. He was here as an observer, despite the very real pull of the dead on his now weary body. The dead had no concept of past or present. Their essences existed in all times, in all places, and in every one of those instances Azrael remained the former Angel of Death.

He watched as the phantom floated toward Sophie, its body moving in strange conjunction with the rest of the world; it walked as if it had feet to push along the ground, but those feet did not touch the earth. Instead, it hovered several inches above it and moved at a speed that belied its odd gait.

Azrael's entire body tensed, his muscles bunched, and the monster in him rushed to the fore, all fang and claw and hunger as the phantom closed in on Sophie and raised its white, withered, semi-material hand. In one clean swipe, the phantom sliced its hand across Sophie's body. But there was no destruction, no open, gaping wound in her torso where the phantom's hand had passed through her. Instead, she simply went limp and fell to the ground.

The gun she'd held in her hand tumbled across the wet grass and slid to a stop a few feet down the hill. Then the phantom moved to the dead body of her foster father and stood over it, looking down.

What the monster did next would have given any mortal a bone-deep chill. The phantom threw back its head and laughed. It was the sound of fingernails on a chalkboard amplified by the hollow-lunged evil of the creature that made the sound. Azrael's heart hammered hard, and his body ached where he fought the petrifying effects of Sophie's memory. But all he could do was watch as the phantom lowered its head and then moved over the dead body.

Its own form began to dissolve into the mists that seemed to make it up. Those mists covered Harvey's corpse, enveloping it in white.

A few seconds later the fog drifted away, and Harvey's body was gone. It was no more than the rest of the mist that coiled and eddied and parted across the rolling hills of the New York cemetery.

# Chapter 18

When Azrael came to, he was lying on his own bed and Sophie was lying beside him, her golden hair spread across his chest and the black satin comforter.

Azrael gazed down at her; his eyes burned furiously in his skull, his teeth ached painfully in his gums, and his body shook – trembled uncontrollably – with need. His golden archess was still unconscious. And he was in agony.

Only twice in his life on Earth had he ever felt this weak and this hungry for blood. Twenty centuries had passed since the initial, hellish moments of his life in this realm. He'd had two thousand years to get over the pain he'd suffered during his transformation. It had barely been enough.

The second time he'd felt this suffering was several months ago. Samael had cast that spell upon Azrael in the cemetery, awakening the spirits so that they clawed at him and ripped apart his spirit. The physical pain it had caused was immense. It had taken days and many feedings to heal.

And now that pain was back.

Azrael rose from the bed in one fluid movement and forced himself to take a step away from it. His entire body ached, *throbbed*. He could actually feel the emptiness in his veins. It was as if they were drying out, cracking, sending searing pain through the very fiber of his physical being.

Sophie stirred on the bed. Her head turned so that she faced him. She frowned in her sleep, and then the lines of her beautiful face smoothed out as if she'd found peace once more. Az's gaze traveled from her plump lips to the smooth curve of her chin and the long, graceful line of her throat.

He caught the beat of her heart, heard the small sounds of her breathing, and smelled the temptation of her blood where it flowed, innocent and waiting just beneath the surface of her neck.

He'd wanted her before. Out on the bay, at the hockey game, as he watched her sleep in her Pittsburgh apartment. He'd wanted her at the wedding, at the restaurant, out on the pier, where she'd strolled across the boardwalk and fed the seagulls what remained of her lunch. Azrael had wanted to taste Sophie from the moment she had appeared in her maid-of-honor gown and walked down that aisle behind her best friend.

And now he was going to have her.

Azrael was already bending over his archess when he heard the distinctive sound of a footfall in the darkness behind him.

'My lord, please believe me when I tell you that you do not wish to do that.'

Azrael froze, the presence of the other ancient vampire rolling over him in all its power. Only Uro could have followed Azrael through the shadows. Only Uro knew of this cavern.

Slowly Azrael straightened. The pain was making him mean. Every ounce of him was the monster now. There was no room for anything else. Uro may have been his best and oldest friend, but he was getting in the way of what Azrael wanted more than anything he had ever wanted in his ancient, worthless existence.

He slowly turned to face the other vampire and then cocked his head to one side. 'Wanna bet?'

There was no warning then. Neither of them was a speaker of unnecessary words. Their bodies blurred into motion and, at the center of the enormous cave, they met, a clash of growls and snarls, fangs bared, claws out, bodies spinning with insane momentum.

No human eye would have been able to follow the progress of their struggles. Several seconds later, something hard hit the wall of the cave and Azrael had Uro pinned, a hand around his throat, his fanged face inches from that of his closest friend.

'I took you from death's clutches, Uro, but I can throw you back just as easily.'

'I know,' Uro said, grinding the words out through clenched teeth. His red eyes flared and his fingers grasped Azrael's wrist tightly. 'If that's what it takes to save you from yourself, so be it.'

Azrael looked into those red eyes and saw the fire of Uro's spirit. It raged and roared and yet only now did it show itself. Only now, when his king and maker needed him most, did he break the facade of calm that composed his outer shell.

Uro had always been there for him.

*If you take her now, you will kill her. And then you will kill yourself,* Uro told him, his words spilling into Azrael's mind with desperate clarity. *You will lose your queen – and we will lose you both.*

Azrael's body shook under the assault of his fierce hunger.

It needled through his nerve endings, forming stars on the outskirts of his supernatural vision. His grip on Uro's throat tightened.

*Leave her blood*, Uro told him, clearly refusing to give up. 'Take mine instead.'

Az stilled. He replayed what Uro had just offered through his head. And as he did, he thought of Michael. Two thousand years ago, Michael had given his blood freely so that Azrael would suffer less. Now Uro offered to do the same.

Azrael considered it for a split second more, and then he moved his hand up so that it tilted his friend's head to the side, and he sank his fangs into Uro's neck.

Uro tensed; the bite hurt. A vampire's blood was not meant to be drained in this manner. But he remained steadfastly silent, and as his pain increased, Azrael's subsided.

He pulled and swallowed, and after a few seconds clarity began to return to his world.

Soon, he withdrew his fangs and took a step back. Uro swallowed hard, remained on his feet, and turned his face to look at his sovereign. The fire in his eyes had retreated to two smaller pinpoints of red light. He looked a tad pale.

But otherwise, alive.

'Thank you,' said Az. He meant it from the bottom of his heart. He turned to glance at Sophie where she still lay sleeping and unsuspecting on his bed.

He'd almost done something terrible.

He turned back to watch as Uro stepped away from the wall and his eyes returned to normal. The wound on his neck had already healed. Uro glanced at Sophie and then back at his king. 'What happened?' he asked.

It was an excellent question. Azrael was still in some discomfort; he felt like a human would feel after not eating for a few days. But he was sane, and now that he was sane, he was able to reflect upon Sophie's memory and the way it had drained him so thoroughly.

'I don't know,' he replied softly. He looked at her sleeping figure. He *didn't* know – not yet. It was one thing to have to fight his way through his archess's mind; she was complicated and intricate and her thoughts went as deep as her beauty. It would have been difficult for him to pull something out of any archess's mind; with Sophie, it was astronomically so. Still, that alone would not have had such a severe effect upon his constitution.

What had done him in was the cemetery. Even in the supposed safety of her memory, the graveyard's spirits posed a threat to him. And something had awakened them.

Azrael thought of the phantom's presence in Sophie's past. He thought of what she had been forced to do – and how the phantom had covered it up. He wondered what Sophie had done once she'd regained consciousness on that misty, fateful day.

Whatever it was, he was willing to bet the phantom had orchestrated many of the things that had happened to her, and influenced her choices. A path had been built for her, and whoever had hired the phantom – for the creatures were always the employees of those more powerful and more secretive than they – had led her down that path with terrible accuracy and skill.

There were forces at work here that Azrael did not understand. His first instinct was to blame Samael. The spell in the cemetery of Sophie's memory and the spell that Samael had cast on him in the graveyard months ago were so similar that it was a natural assumption. But it felt wrong.

Granted, it wasn't as if any of the four brothers ever really had any idea what the hell Samael's game was, but the phantoms and the accident on the bridge – those weren't like Sam. In the two thousand years that he'd been making life miserable for Azrael and his brothers, Sam had never been known to cause humans undue suffering. He'd never killed anyone. He'd never actually even come close.

Either the Fallen One had gone through a major personality shift or this was the work of someone else.

The Adarians?

Azrael moved to the bed and stood over it. He took a deep breath and raised his hand, palm down, to slowly trace Sophie's outline in the air. As he did, her clothing took on a different cast; its threads shimmered and changed, becoming woven through with gold. It never hurt to play it safe, and this was a trick he knew Gabriel and Uriel had both used on their archesses. According to Juliette, gold no longer had a caustic effect on Abraxos, no doubt due to his new vampiracy. However, he was only one Adarian.

When Az was finished, he ran his hand through his hair and realized his fingers were shaking. He turned back to Uro, who was still watching him in silence. There was a companionable warmth to the man, even now, after all he'd been put through that night, that was priceless to Azrael. Uro's dark gaze was as ancient and vast as the night sky. He was the only one of Azrael's created vampires old enough to travel through the shadows and find this cave.

'How many did you have to go through before you found me?' Az asked. His voice was deep and beautiful, but it lacked the strength it normally had. He needed to feed again, and soon.

Uro offered up a small smile and shrugged. 'A few.'

Az returned the smile. 'We have a few hours before sunrise,' he said. 'We could both use more sustenance.' He and Uro could move with incredible speed. They could find a soul to feed from and be at the bridge in very short order. Sophie would be safe in the cave. No one who wasn't able to walk the darkness of the shadows would be able to find her here, a hundred feet below-ground, in a space with no windows and no doors and only magically created oxygen. 'And I need to check in with my brothers.'

'They're still at the bridge,' Uro told him.

'I'm sure they are.'

Michael ran his hand through his hair and fisted it there, frustration riding him hard and mean as he stood on the Golden Gate Bridge. He'd already been under an undue amount of stress. Between the Adarians and Samael – wherever he was – and this rapist making his way across New York, Michael's cortisol levels had been on the heavy side of late.

But there was an edge to this night that cut through him like jagged glass, fracturing reality in such a way that he almost couldn't tell the difference between what had happened and what he was *afraid* would happen next.

Randall McFarlan had met Michael and his brothers, the archesses, and Max on the bridge after they'd used the mansion to transport themselves to San Francisco. While Michael had to admit that he felt less than comfortable around a lot of Azrael's 'creations,' he liked McFarlan well enough.

As usual, he was accompanied by the thin, younger-looking Terrence Colby and the Hispanic Casper MonteVega. According to McFarlan, Azrael had been out on his boat with a woman when an eighteen-wheeler had broken through the cables and guard rails on the Golden Gate Bridge above them and then sailed through the air to crash into Az's boat. The *Calliope*, which Michael *did* feel comfortable around – he'd been on the boat a few times himself – was completely destroyed. The truck had sunk like a rock to the bottom of the bay, and the driver would have been dead if not for the quick thinking of Azrael's vampires – and Michael's healing powers.

Everything had happened so fast.

Michael was in New York, just getting off work when Max called him on his cell phone. He'd just received a telepathic message from Azrael informing him that their help was needed at the Golden Gate Bridge.

After he hung up with Michael, Max called the others. Within minutes Uriel, Eleanore, Gabriel and Juliette, and Michael had all managed to convene in the foyer of the mansion. They stepped through its swirling portal of a door and into the San Francisco night together.

They were met at once by one of Azrael's band mates, Uro. Seconds later, several other vampires showed up and together they led the archangels to the accident scene.

It was a horrible mess.

Michael had seen a lot of devastation in the course of his existence. If that wasn't about destruction, nothing was. However, he'd gone after evildoers and 'mistakes' that the Old Man had created and tossed to Earth to forget about. He'd fought demons, things so ancient and wrong that their names were eventually forgotten because people had refused to utter them for so long.

Human destruction was different. Whether it was caused by man or it *involved* man, it was always . . . *worse*, somehow.

Michael and his brothers never turned their backs on human suffering. Not when they could help it. There was too much pain in the world, all of it happening at once in too many different places, for them to deal with all of it – or even *most* of it. But they did what they could, when they could.

As a peace officer for various countries and states, Michael had actually witnessed more loss and heartbreak than he'd taken in during all of his years as the sword arm of the Old Man. Humans were a tragic lot, trapped in the enormously cruel dichotomy of having minds that allowed them to feel beyond the boundaries of necessity and brains that pushed them to create situations in which these emotions were put into play. They were naturally unnatural.

And the thirteen-car pileup on the Golden Gate Bridge that night was testament to that. Though it was clear that the crash had not been initially set in motion by a human, its ultimate capacity for tragedy was *entirely* human.

A kind of quiet hysteria had taken over the bridge. The stalled vehicles on either side of the massive accident shone their headlights on the scene, outlining the horrors of it in all their gory detail.

Mothers were sobbing, fathers were shouting, and bystanders were wandering aimlessly, too much in shock to know what to do other than call 911. No amount of extra telephoning was going to help at this point; the rescue crews could only move so fast, and Michael was more grateful than words could say that two of the archesses had been found so far. He needed the help.

The vampires helped as well. There were more of them than Michael had been expecting. It made him wonder just how many of the creatures there were on Earth. At the moment, though he might not be entirely at ease with their presence, he was happy to have their assistance. Their mind-bending powers calmed family members and the injured enough that Michael and the archesses could do their jobs.

There were twenty-seven people with injuries, but only nine of those cases were serious. The truck driver that one of the vampires had pulled out of the bay was the first Michael healed. His barely living body had been laid flat on the tarmac of the bridge between two shielding, empty vehicles. Michael saved his life and a vampire promptly put him to sleep.

The pileup was so bad, the traffic so jammed, none of the ambulances dispatched to the location had yet been able to make it through. Helicopters whirred above them, their blades slicing through the sky like the wings of massive dragonflies.

Michael knew they were filming the bridge and he knew that the helicopters and their 'live' hookups would be the first order of business for Max and his unique abilities.

As Max stood near the red-painted railing that divided the road from the pedestrian walkway and blanked out the minds and cameras of any who could bear witness to the event, Michael, Eleanore, and Juliette got to work healing the remaining wounded.

It was a draining endeavor. By the time ten minutes had passed, he'd sealed a ruptured spleen, mended two sets of pierced lungs, and re-formed more than a dozen broken bones. Eleanore had calmed a seizure, rebuilt an entire nervous system, and healed a concussed woman's underlying case of breast cancer. Juliette had perhaps the hardest job of the three of them; her 'patients' had been children for the most part. For some reason, she just seemed to be on the side of the road where there were more of them. And while their little bodies were more flexible and often received less injury because of this, they were also easier to throw through the windshield of a bus.

Michael was rising on unsteady legs and joining Gabriel and Juliette when he felt the familiar presence of Azrael on the bridge. He turned and scanned the wreckage around him until he saw Az and Uro come around the side of a flipped taxicab. He approached them, as did McFarlan and his companions.

'I think we're wrapping up,' he told his brother. 'Max looks wiped out and probably can't hold off the press much longer.'

Az nodded and looked up at the helicopters overhead. His golden eyes began to glow yellow and then narrowed dangerously. The air around them started to stir and a wind picked up.

Michael shielded his eyes and watched as the choppers tipped to the side a little and then began flying off into the distance, leaving the area of the bridge.

'Nice,' Michael admitted. Sometimes it paid to have a brother who had the very wind at his fingertips.

'Damn,' said McFarlan. 'I can't believe I didn't think of that.'

# Chapter 19

Az waited until he was certain that the helicopters were both out of the way and safe and then he looked back down at Michael. His brother's exhaustion was patently obvious. The blue of Michael's eyes was lighter than normal, as if the color had been depleted from their irises. His body swayed ever so slightly and his fingers shook where his hands rested at his sides. The Warrior Archangel's tall, strong form was bent under the burden of weariness.

The stench of disaster was all around them. Human blood and bodily fluids lent a tang to the air, and gasoline, antifreeze, and exhaust made it murky. Not far away, Eleanore, Juliette, Gabriel, and Uriel stood together, the women looking as tired as Michael.

'We need to talk,' Azrael said seriously. It was time his brothers knew about Sophie and about the phantom that had caused this horrendous mess. Someone out there had it in for one or both of them, and he stood a much better chance of figuring out who it was if his brothers and Max were helping him.

'I agree,' said Michael, something dark flashing in his blue eyes.

Az's gaze narrowed thoughtfully. He brushed Michael's mind and caught the floating thoughts there. Michael didn't believe this was an 'accident' any more than Az did. The coincidences were too strong – and Michael had been a cop for too long.

Azrael nodded, just once, and turned to Uro. 'Sophie is alone. Please join her and keep an eye on her until I return.' He was fairly certain that no harm could come to the archess as long as she was sequestered in that hole underground, but there was more here than met the eye and something dank and creepy was riding his skin. He felt what a human would probably feel just before getting goose bumps. And there was always the possibility that she would wake up before he could return to her; she would be alone in the cave and under the full, mind-numbing influence of her retrieved memories. It wouldn't be good. However, she knew Uro and had spent time around him, at the hockey game and on the boat. And since Azrael and Uro had fed on the way to the bridge, Az knew that Uro would be able to help her if she woke up and was overwhelmed.

Uro nodded, and in the next instant, he was gone in a fury of wind and shadow.

'Sophie Bryce?' Michael asked, his expression giving nothing away. But Az didn't have to read his mind to know what he was thinking.

'Yes,' he said. 'I'll explain once everything is stable.'

Michael nodded. 'Can you do anything to get the medics here faster? I can't replace blood, and some of the kids have lost a lot.'

Az turned to Randall, who nodded his immediate assent. The two together would work faster and more efficiently than Azrael alone. At once, they took to the skies. It didn't take them long to find the ambulances, fire trucks, and police cruisers that had either been dispatched to the scene or were on the same route when the call went through. They were trapped in traffic, however, the cars in front of them completely boxed in. Their sirens wailed, their horns honked, but they could only stay where they were, in their useless cacophonies.

Azrael quickly studied the scene and then concentrated. On either side of the stalled vehicles waited a good two to three feet of empty space. Az utilized that space now, lifting the cars and trucks telekinetically and setting them to the side. Randall used the power of the wind to the same effect. The passengers inside the vehicles reacted as one would expect them to. They froze behind their steering wheels, certain that they were trapped in an earthquake or some kind of tornado, their senses of logic forcing them to wonder whether it had been a natural disaster that had caused the wreckage ahead.

Once the vehicles has been moved sufficiently to the side, the EMTs inside the ambulances stared in wonder at the empty space in front of them. But their initial awe lasted only seconds before their sense of duty kicked in. Gas pedals were floored and medic bags were grabbed as the ambulances shot forward through the gaps toward the wounded.

Azrael watched them go, his careful eye sliding anything that might slow them down out of the way. No doubt, the EMTs would think they were living a miracle and that nothing short of the hand of God had aided them on the bridge that night. If Max wasn't able to clear their memories and erase the anomalies from their minds, they would retell the story of what happened, probably embellishing it to some degree.

It was a good thing and a bad thing to have faith in such miracles. On the one hand, it allowed humans to feel as if there were a higher purpose to life and that they were not alone – even when they felt more alone than ever. However, it also made people lazy. When they believed someone or something bigger than themselves would come to save them, would rescue them, would make things 'better,' they were less inclined to do the work to make these things come to fruition themselves.

Azrael frowned slightly at the thought. Hopefully Max would be able to wipe their minds.

A few minutes later, three of the ambulances had made it to the scene and Azrael had sent the order for the others to get his brothers and their archesses and the guardian off of the bridge and to safety.

He met them on Pier 39, where people were gathering to watch the accident on the distant bridge despite the late hour.

'It's going to get messy here before long,' McFarlan told them, his intelligent blue gaze scanning the building crowd.

'Everyone loves dirty laundry,' Monte said. And then he fidgeted a bit and smoothed his gray suit before he muttered, 'Except me, that is.'

Max sighed heavily and adjusted his glasses. He looked as tired as Michael did.

'We've done all we're capable of,' Az told his guardian gently.

'Agreed,' Max said. 'Let's go home. And then you can fill us in on what the hell is going on.' He gave Azrael a sharp look that said no wool had been pulled over his eyes, and then he turned and began making his way through the small crowd on the boardwalk.

Azrael nodded at Randall and the other vampires by way of farewell. A few minutes later, he and his brothers had opened a portal inside a deserted ferry building and were stepping through and into the foyer of the mansion. Gabriel headed immediately for the fridge and its waiting beers. He pulled two from its interior and then turned and handed one to his lovely bride. She smiled a grateful, tired smile, twisted the top off, and put it to her lips.

Michael turned the hot-water heater on for tea. It wasn't as if he actually needed the appliance to boil the water; he could have done so telekinetically. But the act of making tea was often more soothing than the drinking of the tea itself.

Uriel sat on the end of one of the stuffed leather couches in the living room and pulled Eleanore's weary body onto his lap. She instantly curled up against him, ducking her head into his chest and closing her eyes.

Max moved farther into the living room, took off his glasses, rubbed his nose and eyes, and then gracefully took a seat in the large plush chair adjacent to Uriel. Az waited. And Max looked up, pinning him with his knowing, dark stare.

'Sophie is my archess,' began Azrael. Sometimes it was best to get right to the point.

Sophie came awake amid roiling nausea, deep, hard chills, and a terrible need for denial. She moaned low in her throat, overwhelmed by the sickness building inside her, and then rolled over to get off the bed so she could throw up.

A gentle hand touched her chest as she faced the edge of the bed and, a second later, the nausea was gone. Sophie looked up into a set of fathomless black eyes.

'Uro,' she said softly, not trusting herself to speak too loudly should the nausea hear her and return with a vengeance.

Uro smiled a tender, gentle smile, making Sophie's breath catch despite herself. He knelt beside the bed, all grace and strength, and softly placed his hand over hers on the comforter. 'Yes,' he said.

'Are you a vampire too?' she asked, knowing already what the answer would be. No human could take away pain the way he just had. No human was as beautiful as he was or could play the guitar the way he played or could even kneel as gracefully as he had just knelt. She knew he was a vampire. And that probably all of Valley of Shadow were as well.

'Yes,' he admitted readily. 'And yes, the others are as well.'

'Can you wipe my memories from my mind?' Even as she asked it, she felt the sob rising from deep within her chest. And as she spoke the last word of the question, the sob pushed itself out and she gave in to it, curling in on herself as her eyes filled with tears.

A little over a decade ago, she'd killed a man. She'd shot him with his own gun.

*She'd killed a man.*

Everything else paled in comparison to that realization. It was as if she'd been watching a movie about murderers and all this time she'd been sitting back and thinking, 'Wow, that sucks. I'm glad I'm not one of them.' And then she'd awakened to find that the movie was a dream and she was 'one of them' after all. All of life had become a horror movie, a bad dream, a waking nightmare.

'Oh God,' she whispered amid the sobs that wracked her

frame and drenched the satin comforter beneath her with salty pain.

'I cannot, dearest Sophie,' said Uro gently, his voice wrapping around her like a blanket. It slid along her skin, silk on her flesh, and massaged her emotional nerves. 'Or I would.'

'I want to die,' Sophie told him, meaning it with all her heart. She didn't want to live with the knowledge of what she'd done. 'I thought you vampires had magic powers!' She felt angry, desperate, like she wanted to crawl out of the skin that housed the brain and bones that had caused that death on that hill eleven years ago. She couldn't stand herself, didn't want to be her, didn't want to take another breath that would fuel the person she now realized she was.

Beside her, in that distant sort of way people notice things when they're in the throes of any kind of madness, Sophie felt Uro move. She felt his hands on her arms as he drew her to a sitting position.

'Sophie,' he said softly, and his voice curled over her, washed through her, and stifled her next sob. 'Look at me,' he instructed gently.

Sophie wiped her eyes with the back of her hand and looked up. She would have expected her vision to be blurry through the film she'd left on them, but Uro's handsome face was in clear, perfect view. His bottomless black eyes pulled her in, made her want to search for constellations.

She stilled, feeling a sense of calm come over her as she fell into those eyes. Was there a star there? A comet?

'That's it, Sophie,' he said with a pleased smile. His fingers gently brushed a lock of hair from her wet cheek. 'Here,' he said, reaching into the inside pocket of his sport coat. When he produced a genuine woven handkerchief, Sophie was just surprised enough to give him a baffled expression.

'Old habit,' he told her. 'Where I'm originally from, we carried these with us everywhere we went so we could wipe the sweat from our brows.' He paused and the darkness in his black eyes became so deep, so dense with the passage of time that Sophie was struck with a feeling of nostalgia. 'It was long ago.'

Sophie slowly took the cotton cloth from his hand and said, 'Thank you.'

'It is my pleasure.'

'I . . .' She paused, both relieved and bewildered that she felt calm enough to form normal, coherent sentences and that she no longer wanted to kill herself. The pain of her memory seemed distant now, as if it were residing in a room separate from herself and she'd simply closed the door. It was still there – but she couldn't hear it screaming any longer. 'I think I need to blow my nose. It might be gross.'

Uro's dark eyes flashed with something like stardust and he threw back his head and laughed. It was an amazing sound, much like Azrael's laugh – but not quite.

'I challenge you to do worse than what I have seen and heard,' he told her, his smile jovial and light. 'In fact, I used to wake up my brothers by blowing my nose in their ears every morning.' He paused again and straightened. 'Again, long ago.'

Then he stood and moved to the fireplace, turning his back to her. 'If it makes you more comfortable, I will cover my ears.'

Sophie wanted to laugh then. She really did. She didn't know why; it wasn't *that* funny. But he was taking her pain away, and for that, she just about loved him. With a smile of relief, Sophie put the handkerchief to her nose and blew. She was sort of glad, actually, that he was holding his ears.

When she was finished, she folded the handkerchief up tight and shoved it into her jacket pocket. As she did, she realized that she was missing something.

Her leather messenger bag had gone down with the *Calliope*.

'Was the driver okay?' she asked Uro as he turned back around to face her.

He didn't seem surprised by her question, and Sophie wondered whether he was capable of reading her mind like Az could.

'Yes,' he told her. 'He is safe, as are the others who were involved in the accident.'

Sophie frowned. 'How? Did you guys save them? Can vampires heal people?'

Uro looked sad for a moment. 'Unfortunately, no. However, Lord Azrael's brother can heal, as can your friend Juliette and Uriel's wife, Eleanore. They came to the bridge to help.'

Sophie's eyes widened. 'Jules is there?' she asked. She wasn't sure how she felt about that. On the one hand, she felt a little homesick for her best friend and a little left out that she and Eleanore were working together without her. On the other hand, there was a nasty taste budding on her tongue and a strange chill riding up her spine at the thought of the accident. She didn't want Juliette anywhere near it.

And then there was a third issue, a new and unfamiliar sensation. Sophie felt the dawning need, deep down inside, to be there on the bridge with them – *not* as a friend but as an *archess*.

She was just starting to wonder whether it would feel the same and work the same for her as it did for Juliette when Uro straightened. The air in the cavern shifted, becoming abrasive. Sophie stiffened and Uro turned toward the shadows on one side of the room.

Someone stepped through them.

# Chapter 20

Kevin smiled as he turned from the blank apartment wall he used these days for scrying. The image of a sleeping Sophie Bryce on a black bed shimmered and disappeared as he looked away. 'As you can see, she is coming into her powers,' he told his fellow Adarians. Mitchell, with his fathomless black eyes and black hair, reclined effortlessly against Kevin's desk and listened intently, the slight hint of a smile on his handsome face.

Luke, with his classically beautiful face and mass of curly blond hair, sat still in a nearby chair, his expression enigmatic and deceptive. Of all of the Adarians, Luke was the one who found himself appealing to the largest crowd. His surfer-boy good looks made an impression on both women and men, and his bright eyes and easy smile charmed people of all ages. But Kevin knew the Adarian's facade to be particularly beguiling; he was capable of harsh, fast assault the likes of which often left his fellow Adarians in a kind of quiet awe.

Ely, for his part, stood as always – big and strong, his massive arms crossed over his chest, his body radiating pent-up power and the control it took to keep from letting it loose.

Kevin went on. 'When we step through, she'll undoubtedly be alarmed. We'll be underground, so she can't zap you with lightning,' he said, referring to an archess's power over the weather. 'But keep your guard up.' He turned to Luke, whose light blue eyes reflected a little something more this night. Luke, whose original name so long ago had been Laoth, had a host of very useful powers at his disposal. Much like a vampire, he could hypnotize mortals, put them to sleep with no more than a locking gaze, enter and control their dreams, and cast both darkness and silence upon any given area.

Kevin wouldn't have time to knock Sophie unconscious using drugs or any method that wouldn't cause her real harm before Uro was able to contact Azrael about the attack. However long it took them to subdue both the vampire and the archess would be long enough for Uro to send word. Kevin and his men would have to move very, very fast. Because of that, Luke was going to have to overwhelm the archess straightaway and yank her back through the shadows.

She wouldn't be conscious for long. Once she was out, she could be easily transported. As long as she wasn't awake, she wouldn't be fighting, and the Adarians wouldn't have to contend with lightning bolts being called down on their heads or automobiles being thrown at them via telekinesis or tiny flames at the ends of cigarettes or candles being morphed into raging fires that would come after them with a vengeance. Archesses were a very powerful breed. They weren't to be taken lightly.

'You know what to do,' Kevin said, nodding at Luke.

He nodded back, just once, and his ice-blue eyes flashed with cold resolution. Together, he and the others stood and moved to join Kevin in front of the darkened corner of the office.

It had been a frustrating few nights for Kevin. He'd truly believed that by combining the blood of certain Adarians and ingesting it, he would be able to withstand the effects of daylight to some minute degree. However, every attempt he'd made to get the magical concoction right was an epic failure, and he had the permanently scarred left hand to prove it.

It appeared that some things were more powerful than others, no matter what the circumstances. For a vampire, the sun was the ultimate danger. It was the threat of oblivion no matter what steps he took to fight it.

The unfortunate discovery threw a wrench in Kevin's plans like nothing else could have. His attack on the Four Favored and their latest archess was originally going to come during the day, when Kevin knew 'Lord Azrael' to be out of commission. But that course of action was no longer an option for him.

However, when fate closed a door, it opened a window and invited Kevin in.

According to the research he and his men had done over the last few days, most vampires were not able to move through the shadows as Azrael could. It was a peculiar and highly useful skill that came solely to the elusive black dragon – and to vampires with vast age and experience.

Nevertheless, Azrael had apparently possessed this ability since the very beginning. He'd *always* had it.

This made Kevin wonder what made the archangel vampire different from those he created. Certainly, he was the first vampire to exist on the planet. That made him special enough. However, more interesting – and perhaps promising – to Kevin was the fact that Azrael was the former Angel of Death. He was an archangel.

And so were the Adarians.

It was with this knowledge playing through his head that Kevin had approached a shadow in the Adarian headquarters, for the first time seeing it not as an immaterial aftereffect of light and substance and the crossing of the two, but as a *possibility*. A doorway.

He stepped into it, and as he did, the world shifted around him, becoming darker. Color was leached from the furniture in his office, turning reds and blues to black, and yellows to gray. His feet felt light; he could no longer feel the floor beneath them. His body felt less than solid, as if he would not be able to direct it to move or think or even breathe without careful concentration.

The sensations were striking and frightening enough that Kevin instantly found himself trying to step back out of the shadow. It worked; he came out of the shadow and into the 'real' world of his office, and felt the pounding of his heart in his chest as he contemplated what had just occurred.

The second time he tried it, he lasted a little longer. The third and fourth times, he managed to come out elsewhere within the complex. And now he had a new plan. He wasn't going to be able to take the latest archess during daylight hours, but if he played his cards right, he could use this shadow-walking ability to get to her nonetheless.

Using his ability to scry, Kevin and his fellow Chosen waited and watched as Sophie moved to San Francisco and got more or less settled. All the while, the former Angel of Death was one step ahead of her, and his vampires formed a web of protectiveness around her that gave the impression of being unbreachable. It admittedly irritated Kevin that she was so closely shadowed, but he couldn't blame the archangel. Sophie was a rare and precious bird and there were big bad wolves out there. He was one of them.

Finally, the moment he'd been waiting for arrived – and Sophie Bryce was left alone in a cave that Azrael no doubt believed only he and his oldest created vampire, Uro, could enter. He had never been more wrong. Since Kevin had learned how to move through the shadows, he'd helped his brothers master the same skill.

Uro would have been no match for Kevin alone. Kevin had been stronger than any of Azrael's created vampires *before* he'd become one himself. He'd been created with the ability to change his shape, a power he'd used against Uriel months ago. He also had the ability to fly. As an Adarian, he possessed superhuman speed and strength. Now? By absorbing powers from other Adarians, Kevin had acquired the ability to control animals, create fire, call lightning from the skies, manipulate electricity, and create enormous blasts of force that were able to repel large objects as if they'd been struck by a hurricane's wind. As a vampire, his speed and strength were increased many times over, his form could become no more material than mist, and he possessed the power to control human minds.

In a battle between himself and Uro, one on one, the other vampire wouldn't stand a chance. However, Kevin would not even be alone tonight. He would be accompanied by his three Chosen.

Kevin turned toward the long, tall shadow before him and stepped into it. As before, he was dwarfed in darkness and silence and the world shifted into a two-dimensional representation of itself. He concentrated on breathing, on moving, on continuing through to his final destination. He kept the image of the cave in his mind and saw the shadows in the cavern as they had appeared in the scrying vision on his wall. And the darkness responded to this knowledge, pulling him through, guiding him where he wanted to go.

It seemed like a lifetime, but only seconds passed before he was coming out the other side. It was like stepping off an escalator. He shifted his gait, scanned the cave, and came to several split-second decisions even before he'd fully emerged from the darkness.

Sophie was seated on the black bed, obviously having awoken between the time that Kevin had scried upon her in his office and now. Uro, on the other hand, was already rushing Kevin, as he imagined the vampire would do. Before Mitchell, Luke, and Ely even stepped out of the shadow behind him, Kevin met Uro halfway.

There was no give; Kevin's body collided with Uro's with such force that the breath left his lungs and his brain shook inside his skull. The impact was stunning and unexpected, but there was no time to absorb it or recuperate. Uro seemed to know what to do in this kind of fight; he was spinning with Kevin in his arms and Kevin had barely enough time to inhale and flex every muscle in his body before he was slammed painfully up against the stone wall. The torches on either side of them tumbled to the ground, flickered, and went out. On the other side of the room, Sophie quickly got to her feet and began frantically looking around, no doubt searching for a weapon of some kind. Her head snapped back around to face him when Ely and the others stepped into the room after him.

Kevin ignored the archess and the other Adarians; he

knew his men would quickly overwhelm her, and he could afford her no more attention. The pain of his body hitting the wall had a focusing effect. In that moment, he seemed to remember who and what he was. All of his abilities raced to the surface and lined up, ready to be used. With no more than a spike of his will, his body became insubstantial, turning to mist in Uro's strong grip.

Uro backed up. Kevin, miraculously still able to form clear, coherent thought despite the fact that there was no physical brain involved, used another of his powers. A sharp shot of magic rushed Uro, hard and painful. In a blast of forced air, Uro's body went flying back across the cave to hit the other side with incredible force.

Another torch was knocked from its sconce. Kevin quickly took in the status of the cavern's inhabitants: Ely and Mitchell stood back, one on either side of the room, their glowing red eyes focused on Kevin's vampire opponent. Sophie Bryce was unconscious, held firmly in Luke's strong grip. They'd worked fast, as he had instructed them to, but the seconds were not on their side and it was time to end this.

Uro's normally black eyes were glowing a hellish red as he slowly turned in place, taking in the fact that he was surrounded. Kevin waited until Uro turned back around to face him; he was never one to strike a man from behind. Then he pulled his power from inside and focused it once more, heating it with vampire speed to release it in the form of a massive fireball.

He could feel the flame suck the oxygen out of the air in the room with surprising speed; whatever magic had created the oxygen in the first place hadn't been made to keep up with such a thing. The fire raced across the cave as if sent by a flamethrower and struck Uro's oncoming form with a vengeance.

The vampire was lost in the blaze, his body swallowed by the red-orange inferno and once more thrown back across the underground space. Kevin wasted no time, re-focusing his energy in order to surround Uro's burning body with a force field of dark, painful energy.

There was no escape for the ancient vampire. Kevin's force field trapped him within the flames even as it slammed him up against the far wall. The only torch remaining in its sconce tumbled to the ground and went out, but there was plenty of light in the cave.

Lightning struck somewhere aboveground, but the thunder could scarcely be heard over the bellowing roar of Uro's pain.

The world had slipped into slow motion for the occupants of that cave, every movement stretching into a short eternity. But in the real world the fateful fight had taken mere seconds. Still, it was long enough for Uro to have called Azrael. The former Angel of Death could be trusted to be on his way, and Kevin's force field would not last long before it dissipated and Uro was once more free.

With this knowledge hard on their heels, Kevin rematerialized, not wanting to face the enigmatic forces of the shadow world in anything other than his true, physical form. Mitchell and the others joined him in the darkest corner of the cave, their minds united in the knowledge that they had very little time.

There, Luke handed Sophie's sleeping body to Kevin. He was the one who had the most experience traveling through the shadow realm, and *none* of them had any idea what would happen when they tried to take someone who *wasn't* a vampire through with them. It was best to leave the task to their leader.

Kevin hugged Sophie to his chest and took a deep breath before he stepped into the darkness. At once, he noticed the difference. It was strange and difficult enough to pull his own body through the dim, surreal dimension. Dragging an unconscious captive with him was disturbing. At first, it felt as though something were trying to pull her out of his arms. He had to hold on with everything he had. It took him longer to move through, as if his limbs were weighted down or mired in quicksand. This sensation persisted, making it difficult for him to concentrate on breathing, on his own every movement, and he began to worry about Sophie. Was *she* breathing? Would the shadow dimension suck the life from her sleeping body?

Kevin pushed on; every action trailed behind, lagging through time. But after a few difficult seconds, he recognized the solidness of the shadows he was approaching and knew the trip was nearly over.

Not long after that, Kevin was stepping out of the shadows once more, this time with Sophie, and moving into Kevin's office. He looked down at the beautiful woman in his arms and was relieved beyond comprehension to see her chest rise and fall with normal breath. Now he knew.

As the others arrived behind him, he turned and handed the sleeping archess to Luke. Luke smiled and took her with more than willing arms. Clearly, just as Mitchell had taken a liking to Juliette and Kevin had fallen for Eleanore, Luke was more than a little taken with Sophie Bryce.

'Azrael's vampires will be on our tails,' Kevin told the

three of them. 'I don't know whether they can find this building or not,' he went on, referring to their hidden headquarters, 'but it's possible they're familiar enough with shadow walking that they can track us through what we just came through.'

He let that sink in for a moment and then went on. 'We need to keep moving. Gather the others.'

# Chapter 21

Azrael could feel his brothers' frustration like needles against his spirit as he turned from them and Michael hit the light switch. Uro had just called out to him; the cry had been frantic, terrified, and filled with pain. The Adarians had struck without warning – *impossibly* – coming through the shadows and into the cave where he and Sophie had been hiding.

Somehow, Abraxos the Adarian-turned-vampire, had learned to traverse the shadow world, taking three of his men with him through the macabre passageways. They'd managed to find their way into the underground cavern where Sophie was, and then he and his fellow Adarians had attacked Uro and taken her back through the shadows with them.

In the two thousand years that he'd been a vampire able to walk the shadows, Azrael had only ever attempted to take one other being through with him, and that was Sophie. He wouldn't have thought to bring his brothers through now if it hadn't been for the fact that he'd taken Sophie through that same night – and that Abraxos appeared to have done the very same thing.

If Abraxos and his men could do it, maybe Azrael could do it with someone besides Sophie.

That knowledge had Azrael summoning Michael to his

side as he faced the shadows in the corner of the mansion's living room. Uro was on the other side of those stygian passageways, and he would need healing. Michael would not be able to do everything; the ancient vampire would need blood . . . and fire left scars. But the healing he could provide would make a big difference for Uro. Azrael knew this much from personal experience.

As Azrael placed his hand on his brother's shoulder, he called out to his vampires across the globe. Months ago, Abraxos and his men had been at war with four archangels. Now the Adarians would face the entire vampire nation.

Minutes ago, in the temporary quiet and calm of the mansion's living room, the news of Sophie being an archess had affected Azrael's brothers as he'd expected it would. The only one who did not seem to be surprised was Juliette. She'd merely stared at Azrael, and then closed her eyes and nodded. The next words out of her mouth had been, 'I should have known.'

Azrael had been prepared to discuss the importance of the development with Max and the others. There was so much to take into account: The fact that the archesses were suddenly cropping up all at once, the phantom that had caused the accident on the Golden Gate Bridge, the strangeness to the air that hinted at so much more going on than any of them had previously believed. But there was no time.

Uro's call came in hard and fast and desperate. Now Az stepped into the shadows, guiding Michael and feeling as though a trench had been torn through the middle of his soul. The darkness engulfed them, welcoming its king back home.

Behind them, in the space where he and his brothers had been discussing events only moments before, Max and the others scrambled toward the nearest doorway. He could hear their portal opening just as the shadows closed him off from their world.

He wanted to let go and allow the varying degrees of darkness to simply guide him as they normally did. He'd been walking the shadows for so long, they were familiar tributaries and alone, he could have relaxed and let them carry him through as if he were a leaf on the river, and then used his momentum to move faster with the energy he would have spared.

But it was different with Michael, and Az found himself having to concentrate. His golden eyes burned a hellish red in the handsome frame of his face. His teeth absolutely throbbed in his gums. He could feel an anger radiating from his body that went deeper and clawed its way further into his being than any wrath he'd ever known.

All he wanted to do was find Sophie and kill Abraxos for touching her.

But having to take Michael through with him forced him to temporarily put thoughts of Abraxos aside. Azrael hadn't known what to expect when taking someone as conscious and powerful as Michael through the darker dimension. Sophie had been relatively easy, but she was the other half of Azrael's soul, a part of him – and she'd also been asleep. Az was certain that had made things easier.

Michael was another matter. It was an odd sensation, like both pulling and pushing at once, and there was a lag on Michael's body that Azrael had to concentrate hard on getting past. It was as if the black space recognized the Warrior Archangel as a stranger – and it wanted him to leave.

It took much longer than he would have liked to get

through the shadows and out the other side, but within seconds, Azrael was nonetheless pushing past the final murky barriers and entering the cave where he had left Uro and Sophie.

What he found when he stepped once more into the light turned his stomach to lead and opened a second gaping cavity in his heart.

He was beside Uro's fallen form with blurred speed. 'Uro,' he breathed, unable to say anything else. His friend's body was caked with the grime of smoke and blood. His clothes had been shredded by the flames. Miraculously, though there were third-degree burns across his neck, chest, arms, and legs, only half of his face had sustained any damage, and it was minimal. Against all odds, Uro still had a full head of hair.

Not that it mattered.

With a painful slowness, the ancient vampire opened his eyes. Slits of glowing, throbbing red greeted Azrael and a voice echoed softly in his head.

*Go after her now. I read his thoughts, my lord . . . They're going to take her blood. They might kill her.*

'Michael, can you heal him?' Azrael heard himself ask. He was seething inside, going numb with the roaring, screaming, colossal fury battering his soul. And yet somehow he managed to ask the question that needed asking. For some reason, he maintained his place at Uro's side – and even gently took his hand.

'I don't know,' Michael said honestly. He had never tried to heal a vampire before. In the twenty centuries since Azrael had first fed on Michael's blood to ease his pain, the vampire king had never needed Michael's help. Vampires normally healed on their own, so the healing powers of Michael's hands had never been necessary.

But fire was deadly to a vampire. And Uro was near death.

Even if Michael could close the wounds and erase the scars, Uro would need blood – and it would have to be something more than human.

Azrael knew this even as Michael very gently, very slowly, placed both hands palm down over Uro's burned and smoking chest. Az watched his brother close his eyes and lower his head. A moment later, his hands began to glow.

Az felt the pull of time on him; Sophie was out there somewhere – and Abraxos meant to do her harm. But he had no idea where they had gone. He concentrated on zeroing in on her location and scrying her whereabouts, but either the fact that she'd been moved through the shadow realm or the fact that her mind was infinitely complex due to her burgeoning powers as an archess made it impossible to get a fix on her.

To make matters worse, he'd been traveling the shadows long enough to know that if enough time passed after someone had traversed them, there would be nothing left of them to track. Shadow substance was inky and clingy and magical in nature; it warped what moved through it and would erase all traces of Sophie and her abductors.

By this time, the shadows would be completely unable to tell him where the Adarian had taken his archess.

No one left a lasting footprint in a shadow.

Azrael ran a hand through his hair and closed his eyes just as Uro's quick, ragged breathing changed, slowing and growing deeper. Michael's magic was working. There was that, at least.

'I have to leave,' Az said softly, without opening his eyes. Behind his closed lids, he saw Sophie smile. In the hollow, raging silence of his mind, he heard her laugh. Time ticked across his skin, raising his hairs, scraping his nerve endings.

'I know,' said Michael. He sounded more tired than ever.

Azrael opened his eyes to find his brother's head bowed, his hands at his sides. Uro gazed up at Azrael. His clothes were still destroyed – but beneath them, his body no longer bled. His wounds had been closed. Angry red scars criss-crossed across his chest, ran up his side and down his right arm. A thick raised line marred his left cheek and trailed down the left side of his neck to disappear under the ruined shreds of his shirt and jacket.

Azrael wondered whether Michael might have been able to do away with those as well had he not had to heal dozens of injured people on the Golden Gate Bridge earlier that night.

'Go,' Michael said. His voice sounded hollow, empty.

'You're coming with me,' Az told his brother. Michael wouldn't be able to escape the cavern without a vampire to lead him through the shadows. And despite his love for Uro, there was no way he was stupid enough to leave Michael alone with the other vampire when they were both so drained. Uro needed blood and the hunger for it when a vampire was this injured could be overwhelming. The last thing Az needed was to have his brother and his first created vampire fighting in his absence.

Michael seemed to be in no mood to argue. He nodded and slowly stood on shaky legs. Azrael steadied him with one strong hand and led him quickly to the nearest shadow.

He turned back to Uro, whose brow was furrowed in concentration. He was trying to draw his legs in, trying to get to his feet.

'Stay here,' Az instructed softly. 'The others will be here soon. Randall will take care of you. Do as he says.'

Uro's dark eyes met Az's for a moment and throbbed a dull red once, twice, and then closed.

Azrael's grip on Michael's shoulder tightened – and then he was moving once more through the shadows, pulling his brother along beside him. It was even harder this time; Michael's body was fighting not only Az but himself. The blond archangel was exhausted.

By the time Az was stepping back into the living room of the mansion, Michael's form had begun to tremble.

Max and the others were gone, most likely meeting up with Randall, Terry, and Monte at the cave. The vampires would have had to use brute force to create a passage through the ground and into the cave for the archangels and archesses, as none of them could move through the shadows as he and Uro had. But Az knew they'd find the Adarians were already gone and Uro the only one left inside. Az knew Randall well enough by now to know that the ex-cop would offer up his own blood to replenish Uro's. Uro was now under direct orders to do as Randall instructed, so he would drink. It would be enough to get him back out through the shadows. After that, it was possible that an archess would be able to heal what burns and scars remained on his body. Az had a feeling that both Juliette and Eleanore would insist on at least trying.

Right now, the mansion was empty and to Azrael, it felt cold. Which was strange – he never felt cold. The knowledge that Sophie was in enemy hands was turning the blood in his veins to ice.

Azrael took his brother around the waist and draped Michael's arm over his shoulder to walk him to the nearby couch. Michael didn't argue; he didn't say a word.

'See that you eat something,' Azrael instructed.

Michael nodded. 'Where are you going?'

Azrael waited before answering, truly not wanting to give voice to his response. In all of this chaos, there was only one being that Az was aware of who stood a real chance of knowing *exactly* where the Adarians had taken Sophie. And right now, Azrael was devoid of pride.

'You don't want to know,' he told Michael. To his own ears, his voice sounded strange. There was a deepness to it reminiscent of the very shadows he'd just traversed. It was as if he was being tailed by darkness.

Without another word, he turned from Michael and stepped back into the shadows. He moved so fast, the Warrior Archangel never had a chance to object. If he made a sound of protest, Azrael didn't hear it.

# Chapter 22

Sophie came awake slowly and comfortably. Her body was warm, the surface beneath her felt soft, and there was an aura of safety enveloping her that made her want to keep sleeping.

But she couldn't sleep. Something tapped at her brain, knocking repeatedly, trying to get her attention. She kept her eyes closed and tried to ignore the sensation, ducking her head deeper into the softness beneath her cheek. But it grew more insistent, morphing from a gentle tapping to a kind of buzzing that circled around the base of her skull.

A flash of something raced before her mind's eye. It was a sliver of a memory, a bit of a dream. It was dark and harried and red.

She was forgetting something. The buzzing grew and a thrum of apprehension went through her middle, forcing an extra beat from her heart and clenching her stomach. She frowned and blinked her eyes open. The room was dim and her vision blurred.

*Where am I?*

She rolled over to survey her surroundings. She was on a small bed and it was indeed fitted in the finest sheets, composed of a thread count that she was sure she would never be able to afford. The pillow cradled her head with a loving tenderness that only big bucks could buy. The duvet over her was thick, keeping the world's chills at bay.

But the bed and its linens were where the comfort in the room stopped. Beneath the edges of her bedspread, the warmth surrounding her dispersed into the cold and damp of what could not be mistaken for anything other than a prison cell.

'What the . . .' She sat up slowly, her mouth dropping open as she took in the peeling paint on the walls, the rusted bars of the door, and the dented metal that had obviously been used as a mirror above a broken sink on one side of the closet-sized room.

A single bulb hung from the ceiling, shedding an eerie, unpleasant light on the cramped quarters. Beyond the bars at one end of the room, the darkness of the hallway loomed, deep and ominous.

Sophie's body was beginning to tremble with fear as she pushed back the covers to slide from the bed. It was out of place in this room; that was clear now. Someone had put it in the cell for her to sleep on.

The dichotomy of the small kindness and the cruelty of locking her up in such a place struck her a confusing blow. She moved from the bed toward the bars on feet that still wore boots. They'd left her clothes on . . . To further protect her from the cold?

Sophie gritted her teeth, frowning deeply as she wrapped her fingers around the bars and pulled. There was no give. Her movements clanged against the metal and the sound echoed through the halls beyond, seeming to go on forever.

In the distance, a foghorn sounded. A hard shiver rushed through her and she released the bars to hug herself.

'Oh God,' she whispered. *What's happening to me?*

Where was she? What had happened? She tried to remember, tried to make sense of her surroundings . . . She squeezed her eyes shut – and moved back from the bars as more flashes of memory overtook her.

A cemetery, her stepfather – a gun.

Her heart slammed painfully as, all at once, everything came rushing back. A strangled cry escaped her throat and she stumbled back until her hip hit the top of the bed and she lost her balance.

Collapsing like a rag doll, Sophie landed hard on her bottom. A second later, she was curling her legs against her chest and cradling herself. The rocking came naturally – back and forth, back and forth – as the realization of what she had done struck her once again like a bomb.

She'd killed a man. He had been a horrible man and he'd been planning on raping and killing her, but somehow it seemed to make little difference. The feeling was the same. It was like a sticky, inky black blanket that draped itself over her and then began to tighten. She felt smothered in the truth.

And the truth wasn't done with her yet.

*Azrael's a vampire.*

The fact floated, immaterial at first.

*Azrael is a vampire.*

It was more solid this time, less two-dimensional.

*Oh my God*, she thought. *Azrael is a vampire.*

None of Azrael's brothers were aware of the former Angel of Death's ability to traverse the boundaries of Sam's fortress and enter unbidden. Samael knew. But Samael knew everything. Or he seemed to.

And there were many things about Azrael that Michael and the others were not aware of. It was a symptom of the man and creature and angel that he was, this solitude of sorts. He was a being apart, separate and mysterious. He knew this. There was no helping it. So he had embraced it.

When Az exited the shadows and stepped into Samael's sixty-sixth-floor office in the former Sears Tower, Sam continued writing at his desk without looking up. When he was finished, he put down the pen and only then looked up from his desk. There was not the least bit of surprise on his incredibly handsome face. The stormy gray of his charcoal-colored eyes swirled and taunted; his expression was unreadable.

He was conveniently alone in the room. Normally the man was accompanied by one or more of his servants, monsters of the supernatural world who were sworn to do his eternal bidding. However, at the moment, none of these people were around, and Azrael wondered whether it was so that he and Samael could conduct their business in private.

Az left the corner beside a solid wood bookshelf and approached the center of the office on silent booted feet.

'I'm assuming the situation is dire indeed to bring you to my door,' Samael said softly as he pushed gracefully away from his desk and rose to his full impressive height. He was dressed, as usual, in a dark gray suit, expensively tailored. 'So have out with it at once, by all means.' A tiny hint of a smile graced the corners of his lips as he smoothed the front of his suit and moved around his desk.

He and Azrael slowly approached one another, their essences colliding, circles of power that chafed against each other, setting off invisible sparks of negative energy. They stopped at three feet and Azrael considered the infamous archangel with great care.

This was a mistake.

'Of course it is,' Samael told him, flashing a bright white smile that would have left women swooning. 'But you knew that before you stepped into my shadows.'

He did. He also knew he was out of his league here. But it didn't matter; he had no choice.

'The Adarians have taken Sophie,' Azrael told him, aware that as he said it, it was probably something Samael already knew. 'I need to know where they've gone.'

Samael cocked his head to one side, his dark gray eyes glittering. 'I'm sure you do. I'm sure you also know that my assistance comes with a price, "Lord Azrael".' He said the name softly, almost teasingly, and Az tasted blood in his mouth.

His jaw was too tight, his teeth too sharp, and his patience officially at an end. 'Name it.'

Samael's brow lifted. He considered Az for a moment, and not for the first time since coming to Earth, Azrael wished he could read the archangel's mind as he could that of every other creature on the planet. And as *Sam* could so easily read *his*.

Then Samael's smile faded and Azrael felt as if there were storms brewing in the Fallen One's eyes. There was a building darkness there, a depth that hinted at . . . problems. Az wondered if there was something going on with Samael that failed to meet the eye.

Sam turned away to sit on the leather sofa on one side of the massive office. Az glanced at the giant windows that outlined a view of the lake and Chicago's night lights below.

The sky was lightening a little; dawn was fast on its way and the impending daybreak added to Azrael's discomfort. Other than that, it was a stunning view. Samael had never settled for anything but the best.

'Which brings me to the subject of my price,' Samael said, his words cutting through Azrael's thoughts. Az turned to face him. 'You're right, Azrael. I settle for nothing less than the best. I go for the gold in everything I do.' He shrugged, rather nonchalantly, and his perfect suit moved effortlessly with him.

'Sophie is mine,' Azrael told him simply.

Sam's smile was back, but it was a smaller echo of the one he'd worn before. 'You misunderstand me,' he said. 'Sophie Bryce is absolutely priceless and an amazing catch, don't get me wrong. But she's right for *you*, Azrael. Not me.'

'Spit it out, Sam. What do you want?' Az could feel the weight of time settling over him, a shroud that grew heavier with each passing second.

'Your brother possesses the ability to heal,' Samael said. 'I want you to take it from him.'

Azrael stared at Sam as the silence stretched between them. He would have assumed that he'd heard incorrectly, that he was imagining things, but he had very good hearing.

'Mind you, it won't be permanent, if that's worrying you,' Sam said, his tone so utterly casual it was not as if he'd just asked Azrael to do something so wrong it was nearly sacrilegious. 'Take Michael's blood,' he went on, 'and concentrate on taking the healing ability with it. He will be without the power for several days.' He paused, let the weight of his request sink in, and then straightened on the couch, leaning forward to rest his elbows on his knees and lace his fingers together. He eyed Azrael with cold, hard eyes. 'That is my price, archangel. Take it or leave it.'

'Done,' Azrael said as he felt the world drop out from under him. Michael was the silent leader of their brotherhood. He was the one who kept them together. He was the spiritually strong one, the giving one, the brother who always had everyone else's back. When Azrael considered everything that Michael had done for him over the years – the way he'd stood by him in those first few agonizing moments on Earth – a sort of sickness stole over him and he felt as if his chest would cave in.

But Abraxos had Sophie. And quite simply, Azrael would do anything to get her back.

Samael stood once more, gracefully rising from the couch and reaching into the inside pocket of his suit coat. Azrael watched in unexpressed misery as Sam produced the infamous diamond pen he'd used on so many of them before and held it up to the light.

'You'll understand if I don't take your word,' Sam spoke softly.

'Why would you?' Azrael replied just as softly as he strode across the room to take the pen from Sam's outstretched fingers. Its tip was wickedly sharp, and Samael's other victims had no doubt seen it as an object of perilous and menacing design. To Azrael, it was the period at the end of a sentence that condemned him to hell. Nothing more.

Sam waved his hand over the surface of the coffee table and the piece of furniture transformed. In a warping, dizzying display, the table became taller, morphing into a black stone altar. Atop the altar rested a contract composed of intricate and puzzling lettering.

'Unfortunately for you,' Samael said with a devious smile, 'you *will* have to take me at mine.'

Azrael knew how this worked. Uriel had been in this position once, and for almost the same reason. Uriel's account of his own signing with Sam had filled him in on the details. This particular pen used blood.

Az said nothing as he glanced at the contract and then pressed the pen's tip into the vein on the inside of his wrist. The sharp nib broke the skin at once, drawing his blood into the diamond vial attached to it. Uriel claimed that when he'd signed his contract with Samael, the pen had drawn his blood painfully. However, Azrael felt nothing but a deepening sense of loss as the pen went from clear to crimson red. When it was filled, he removed the tip and turned to the altar. Sam remained stoically silent and watchful as Azrael pressed the tip of the pen to the first of two lines that waited at the bottom of the document.

He signed.

When he was finished, he handed the pen to Samael. It was empty. Sam lowered it to the document and as he did, it once more filled with blood. Azrael's ears roared with the sound of his own blood rushing through his veins. The world seemed distant in that moment, out of reach. He was traversing the passageways of a nightmare.

Sam finished signing his own name in scrawling, perfect script and pocketed the again empty pen. And then, out of the inside pocket on the other side of his expensive suit coat, he extracted a small book.

'You'll need this,' he said, handing the book to Azrael. 'And I have a message for the Warrior Archangel.'

Az looked down, turning the book over in his hands. It

was a tour guide for Alcatraz Island. The impatience abrading his skin got worse; the air was turning to steel wool around him. He looked back up and was caught in Samael's mercurial gaze.

'Michael has been hunting a rapist,' Sam told him, no hint of emotion one way or the other on his handsome face. 'Tell him to take a walk in the park.' He turned away from Azrael to casually make his way back to his desk. 'Many people claim to find the answers they seek there.'

# Chapter 23

*There are vampires.*

Sophie had always believed there was more to life than what met the eye. She'd always had an open mind. Ghost stories intrigued her; haunted houses sparked her imagination. She'd seen every vampire movie and read every vampire book she could get her little orphan hands on while growing up. Not because she knew they were pretend and she had fun staring at the actors. But because they made her wonder. That was just the kind of girl she was.

But now, sitting on the cold stone floor of a cell God-knew-where and facing the very real fact that there were not only archangels but vampires as well, she realized that she was feeling . . . rather strange. As if she were composed of stuff as insubstantial and make-believe as the books and movies she'd loved so much. She was living in a fantasy world. She remembered teachers accusing her of that from time to time. If they could only see her now . . .

A loud clanging sound drew her head up and had her hastily wiping her eyes. She hadn't realized she'd been crying until now. She spun around to face the bars on the other end of the cell and wasn't surprised to find herself face-to-face with someone she didn't recognize. Nothing surprised her now, she guessed.

He was a man of average height and build, had slightly thinning brown hair, and his unremarkable blue eyes looked out from behind wire-rimmed glasses. He was dressed impeccably in a three-piece suit the same color as his hair.

The man waited until the bars finished sliding to the side, and Sophie noticed that the bars moved in time with those of other cells across the hall. She could see them all now; someone had turned on the lights, and there was also a softer edge to everything, as if the sun were rising. Row upon row of tiny concrete rooms stretched down the corridor. As the doors slid into their open place, the sound rang loud and clear through the hollow emptiness.

'Miss Bryce.' The man greeted her, his voice gentle. He stood in the open doorway, his hands clasped before him in a friendly manner.

Sophie frowned and blinked, coming to her feet.

'I do hope you rested comfortably,' he went on, gesturing to the bed behind her with one well-manicured hand. 'I'm afraid this bed was the best I could come up with on such short notice.'

'Who are you?' Sophie asked, speaking before she realized she was going to do so. Her voice shook horribly. She was more of a mess than she'd realized.

'I'm John Smith,' he said. 'But please call me John. I'm here to escort you to my employer. He's been waiting patiently for you to sleep off the remainder of the influence the Adarian put you under. He would have awakened you, but he felt you most likely needed the rest.'

This took a moment for her to digest. Employer? Adarians? The employer wasn't an Adarian? 'Where are we?' she asked next, her subconscious clearly wanting to tick off the questions in order of importance.

'An old prison,' Smith replied with a glance at their surroundings. He made a slightly displeased face, but the look was quickly gone and his expression was once more emotionless. 'It was not our choice, believe me. But time was of the essence, and this was where fate brought us.'

Sophie had never felt more confused or wrung out. She wondered if she looked as crooked and stringy and crinkled as she felt inside.

'Please,' Mr Smith said as he stepped to the side and gestured for her to exit the cell. 'Come with me.'

What else was she to do? It felt strange to step through that space and out into the hall; as her body crossed to the other side, it almost felt as if something pulled on it for the briefest moment – trying to draw it back inside, hold on to it. Keep it forever.

But it must have been her imagination. Unless ghosts existed too. Just like angels . . . And vampires.

'I imagine you are very confused right now,' said Smith as he led her down the long gray corridor. On either side the cell doors lay open, revealing empty rooms beyond. 'And more than a little frightened.'

Sophie barely heard him; she was half listening and half stuck in her own numb, overcrowded world. She knew where she was now. She'd come here when she was very little. She had visited with her mother.

Back then, she'd been surrounded by other tourists, and the halls had echoed with the sounds of children and women whispering and men snapping photographs. Now the hallways were hollow. The only people here were her and John

Smith – whoever he was – and the ghosts of the men who had been imprisoned here so long ago.

Smith walked Sophie to the end of the corridor, a hall she seemed to recall was named after Broadway. As they crossed the threshold of the doors that led to another room, Sophie looked up to see a red handprint, faded but memorable, marking the peeling paint. No doubt it had been left there by Native Americans in the sixties when they'd occupied the infamous penitentiary. And it was still there now.

'I'm in Alcatraz,' she said softly, more to hear herself say the words than for any other reason.

'Yes, I'm afraid so,' said Smith. 'But though he felt it would be too cold there for you to rest comfortably, my employer prefers the open air, so we will be meeting him in the yard.'

'Who are you?' Sophie asked.

Smith glanced at her over his shoulder and offered her a warm, understanding smile. 'I'm assuming you actually mean to ask, "what" am I. And I can understand why.' His smile broadened, touching the blue in his eyes and lightening it. 'You've been hit with a lot lately. Angels are one thing. Vampires are another, no?'

'Are you a vampire?' she asked.

He chuckled. 'No,' he said, as if the very idea were too nuts to consider. 'I am not.'

They pushed through a final set of doors and then stepped out into the frigid temperatures of an Alcatraz Island dawn. At once, Sophie was hugging herself. She still wore the warm clothes and army jacket she'd put on before she'd left her apartment what seemed like ages ago, but out here, in the middle of the bay, the temperatures were always much cooler

– and the winds much stronger – than they were on the mainland.

She closed her eyes for a moment against a blast of cold, and felt something heavy being laid across her shoulders. She opened her eyes to see that Smith had moved behind her and was draping the coat of his suit over her. 'Sophie Bryce,' he said, and she glanced over her shoulder to see that his eyes were on something ahead of her. 'May I introduce my employer.'

He paused as Sophie peered through the stray strands of her hair to see a tall figure in white standing at the end of the long yard, his back to her.

'Gregori,' Smith finished.

He was very tall, though that didn't surprise Sophie any longer. In fact, if anyone stood out in her world of late, it was Smith because he was less than six feet tall. Gregori had a strong, slim build and broad shoulders that gave Sophie a strange flutter in her stomach. His hair was shoulder length, jet-black, and thick. At the moment, he seemed to be gazing out across the bay; she couldn't see his face. But for some reason . . . she imagined he was quite handsome. Beautiful, in fact.

He wore a white suit, tailored to fit his strong, athletic figure. His hands were hidden in the pockets of his suit pants, his posture that of a man completely at ease – or lost in the depths of his own private thoughts. For the briefest of moments, Sophie was struck with an image of Al Capone gazing out across the waters that had held him captive.

The atmosphere of the timeless, infamous prison was getting to her.

Smith left the coat over her shoulders and moved around

her to approach his employer. A short flight of stairs led up to the platform on which the man in white stood. Smith took these stairs with the slow and measured care of a man approaching one much more powerful than he.

The wind whipped across the small length of yard between them and Sophie couldn't hear what Smith said to his boss. However, Gregori's head tilted as he caught his employee's words, and Sophie glimpsed the strong line of his jaw. It caused her heart to skip in her chest. And then the man pulled his hands from his pockets and turned to face her.

*Oh no*, Sophie thought as her heart again skipped and began racing. *I was right.*

Even from this distance, his nearly cruel beauty struck her with almost tangible force. She could see that his eyes were the color of thin blue ice. They seemed to almost glow in the somewhat swarthy frame of his sculpted face. She felt locked in their pull; something about his gaze was both mesmerizing and unsettling. There was something wrong with it . . . but she couldn't tell what it was. She wanted to stare forever, for as long as it took to figure it out. He was a puzzle that entrapped her, and she'd seen him for only three seconds.

*I can't move*, she thought. She felt stuck there, immobile, glued to the spot as she gazed up into his light, light, *light* blue eyes. They were nearly white. And at their centers . . .

A gentle wave of cologne wafted toward her, clean and masculine. 'You look positively frozen, Sophie,' he said, his voice like deep black silk. She heard the words as if they'd been spoken intimately into her ear. She blinked and straightened. Somehow, Gregori had come across the yard and was now standing in front of her. She didn't even remember seeing him move.

*Frozen*, she thought. Yes, she was frozen. *Petrified*.

And then she realized what it was about his eyes that both intrigued and troubled her so. His pupils were not round; the black, bottomless pools were the shape of stars . . . many-pointed stars, deep and dark and deadly. When he smiled then, it was with teeth as white and predatory as Azrael's, his canines ever so slightly longer than they should have been.

'What are you?' Sophie found herself asking. She felt a tremor moving through her, quivering the marrow in her bones. Standing before Gregori on this isolated rock in the middle of a cold, deep sea was rocking her to her core. She was terrified and her body knew it.

'I am a messenger,' he told her. 'A warrior, a guardian,' he went on as he slowly began to pace around her. She found herself turning in place to maintain eye contact. She would have done anything in that moment to continue staring into the stars in his eyes. 'I am a judge, a rectifier.' His smile slipped just a little, and a dark shape moved beneath the frozen ice of his eyes. 'I am death.'

He said it so softly, so intimately, Sophie was utterly and completely thrown. If she'd known what to say, she wouldn't have been able to say it. Not here, not now, not trapped and breathless in the pull of Gregori's presence.

'Sophie,' he said as he turned to face her fully and gently took her arms in his hands. His touch was strange. Even through the layers of her clothing and the protective warmth of Smith's jacket, Gregori's hands . . . *hurt*. The sensation of his gentle grip felt as though she were touching a fork to the coils of an electric stove. There was a slight buzz going through her body now and it wasn't pleasant.

It was nothing like being touched by Azrael. But Gregori's

touch was nonetheless more powerful. *That* she knew with every fiber of her being.

Whoever and whatever Gregori was, he was awe-inspiring. And incredibly dangerous.

*I am death.*

'I'm here to help you, Sophie Bryce,' he told her.

'You now know that you're an archess. You know because the powers-that-be *deemed* that you would find out now. *Now*,' he said with slightly more emphasis, 'that you have grown and your painful childhood is over. *Now*,' he said again, 'that your helplessness has come to fruition and set you upon your path.'

Sophie couldn't help but think of the gun in her hand, the heavy weight of her foster father's body over hers, the pain of the grave beneath her as its sharp-edged stones angled bruises into her back. She heard his labored breathing, his swear words that sliced across her mind, felt his fingers gripping the top of her jeans. Then she heard the bang that split the fog and cast her into a decade of forgetting and denial.

She'd been a child. Completely helpless. If she'd had the powers of an archess then, when she'd needed them most . . .

'But you didn't have them, did you, Sophie?' Gregori asked. He raised his hand to curl his forefinger beneath her chin, tilting it up. Again, his touch was unnerving, setting off currents of electricity across her skin.

She stared up at him, feeling bewildered. He looked concerned and the emotion was completely at odds with the mesmerizing stars in his eyes. 'You have never had what you needed, not until now – because some other being out there is pulling your strings. Someone *else* is planning your fate.

That someone has deemed that the time is finally right for you to come into your abilities.' He smiled tenderly and cupped her face with his hands. Sophie felt as though she were watching the cobra sway gently from side to side. 'So that you can become an archess and give your life to the man you were made for,' he finished.

Gregori brushed his thumb across her cheekbone in a loving gesture. Sophie's teeth clenched, her jaw tightening. She felt the stirrings of something wholly uncomfortable swirling within her.

'Everything has been decided for you, young Sophie. Your entire life has been dictated. You have never had any choice, any control — any freedom.'

He released her suddenly, and Sophie blinked as he took a step back from her. The cold rushed in at once, cutting straight through the jacket Smith had given her. In her peripheral vision, she could see Smith watching the exchange in careful silence.

'Until now,' Gregori went on. 'Now you have the means with which to do *anything* if you're given the freedom to do it. For instance, you can do something about *this*. If you try.'

With that, he took a step to the side and turned. As he did, he revealed a young woman tied to a pole behind him. She hadn't been there before. The space had been empty until now.

The girl must have been no older than eighteen; a slight smattering of acne marred her forehead, but otherwise her skin was young and smooth. Her long black hair had been fishtail-braided at one point, but bits of it had come out, and mascara smeared her cheeks. She was gagged, and ropes cut into the sweatshirt and jeans over her body where they bound her tightly to the metal column behind her. The old column stood alone in the yard and supported nothing now but the young female captive.

Sophie's eyes widened.

And then Gregori was swiping his hand across the girl's throat. Something metal in his grip glistened in the dawning sunlight just before the blade sliced clean through the girl's neck, opening her artery to the world.

'Noooo!' Sophie's cry of shock and alarm ripped from her lungs. For the most horrid moment, she was frozen in time and space, unable to move, as if held there in place by the greedy, envious hands of the long-since dead. But the moment passed and Sophie found herself rushing forward.

The girl's eyes were golf-ball wide, her sweatshirt quickly turning red with the drenching of her blood. Sophie wrapped her hands around the teenager's neck, her fingers fumbling for something to close. But it was like trying to grip the fins of a fish; her flesh was wet and open and Sophie's hands slid along the surface, dipping ineffectually into the gap of death Gregori's blade had carved.

'No! God, please, no!' Sophie cried. Somehow, the girl's ropes had come undone and she now slid to the ground. Sophie followed her down, her arms trying to catch her limp body and seal her wound at the same time. It seemed the world had shrunk to only the victim and Sophie.

The girl's eyes were rolling back in her head. 'No, no, no, no, no.' Sophie had no idea what she was saying any longer.

*You can heal her, Sophie. You can fix this. If you try.*

And then Sophie's hands were moving from the girl's throat to her red-soaked chest. There was no thought, no premeditation. Her head was filled with the roaring of her own blood through her ears; the universe had receded. She simply saw the wound, felt the impending death, and knew she didn't want it to happen.

*Fix it.*

Whether or not the thought was her own she would never know. She closed her eyes when her hands began to heat up. The warmth spread from her palms to her fingertips and intensified, instantly drying the soaked material beneath her touch. It moved up her wrists and into her arms, chasing away the chill of the Rock's whipping winds like a friendly flame.

As it spread across her chest, Sophie let her head fall back. She felt weak and a little dizzy . . . but she also felt warm and tingly and the terrible, gripping fear that had possessed her moments before was now gone. There was no sound or outward indication that the task had been completed, but Sophie knew it was all right when she slowly removed her hands, lowered her head, and opened her eyes.

The girl was still gagged. But her eyes were not quite as wide, and her breathing had gone from desperate, ragged breaths through cloth to a more even, relaxed rhythm. Sophie looked from her face to her neck. The clean-sliced gash that had been there seconds earlier was gone; the girl's throat was whole, the skin healed.

'Imagine what you could have accomplished on that bridge,' said Gregori. His voice poured over her from behind, deep and melodic. Sophie closed her eyes, picturing the accident, the semi truck dipping through the sky, the *Calliope* shattered. 'Or what you might have done when any one of your foster fathers got out of hand.'

Sophie's eyes shot open, her stomach gripped with the

instant memories and the loathing that came with them. 'I don't understand,' she whispered. She didn't understand what she was doing there on that rock in the early-morning hours. She didn't understand why Azrael, the Masked One, the former Angel of Death, was in her life. She didn't understand why she was an archess, why she had these powers, or why they had arrived only now . . . when it was too late for so very much.

A part of her didn't understand the world and couldn't comprehend what it had become with all of its supernatural beings and magic and fated romances. That part of her mourned the loss of her best friend to an archangel and the loss of her own freedom to the same destiny.

There was another part of her that seemed to sit back, take a deep breath, and rest easy under the knowledge. It was as if she had been waiting all her life for this secret to be told, for this reality to finally make its appearance. That part of her was okay. But it was far too small for her liking.

'Of course you don't understand,' said Gregori. 'Why would you? It isn't important to the powers that be that you understand why this has been done to you. The one who created you doesn't care if you're confused, or that you suffered.'

Sophie turned and looked up at Gregori. His dark stars beckoned, his ice blue eyes mesmerizing. He shook his head, just once, and knelt gracefully beside her. Sophie experienced the briefest fear that he would dirty his beautiful white suit. But then his cologne was wafting over her and his body was inches from her own, and all she could do was gaze up at him, her lips parted, her entire being in awe.

He'd almost killed this innocent young girl, and yet she

couldn't hate him. She feared him and respected him. But the anger sat in the back of her mind and refused to stand.

'This is what I have come to give you, Sophie. I've come to give you the choice that your maker took from you two thousand years ago.' He smiled a charming, friendly smile, as if they were about to share an inside joke, and it took Sophie's breath away. And then he raised his hand and Sophie saw that between his fingers he held a single flower.

It was a dandelion. It was the lowliest of blooms, a weed, a bane to gardeners and groundskeepers across the globe. But it was perfect, every petal smooth and long and rounded.

It was also black.

# Chapter 24

'You have to rest. We'll go after her.'

Azrael's skin hurt. His head hurt, his heart hurt, his very blood hurt. The sun had come up and he wasn't below ground, sleeping. Each passing millisecond drained him more completely, more painfully than any mortal could have imagined.

'Just tell us where she is.' Michael's sapphire eyes glittered with knowledge. He was well aware of where Azrael had been. He knew whom Az had gone to for help.

The Warrior Archangel still looked very tired; the bridge and Uro had taken their toll on him. But he'd had an hour or two to rest and eat and drink and Max had no doubt seen to it that he'd had the very best of all three. His quick police-officer mind may have been able to guess where Azrael had been during that time, but Michael had no idea what it was that Sam had asked of him.

Now Michael stood at the exit of the foyer, his arms at his sides, his gaze one that would brook no nonsense. He was in archangel mode, giving Azrael an order. And he wasn't alone.

Uriel and Gabriel stood at either side of him and back several paces. Uriel's eyes cut hard emeralds across the space between them. Gabriel's flashed cold metal. None of them were in the mood to barter.

'We know he told you where she is, Az,' Gabriel said, his brogue deep now that he'd been back in Scotland for a while and he was feeling emotional. 'An' we also know you're plannin' to go after her yerself. An' we're tellin' you it won't happen.'

Azrael's brain was beginning to boil. Gabriel was right. In his fury, he'd been planning on going to Alcatraz himself to face off against the Adarians. He would have taken the shadows, hoping for a path that would lead him past the sun, the water, and deep into the cold metal corridors of the infamous jail. But even as he'd planned it, he'd known it would either kill him or come very close.

Even without exposure to direct sunlight, any vampire awake during the day suffered the consequences, including him. It was not their territory, not their world. They were unwelcome blots of darkness on the sunburns and freckles and sunglasses glare that existed between dawn and dusk.

'Alcatraz,' he said softly. Traces of pain edged his perfect voice, tilting it ever so slightly. 'Take the archesses. Take everything you have. The Adarians are not playing alone.'

Michael moved then, grabbing Azrael under the arm just as Az realized he was swaying. Gabriel took his other side and Uriel turned to face Max, who was watching his charge through calculating brown eyes.

'Azrael, you have to stay awake for another five to fill us in. Can you manage that?' Max asked. His tone was angry but calm, like that of a parent who was more than a little disappointed in his child.

Az nodded, not bothering to waste his breath.

'Get him below,' Max ordered.

Michael and Gabriel moved fast, ushering him through

the house and down the corridor that led to his chambers under the strange, magical foundation of the mansion. Once they were sequestered three stories down and the only light touching any of them was shed by the torches that spontaneously sprang to life along the walls, Michael and Gabriel helped Az to the altar upon which he slept. There they released him.

Az pulled himself up on top of it and wasted no time lying down. He even closed his eyes. And then he said, 'Abraxos somehow turned at least three other Adarians into vampires,' he said, beginning to fill them in on everything he knew. 'And they've developed new powers.'

Sophie looked at the dandelion, fascinated by its intricate black petals that shimmered like a raven's wings. Without thinking, she raised her hand, her finger poised to take the flower from him. She had to stop herself before she actually did so.

What was he offering?

'What is it?' she asked.

'A gift,' he said. 'A reminder.' He smiled. 'A way out.' He raised his other hand, took her fingers in his, and placed the flower in them. Again, the odd buzzing sensation passed through her skin and up her arms, both intriguing – and almost hurting – her.

As soon as she held the flower, he released her hand. She looked down at the black dandelion and felt as though she was holding something truly precious. Something unique. 'It's beautiful.'

'Freedom always is.' Gregori stood then, and Sophie watched him come gracefully to his full height. The imposing cut of his figure and the coldness in his eyes reminded her.

She turned to look down at the teenage girl whose life he had nearly taken, the one she had just saved.

The girl was gone.

'She was a lesson, Sophie,' Gregori told her quietly. Sternly.

Sophie turned back to face him and came to her feet, her fingers still clutching the black flower.

'Some lessons are harder than others.' With that, he took a step back and Sophie felt the world tilt beneath her. She moved, trying to catch herself. There was a blurred flash, a warping of the air around her, and she stumbled to the ground, pulling the bedspread off her bed as she fell.

The hardwood beneath her knees pressed into her knee-caps. Her gaze took in a knot in the wood, the gaps in the slats, a dust bunny she'd missed the last time she'd swept. She blinked, sitting up and looking around. She was in the bedroom of her apartment on Hemlock.

Sophie swallowed hard and closed her eyes, wondering if everything she'd gone through over the last twelve hours had been no more than an elaborate psychotic dream. Maybe she was under too much stress. Starting school at her age, with classmates who were much younger, wasn't going to be easy. Maybe she'd forgotten how to study and would flunk out and lose her scholarship. Maybe being back in San Francisco, her mother's favorite city, was too hard on her. Or maybe it was Juliette and her band of angels who were screwing with Sophie's head. It all seemed a mishmash inside her, fooling her subconscious into reveries of spectacular proportions.

She'd always had a wonderful imagination. Maybe it *was* a dream.

A knot of foreboding pulled her stomach muscles taut and

she gritted her teeth as images of guns and foster fathers and graveyards skated through her mind. But how *much* of it was a dream?

*Not that*, she thought. In her heart of hearts, she knew that much had been real. She knew she'd been attacked by her foster father at the age of fourteen. She knew that he'd taken her to the ground in the middle of the cemetery where her parents were buried. And she knew that rather than allow him to rape and murder her on her mother's grave, she had had taken his gun from him and shot him.

With an odd, choked sound, Sophie opened her eyes and looked down at the cuff of her sleeve. It was stained red with the blood of the girl she'd just saved.

None of this was a dream. All of it had been real.

With a start, Sophie realized that some of the blood staining the cuff was actually her own. It streamed in two thin rivulets down the meat of her palm to the wrist of her sleeve. Sophie blinked and uncurled her clenched fist. She'd been squeezing so tightly, her short nails had carved scarlet moons into her life line. She fully expected the dandelion she'd been holding to be squashed and lifeless now.

However, the dandelion was gone.

Lying within the rising crescents of blood on her palm was an artfully painted tattoo. At first glance, it looked like the black dandelion with a host of perfect petals. But as Sophie opened her palm and looked more closely, she realized she'd seen this shape before. It was a many-pointed star, as black and bottomless as Gregori's fathomless pupils.

There was no telling where the mansion would leave them in the labyrinth that was Alcatraz the prison. The best they could do was hope to open a door that didn't lead them directly into an ambush.

The portal swirled to life before them, waiting for them to step through. Michael turned back to glance over his shoulder at his brothers and their wives. Eleanore's deep indigo eyes had never been more serious. She was dressed as usual, which meant she was ready for battle in jeans, a black sweatshirt, and combat boots. Uriel's left hand was wrapped around her waist. In his right fist was a gun with gold bullets. None of them knew how much of an effect the gold was going to have on the Adarians now that they were becoming vampires. But the archangels were going to try every tactic they could think of.

Gabriel and Max both had black bags slung over their shoulders; the bags contained everything from gold grenades to cartridges with more gold bullets. Michael turned to Juliette, who met his gaze unflinchingly. The green in her hazel eyes was more pronounced when she was angry, and right now they were more green than he'd ever seen them. There was also a darkness beneath them that hadn't been there before. In the beautiful frame of her lovely face, it made her look like a Luis Royo painting: angry and frightened, but tough as nails.

Sophie Bryce was Juliette's best friend. Michael's gut clenched at the thought. Juliette stood to lose too much here. Azrael stood to lose everything. This was a waking hell.

He turned back to face the portal and stepped through. At once, he was enveloped by the twisted light that manipulated space and time. He was used to it, so he knew to adjust his step as he moved through the magic and exited into the cold and damp of Alcatraz's inner sanctums.

Michael stepped to the side to make room for the others even as he took a moment to look around. One of the few vampires Azrael had created that Michael really got along with had actually put a few men on the Rock himself. Randall McFarlan had traversed the passageways of Alcatraz many times. It was one of the things he and Michael spoke about on the very rare occasions when they both possessed the leisure time and proper mindset for casual conversation about law enforcement. Cop talk. San Francisco's cop talk somehow always found its way back to the Rock.

Now the dawn light cast dusty beams through the filthy windows of the large open chamber in which Michael stood. A chain-link fence painted a dull beige caged the room in on two sides. Up against the other two walls were the remains of wooden bookshelves. This was the Alcatraz library. If the bookshelves hadn't made it obvious, the signage would have. A poster-sized photograph on one of the chain-link walls showed what the room had looked like fifty years ago, complete with the portable bookshelves that had once filled its now empty space. And on the support beam at the center of the room hung a single yellow sign that read LIBRARY.

At this time of morning, before the arrival of the first tourism ferries, the silence in the prison seemed amplified by the sounds of sea life beyond its walls. There were no footsteps and no voices, but the halls were nonetheless filled with echoes of the past.

There were three exits from the library. But only one of these had a trail of stark red blood.

That blood stained the floor in splotches and left grisly designs along the walls and gate, reminding Michael of the scene in the missing girl's bedroom. A hard, cold chill began to settle deep inside the Warrior Archangel.

Once Michael's brothers, the archesses, and Max came through the portal and it closed behind them, Michael made his way toward the winding chain-link fence that would take him out of the library and into what was once the D Block of the prison. This was where Alcatraz's more infamous and violent prisoners had spent their hard time. As he moved down the corridor, the blood became more plentiful.

'Oh my God,' whispered Eleanore.

'This bodes ill,' Gabriel muttered. Michael glanced at him to see that the former Messenger Angel had pulled out his own firearm and his body language was rather more protective of the archess beside him than it had been moments ago.

Michael turned back to face the row of open cells to his right. There were two kinds of rooms on D Block. Those to his right were isolation rooms.

These doors were never closed any longer, not unless a tour guide was jokingly locking some tourist in just for the fun of it. These were the roomiest, most state-of-the-art cells in Alcatraz and always had been. They were also the most miserable.

Though their occupants would have had twice the space they would have had in A, B, or C Block, the rooms were so cold and damp that life within their walls had been unbearable. The wind whipped through the windows and across the cells with a moaning, whistling vengeance, tearing through the inmates' thin clothing and chilling them to the bone. It was never quiet here, not even on the calmest of days. The wind always sang its eerie song.

To make matters worse, though regulations stated that the lights were to be kept on, they often weren't. The prisoners were left in the dark for endless hours. Day upon day, night upon night. Alone.

Michael stopped at the entrance to the final isolation cell on the right. At one time, it had housed a single unlucky soul. Now it housed three.

'Jesus,' Uriel muttered.

'What happened to them?' Juliette asked, her voice a monotone. Michael glanced at her, noting her pale complexion and widened eyes. She was staring fixedly at the mess that waited beyond the large metal door and sliding metal bars of room number nine.

Three Adarians lay dead on the damp, bloodstained floor. Their bodies were mangled, their clothes drenched with red. So much blood had been spilled, it pooled beneath them and dripped through the drain at the center of the room. Michael could hear it hitting the sewage pipes in the corridors below them. *Drip. Drip. Drip.*

Michael recognized the men inside, though barely. Having gone up against the Adarians a number of times before, the archangels were now familiar with each one and his abilities. One of the dead had been capable of creating ice. Michael was fairly certain he'd also been able to fly. Another had possessed odd abilities such as creating magnetic force fields and the like. Azrael seemed to think that it was this same Adarian's ability to find people that had helped Abraxos locate Sophie. Michael believed the third one went by the name Astaeroth and had been the most powerful of the three, capable of creating and using fire against his enemies. Azrael had feared this Adarian a little more than the others. But he wouldn't be fearing him now.

Eleanore was the first to turn away. Her hand was over

her mouth and her eyes were closed. It hadn't been long ago that these same three men had tried to rip her apart from Uriel. They'd tortured her husband and kept him confined in a prison no better than this. And yet to see them destroyed in such a manner was traumatic.

'What in bloody hell are we dealing with?' Gabriel asked, his brogue in full, emotional tilt.

'There's a note,' Max said, his voice cutting through the silence. He moved past the brothers and lifted a small Post-it off a sewing pin that had been pressed into the dead Astaeroth's chest.

The yellow square of paper was dotted and curled with blood, but still legible. In neat black print was the word: 'Check.'

Max studied it for a moment and then lowered his arm to look carefully around the room. 'Where do you suppose the others are?' he asked.

'Sleeping, if Az was right about the vampire thing,' Uriel said. He had his arms around Eleanore, whose face was buried in his chest. His green eyes flashed with dangerous emotion.

'And Sophie?' Michael asked. Someone had to do it.

'I'm guessing she's back at her apartment,' said Max, who then handed the Post-it note to Michael without looking at him. He was too busy taking in their surroundings with the careful attentiveness of someone who needed to know who and what they were dealing with.

Michael looked down at the note. Something was written on the other side. It was an address. 'Sophie's address?' he asked, not knowing it himself.

'Yes,' said Max. 'Whoever did this is not only capable of easily overpowering the Adarians; they also have the ability to either move through the shadows as a vampire would or they have a portal of their own.'

'Or they don't *need* a portal,' said Eleanore in a muffled voice from behind Uriel's T-shirt.

Max glanced at her. 'Indeed,' he agreed.

'I know we're all thinkin' it, bu' I'll say it anyway. This was no' Sam's doin'.'

'No, it wasn't,' said Max. 'It doesn't fit him.' He shook his head and sighed. 'And he was the one who tipped Azrael off as to Sophie's location. In fact, I'd wager a guess that Samael doesn't know she's no longer here.'

'She'll be alone,' said Uriel, clearly speaking of the fact that Sophie was at her apartment now.

Michael had to agree with him. If the beings responsible for the Adarian killings had wanted to hurt Sophie, they would have done so here, on Alcatraz Island. There was no reason to draw the fight to the mainland. Sophie was most likely unaccompanied, and this was all some kind of elaborate game to someone much more powerful than they were.

'My thoughts exactly,' said Max. He looked at Juliette and his expression softened. 'Juliette, I think it would be best if you go to her alone. I cannot even imagine what must be going through her head at the moment.'

Juliette nodded resolutely. 'My thoughts exactly,' she echoed. 'If I can't convince her to come back to the mansion with me, I'll let you know.'

'And we'll bring her back ourselves,' said Michael. Whether Sophie could see the reasoning in it or not, she wasn't safe anywhere else.

# Chapter 25

Sophie jumped when there was a knock on her door. She looked up toward the living room and a thousand thoughts chased each other through her head.

'Sophie?' came a gentle voice from the other side. It was Juliette!

Sophie's chest swelled with warmth, but she remained where she was, frozen beside the bed. She glanced down at the suitcase and large leather messenger bag she'd been packing and blinked. The inside of her right hand throbbed. She opened it and gazed at her palm She'd healed the crescent marks her nails had made; it had been easy. But the dandelion dark star remained. She'd forgotten about it; it hadn't hurt until now.

'Sophie are you home?' Juliette called again.

A frisson of irritation thrummed quickly and unexpectedly through Sophie. Her palm twinged with a quick, mild pain, and she blinked. 'Yes,' she replied, her mind spinning furiously. 'Yeah, give me a sec, Jules! Just getting out of the shower!'

*That was stupid*, she berated herself. *Your hair's not even wet.*

Thunder rumbled over the apartment building. She wasn't thinking clearly. She felt strange. With a frustrated sigh, she ran her hands quickly over her face, shoved her hair out of her eyes, and turned to the hallway that led to the living room. Her leather-soled boots sounded loud on the hardwood floor. A few seconds later, she was unbolting the door and opening it.

Juliette stood on the threshold, her face pale, her eyes enormous in her beautiful face. She was alone.

For several long moments, the two young women simply stared at one another. Sophie thought about telling Juliette everything – *everything*. A part of her was screaming inside, begging to be released so that she could tell Juliette about her foster father and the gun she'd used on him and about Azrael being a vampire and the fact that she was his archess and the bridge and the Adarians and Uro and the fire and finally about the stranger on Alcatraz Island. The man in white.

But the rest of Sophie was wrapped in silence, strapped down in indecision and a strange, uncomfortably building ire.

And so she said nothing.

'Sophie, are . . . are you okay?' Juliette asked, her expression one of baffled hurt and a little fear.

*What am I doing?* Sophie asked herself, suddenly realizing that she hadn't said anything and that there was far too much to say for her to be remaining silent.

'I . . .' She fumbled for the right words, but her palm ached now and the thunder outside was drawing closer and her mind felt stuffed with cotton. 'I don't know.'

With that, Juliette was moving forward and pushing Sophie back into the apartment at the same time. Jules shut the door behind her and led Sophie to the couch. Sophie didn't argue.

They both sat down and Juliette turned to face her, all seriousness now. 'What happened on Alcatraz?' she asked.

*On Alcatraz*, Sophie thought. She stared into her best friend's eyes and it seemed that a bit of the murkiness in her head cleared up a little. She saw the teenage girl . . . and the man in white slitting her throat. And suddenly, without warning, she felt a shuddering sob shake her slim frame to her core.

Thirty minutes later, Sophie was blowing her nose for the twentieth time and Juliette was handing her a freshly brewed cup of chamomile tea. Juliette had brought a stash of the tea in her purse; obviously she'd known what kind of state Sophie would be in. Juliette was good at that kind of thing.

Over the course of the last half hour, Sophie had told Juliette everything that she'd wanted to tell her upon seeing her on the threshold of her apartment. She told her about her foster father and her life afterward, about Azrael and the accident on the bridge, and about Gregori and what had happened on the Rock. And then Juliette had told her about the three murdered Adarians found in the jail cell in the prison, which brought the subject back to Gregori.

'He has stars for pupils,' Sophie found herself saying. She'd already told Juliette about how Gregori had nearly killed the innocent teenage girl. She'd described the occurrence in vivid detail; she couldn't help it. Everything about the incident was painfully clear in her mind's eye.

'Jules, you just can't imagine what he was like. He was simply overwhelming.' She felt out of breath just thinking about the man in white. The way he'd crossed space and time in the blink of an eye, the way he'd gotten into her head, to say nothing of the way he looked – and what he'd done to that girl. She shook her head and shivered violently before closing her eyes and running a shaky hand through her long blond hair.

Juliette watched her in silence for a moment and then her already troubled expression became decidedly more so. 'We have to tell Max about him,' she said. Then she took a deep, bewildered breath and shook her head, briefly closing her eyes and pinching the bridge of her nose. 'Now we have a name and a face to put behind the Adarians' murders. It's not much, but it's something.' She sighed, dropping her hand. 'Who the hell is he, and what does he want?'

Sophie watched her friend, taking in the small changes that had come over Juliette in the last few weeks. Jules was a small woman, but her stature seemed to have grown. She radiated a kind of power and confidence that Sophie was fairly sure she herself would never have. Juliette had found where she belonged in the world. She'd learned who she was meant to be and had moved into that role with flawless ease. She'd found happiness . . . that much was clear. And now something threatened that happiness.

Sophie couldn't help but wonder how much of it was her fault. If she hadn't been born an archess, if she hadn't somehow found her way to Juliette's side, if she hadn't been as messed up as she was, as much of a magnet for trouble as she was – none of this would be happening.

Her hand tingled, the pain that had been ever present in her palm over the last half hour spreading and lessening, becoming more of a warmth that inched up her wrist.

Or maybe it *would*. If Sophie hadn't been born, then Juliette would still be an archess and the Adarians would still be out there and the man in white might still be playing whatever game he was playing, but playing it with Juliette instead. Or Eleanore. Or some other woman who had been born the archess instead of Sophie.

And Azrael would be chasing after someone else.

Sophie felt a rush of heat go through her at the thought of the tall, dark archangel. She was powerless against the image of him, dressed in black, surrounded by an aura of power and calm and unimaginable strength. She caught a whiff of his scent, like night – sandalwood and leather and soap, and her mouth watered. She saw his long, thick jet-black hair and felt his vivid eyes bore into her. The chiseled perfection of his features threw her for a moment, as she imagined him staring at her from behind her own lids . . . and speaking her name.

'Soph?'

Sophie jumped a little and opened her eyes, realizing that she'd shut them in the first place. 'Yes?' she asked, blushing as if Juliette had been privy to the scene in her head.

'Where were you planning on going?'

Sophie turned to look at her friend and noticed that Juliette was staring at something down the hall. *Damn*, she thought as she glanced back and caught the edge of her suitcase on the bed. It sat open, its contents partly folded.

The truth was, she'd had no idea where she was going to go. She only felt that she needed to get away – from Frisco, from the bay, from . . . Azrael.

She was positively obsessed with him. Her most recent thoughts proved as much. She had hated being obsessed when she'd thought it was her own doing, her own weak will that left her drooling over the lead singer of Valley of Shadow like some lovesick teenager. But now that she knew she was an archess and that she was *destined* to feel this way about the man, it was worse. It was worse because she realized that she had never had any control over the fact that she would one day end up lusting after the Masked One. She'd never had any say in whom she was going to fall in love with. She'd never been given any freedom.

And that pissed her off.

Thunder rumbled overhead again, closer still. A storm was coming.

Juliette glanced up at the sound, her brow furrowed. Sophie ignored her. She was too wrapped up in the feeling of helplessness that she had where Azrael was concerned.

She resented him. She lusted after him and dreamed of him and fantasized about him . . . and a part of her felt as though it hated him. She needed to get away from the power he had over her. And the only way she knew to do that was to run.

The heat in her wrist spread up her arm, tingling pleasantly. She ignored that too, despite the fact that she could see Juliette staring at her hand. She was caught up in her emotions now – damn everything else to hell.

Running was what Sophie had done when she was fourteen. She killed her foster father, and when it was done, she awakened on that cemetery hill to find herself alone. She didn't remember how she'd gotten there. There was a smoking gun still hot in her hand. She had no idea where it had come from or what she'd used it for, but a horrible feeling crept along her skin and brought her to a decision: whatever she'd done, she wasn't going to hang around long enough to find out.

She took off then, shoving the gun into her jeans and heading into the woods that surrounded the graveyard. She buried the gun, not knowing what else to do with it. And then, when she was finished, she went back to her foster mother's home.

Sophie realized now that when she'd gone home, she'd expected to find only her foster mother. No father. It was like it had always been that way. And the truly bizarre thing was that her foster mother felt that way as well. Neither of them mentioned Sophie's torn jeans or the grass and mud in her hair. It wasn't like her foster mother would have noticed these things anyway, but in the light of the reality Sophie was now faced with, there was no denying that her foster mother's actions that day had been beyond bizarre. It was as if Sophie's trauma-induced amnesia had been infectious. Neither of them mentioned anyone named Alan Harvey. No one did. Not the neighbors, not the unemployment office or the utility companies, not the orphanage – no one. As far as the world was concerned, Alan Harvey had never existed.

Life went on and, for a change, there were no horrible men in it. At sixteen, Sophie's foster mother moved to Pennsylvania and Sophie enrolled in high school there. On the side, she landed a job in Pittsburgh as a maid to make extra money. Two years later, she met Juliette.

And now here she was, in a life that seemed utterly foreign to her. She felt like she should consider herself the luckiest woman in the world. She had magical powers, she was an angel, she had an awesome best friend and a love interest who was quite literally the most famously charismatic man on the planet.

She also felt completely confused and positively furious.

What the fuck had happened that day? What was going on with her life? Who the hell was in charge here?

Her existence was a circus, replete with a smoke-and-mirrors magic act, and she was both clueless and powerless as to how it played out.

How dare the world do this to her? How dare it leave her to fend for herself as a child and then, when it mattered least, pop her with powers she'd always needed? Just when she was about to be strapped to someone who would *still* be more powerful than she was?

And that was why she had been planning to run.

When she turned back around, it was to find Juliette staring fixedly at her. The hazel-eyed archess glanced down at Sophie's hand. Sophie followed her gaze to the dandelion star on her palm. Reflexively, she curled her fingers and tucked her hand under her leg.

Lightning crashed just outside the windows. It was time for Juliette to go.

Sophie had every reason to be angry. Juliette had always known that her best friend's life had been hard — very hard. But now that she knew the whole story, she was baffled by how well adjusted Soph had always been. That Sophie could even function like a normal human being after having killed the man who nearly raped her at fourteen was beyond Juliette. She'd always had immense respect for Sophie Bryce, for her strength, her will, and her refusal to let life get her down. Now that respect was amplified to a heart-wrenching degree and Juliette could not blame Sophie for her fury and resentment at all.

But . . . something was wrong. There was more to this.

Not only did the fact that no one remembered Sophie's foster father's existence spell 'supernatural' in Juliette's book, but there was an aura around Sophie now that was distinctly un-Sophie-like. Granted, the girl was no doubt beyond stressed out. But this was different.

The man Sophie described – the man in white – well and truly frightened Juliette, and she had never even met him personally. What he'd done to the Adarians would have been enough. But when Sophie told her what he'd also done to the innocent teenager, coupled with her description of the white, perfectly tailored suit, and the nearly white color of his ice-blue eyes, Juliette had felt an unpleasant sensation unfold within her. It felt a little like the beginning of a panic attack. There was a buzzing sensation, a tightening in her chest, and her heart felt heavy, as if it was turning to lead.

She didn't like Gregori. Hell, she didn't even like thinking his name.

She would rather refer to him as the man in white.

To make matters worse, it was becoming increasingly clear to Juliette that the man in white had done something to Sophie. The mark on the inside of Sophie's hand had never been there before. Unless Soph had gone out and tattooed a dark star on her palm at some point after the wedding at Slains Castle, the mark was new – and it wasn't Sophie's doing. In fact, it looked an awful lot like the stars-for-pupils that Sophie had said Gregori possessed.

It was unnerving. And so was the way Sophie was behaving.

Anger would have been one thing. Juliette could have understood that – empathized with it – and forgiven it easily. But Sophie was distracted and becoming more so by the second. Sophie Bryce had never been the airhead type. She'd never been anything but quick-witted, full of energy, and sharp as a tack.

Yet even that, Juliette could have dismissed as probably having to do with lack of sleep and an overwhelming boatload of information and nastiness being dumped on her best friend's head.

What she couldn't forgive or dismiss or even understand was the way Sophie was closing herself off from Juliette.

Right now.

'Jules, I just need some time to think. Please.'

Juliette wasn't stupid. Sophie was trying to get rid of her. 'You do know that if you leave, you won't get far. Not with Az on your tail.'

Sophie blinked, and her expression hardened. Her beautiful golden eyes felt like amber in that moment, and whatever intentions she'd had were now frozen within them. 'Please leave, Jules.'

'It isn't safe out there, Soph. The Adarians are bad enough. But this Gregori guy?' Juliette flinched, unable to help herself. She couldn't stop seeing what he'd done to the Adarians in that cell on Alcatraz. 'Azrael will never leave you unprotected. Not now. I'm sorry, Soph, but you just happen to have gotten paired up with the most intense archangel in existence. The man was willing to go after you during the *day*.' She shook her head, her eyes wide. 'It would have killed him, and Max had to seriously talk him down.'

Sophie stared at Juliette, and as she absorbed what Juliette had told her, the expression on her face softened a little. The amber in her eyes melted, appearing warmer, like honey. She seemed to be momentarily at a loss for words, but then she flinched and Juliette noticed that she clenched her fist harder where she hid her hand beneath her tight blue jeans.

'Jules,' Sophie said, looking away. 'When you first met Gabriel, did you warm to him right away?'

Juliette realized that Sophie already knew the answer to that question. Soph was well aware of the power struggle Juliette and Gabriel had gone through in Scotland a few months ago. She was only asking the question to make a point. Juliette wasn't sure she wanted to know what point that was.

'No,' she replied.

'No,' Sophie echoed. 'And he wasn't a vampire.'

'No,' Juliette admitted.

'And you had never killed anyone,' Sophie added.

Sophie looked back up at Juliette then, and saw a new expression on her lovely features. It was a look Juliette had never before seen there.

'No.' Juliette's voice fell, along with her hopes. 'I had never killed anyone.' She'd never had real cause to feel fury toward Gabriel the way that Sophie might feel toward Azrael and the archangels. As an archess, Sophie had possessed the intrinsic ability to stop her foster fathers from attacking her all those years ago, but her archess powers hadn't actually appeared until now. She most likely felt cheated. She probably felt as if she'd never had control over her own life. And she no doubt blamed the archangels and their creator for this sense of helplessness.

Juliette fell silent, unsure of what to say or how to say it.

'Jules, I need some time alone.'

Juliette straightened, gazing long and hard into her best

friend's beautiful eyes. She saw a desperation there, a sadness, and a pain. Maybe Sophie was right. Maybe the solitude and time she was asking for were what she needed more than anything else right now.

But Juliette couldn't overlook the fidgeting and the twitch of Sophie's right hand. The man in white was pulling her strings; Juliette would have bet her castle on it. This was beyond her capabilities. It was something she couldn't handle alone. It was time to call in the big boys.

'Okay,' she said softly, rising from her seat on the couch. 'I'll leave you. But please remember that I love you, Soph. You're a part of us now – and you've *always* been a part of me.' She leaned over and pulled Sophie into a fierce hug. She felt her friend relax against her, absorbing the warmth of the embrace. And then Juliette let her go and headed for the door.

She didn't wait for Sophie to walk her out or close the door behind her. Instead, she left the apartment and went directly to the nearest alleyway. Once there, she glanced over her shoulder to make certain she was alone. Then she turned toward a metal door in the wall that led to a small shop beyond. The door was for employee use only, according to the white and red metal sign hanging above it.

Since Eleanore and Juliette had each 'earned their wings,' they had been capable of using the mansion for transportation, just as their archangel mates could. Max's thoughts on the matter were that the mansion had been created for the archangels to use as they searched for their archesses. It wouldn't make any sense to limit its use to the archangels once the archesses had been located; therefore each archess was able to use it as well.

The mansion's transporting powers were available for Juliette to use now, just as they were for Eleanore. All she needed was a door.

Juliette raised her hand toward the door in front of her in the alley and opened a portal to the mansion.

# Chapter 26

The sun would soon dip into the Pacific, but no one could tell. The sky was laden with clouds, heavy and dark. Thunder rumbled along the West Coast and the wind sent sailing ships scurrying for the harbor.

Azrael tossed in his sleep as images flashed across his mind. He felt an anger stirring his blood as if it were his own – but it wasn't. It was Sophie's. He knew it as if she were a part of him, body and soul.

In the distance of his dreamscape, lightning split the sky and tore holes in a land parched and destroyed. Wind howled, rushing through his hair. He reached out to settle it and it fought him, but eventually obeyed.

He heard a gunshot and turned toward the ancient cemetery sprawling behind him. Black dandelions coated the once green hills, surreal and beautiful and terrifying. Fear gripped him hard and cold, squeezing his soul in its taloned fingers. To step into another person's mind and see the headstones was bad enough. To dream of them himself . . .

He needed to wake up.

It was too soon; he knew this, but Sophie's spirit called to him, shuffled through his subconscious, and unsettled his mind. He was sinking into death, into what he once was. He needed her. His sunshine. Only she could pull him back from this precipice.

Ten minutes before the sun set, Azrael opened his eyes where he lay on the stone altar that served as his bed. At once, the torches that lined the walls leapt to burning life as if they recognized the conscious presence of their liege.

The shadows shifted and Azrael rose in one fluid motion, his gold eyes glowing hot in his face. Despite the instant weakening effect it had on him to be moving even this late in the day, the vampire archangel was blurring through the corridors of the mansion at an incomprehensible speed well before the final rays of sun winked out and twilight took the land.

His brothers were waiting for him, as were Eleanore and Juliette. The curtains and blinds had been drawn tight; they'd known he would be up early.

'Where is she?' he asked. It was all he cared about.

Juliette rose from the couch. Her expression was pained, worried. Gabriel stood beside her, his well-muscled arms crossed over his chest. His silver eyes flashed warily. Alarm bells went off in Azrael's head, deafening in their warning.

No one answered his question.

'There is much we must discuss, Azrael,' said Max. He stood at the opposite end of the couch, once more dressed in the brown three-piece suit he normally wore. A serious expression settled over his features, and in his hands he held one of the four gold bands that the Old Man had given them so long ago. The bracelets possessed the power to trap a supernatural being's abilities within their body, rendering them useless. The fact that Max was bringing one of the bands out now no doubt meant that Az would soon be faced with an archess who would fight him.

'I just left her a little while ago,' said Juliette, drawing his attention. 'She's fine,' she assured him. Then she shook her head. 'But the situation is not good.'

The final minutes of the day had taken a proverbial bite out of Azrael's constitution, but he'd healed rather resolutely once the sun had gone down. And then he'd fed.

Now he stood on the roof of the apartment complex directly across from Sophie's and let the angry wind whip through his hair and trench coat. Beside him stood Michael and Max. Gabriel and Uriel had remained at the mansion with their wives. They'd insisted that the archesses stay behind, and because none of them knew how powerful their new enemy was, the archangels remained with them. The archesses could not be left alone.

Behind Azrael on the rooftop were the members of Valley of Shadow, his oldest friends and created vampires. Uro, for his part, had been the fortunate recipient of the healing powers of two archesses and had not a single scar to show for the attack Abraxos had mounted against him. He was as handsome as ever, but the event had struck a serious chord with them all. They knew what they were up against now and it was far more powerful than any of them would have believed. It went without saying that Uro was on guard, and his band mates echoed the sentiment. If Abraxos had been more than Uro could handle, the man in white who had so effortlessly killed the Adarians was an unmeasured threat.

Az peered down at the windows of Sophie's second-story apartment. There had been no movement within the rooms, but he could feel her there. She was like a piece of a star, bright, volatile, and barely contained. He could also feel the presence of his other subjects all around him, on rooftops and bridges for miles in every direction.

Down below, on the street in front of Sophie's building, stood Randall, Monte, and Terry. Vampires preferred dark clothing, and their figures blended with the shadows around them. As one, they looked up, their eyes glowing as they locked gazes with their king.

They were waiting. Everyone was waiting to see what Azrael would do.

The good people of the world were tucked inside this night. The storm raged, windows rattled, and the tide brought with it froth-filled, crashing waves that beat against the piers and threatened anchored boats in their docks. The air was cold; to a human, it would have been frigid, leaving rime where the salt water coated the wood of the boardwalks.

For *any* time of year in San Francisco, freezing weather was rare. In mid-May, it was practically unheard-of. Sophie Bryce had come into her powers, all right, and they were stronger than anything Azrael had encountered with an archess.

Az had a feeling that the extra help was coming from the man who had left the mark on the palm of her right hand.

Azrael slipped his own hand into the pocket of his trench coat and fingered the gold bracelet waiting there. Once more, the vampire archangel was faced with a choice. He could do this the easy way, the way he wanted to do it, and use everything in his power to overwhelm Sophie until she submitted to him. Or he could rein himself in . . . and do things the hard way. He'd tried so hard to play nice; he'd come so far. It meant everything to him that Sophie trust him

– that she grow to love him on her own terms. He wasn't ready to lose what he'd gained now.

But archesses were a difficult and dangerous breed to scuffle with. On the battlefield, they were every bit as powerful as their archangel counterparts, if not more so. Sophie was not to be taken lightly now – especially not while she was under whatever influence Gregori had over her.

Azrael considered the stranger Juliette referred to as the man in white. He thought of the dead Adarians and wondered where Abraxos and his three Chosen, the Adarian-made vampires, were at that moment. He couldn't feel them; wherever they were, it wasn't here, in the midst of Sophie's tempest.

Not yet.

'You already know Abraxos can move through the shadows,' Az said. 'If he comes tonight, he will bring the others through with him again.'

'Do you think if I killed him and took his blood, I could do the same?' Rurik asked, his voice deep and his tone laced with acid. Az glanced back at him. The Viking's eyes glowed a hellish blue, like the center flames in a bonfire. His fangs were fully extended, and at the moment the scar above his left eye seemed redder than usual.

The four band members together reminded Azrael of the four horsemen of the apocalypse. Rancor was moving through the vampires of the world that night. They were angry that someone had attacked their queen – and marked her. They were also angry that the Adarian general and his three Chosen had joined them in the night uninvited. The fact that Abraxos and his turned vampires could move through the shadows sat particularly unwell with them.

And they wanted vengeance for what had been done to Uro.

Max, who was now dressed in fatigues, as he always was for a battle, turned to look at Rurik as well. 'Just try not to get yourself killed,' he said. 'You have a concert on Saturday.' He looked back at Azrael and his brown eyes softened with genuine concern. 'The same goes for you.'

Az shifted his attention from Max to Michael, who was standing at the edge of the roof and surveying the alleyway beneath them. Az brushed his mind. Ever the cop, Michael was thinking about power outages and the problems they would cause for mortals throughout the city. But he was also thinking of how the four brothers had been forced to fight for every one of their archesses so far. He was wondering what would happen when, and if, he ever found his.

Looking at his brother now, Az couldn't help but remember Samael's contract and the promise he'd made. His heart turned to lead as he listened for and caught the sound of the powerful archangel's blood running through his veins. It was blood Sam wanted him to take – along with the power inside of it.

But now was not the time.

With a hardened resolve, Azrael faced his band mates. They met his gaze resolutely. 'Keep your heads,' he told them, trying his best to keep his own. And then he turned and leapt off the building. His trench coat billowed as he descended. Lightning crisscrossed behind him; he could feel the heat of it sizzling through the air. He landed with a cat's quiet, easy grace, as if the world moved for him to make it easier. And then he straightened and looked up at Sophie's second-story window.

It struck him as odd that there was no rain – or sleet, rather – accompanying Sophie's storm. It was dry . . . like a tearless rage.

Azrael strode to the front door of the building, passing Randall and the others on the way. He moved through the front gate into the enclosed courtyard beyond. Quickly he found the stairs that led to Sophie's floor, and within seconds he was standing before her door. He didn't bother knocking. It opened for him with no more than a thought, and the cold entered Sophie's world on mist and wind and lightning-streaked darkness.

Sophie looked up from where she sat on the couch. Her beautiful golden eyes were unnaturally bright, her teeth were clenched, and her gaze was narrowed.

'Let me guess,' she said. 'You've come to collect your little archess.'

Something hard and mean ramrodded through Azrael, an animal reaction to the defiance he saw in his mate's eyes. He watched as she slowly stood, her hands curled into fists at her sides, her glorious golden hair whipping about in the wind he'd let in along with him. She glared at him – and the vampire inside of him raised its head and recognized the challenge. He wanted to take her then, to slam her up against the wall and sink his fangs into her neck and drink her in until she surrendered.

But part of him recognized the emotion in her gorgeous eyes for what it was. It was enough to hold him in check.

Barely.

'You got it in one,' he said calmly, turning to glance at the door so that it slammed shut behind him. 'Now it's my turn,' he said as he moved farther into the room.

A flash of uncertainty skated over her perfect features. She took a step back beside the couch, her gaze wary.

'You met a man on a rock and he reminded you of how you've had a hard life filled with pain and loss, and how you've been helpless to stop it until now. And you hate that.' He stopped and cocked his head to one side. 'Am I right?'

Sophie's gaze hardened. 'What I *hate*,' she said, again speaking through clenched teeth, 'is *you*.' She paused, allowing her words to sink in.

Azrael's chest tightened and his eyes flashed, but he took her attack in stride. He knew this wasn't Sophie – not completely, anyway.

Relentlessly, she went on. 'I hate you and your brothers and your stupid Old Man and the way he thinks he can create people and toss them away and then play *games* with them like fucking chess pieces on a board.'

Azrael raised his head and took a slow, deep breath through his nose. He felt his eyes burning in his skull and knew they were glowing like suns. His gums throbbed, his fangs begging to be released. Somehow he kept them in.

'So what will you do, Sunshine?' he asked as he took a step toward her. The darkness followed him as he moved, wrapping around him, swathing him in its power as if dressing him for war. 'Will you run?' he asked. 'Hide?'

'If I could, I would,' she hissed.

'But you know you can't, don't you?' he continued, taking another step. 'You know that it's pointless to run from me. No one escapes me, Sophie. Many have tried.' He shook his head. 'All of them have failed.'

She watched him take another step toward her, so close now, and her gold eyes flashed. 'Only a cruel and heartless bastard would consider that something to brag about,' she told him fiercely, shaking her head. 'You think it's funny that everyone dies eventually? You think it's something to shrug off and laugh at?'

Azrael stilled. He stopped two feet away from her. 'No one is laughing, Sophie.'

Sophie's gaze flicked past his eyes to his lips. He watched as she couldn't help but take in the curve of his neck, his shoulder, the broad expanse of his chest. He wanted to absorb that attention and crow, but Sophie shut her eyes tight and turned away from him, showing him her back.

'Get out,' she demanded, her voice shaking with pent-up emotion. 'Go away.'

Azrael closed the distance between them and gazed down at her. Despite her long, lean body, he towered over her. His darkness shadowed her and he saw her shiver beneath the weight of his nearness.

'That's not going to happen,' he told her.

She had known he was there, but the sound of his voice so close had an effect upon her. He could hear her heart rate speed up, her breathing change. He knew she could feel him behind her. He watched her fingertips press into the sleeves of her sweater.

'Sophie, turn around and look at me.'

'No.'

If it had been a stubborn refusal and nothing more, it might have made him smile. But her anger was still there, lacing the edge of her tone like poison.

The heat of her ire warmed her veins and Az caught the sweet scent of promising magic that coursed through them. His gums throbbed and his fangs slid partway to freedom. He closed his eyes against their invasion, trying desperately to find the strength he needed to hold back a little longer.

'Please leave me alone, Azrael,' Sophie told him. 'Despite what you and your brothers and your guardian think, I have a choice now. And I've made it.'

'Oh, Sunshine,' Azrael said, his tone hardening, 'you have never been more wrong.'

She stilled before him and straightened. She could hear the change in his voice and recognized it for the resolve that it was. He noted the thump of her heart and the catch of her breath as instinct shoved her into defensive mode.

But she wasn't fast enough to avoid him. It took only a fraction of a second for Azrael to wrap his arm around her neck and shoulders and pull her back hard against his chest. When she raised her hands instinctively to grab his arm, Az slammed the binding bracelet onto her right wrist. It flashed brightly as it separated and then remolded around her.

Sophie struggled in his grasp, but he tightened his hold and, as he'd known she would, she calmed down for fear that he would choke her. He held her there for a moment. He couldn't help it. She felt good pressed against him and he wanted to be closer.

As her fingernails curled ineffectually into his arm, he lowered his lips to her ear. 'We need some alone time, Sophie,' he told her. He was about to go on when he noticed the chipped, crooked coffee table rattling where it rested beside them. He glanced at it in surprise as it suddenly shot up from the ground and then sailed straight toward them.

He could have used his own powers to stop it, but his first instinct was much faster, and he was ducking with Sophie, taking her down with him. The coffee table soared over them to slam into the opposite wall. Az rolled with Sophie and pulled her back up to a standing position with him just as the card table she'd been using for a dining table picked itself up and flew across the room toward them.

Az narrowed his gaze at it and it warped, turning to a mass of black feathers that floated slowly to the ground.

In his grasp, Sophie screamed in frustration. Thunder rocked the apartment complex. Azrael ignored it. His mind was spinning. How could she control these things while wearing the bracelet?

Suddenly, the couch behind him slammed hard into his back, surprising him enough that he loosened his grip on his archess. She took the opportunity to break free and then spun to face him. Azrael lowered his arms and watched with wide eyes as Sophie glared at him, gave him a wicked smile that both terrified him and turned him on, and then yanked the bracelet off her wrist in one bright flash.

# Chapter 27

Kevin knew something was wrong before he opened his eyes. There was a heaviness on his chest, as if an anvil had been left there during the course of the day. But he sat up free of physical weights and frowned into the darkness.

With a wave of his hand, he brought the overhead lights on, adjusting them to a dim setting. Ely, Mitchell, and Luke were belowground with him, each in his own wing of the man-made tunnels far beneath the surface along the West Coast that spanned what he'd jokingly begun to call their lair. He sent out a mental call to them now.

Within seconds, Mitchell's dress shoes could be heard on the cold stone floor. He stepped into the light of the main room and Kevin caught a whiff of lighter fluid and smoke as Mitchell lit the end of the cigarette he had between his teeth.

The Adarian vampire's gaze was on the ground as he took a pull off the cigarette and lowered it between two fingers. He blew out a cloud of smoke, then paused – and looked up at Kevin. 'Something's wrong.'

'I feel it too,' said Luke as he emerged from his own wing.

'It's Adam and the others,' said Ely, who appeared a split second later.

Kevin knew he was right. As Ely said it, Kevin realized he'd known it even upon waking.

Adam and two other Adarians had not yet made the change to vampire. Kevin had his reasons for this. Though being a vampire made an Adarian much more powerful in most respects, it made him weaker in another. Kevin needed someone close to him who could move about during the day, and as a vampire this was impossible.

Once the Adarians had successfully taken Sophie from Azrael's cave, they had regrouped on Alcatraz Island. Dawn was breaking, so Kevin and his three Chosen had taken off for safe haven underground. In the meantime, Adam and the others promised to take Sophie somewhere safe. Kevin didn't want the archess resting with him and his Chosen; if Azrael was at all able to stay up during the day – which Kevin was fairly certain he couldn't do – then the vampire king might use his scrying ability to track his archess down while Kevin and his men were unconscious and helpless. Sophie could inadvertently lead Azrael directly to them, and during the day the Adarians would be sitting ducks.

Instead, Kevin had to rely upon Adam's inherent Adarian intelligence to get Miss Bryce far enough away from San Francisco to pose a problem to Azrael's brothers and hope against hope that Az was as helpless during the daylight hours as Kevin was.

But now . . .

With a glance at the others that tied them together in purpose, Kevin turned to the nearest shadow big enough to hold his tall, strong form and stepped through it. A few minutes later, the four of them were exiting the dark realm and leaving behind the shadows to step into the Spanish fort on Alcatraz Island, a much older, more crude part of the establishment that was located beneath the prison.

The cold, hollow air was quiet but for the occasional echoing cry of a seagull and the howling of the wind over the land above. Kevin turned to Ely, gave him a nod, and the four of them made their way up several flights of stairs and into the cold night. The wind whipped through the trees and across the shrub-covered hills of the island, knocking birds askew in their flight and preventing them from finding suitable perches. Kevin glanced up to watch low-lying clouds sink lower, dip, and dive, driven by a nearly unholy wind. A faint dusting of frozen precipitation floated around them, eddying with the backdrafts that brushed Kevin's black hair across his forehead.

Lightning flashed over the city of San Francisco in the distance. Kevin watched it decorate the night, ominous in its bright white intensity. Thunder rolled across the bay. He narrowed his gaze on the out-of-season storm and closed his eyes.

In the silence of his mind, he called out for Adam and the others. There was no reply. Instead, there was an emptiness where there had been a feeling of brotherhood and stability. Kevin opened his eyes with a sinking, dreadful realization.

His men were dead. After thousands of years, all that remained of the Adarian race were the few men with him now, out here on this rock in the early evening hour, gazing out across a lonely, cold sea.

Kevin turned to speak with Ely, to tell him what he knew in his heart, when he caught the faintest whiff of blood.

In weather like this, in cold this strong and wind this angry, any other kind of blood would have gone unnoticed. However, the blood Kevin scented now was Adarian blood. Strong. Powerful.

Without a word, Kevin blurred into motion, following the scent to its source. Along the way, he encountered two gates. He didn't slow, simply turning to mist in order to pass them by. And then he was standing in the D Block of Alcatraz and his three Adarian Chosen were solidifying behind him.

Before him stood cell number nine, the first of the isolation chambers used to punish particularly nasty criminals. The inside was clean, devoid of object or decoration. However, the scent of disinfectant was stronger here than anywhere else in the penitentiary. And even so, it couldn't hide what had once been spilled upon its floor.

Adam, Thane, and Raze were indeed dead. He could smell them all, scent the magic in their blood, and feel the remnants of their spirits here, where they had been snuffed out like candle flames in this god-awful tempest.

'The archangels?' Ely asked softly. His voice sounded tight, strained. They'd all lost so much – so many men. Of the twelve original Adarians, only four remained.

Kevin tried hard to consider this logically. He tried to think things through. Something about the scene didn't look right. Something about the amount of blood he could tell had been spilled just didn't seem like the archangels. If he'd been able to think past the dawning realization that he, Ely, Luke, and Mitchell were now alone in the world, he might have been able to put the puzzle together.

But his chest felt tight and his gums ached where his fangs had erupted in his mouth. His eyes glowed hotly in his face, sending everything into the sharp contrasts of a predator's vision. There was so much pain inside him at that moment, he wanted to rip his own body apart to make it stop. He wanted to walk into the sun.

Beyond thought, his rage turned to his age-old enemies. He really, really wanted to kill four particular archangels. They'd taken everything from him.

Kevin wasn't consciously directing his actions when he spun, dissolved into a blue mist the color of his glowing eyes, and rode the current of his anger through the prison once more. It was by chance and no premeditation that he wound up in the yard where inmates had once played games at all hours and in all weather in order to avoid the chilling loneliness of their cells.

Here Kevin re-formed – and stood in raging silence on the platform overlooking the walled courtyard. His lungs drew hard, deep breaths of air. His teeth were clenched so tightly he feared they would break.

But his mind paused for a moment in its inner tirade. Down below, where grass and concrete normally paved the long-deserted yard, he saw thousands upon thousands of black dandelions carpeting the ground.

Azrael watched as Sophie raised her hand, the gold bracelet pinched between her thumb and forefinger.

'What's the matter, big boy?' she asked. 'You weren't expecting that?'

Az's blood thrummed to delicious life at the challenge in Sophie's eyes. It was a beautiful thing. It was her own inner fire, finally freed and loosed upon the world. He'd always known she had it inside herself. Her life and its misfortunes had taken that fire and beat it until it was a pile of smoldering embers – still there, still vital, but barely simmering in the careful dark of her soul.

But now it blazed. He knew that it wasn't her doing, not completely. He could feel the influence of another all around her, coaxing out the flames, breathing oxygen on the conflagration until it was an inferno. But it was all Sophie who locked gazes with him now and held her very powerful ground.

He smiled. It was the vampire in him – awakened to the moment. He looked from her eyes to the bracelet, and the hand that held it. A dark star of a mark graced her palm; it was the mark that Juliette had spoken of, given to Sophie by the man in white.

'Very well,' he said, lowering his gaze and letting his power wash over her. 'We'll do this my way.' He let his fangs grow to their full length, and Sophie's expression changed. Uncertainty flitted across her features.

She should have given in then. If she'd been mortal, she would have been utterly and completely mesmerized, lost to his command no matter what it was. But Sophie, in all her newfound power and under Gregori's malevolent influence, stood her ground, though she dropped the bracelet from between numb fingers. Her other hand clenched and unclenched at her side and she licked her lips.

He could smell the adrenaline now. The cortisol. She was frightened. But there was another scent as well, faint and sweet and precious. Little Sophie Bryce, all fire and sunshine and defiance, was indeed afraid of him.

But she was also turned on.

The combination was like a siren song to his blood; there was almost no sweeter solution.

No being on Earth had ever withstood his power. The fact that his archess was able to stand up to him was both a curse and a blessing. He didn't want to hurt her – but he loved that she was giving him no choice.

His fanged smile broadened as he raised his hand and crooked his finger in a come-hither gesture. 'Make this easier on yourself, Sunshine,' he said, his tone taunting, his voice deep and beautiful. 'Come to me now and I'll only bite you once.'

Sophie's eyes widened just a little. She straightened and he watched her fidget, no doubt considering retreat. But her heart continued to pound and her blood continued to race through her veins, and the fire that licked along her being was still there, still hot, and still magnificent. Another roll of deafening thunder shook the apartment complex, testament to the fact that her storm yet raged.

'I'm not afraid of you,' she lied. And then, as if to prove her lack of fear, she looked to her right, zeroed in on the nearest piece of furniture, and using telekinesis, lifted a cinder block from the makeshift shelves she'd created against the wall.

The heavy piece of rock moved with incredible speed, expertly aimed directly at his head.

Azrael waved his hand and the block was redirected. It sailed across the room to smash into one of the walls, taking an enormous chunk out of the paint, plaster, and wood before it dropped to the floor and cracked the wooden planks beneath it.

Not to be defeated, Sophie turned toward the window and her gold eyes flashed with bright power. Azrael whirled, transforming his body into mist just as a bolt of lightning shot through the window, illuminated the world in bright white, and knocked out all sound. Electricity buzzed through the particles of his being, threatening their makeup with the heat of a thousand suns. He managed to move around it as it cascaded through the apartment, fractured into a hundred different static points, and fizzled out.

The lightning strike took only a split second, but for a vampire, it played out in slow motion. Azrael re-formed, whole and untouched by the electrical attack. And then he rushed Sophie. Flying bricks were one thing – fire was another.

Sophie may have had the heavens at her command and impressive powers of telekinesis, but for the most part, she was still human; she possessed neither the strength nor the speed of an archangel, to say nothing of a vampire.

She never saw him coming. Azrael took her before she could blink, wrapping one arm around her waist and fisting the other hand in her hair. She cried out in surprise as he yanked her head back, exposing her throat. Her fingers curled into the leather jacket under his trench coat and she closed her eyes in what he knew was both fear and desire. At once, he was awash with the scent of her, the *feel* of her.

For two thousand years he had been waiting to sink his fangs into just one woman. He'd searched for her, hunted for her, nearly given up on finding her. Now she was here, in his arms, and immune to every part of him but one. He had no choice but to do what he was about to do – and right now, he wouldn't have it any other way.

'You were warned, Sunshine,' he told her, whispering the words in her ear as her quick breaths fanned his own cheek. He chuckled deep and dark. 'So here's the first of many.'

With that, he tightened his hold, raised his head, and drove his fangs deep into the side of her throat.

She made the sweetest, most helpless sound as his teeth

found purchase in the taut flesh of her neck. He opened the vein beneath him, baring it to his hunger, and his body roared to delicious life. And then the first drops of her precious blood spilled across his tongue, and his vision went red.

Never in his wildest dreams could he have imagined that she would taste like this. He swallowed and felt as though he were swallowing hope. Salvation. He took it into himself rapaciously, growling deep and low as precious healing fire spread throughout his body and soul, searing it clean and perfect. There was nothing wrong with the world in that moment. There was no danger, no death.

*No Death*.

Soft and sweet, she moaned against him, her body shuddering as her power left it and made room for his. He flooded her with it, overwhelming her with the bliss that came from submitting to the vampire king. He could feel her magic crackle around her, warm and sparkling and fading. As he drank, the darkness that had invaded that magic slipped away as well, ebbing in its strength until Sophie relaxed against him.

Her body was hot; it radiated heat and passion – and he was so hard, he was in pain.

Slowly, sensuously, Azrael released his hold on her hair and she lowered her head to breathe softly against his neck. With his free hand, he pulled her more tightly against him. He swallowed and she moaned and his grip tightened with a nearly crazed need.

*I have to stop*, he thought. She was filling him with life and it was something he had never felt and he didn't want to give it up for anything. But if he didn't slow down, if he didn't ease off, he would drain her dry.

Azrael had always had control over his world and those around him. But Sophie Bryce was changing him to his core. He had to regain the control she was making him lose and he had to do it *now*.

With great effort, he pulled his teeth from her neck. She shuddered against him, and he absorbed the emotion as he looked into her eyes. They were heavy-lidded and glassy with lust; the scent of her desire teased and tempted him. If he so chose, he could lay her down right here on the floor of her destroyed apartment and have the rest of her.

But that wasn't the point of all of this. It wasn't why he had bitten her.

Was it?

He needed to get her out of here, away from people that her immense power could harm, away from the prying eyes of whatever monsters Gregori had lurking around. Az had managed to take the fight out of her, but how long would that last? Even now, he heard the rumble of thunder that threatened to become more. He heard the first few drops of rain hit the roof above them as Sophie's storm finally broke open and wept.

And as it did, he watched a single tear loose itself from Sophie's golden orb to trickle down her perfect cheek.

Azrael's vision shifted into normal hues, his gut clenched, and his chest felt strange. Slowly, tenderly, he lowered his lips to her cheek and tasted the salt of her pain. As he did, he closed his eyes and reined his monster in. Sophie's soul was in turmoil. The world made no sense to her just then. She would never admit it to him, not here and now, under the spell of the anger and regret she had moving through her, but she needed her archangel as much as he needed his archess.

'Hold tight to me,' he whispered to her.

Maybe it was instinct, maybe it was need. But whatever it was, Sophie responded by ducking her head against him and wrapping her arms as tightly as she could around his chest.

Azrael glanced up and then shot through the ceiling, shielding Sophie's body as he went. The plaster, beams, and insulation shredded around him, fanning out in every direction like shrapnel from a grenade. He took them high, moving so fast that no human eye could have noticed the figures blurring through the night sky.

And Sophie, safe in his grip, made not a sound.

# Chapter 28

Mitchell watched his general move slowly through the strange field of black dandelions in the old prison yard. Kevin had changed a lot since he and the other Adarians had been cast to Earth. The twelve of them had once been a tight band, brothers in purpose and creation, bound by what they were and what they'd gone through. Now only a handful of them remained. It had all happened so quickly.

And Mitchell couldn't help but wonder how much of it was Kevin's fault.

Going after Eleanore Granger was one thing. She'd been the first being they had come across who possessed the ability to heal, a gift they'd desperately yearned for. Eleanore was not only blessed with the very power that the Adarians needed, she was also astonishingly beautiful. That Kevin had fallen in love with her was something Mitchell could wholeheartedly understand. Their consequential hunt for the woman across the span of more than a decade was a mere drop in the bucket of time for them and well worth the possible rewards.

However, once they'd found her and faced off against the Four Favored archangels, things had taken a turn for the worse for the Adarians. After their initial battle several months ago, everything had changed.

Kevin Trenton had always been a good leader. He'd

always had a plan that favored the Adarians, kept them alive, and furthered their purpose. Kevin was a charismatic man, and Mitchell and the others had followed him blindly, knowing deep down that Kevin would do what was best for them all. And that was why when the general suggested that Mitchell attempt to become a vampire himself by draining a mortal of all of his blood and ingesting it, Mitchell was able to see the benefit of such a plan. As a vampire, he would be able to heal – hence, no more need for the archesses' powers. As a vampire, he would be able to move through the shadows, fly, and read people's minds. He would become stronger and faster and, for an Adarian, that was incredibly impressive. The benefits seemed to outweigh the drawbacks – that he would have to feed on a regular basis and that he would never again see sunlight. He'd never been overly fond of the sun anyway.

But now there were only four Adarians remaining out of the original dozen. And those four were vampires. They were stronger, yes. But they were mere shades of the angels they'd once been, relegated to the darkness and the shadows, so far from the grace of the one who had created them that Mitchell had the disquieting sensation that he'd never been created in the first place.

It was with a sinking feeling in his gut and a cold numbness in his soul that Mitchell had this one thought: *This has gone too far*.

He watched his leader stride over the field of unearthly black dandelions, his once intelligent blue eyes glowing red, and Mitchell knew – he simply knew – that Abraxos was no more. The man he'd once been had been lost somewhere. There was a madness to Kevin now that threatened them all.

Mitchell had been a fool to let it go as far as it had. They were in over their heads. Seven Adarians were dead. One – Daniel – had gone missing. How many needed to be lost before the rest learned their lesson?

Mitchell felt shockingly stupid in that moment. The universe had been screaming at him, insistent in its plan, and he'd all but turned a deaf ear to its warnings. Adam's death – the mutilation of him and his companions – it hadn't been the archangels' doing. These dandelions were a sign. Nothing here was right; the entire island smelled of evil. The Four Favored were a thorn in every Adarian's side. But they weren't evil.

Something more was going on here, and Mitchell's instincts were telling him to get out now. Before it was too late altogether.

'It wasn't them,' he said softly, his eyes fixed on the lone figure of his leader.

There was a moment of silence in which no one said anything. And then Luke moved beside him, glancing once over his shoulder at the exit they'd come through. 'No,' Luke said. 'I agree.'

Ely sighed wearily. Mitchell and Luke both regarded the large black man with expectation. His glowing eyes were focused on Kevin and the eerie field of black he moved through. His expression was one of deep sadness and hard resolve. But he said nothing. Before Ely had become a vampire, Mitchell would have been able to read his mind. But now Mitchell was relegated to the thoughts of mortals; vampire minds were too difficult to traverse.

And then Mitchell sensed a change in the air. He looked back at Kevin, who had stopped in the field, his back to his men. He wasn't moving. He simply stood there, tall and dark and filled with something both unknown and powerful.

As if he was waiting for something. Or listening for something.

- Mitchell frowned and descended the steps to join him. The others followed. When they were right behind him, Kevin asked, 'Mitchell, Luke, I'll need your blood again. We're going after them.'

Mitchell's stomach clenched. He glanced at Luke and noticed that the blood had drained from Luke's face. As Adarians, Mitchell possessed the ability to read minds and Luke had the power to enter people's dreams. When their blood was combined, it produced new abilities, among them the power to scry a being's whereabouts.

It was how Kevin had located Sophie Bryce the first few times. Clearly the general wasn't ready to give up.

*It's now or never*, Mitchell thought. He'd been blind until now. If he continued to hold his tongue, he wouldn't be blind. He would be a coward.

'No,' he said. His heart hammered and blood rushed through his ears. He went on, though the next two words out of his mouth were the hardest he had ever uttered. 'We're not.'

Mitchell felt the world come to a stop beneath him. It simply ceased to spin. The air froze, each molecule petrified in place. Watches everywhere slowed down.

And then Kevin turned around, just as slowly, and Mitchell felt the wall of his power turn with him. It enveloped Mitchell like a blanket of electrons, filling him with dread.

'Is there something you'd like to share with the rest of the class, Morael?' Kevin asked, using Mitchell's original name.

'Such as the fact that you believe this has gone too far? That the murders of our brothers were not performed at the hands of the Four Favored?' His voice was soft – *too* soft.

Kevin took a step forward, closing the distance between them and entrapping Mitchell in a space without air. He seemed to be pulling his words directly from Mitchell's mind – and it hit Mitchell that possibly Kevin was capable of doing just such a thing.

'Or maybe you'd like to give voice to your notions of my madness. Please,' he said, cocking his head to one side, 'do expand upon your theory that the deaths of our brethren are my fault.'

Mitchell's world was turned on its side. Every single thing he had been thinking for the last few minutes, Kevin had heard. He'd been in his mind, and Mitchell hadn't even felt it. For a man who had spent centuries reading the minds of others, Mitchell was particularly un-adept at noticing when such a thing was being done to him instead.

He expected it to end then. He would put up a fight of course, but Kevin was the stronger, and he had no misconceptions about who would win in the end. It was a cold, hard sensation to know that the life you'd grown accustomed to for the past several thousand years was about to come to an end in one form or another. Either he was going to die or he was going to live and everything he had ever known would change.

He would no longer be a part of the Adarian family, what there was left of it anyway. He would no longer be led by a man he trusted. He would no longer be that man's confidant and friend. He was going to lose all that he was and all he had ever been.

Right here, right now.

But then Kevin straightened, and the lines in his forehead drew together. Suddenly, unexpectedly, the Adarian leader looked *surprised*. He took a step back from Mitchell and turned his glowing blue gaze upon Luke beside him.

'*Et tu, Brute?*' Kevin asked softly. He looked less sure than he had a moment ago. Less angry and more hurt.

A second later, his eyes widened, just a little – and he turned his gaze upon Ely. Ely immediately blinked and tried to look away, but it was as if Kevin's eyes were gravitational, and Ely was once more locking gazes with the general. '*You*, Ely?' Kevin shook his head, his expression bewildered. 'Of all people.'

Ely licked his lips and rolled his shoulders. 'Adam is dead,' he said. 'Raze, Thane, Paul . . .' The large Adarian shook his head, his amber eyes flashing. 'We've lost almost everyone. This has to stop now. You have gone too far. There's nothing left.'

Kevin stared at him for a very long time. Even the seagulls were silent, and the waves that should have hit the shore decided to stay out at sea.

'Very well,' said Kevin finally. He looked from Ely to Luke and then to Mitchell. There was something strange in his blue-eyed gaze. 'I'm sorry to learn you all feel that way.'

Mitchell watched as his leader turned away from them then. He watched as Kevin moved back out across the field of black dandelions, nothing but the faint beams from the dim, cloud-covered moon to light his way. But Mitchell knew it wasn't over. There was not a snowball's chance in hell that it was over. He knew damn well what was coming – he could have timed it to the very second.

This was how it had to be. This was what it had come to. They had started with twelve brothers and one leader; and in the end, they were just three brothers and one madman. It was the end of their era, the epilogue to their tale.

So when Kevin suddenly spun, blurring with inhuman speed, and his power fanned out in the mother of all offensive attacks, Mitchell was ready for him. And so were Luke and Ely.

Because they knew it too.

*My heart isn't beating.*

It was a strange thought to wake up to, but it was the first thing he noticed. Kevin had always been one of those people who could feel their own heart beating. It throbbed through his temples and the insides of his arms and the backs of his knees. His pulse was a constant companion – there, but dull and in the background. It was a gentle and welcome reminder that he was alive.

But now there was nothing flowing through the insides of his arms. There was no taut pull through the artery in his neck, no comforting *thud* deep within his chest. His heart wasn't beating.

*How can this be?* How could he be thinking? How could he feel the damp dandelions beneath him and hear the seagulls on the island if he was dead?

Kevin opened his eyes, utterly baffled as to how he was able to do so. The horizontal plane of the ground beneath his head slowly came into focus. As it did, he found himself staring at a pair of shining black dress shoes and the perfectly cuffed hem of dark suit pants.

'Welcome back,' came a stranger's voice.

Kevin frowned and slowly pushed himself up. His body felt light and that confused him. He felt as though he should be stiff, seized by something like rigor mortis. But everything moved as he wanted it to and there was no pain.

As he got to his feet, he took in the figure before him. The man was of average height and average build, not pudgy but not overly cut or thin. His brown hair was thinning on top, and his blue eyes were without any special vibrancy. Yet there was a feel to the man's aura that struck Kevin right off the bat. It made no sense, but Kevin knew that he would be dead if not for this man. He knew it without needing to be told.

'Make no mistake, general,' said the man, his lips turned up in the slightest of smiles. 'You are very much dead.'

It would have been a chilling thing for most people to hear. It not only meant that the man was reading Kevin's mind – which no one had ever been able to do – but it also meant that Kevin was right. He was dead. But for some reason Kevin felt next to nothing, and he certainly felt no fear.

'You have no reason to fear anything any longer,' said the man. 'You have nothing left to lose. And that's why you are not afraid.'

'Why did you bring me back?' asked Kevin. It seemed the only reasonable thing to ask at that point. Most of his brothers had been murdered over the last several months, the Four Favored were undefeated and claiming their archesses, and the only three other Adarians left in the world had turned on him and killed him. And yet all he could seem to care about was why this stranger had animated his dead corpse. 'And will I start rotting now?' he asked, almost as an afterthought.

The man's brow lifted and his look became both incredulous and very serious. 'No,' he said firmly. 'It wasn't I who animated you, but my employer. And of course you won't rot. He doesn't make such messy mistakes.' Then the man clasped his hands behind his back and moved around Kevin, his gaze on the ground and its black dandelions, and then on the bay and the city that sparkled beyond. The storm had passed, Kevin noticed. Offhandedly, he wondered where the archess who had caused it was.

'He brought you back because there is about to be a war, general. A culmination, if you will.' The man in the suit stopped and looked at Kevin once more, pinning him with his beady eyes. 'He is going to need someone experienced to lead his army, and he believes you are the right man for the job.'

Kevin considered this, realizing at once that there was nothing to consider. And then, as if it had been sitting on his tongue for thousands of years, simply waiting to be said, Kevin replied, 'I am his to command.'

# Chapter 29

The storm followed her. It remained on the outskirts of the world, but Az caught the lightning flashes in the distance, lighting up the horizon. It sat there, a massive gray beast, and watched its archess, waiting to roll in at the slightest provocation.

He could handle the storm. That wasn't what worried him. It was the anger behind it that troubled him.

He could read her thoughts once more; that barrier at least had been broken. Azrael had her blood in his veins now. It was the first time he had ever had a woman's blood in his veins, and the fact that it belonged to his archess made it a tie that bound them inexorably.

Azrael relished how much more easily he could breach the walls of her mind, but he was torn by the things he read there. He'd never been inside the head of someone who had been through what Sophie Bryce had been through. It was like watching a movie loop. Images continued to flash before them both: police officers taking her by the hand after her parents' death; headstones in a cemetery; one leering male face after another; a gunshot that rang out through her soul like a firecracker in the night. And then the man in white.

Now Azrael knew what Gregori looked like. It was an unsettling observation, to say the least.

Az brought them to the location he wanted and headed for the shore, gently setting Sophie down in front of him on the deserted Northern California beach that was protected by a tall line of cliffs on one side.

Sophie got her legs beneath her, a little wobbly at first. Then she straightened, looked around for a second, and ran a shaky hand through her long, beautiful hair. The ocean breeze immediately caught it and blew it back across her face once more.

She ignored it and turned to look up at Azrael. 'Where are we?' she asked. He could hear the slowly returning fury tiptoeing around her voice, ever threatening.

'Just north of Trinidad,' he told her. 'I have a place here.' He watched her carefully.

Sophie seemed to consider this for a moment and then tore her gaze from his. He felt literally colder when she did so, as if the temperature around him dropped in the absence of the heat in her eyes.

'What are you going to do with me?' she asked softly.

It was a good question. It was a *fair* question. 'I don't know,' he told her honestly. He looked out at the dark expanse of ocean and the faint outline of the horizon where the clouds slowly crawled in. 'That depends on you.'

'What's that supposed to mean?' she shot back.

Azrael wanted to sigh in frustration, but managed to simply walk a few paces away instead. Clearly, her ire was returning fast. At this rate, she would be using telekinesis to slam boulders into him within minutes.

He stopped at around five feet and turned back to look at her. His gaze fell to her right hand, which rested at her side. The mark on her palm was faded, but definitely not gone.

This Gregori had far too much control over Azrael's archess for his liking.

'You need to look inside yourself, Sophie. This isn't you.' He took a deep breath and went on. 'You have every right to be upset. But this fury that is racing through you is like a poison and it's spreading. It doesn't belong in you, Sophie. Someone else put it there.'

Sophie stared at him for a moment, her expression vacillating between a building wrath and a dawning comprehension. She bit her lip – just briefly – and Azrael's hand curled into a fist. And then she shook her head and said, 'What would you know?'

'About poison?' Azrael asked matter-of-factly. 'About something evil that burns through your veins, eats its way into your soul, and bores a hole in your spirit that almost nothing can fill?' He paused, trying for the umpteenth time to regain his composure. 'More than you can possibly imagine.'

He knew it was a mistake as soon as he'd said it, but it was too late.

Sophie turned on him and he could feel the clouds pouring in now, racing across the ocean's expanse like an army of darkness. 'What the hell would you know about me, "*Lord Azrael*"?' she cried. 'You don't know me! You have no idea what or who I am!'

'I know you more deeply than you know yourself,' he told her, meeting her halfway on the anger front.

Sophie's golden gaze narrowed dangerously and Az felt the first wet wind of her rising storm kiss his cheek. 'Oh, that's right,' she said vehemently. 'Because you've been reading my *mind*.'

Az matched her narrowed gaze with one of his own.

'That's funny,' he said, flashing her a mean smile. 'From what I've learned by being in there, I would think you'd *like* it.'

Sophie's gold eyes sparked and lightning crashed into the sand three hundred feet away. Ruthlessly, Azrael kept going. 'After all, having actually *been* inside your mind, I happen to know that one of the things you love about the big bad vampire is the fact that he can read your mind in the first place.'

He moved then. A blur and a gasp from Sophie, and he was standing over her and she was reeling back to get away. He stopped her cold with a strong arm around her waist. 'Because then he knows just what to do to you, doesn't he, Sunshine? He knows *how* to do it – and *when*.' He punctuated his words with a tightening of his grip on her.

Sophie's hands found his chest, automatically pressing against him defensively. But he could tell what she was thinking now. She couldn't hide anything from him any longer. Her efforts to defy him were not only useless, they were a lie.

He had seen inside of her. The hatred that was scorching her inner being to ash was unwelcome. She was a slave to it, as helpless as if it were whipping her into submission. She wanted to be free of its influence as desperately as Azrael wanted her to be.

She glared at him, her eyes shooting daggers, but a very large part of her liked being trapped in his arms. Even if he hadn't been able to read her innermost desires, he could sure as hell smell them. A sweeter, more tempting nectar did not exist.

Azrael was a patient man. Thousands of years had sanded down the edges of his temper. But Sophie was another matter entirely. She was temptation and frustration and seduction all rolled into one amazing body, and there was only so much even Azrael could take.

So, as she glared at him and the sky boiled in her mounting anger, he gave in to his monster and put out a quick mental call. One vampire's bite had faded the mark on her hand and whittled away at her defenses. Az couldn't help but wonder what two bites at once would do.

It was something she had always fantasized about.

Within seconds, he glanced up through the building fog of Sophie's storm to see something tall and dark emerge from the shadows beneath an outcropping of boulders against the cliff face. His wicked smile broadened.

Sophie didn't want to be angry. A part of her honestly empathized with Azrael and his brothers. It wasn't their fault that they were here, on Earth, searching for something that had been created for them, waved under their noses, and then torn from them two thousand years ago. It wasn't Azrael's fault that he'd been made the Angel of Death in the first place.

Someone else had been pulling his strings, just like someone else was pulling hers. She didn't mean to be furious at Azrael. But he was here right now and the storm that raged inside her wouldn't stay put. It leaked out through her pores, through her eyes, through her words – and Azrael was right. It was like a poison, eating away at her while she tried so desperately – and failed – to let it go.

Now he held her tight and no matter how she tried to pull away, her body felt every hard inch of him against her . . . and it was driving her crazy. The weather echoed her emotions, the wind racing, the clouds boiling until they were too heavy to remain in the sky and dropped to the beach instead, covering it in a thick, impenetrable gray. Through the fog, she heard thunder rumble, shaking the sand beneath her boots.

It was all too much, and Azrael was the icing on the madness cake. From afar, on a stage, and even over the radio, the man's presence was stifling in its charisma. Up close and personal, he was overwhelming. There was no other word for it.

His power was a nearly tangible thing. It wrapped around her like silk cords pulled taut. She felt like the fly in a spider's web, and every wiggling attempt she made at freedom only tightened the trap around her.

But despite the fact that she knew it was her defiance that had Azrael on the offensive, she couldn't reel herself in. The fury poured from her like water from a broken dam.

She glared at him helplessly when all she really wanted to do was kiss him . . . *taste* him. What she yearned to do was run her hand through his hair while he sank his fangs into her throat again.

*My God*, she thought. There was no description for that kind of pleasure. The moment Azrael had pierced her skin, she'd been awash in a rapturous bliss so deep, she'd gone instantly weak in his grasp. Only that pleasure seemed to have the power to take the fight out of her.

*Do it again*, she thought desperately. She wanted to cry out, even as she tried again to pull out of his arms. She wanted to beg him for the mercy that only he could deliver, even while she instead turned her attention to the nearest sea-weathered boulder on the beach. Her powers were out of control; the boulder began to rise from where it had been pounded into the earth by a trillion waves. Sand shifted and cracked, then cascaded around its circumference as the stone rose. Sophie squeezed her eyes shut against the fury. Lightning crashed somewhere nearby, rolling over them like a warning.

*No*, she thought. *Take this hate away from me* . . .

'With pleasure, Sunshine,' said Azrael.

Sophie's eyes flew open. Her head whipped around and she caught the flash of fang and the spark of red at the centers of Azrael's dark pupils. In the next heartbeat, a magical warmth hit her from behind and a second pair of strong hands wrapped around her wrists to pull them to her sides. A hard chest pressed to her back as her arms were held tight. Her eyes widened and she inhaled sharply as if to scream.

'Shh,' whispered a voice in her ear.

*Uro!*

The stone to her right dropped with a thud, sending sand flying.

Sophie shivered; the feel of another strong body at her back brought her breath up short, silencing the scream that had lodged in her throat. She was trapped between them, held immobile by the pleasure that was already riding through her body at their very closeness.

She gasped as Uro tightened his hold and moved in. Sophie made a shuddering sound and caught Azrael's smile. It was lascivious, unforgivable, and breathtakingly beautiful.

She felt him loosen his arm around her waist and watched in disbelief as he deftly brushed her hair from her neck. His fingers touched her skin as he did, sending electric rivulets of pleasure across her flesh.

She choked back a moan; the dichotomy of feelings was too intense. She was terrified and angry, and she was burning with a sexual longing unlike any she'd ever known. She couldn't believe Azrael was doing this to her, couldn't fathom that Uro had joined in. The power washing over her built up an anticipation that was so intense it had to go some-where – it had to do *something* – or she was afraid she might honestly die.

Lightning slammed into the rocks at the base of the cliffs behind them, sending pebbles flying in a shower of shattered stone.

The men waited as the thunder rocked over them and rolled away. And then Uro whispered, 'Trust him, Sophie.' His breath caressed her ear. 'Trust *us*.'

*Oh God, oh God, oh God . . .*

Sophie closed her eyes. Azrael slid his arm around her waist once more, his hand spanning her back to press her against him. She felt his free hand shove through her hair and fist gently at the back of her head. He pulled – and she rested her head against Uro's strong shoulder. She could actually *feel* Azrael's triumphant smile through her closed lids. She sensed him bending over her, closing in on her. He was everywhere, all around her. His presence was too strong to block out by simply shutting her eyes against it.

And then she felt his breath on her other ear and she gasped, but there was nowhere for her to go. They had her now. She was well and truly trapped.

'Remember my promise, Sophie,' he told her softly, his words sending delicious chills across her entire body. 'Last time was the first of many.'

She tensed; she knew it was coming. And then she felt the

men do the same. Their bodies went taut with purpose, their grips on her tightened, and Sophie cried out.

Their teeth pierced the tight skin on either side of her neck at the same time, driving deep. Sophie's eyes flew open, but she didn't see the sky. There were stars and planets and something that tore through time and space the way she'd imagined it would look at the end of the universe, but it wasn't the sky. It wasn't here. She was on another plane, in another universe that consisted only of extremes. Colors exploded before her, flowering like fireworks. She fell into them, light as a feather on the wind. There was no pain here, no discomfort. The anger she'd felt rushing through her only moments before was ebbing away. In its place was a pleasure both tranquil and restless, anticipation made tangible.

As the pain left, her pleasure grew. Deep down, a tension swirled to life, throbbing with every beat of her heart. It pulsed and ached, never hurting, only demanding.

She wanted more.

# Chapter 30

He could sense the change coming over her. As the darkness lifted from around her it simultaneously grew within him. He had been made an archangel eons ago, a winged warrior of immense power. But here and now, in this telling moment, Azrael was the vampire king. The need inside him shoved all else aside and left no room for subtle kindnesses.

He was all monster, his sole saving grace the absolute love he felt for the woman in his dangerous embrace. Had it not been for this tempering compassion, Azrael would have turned her. No hesitation, no remorse. He had never created a female vampire. Sophie would have been his first. All it would have taken was a thought: *Turn and join me*. And Sophie would never again walk in the sun.

But his love for her left him settled somewhere in her warm and welcoming mind, simultaneously experiencing the hope and loss, the ebbing anger, and the growing peace. Her sweet, heartfelt emotions collared the beast within him just enough.

In his peripheral awareness, Azrael noticed Uro pulling away. The vampire released Sophie's wrists and stepped back. His job was done; their combined attack had diminished Gregori's influence on the archess and obliterated Sophie's defenses, and Uro knew when to call it good. He would leave now and rejoin the others. Az had to commend him for being able to stop. It was something Az himself could not do. Not with her. They were too tightly bound. She hadn't been made for Uro, after all. She'd been made for Azrael.

Az stayed put, his grip ever tight, his teeth firmly planted in her throat. He drank slowly, sparingly, and Sophie's sweet, sweet blood drifted slowly over his tongue. It set off a flickering of delicious fire that burned down his throat and spread throughout his tall, strong body. *Divine.*

That was the only word for it.

Azrael was held prisoner by his desire, trapped between his yearning to go further and his need to avoid bringing Sophie any further harm. But his hunger was undeniable. He needed more. If he didn't get it soon, he would lose his already tentative grasp on control.

*Sophie* . . . his mind whispered. He knew she heard him when she exhaled softly, her breath caressing the curve of his shoulder. *My sweet Sunshine* . . .

The ground released its hold on them as Azrael took them to the sky. They rose gradually through the mist and clouds of Sophie's waning tempest. Moisture licked at their hair, dampening their locks and pressing them to their cheeks.

*Az* . . . Her mind called to him. She did it without realizing she did so.

He felt her arms slide around him, warm and tight and welcome, and the vampire king's heart cracked a little, a genuine ache that was both the most wonderful and the most horrible thing he had ever felt.

Lightning sizzled around them, somehow changed now. It

was no longer an angry energy that arced from the earth to the sky. It was hot and languid and crackling, and it bounced off of the dense walls of the low-lying clouds.

Gently, Azrael released Sophie's now damp hair and brushed his fingers down the back of her neck. She shivered beneath the caress. He wanted to touch more of her. He used his control of the air to help him hold her aloft, and with a simple thought and flux of will, he did away with their clothing. It was there one second, gone the next. The clouds swirled in to dress them, leaving droplets of moisture on their skin.

Instinctively, Sophie pressed herself against him, a soft moan escaping her lips. Az felt his chest shudder, his body clench tight. He was hard as steel, pulsing hot, and they were skin on skin, her warmth taunting him. His fingers moved lower, grazing the smooth, perfect plane of her back to the tight curve of her bottom. Rivulets of rainwater built and trickled, running over his hand.

Sophie gasped and involuntarily arched her back as he cupped her cheek and continued further, his fingers taking her in, absorbing her heat. When he reached the valley between her legs, her fists curled into his back, her nails threatening his skin.

In response, he sucked harder, his teeth claiming her throat, taking her blood now with a renewed sense of urgency. *More* – he wanted *more*.

Humidity blanketed them, leaving them drenched. Azrael's cock throbbed against her taut stomach, now so painfully engorged that he could no longer ignore it. His hand slid over the slick, honeyed entrance to her core, the scent of her arousal wafted toward him, and her nails broke through, drawing his blood. Her body arched desperately against his as he growled against her throat and pressed further, dipping into her heated wetness.

One finger . . . Two . . .

Sophie cried out; he drank deeper. *More*.

He felt her clench around his fingers, mind-blowingly tight and so very wet. Another sizzling bolt of lightning crisscrossed the dense fog, charging the air with heat and static. It sliced through the spaces beside him, threateningly close. He ignored it, his attention focused solely on the sweet, responsive woman in his arms.

*Sophie, I need more*, he thought, sending the words careening through her mind. It was the plea of a starving man – a dying man – who had been given a taste of salvation and would perish without another life-giving swallow.

Sophie coated his fingers with the nectar of her desire, urging him on without another word. But she was so tight, so small.

With tender care, Azrael pushed harder, subjugating her body to his demanding, expert touch. Then his vampire took over and he pulled his fangs from her throat.

She cried out at the quick retreat and her fingernails drew more of his archangel blood. It ran down his back now, thin rivers of crimson pleasure.

He leaned back, taking her in from head to toe. No woman on Earth should have looked as good as she did, from the tips of her toes to her long, slender legs and the triangle of golden curls between them. His gaze burned over her tapered waist to her perfect round breasts to the graceful lines of her collarbone. As he looked at her, she moaned in frustration. His eyes shot back to hers. Her straight white teeth were bared and she was writhing in his embrace, waiting to accept everything he wanted to give her.

Slowly, almost menacingly, Azrael ran his tongue over his fangs and watched as Sophie's glassy, lust-filled eyes widened. Her breathing became short and quick, her body moving desperately upon his fingers. She was trapped in his gaze, held captive by his influence, and nearly frantic for release.

She was all his.

He struck with vampire speed, lowering his head and sinking his still glistening, razor-sharp fangs into the smooth flesh of her left breast. Sophie's piercing cry split the night and lightning sizzled, an impossible tornado of electricity that coiled around their bodies like a spiral cocoon. At the same time, her hand shoved through his thick, dark hair, holding his head to her chest – as if he would consider letting go.

But he *was* going to let go. Because there was another place on her body he wanted to sink his teeth into. Gently, he extracted his fangs once more and again brushed his thumb across her clitoris as his fingers moved inside her. Sophie's head tossed to the side, her now fully wet hair flying around her like a glorious golden halo. Azrael took it in, never wanting to forget what she looked like.

The air responded to his command once more, holding her aloft as he released his hold on her waist and slowly pulled his fingers from her molten core.

'No . . .' she murmured, her forehead furrowing in disappointment.

His smile broadened, becoming well and truly cruel. She took one ragged breath after another and floated, captive to his web of air as he slowly moved down the length of her body until the dark blue vein on the inside of her leg was in his sights.

He ran his hands up the backs of her well-muscled legs, then curled his fingers around them to hold them open. Sophie resisted him, perhaps instinctively, for a fraction of a second. Her breath caught and he looked up. Her eyes met his – and he knew that she was fully aware of what he was about to do.

She made a helpless sound, one he could never hear enough, as he pulled her legs apart and lowered his head to slowly, teasingly, run his tongue across the slick, smooth lips of her womanhood.

She bucked in his embrace, as he had known she would, but his grip was firm – and his mind was headed toward delirium. He tasted her a second time, wanting to drink her in every possible manner, wanting to absorb everything that was Sophie Bryce, body and soul.

*Divine.*

The word floated through his mind once more and he closed his eyes as his tongue continued to taste and Sophie continued to writhe in his fast grip. He was in heaven. But heaven was a pleasure so severe, it was painful. His body was so hard, sweat had broken out across his skin, joining the rainwater that coalesced on them and soaked them both. Azrael raised his hand and pressed gently on the swollen nub of Sophie's clitoris. She cried out in both frustration and ecstasy and quivered under his hand, her movements more furious now. The clean, wanton scent of her was maddening. She was dripping for him.

Without warning, he turned his head and sank his fangs into the vein on the inside of her thigh. As he did, he shoved his fingers into her once more and was rewarded with the tight, frantic clenching of her core around his hand. Her climax drew a harsh cry from her throat, but that cry was totally absorbed by the thunder that echoed off the clouds as a second spiral of lightning enveloped the airborne lovers.

Azrael watched her through his glowing eyes as he pulled and swallowed. Pulled and swallowed. If he drank her dry, it wouldn't be enough.

*Careful*, he told himself. She was an archess and made of stronger stuff than a mortal, but she could still be killed, and he'd taken enough blood.

And there was something else he wanted just a little bit more in that moment. He couldn't wait any longer.

In one swift movement, Azrael pulled his teeth from her vein and his fingers from between her legs. Then he rose on the wind and pressed the tip of his painfully swollen member to the slick opening between Sophie's legs. He could feel her still clenching, still coming down from the tidal wave of pleasure she'd just experienced.

He drew her against him, wrapped his arm around her waist, and cupped her face, leaning over her, demanding that her eyes meet his. He felt her hot little breaths across his lips as he brushed his thumb along her cheekbone and marveled at her perfect beauty.

And then he drove into her, shoving into her slick, tight heat in one hard thrust. He swallowed her scream of pleasured pain with a kiss just as demanding, just as powerful. And lightning struck.

This time it hit home. The heavens opened and the bolt of white-hot heat cascaded over Azrael and Sophie with direct aim. But they were completely drenched in rainwater and perspiration, and the electricity sizzled around them, moving over and off of them, kept at bay by the layer of moisture they wore.

Az let it go without so much as a second thought. All he could feel was her heat wrapped around him, enveloping him with a succulent, velveteen rapture.

For a moment, he rested there, lodged deep inside his archess, his entire world one of intense bliss. Her arms had come tightly around him, her fingers flexing against his strong back. He drank her in through his kiss, his tongue drawing forth her pleasure with thousands of years of practice as they both grew accustomed to his impressive size – and her incredible tightness.

Long enough.

Azrael drew back, pulling out of Sophie until his cock was nearly free. And then he drove into her again. Once more, she cried out against him. He took the sound and absorbed it, silencing her cry with his kiss. His teeth threatened her lips, poked at her tongue, dominant and fierce.

And he pulled back . . . and drove into her again.

*And again.*

Sophie's precious little sounds settled down into a rhythm along with his thrusts, each sigh and gasp and moan coming with euphoric perfection. Azrael ended the kiss and tilted her head to bare her already pierced throat to him one final time.

He sank his teeth into the marks he'd already made, driving his fangs deep as he shoved more fiercely into her sex. His power broke free as Sophie's second orgasm drew near and his own followed. The two of them began to rise through the fog once more.

Fingers of mist swirled around them, eddied before them,

and then pulled away as Azrael unknowingly broke through the cloud ceiling and brought them into the starry night above.

It was quiet here. Sacred. This, up here, beneath the halo of the moon and the blinking, diamond stars was a soul expanse, pure and deep and dark.

Azrael and his archess filled that sacrosanct dark with the combined sounds of their climaxes as Azrael took his final swallow of her precious life force and pulled his fangs from her throat. Sophie bucked violently in his fierce grip, her body convulsing around him as his molten seed filled her womb.

Azrael threw back his head and howled into the night. The Masked One's voice echoed off the stars, alerting the universe to his pleasure. The Angel of Death had found his archess, and after two thousand years, he had at last claimed his mate.

# Chapter 31

He'd clothed them both again. The sea air was cold, and though he couldn't feel it, Sophie certainly could. He also created a few extra blankets, and he snuggled beneath them on the beach with her now.

The night was in its winter hours and dawn would approach soon. He would have to take them to his resting place up the beach; a multi-roomed chamber he'd fashioned long ago from the very rock of the cliffs. But for now, they rested beneath the moon and stars, and Azrael was at peace. The only magic he had to use was the occasional burst of warning toward any sea or sand creature that threatened the edge of their blankets.

They lay on their sides, he spooning her. In his arms, Sophie breathed a sigh, her hand moving atop the soft coverlet, and Azrael glanced up at the movement. When he did, he caught sight of the mark on Sophie's palm. It had faded significantly, but was still there.

Azrael couldn't help the twinge of fear he felt at the sight of it. What more could he do to rescue his archess from the influence of the man in white? Trepidation wedged its way into his heart as he hugged Sophie close and closed his eyes, wanting only to make this moment last a little longer.

But Sophie shifted uncomfortably, and Azrael loosened

his hold, the fear in his chest growing. 'Are you okay?' he asked, not knowing what else to say.

'Yes,' she said quickly. 'I think I just need to stand up and walk around.'

She was feeling suddenly antsy. It wasn't a good sign.

Azrael felt a flash of heat go through his eyes, momentarily lighting them up. But he shut them tight again, pulled his power in around him, and forced himself to take it easy.

He let her go and Sophie rolled over to rise from the blankets. He stood after her.

'Let's go for a walk,' he said, taking hold of her marked hand. She didn't pull away, but he felt her stiffen a little in his grip.

Azrael turned and began leading her down the beach as his blood heated in his veins. If he ever came face-to-face with the man in white, he was going to do everything within his power to kill the bastard.

They were silent for several minutes. The tide was low and myriad seashells littered the wet sand. Azrael noticed a perfect white sand dollar beside a boulder and remembered something he wanted to share with Sophie, but she stopped beside him, pulling his attention back to her.

'Az . . .' she started, and then paused. She licked her lips, pulled her hand from his, hugged herself, and looked away. 'I feel so confused right now.'

Warning bells went off in Azrael's head. 'I know,' he said, moving forward as her distress drew out the need in him to protect and comfort her.

But she stepped back and immediately held up her hands. 'No, you don't,' she told him gently but firmly. 'You've always been an archangel – and then a *vampire*, Az. You can't really have any idea what it's like to be *powerless*, to have your destiny picked for you while you stand there and have one load of crap after another dumped all over you.' She shook her head, turning her back to him in a show of hastily renewed frustration. 'Az, you . . .' She trailed off, as if afraid to finish.

Azrael was no longer able to tell what she was thinking. Once again, she was closed off to him – just like that. Whether it was a side effect of Gregori's influence over her or she was simply coming to be Azrael's equal in her archess abilities, he found it impossible to read her mind in that moment. And he desperately wanted to hear what she'd been about to say.

Even while he was terrified of her saying it.

'I *what*, Sophie?' he asked softly. The night grew silent as the sea and sky and sand waited for her reply.

Sophie shuddered and he saw her fingers go white where she hugged herself tightly. 'You took my parents from me.'

A wave crashed onto the shore. An arc of pain sliced through Azrael's chest. *No*, he thought desperately. Sophie couldn't be more wrong. Azrael had nothing to do with her parents' deaths. He had no control over that aspect of existence. He hadn't worn that particular uniform in two thousand years, and even when he had roamed the universe as the Angel of Death, he'd wielded an unexplainable power, immense yet severely limited.

He'd taken souls from one place to another, but they came when they came and not a moment sooner or later. Sophie spoke of destiny. But destiny was something no being had ever escaped. It was as much a part of existence as was conscious awareness. Everything and everyone was a slave to some kind of fate. Fate moved through life and twisted it around and pushed it through to the other side.

Azrael had never had any power over his own destiny. If he *had*, if he'd been given the choice – he would not be what he was . . . what he had once been. If he could change his past and present and future, he would no longer be hated by those who had passed – and by those they had left behind.

That he had never had any more control over a being's death than *they* had was something no mortal could comprehend, much less accept. There was too much pain involved with the phenomenon of death.

Azrael had not taken Sophie's family from her. But she was trapped in the idea of having lost what she might have had, and nothing burned so much as the acid of resentment.

'Sophie,' he whispered as he moved forward again, coming to stand just behind her. 'Sweet Sophie.' He closed his eyes, which now burned bright and hot in his skull, and he swallowed hard. 'I didn't kill your parents,' he said. 'And if I had been there to take them when they died, I would have moved heaven and earth to change things.'

He shuddered and looked up, as if expecting lightning to strike as he realized the full weight of what he was about to say. And then he didn't care, and he said it with the fierce resolve of a man who is both telling the truth and making a promise. 'I would have laid down my wings to save you from that grief. Sophie . . . I would have stepped down and turned away from everything I'd ever known if it meant that you could know the warmth of your mother's smile and your father's laugh for even a minute more.'

In front of him, Sophie went completely still. The surf climbed the sand a hundred feet away and seagulls rounded a band of rocks up ahead, searching for a washed-up meal. The sky was more or less quiet . . . but Azrael could hear Sophie's blood rushing through her veins, pushed hard by a heart that raced maniacally. It pounded with deafening ardor, testament to her complete surprise.

Slowly, stiffly, she dropped her arms and turned to face him. He stared down at her through gold eyes filled with so much emotion that they burned painfully in his skull. He heard her breath catch and wondered if he was frightening her.

'Az . . .' she began, her voice shaking, 'are you telling me—' She broke off, blinked, and started again. 'Are you telling me you would have stood up to the Old Man in order to . . .' Again she trailed off. It was as if she was just as afraid of saying it as he had been of thinking it.

But there was no hesitation now as he replied, 'To protect you, Sophie, I would do anything.'

Sophie couldn't speak. She could barely think. Azrael stood before her a monument of a man, tall and dark and incredibly dangerous. His inhumanly beautiful eyes glowed with a hellish gold fire, bright and hot. They pulled her in with their blazing emotion, scorching her from the inside out.

She couldn't move while trapped in that sway; she could only stand there and let the wind whip through her hair as her mind tried to come to grips with what Azrael had just told her. It literally took the breath from her lungs.

But Azrael spared her any further speech by looking away for a moment and composing himself. Then, with paramount grace, the tall, dark archangel brushed past her to move several feet down the beach. Sophie, wrapped in her stunned and heavy silence, could only turn and watch him.

Az stopped beside a smooth black stone that rose from the wet sand like the back of an Orca whale. Then he bent gracefully and Sophie saw him pick something up. He straightened, coming back to his full impressive height, and gazed down at what he held in his hands. But his back was still blocking her view, and curiosity pulled her across the sand toward him.

When she was three feet away, he turned and held out his hand. In his palm was the perfect white disc of a large sand dollar.

'It's been years since I thought about it, but the Old Man made these for us,' he said. 'Sand dollars.'

Sophie blinked, her brow furrowing, her voice entirely gone. He'd completely changed the subject, as if he couldn't bear to think any longer about her loss and the part she felt he'd played in it.

In the silence, he went on. 'He made them for me and my brothers.' He smiled, just a little, and the moonlight sliced across his piercing eyes. 'In other parts of the world, they're known as sea cookies or snapper biscuits. Some people believe they're the coin of merfolk. In reality, they're the skeletons of echinoids, nothing more.' He paused, running his thumb idly over the surface of the endoskeleton. 'But the Old Man had always been most proud of our wings.' He chuckled, and it was a melancholy sound, sweet and lilting and filled with unspoken sadness. 'So, in secret, he reproduced them.' He looked up as Sophie inched closer. '*Here.*'

Sophie watched as the perfect sand dollar split slowly in half, a hairline crack forming across the middle of the object from one side to the other. When it was finished, Azrael pulled the separate pieces apart and tipped one of them over his open palm. Five tiny objects poured out.

Sophie leaned in to see better. 'They're angels,' she whispered, finding her voice at last. Tiny white objects that honestly looked like miniature angel sculptures rested in his open hand.

Azrael chuckled again. This time it was a little less sad. 'There are five in every sand dollar,' he said. Sophie looked up at him, her gold eyes meeting his. 'Four represent Michael, Uriel, Gabriel, and myself. The Old Man wouldn't tell us what the fifth was for.' His voice had dropped to a whisper at this point. Very gently, he took the tiny white delicate angels between his fingers and dropped the sand dollar casings. Then, with a gentle touch that sent a rush of warmth up Sophie's arm and across her chest, Azrael took her right wrist in his fingers and turned her own hand over.

The mark that Gregori's black dandelion had given her was still there, but it was greatly faded, as if the ink had washed away with time.

If Azrael saw it now, he made no mention of it. Instead, he very carefully set one of the tiny angels in the middle of her palm. It lay atop the black dandelion, stark in its whitewashed beauty. 'But I've figured it out,' he said softly, drawing her gaze to him. His eyes were searching, deep and mesmerizing. 'The fifth is that which the four of us search for. It's that piece of us that was made with us, surrounds us in spirit, and leaves us incomplete until we find it again.' He paused, allowed his next words to be said in the waiting silence, and then spoke them aloud for good measure. 'For me, that's you, Sophie.'

Sophie stood numb and still for a long while. Then she looked down at the tiny angel in her hand. It seemed so small

– yet so significant. Finally, she looked back up at Azrael. Her chest ached. It was a real, physical kind of pain that gnawed at her and yet filled her with something for once substantial. There was a brief moment, a pulse in time – eternally long – that was gone in an instant.

And then Azrael was kissing her.

No. That wasn't right. *She* was kissing *him*.

She wasn't sure what had given her the push, but she stared up at him standing there, wrapped in regret and wishes as thick as her own, and knew that she was gazing at not only the most outwardly beautiful man in the world, but the most inwardly beautiful as well.

She suddenly realized that while she had been trapped in her own destiny – so had he. They were angels in a sand dollar, adrift in a sea and split apart to be lost and separated for two thousand years.

And now here they were, standing on the shore once more. And Sophie knew – she *knew* – she'd loved this man from the very beginning. She'd loved him from the moment she'd heard his voice crooning over the radio. She'd ached inside, wanting to pull back the mask he wore onstage so that she could look into the face that she had already fallen for.

She loved him. Despite the fact that he'd been the Angel of Death, despite the fact that he was tied to her through some divine destiny, and despite the fact that he was a vampire. Despite everything – or maybe *because* of it.

*I love you*, she thought.

And then she was moving forward and standing on her tiptoes to shove her hand through his long, thick black hair and pull his lips to her own. It took no time at all – none passed – before Azrael was sliding his strong arm around her waist and using it to pull her body against his.

She melted into the tall, hard frame of him, at once enveloped in his warm darkness and his incredible surge of power. She gave herself up to it – to him – and let him take control for the second time that night. She had no choice.

His lips claimed hers in a way that chased the uncertainty from Sophie's mind like the sun on the fog. His grip on her was tight with desperation; his kiss was just as desperate. She caught the scent of leather and felt his hair brush her cheek as his tongue expertly, insistently, opened her up beneath him.

And just like that, once again, she was delirious. The night danced around her. She felt his hand in her hair, tilting her back as he drew her every breath into himself, devouring her heart and soul. She heard a moan and knew it was her own but could not remember making the sound.

There was sudden sharp pain in Sophie's palm and she jerked slightly in Azrael's embrace. At once, he broke the kiss and gazed down at her, concern clear in his handsome features.

Sophie frowned and looked down at her hand, which was curled tightly into a fist. With a rapidly pounding heart, she uncurled her hand and stared at her palm. The mark Gregori had given her was now gone. But so was the tiny white angel Azrael had given her. In their place, etched perfectly into the skin of her hand, was a shimmering pair of golden wings.

# Chapter 32

In a large white marble chamber, complete with round marble columns and firelight flickering off the polished marble surfaces, a man sat cross-legged in the center of a circle of white candles. His thick black hair curled over the collar of his crisp white button-down shirt. His incredibly strong body was at ease, relaxed. And his beautiful but frighteningly different eyes were closed.

The flash of an image passed before those closed eyes – and they flew open. Pupils the color of ice surrounded dark stars born of a darker magic that was capable of spreading like wildfire and growing like a weed. The man gazed through those eyes into a scene of a vampire on a beach – and a woman who had escaped her bonds.

*So be it*, the man thought. *It is time.*

*I love you.*

He heard it loud and clear. The single, short thought cut through the thick fog that was the rest of the world as if those three words were the only three words any being had ever uttered in the history of time.

In that moment, everything bad that had ever happened in his existence was nothing. It was gone, blown away like dust in a hurricane. All was forgiven, all was right, and all he wanted to do was kiss the woman who had made it possible.

*I love you.*

She jumped up on her tiptoes and ran her hand through his hair and for the briefest of moments, he was so stunned, he simply stood there and let her pull his lips to her own. And then he was taking over, every fiber of his archangel being roaring to life once again.

She flinched and he felt a thrum of quick, sharp pain move through her as if it was his own. He pulled out of the kiss, regretting it at once, and looked down at her. She was staring at her palm where Gregori's mark had been replaced by a shimmering golden tattoo.

Of a pair of wings.

It was the sudden shifting of the air on the beach that prevented him from grabbing her hand for a closer look. A disturbance around them drew his attention and switched on his defenses. He straightened and turned, holding his breath as his now glowing gaze skirted the shadows of the shore.

There was a popping and then a sucking sound, and everything changed. Azrael was moving so fast that his body blurred, his vampire-archangel reflexes spinning him around and drawing Sophie behind him in the blink of an eye. He took in the scene and processed it in no more than a millisecond.

Phantoms swarmed the beach, a handful of wraiths among them. Their presence warped and froze the air, sending out negative energy so thick it was stifling.

Azrael's fangs erupted, his eyes shifting to red. His breath formed icicles in the phantom-chilled night. The presence of these monsters was inexplicably wrong. They were obviously there for Sophie. If they'd wanted Azrael, they'd had thousands of years to attack.

The milky-white bodies of the phantoms turned toward the couple, their grisly visages twisting into black, razor-toothed smiles. They stood seven feet tall, and their skin slithered and swirled as if it were coated with a thin layer of fog. In some respects, they looked like photo negatives of mortals, though they stood taller.

Their shoulder-length blue-white hair was so fine, it looked like feathers in the breeze. Their eyes were no more than pools of bottomless black. Their broad chests were bare, and around their tight abdomens were tattooed strings of arcane symbols inscribed in glowing blue-white ink.

Phantoms were the bane of the supernatural community. They could disappear at will, transport through a space of any size in the blink of an eye, and when they touched a victim, the victim was sapped of strength and chilled from the inside out, resulting in a painful, frozen death.

One phantom alone was a challenge none of the archangels would have taken lightly. *Many* phantoms was an apocalyptic nightmare. Fortunately, phantoms were known to be solitary creatures and had never before worked in any kind of group. What Azrael saw before him now, he'd previously thought impossible.

The wraiths among the phantoms moved more slowly. They were less powerful than the notorious assassins, but their figures stood out more. Their power was simple and horrible: they possessed the ability to literally open old wounds simply by touching their victims. Any injury ever sustained in a being's lifetime could reappear, tearing holes in flesh and cracking bones within seconds.

Long ago, when the Old Man had first created the wraiths, he'd realized his mistake, and he'd taken the hands off every wraith and then cast the monsters to Earth. However, once on Earth, the wraiths had quickly found substitutes for their missing hands, turning their stumps into working appendages once more by robbing what they needed from the dead.

Now they existed as black-cloaked figures with faces like wax, bleeding red slits for mouths, eyes of stone – and skeletal hands. One touch from those skeletal hands and every wound Azrael had ever suffered would begin to resurface.

Az did a quick count: at least a dozen phantoms, and half that number of wraiths. And then a flicker of movement caught his eye and he glanced to his left toward an outcropping of wet black stone.

Icarans. He sensed at least three, although their black skin camouflaged their presence in the dark night. Icarans were also known as leeches because they fed on magic. They were attracted to it; it was their sustenance, and they tended to gorge on it, often to the point of a grisly, explosive death. They were no doubt drawn to the beach by the massive amount of supernatural power gathering on it at that moment.

Sophie's fingers curled around Azrael's right wrist as she peeked out from behind him at the small army of monsters closing in on them.

'Holy hell,' she whispered, her voice shaking with both cold and terror. 'What in G-God's name are th-those?'

Azrael didn't reply. He was too busy trying to figure out how to deal with their situation. The phantoms could transport at will; their presence here was easily explained. They'd mostly likely brought the wraiths with them; it was the only logical explanation for the wraiths' synchronized appearance, despite the fact that it seemed to go against phantom nature. The Icarans had probably been somewhere nearby and had simply followed the magic.

There was little time. Azrael didn't know why the monsters had gathered, but he knew he had to get help very quickly. It took seconds for him to send out a mental call. Unfortunately, there were no archways or anything even remotely door-like on the beach that could serve as a portal. His brothers and Max would not be able to use the mansion to get to him in time. Only Azrael's vampires could come to his aid fast enough. But first he and Sophie needed to survive the seconds it would take for help to arrive.

He could take Sophie and escape through the shadows to someplace safer – but the phantoms would only follow him. It was one of the many, many things that made them so dangerous. They could track anything, anywhere. Only vampires and black dragons could traverse the dark web of passageways in the shadow realm, but phantoms could sniff out who had been *through* them, when, and where they were headed next. They would know where Az was going before he got there. Then all they had to do was transport to that location. If Az disappeared through them with Sophie, he would come out the other side only to find himself walking into an ambush of terrible proportions.

His only other option was to take to the skies with her. Both phantoms and wraiths could fly, and they would be hot on his tail. But vampires, at least, were faster.

Az had decided to do this and was turning to face Sophie when she was suddenly ripped from his side. He spun, blurring with the motion, but too late.

Sophie was caught fast, a strong arm around her shoulders

both pinning her to her captor and covering her mouth so that she couldn't scream. A second hand fisted in her hair to expose her neck to the now frigid air. A pair of glowing blue eyes glared at Azrael over Sophie's head, and a set of sharp white fangs threatened her throat.

Azrael froze. 'Abraxos,' he whispered.

Abraxos grinned at him through those misbegotten teeth as Sophie struggled ineffectually in his strong grasp. The Adarian vampire winked at Azrael and stepped back into the shadows behind him, taking Sophie with him.

Az was rushing forward to follow him into the darkness when something cold and horrible struck him from behind. An arc of freezing pain shot through his chest, clutching at his heart. He stopped in his tracks, fighting not to fall to his knees. Unsteadily, he attempted to inhale, but his lungs felt frozen. He looked down to see icicles forming across the black clothing over his chest, and he knew that the flesh and bone beneath it were freezing just as rapidly.

From the center of his chest protruded a taloned, slithering white hand shrouded in magical mist. As he watched, the phantom slowly twisted its arm in Azrael's chest, and then yanked it back out again, sending Az to his knees after all.

The pain was excruciating, but Azrael's worry for Sophie was stronger. It shoved his legs back underneath him and brought him once more to his feet. But the moment he again attempted to blur into forward motion, he was met with another, different kind of pain that brought him to a fast halt for a second time.

He cried out as the left side of his neck was embraced with lightning speed by the skeletal hand of a wraith. The touch sent a malevolent, magical poison through his system, turning back time to wrong all rights.

Azrael had been battling the monsters of the universe for thousands of years. Over that time, he had sustained many injuries. Several of them reopened now: a claw rake across his back that left four deep gouges and was instantly welling blood, a blade's clean slice across his left quadriceps that nearly disconnected two halves of the muscle, a burn on his right shoulder left there by a red dragon before Az was a vampire.

Azrael's back arched with the pain and he stumbled, bending to clutch at the wound in his leg. He was not only an archangel but a vampire, and the wound would heal, as would the claw marks across his back. But the last wound was the one that frightened Azrael the most. It had been born of fire, and his vampire-archangel blood could not heal it like the others. Worse yet – the bite was poisonous. The fire would spread, burning across his skin and scorching it to a crisp until it could be magically halted in its tracks. This hadn't been a problem for Azrael the archangel; his blood had healed the wound before it had a chance to spread.

Now, however, things were different.

Azrael gritted his teeth, his fangs aching in his gums. He spun on the wraith, fury and fear fueling his movements. The monster reeled back, realizing his mistake in remaining too close for milliseconds too long. Azrael grabbed the creature's thin, waxy neck with one hand and twisted with fierce, violent momentum. The wraith made a wretched choking sound and dropped to the ground.

But it was quickly replaced. Another phantom raked its icy-death claws through Azrael's already churning midsection while he went for the neck of yet another supernatural monster. Azrael felt the fire of the red dragon wound spreading even as his others healed. He couldn't get near the shadows that Abraxos and Sophie had disappeared into. If enough time passed, he wouldn't be able to track them. And he wondered for the first time if he was going to die on that beach.

*At least she loves me*, he thought.

*And that's reason enough to live, my lord*, said Uro, his voice a stunning comfort in the confines of Azrael's spinning mind.

Az turned, having to peer over the shoulders of two phantoms who simultaneously attacked him in order to catch sight of the vampires who were now stepping out of shadows of their own. Uro was the only vampire Azrael had ever created who could move through the shadows. But the Egyptian had not come alone. He'd brought the entire band along with him, no doubt having to concentrate to the point of pain in order to move so many bodies through the murky, confusing labyrinth that was the shadow realm.

Az had rarely seen a more welcome sight. Just as he was ducking to avoid the reach of another wraith, Uro attacked, yanking a phantom back by its hair and taking it to the skies in an angry white blur.

Azrael's attention was divided then. Half of him fought with the creatures around him, as did Rurik, Devran, and Mikhail. But the other half of him was fast becoming a slave to the pain of the burns moving through his body.

He needed to get to Michael or one of the archesses. Sophie would have been able to heal him, but he would have to go through Abraxos to get to her. In his current state,

Azrael honestly didn't think he was up to the challenge.

The red dragon's poison was moving inward. He could feel it edging toward the arteries of his heart. It wouldn't be long before the muscle was burned. And when that happened . . .

Azrael pulled his thoughts from the possible dark fate and concentrated on his other option. A phantom shoved his fist through his shoulder, Azrael pulled it back out again, broke the arm at the elbow, and then backhanded the phantom so hard that the monster went sailing across the beach.

It was either up to Az to move through the shadows to the mansion himself in order to find Michael, Ellie, or Jules – or up to Uro to bring Michael to him there on the beach. The former was far more likely and far faster than the latter.

So that was what he concentrated on. All he had to do was make it through three more phantoms and a wraith before the fire could take his heart, and the shadows would be his to traverse.

# Chapter 33

Sophie closed her eyes against the feeling that moving through the strange darkness gave her. She was torn between wanting her abductor to release her and wanting him to hold tighter to her so that he wouldn't lose her in the miasma of shadows.

When they finally stepped through the other side and her captor shoved her into a bright white room of pure marble, Sophie felt like crying with relief. And just plain crying.

Her wobbly legs crumpled beneath her. She went down hard, landing on her knees on the smooth white stone before she could get a good look around. As she hit, she sucked in a breath of pain and bit her lip. Then she took a shaky breath, raised her head, and shoved her hair out of her face in order to more fully take in her surroundings.

She saw that there were people in the room, but at first she couldn't focus on them. Instead, she was distracted by the strangeness of the space itself. The room was octagonal and divided by several tall white marble columns. Veins of gold and what looked like crushed diamonds were woven through the polished stone. At the center of each wall was a large arched window, apparently gilded in gold.

Whoever had abducted her couldn't have been an Adarian. From what Juliette and the archangels had told her, Adarians would never have surrounded themselves with anything resembling gold.

Beyond all eight windows stretched the same stark landscape: mountains and canyons of pure white ice climbed from valleys of pristine, glimmering snow. The sun's twilight rays nearly crested the tops of the spiked, crystalline hills, lending the view a pinkish orange glow. In a few minutes, the fiery orb would rise and the land would reflect its brightness in blinding brilliance. Sophie experienced the temporary urge to simply stare out the windows for a while until the sun did so. She was certain it would be spectacular beyond her wildest dreams.

The frigid landscape waited beyond the open arches of the windows and yet she was warm, which was disconcerting. She'd only recently come into her archess powers, and she had yet to fully digest the fact that she *was* an archess, but she understood enough through Juliette and through what she'd done so far to know that this room seemed made specifically with her powers in mind. There was nothing in the room to throw around with telekinesis. There was no fire to manipulate. And the fact that she couldn't feel the outside world through the windows meant that the room was magically shielded from its location. Any storm she caused around them would have no effect upon the inhabitants of the marble chamber. She was powerless here.

As she considered this, Sophie tried desperately to ignore the tower of energy she felt radiating from the man in white several feet away.

'I can't deny that I'm disappointed, Sophie,' came his familiar, eerily beautiful voice.

Sophie tried not to look at him. She didn't want to get

sucked into Gregori's ice-rimmed dark stars. She knew him now. As she knelt there on the floor, her body shivering with fear, she felt that she could finally think clearly enough to see the man in white for what he was.

He'd done something to her last time. He'd marked her, and that mark had taken her over, turning her against the man she loved.

*The man I love*, she thought, the words stunning her and empowering her at the same time. Here she was, kneeling before a creature who would most likely kill her – *why*, she had no idea – and yet her recognition of the love she had for Azrael seemed paramount.

'Disappointed.' Gregori sighed, sounding so truly sad that Sophie couldn't help but look up at him at last. 'But I cannot fault you,' he continued, tilting his beautiful head to one side and giving Sophie a gentle, understanding smile. 'If your feelings are true.'

To say that Sophie was confused would have been an understatement. Who was Gregori and what the hell did he want with her? What was his game?

She chanced a quick glance at the other occupants of the room. There were four other people in the room with them. One was the man who had taken her from the beach. Sophie glanced at him over her shoulder. If she had to guess, she would peg him as a vampire. He was tall and broad, with jet-black hair and very blue glowing eyes with fiery red pupils. There was something strange about those pupils, but Sophie couldn't bring herself to look into them long enough to figure out what it was. She didn't want to turn her back to Gregori for any significant length of time.

Two other men in the room stood on opposite ends of the

chamber. Each was nearly seven feet tall, appeared broad and strong, and possessed skin that was pale to the point of translucence. One had brown hair with green highlights running through it. The other had black hair with blue highlights. Their eyes were . . . *reptilian*. Instead of the round pupils of a human, their slightly reflective eyes possessed slits like those of a lizard.

Sophie knew she shouldn't, but she stared at them in stark fascination while they gazed straight ahead at nothing in particular. They were as still as statues, their hands at their sides, and each was dressed in blue jeans, engineering boots, and a leather jacket encrusted with what looked like genuine gemstones. They were simply too deep in color, too refractive of the light to be crystal or cut glass. One of the jackets contained gemstones of green – emeralds? The other had blue sapphires.

*Jesus*, thought Sophie, *those jackets must be worth a fortune*.

Finally, she looked away. The other person in the room she recognized as John Smith, the man who had taken her from her cell on Alcatraz. Smith now watched her with an enigmatic expression on his face.

'Why am I here?' she asked, choosing to meet Smith's gaze since it didn't make her stomach feel as if it was boiling.

'You would find this hard to believe, but the truth is, I bear you no personal ill will, Sophie Bryce,' said Gregori, at once stealing her attention. She turned back to look at him and slowly stood in the hopeless attempt to not feel so small in front of the man.

He watched her rise, his expression unreadable.

'If I did, I would not have watched over you for the past

twenty years.' His voice was level, his tone filled with meaning. 'I would not have kept you safe when your parents died or protected you from the authorities when you killed your foster father.'

Sophie stared at him, dumbfounded. *It was you?* she thought.

Gregori nodded, just once. 'You see, for many years, I blamed Azrael for my misfortune. He was the Angel of Death. And I lost someone very dear to me. I had an ultimate plan, of course, but I saw no reason why Azrael shouldn't suffer in fulfilling that ultimate plan. And what could make him suffer more than losing the one he loved as well?'

Sophie's gaze narrowed. A riddle here and there was one thing, but this was going too far. She was sick and tired of not knowing what was going on. 'You lost me,' she said honestly, her own tone low with impending storm. She was furious at being ripped from Azrael's embrace, and she was more than a little worried for the archangel's safety. The monsters that had been swarming the beach before her capture had not looked at all friendly.

Gregori's brow raised, whether because he was impressed or amused, Sophie couldn't tell. She found her throat going dry as the man in white watched her for a moment in silence.

Finally, he took a deep breath and let it out in a weary sigh. 'Many years ago,' he said, turning to pace a step away and then pausing to glance back at her. '*Many* years,' he repeated with emphasis, 'I fell in love with a mortal woman.' He paused again, and his expression changed, his voice taking on a softer tone. 'Her name was Amara.'

He smiled wistfully and for a fraction of a fraction of a

second, Gregori was no longer frightening. He looked human – and sad.

But then the impression was gone and he laughed softly but harshly, shaking his head. 'The name means "eternal." It was unfortunately ironic, as her life was to be anything *but.*' He resumed pacing then, his gaze on the pristine marble floor in front of him, his white wing-tipped shoes making soft clicking sounds as he moved. 'In my realm, we were forbidden from mingling with the mortals of Earth. The Old Man decried them as unfit and did not want us to be tainted by their wayward spirits.'

*The Old Man*, Sophie thought. *So Gregori's from the same realm as the angels.*

Gregori stopped and looked up at Sophie, his eyes boring instant holes through her. She ceased breathing.

'Oh, we are most definitely from the realm of the angels, Miss Bryce.' He smiled grimly. 'In fact, we were there long before the archangels were created. Long before the Adarians.' He waited and the silence stretched. 'We were the first.'

*I made it.*

It was a simple thought, free of embellishment, but it meant everything to Azrael. It had been a long while since he'd had to fight so hard to do no more than survive. Whoever Gregori was – *whatever* Gregori was – he meant business. Not even Samael had ever come after the archangel brothers with such ferocity.

By the time Azrael was stepping out of the shadows and into the mansion's foyer, the red dragon fire in his system was inches from taking his heart. It was only by some twist of luck and fate that once Az had taken off with Sophie after pulling her out of her apartment, Michael himself had decided to return to the mansion. There were so many places he could have been, and Az didn't possess the strength to track him down. Fortunately, he didn't have to.

Az stumbled through the archway that led to the living room where all three of Azrael's brothers, Eleanore, and Juliette now sat with Max. Some of them held steaming cups of tea in their hands, and all wore decidedly worried expressions. They also looked tired; it had been a long few days.

Everyone turned toward the foyer's entrance as Azrael appeared. Heartbeats later, Michael was up and out of his seat and racing toward Azrael. Gabriel joined him, and the two of them helped Az to the nearest couch as Uriel cleared away the pillows and throws to make room for his tall frame.

'You look like rubbish,' Gabriel breathed.

Azrael lay back with a wince. He was being eaten alive by fire poison, and more than a few phantom and wraith wounds were still attempting to heal themselves.

Michael took one look up and down Az's normally strong body and his expression became grim. At once, he knelt beside his brother and placed his hands atop Azrael's abdomen.

Az bit back a curse of pain.

'Where is Sophie?' Max asked as he approached the couch and Michael shut his eyes to concentrate.

Azrael's head spun and his heart physically ached, as though the poison had already reached its mark. 'I don't know,' he said honestly. 'Abraxos took her.'

'Bloody hell!' Gabriel exclaimed gruffly. 'Again?'

Michael opened his eyes, his concentration clearly interrupted.

'Not helping,' Uriel said softly as he and Max shot Gabe a warning look. Gabriel shut his mouth, his silver eyes flashing.

'Move, sweetie,' said Juliette. She and Eleanore pushed their way past the Scot in order to kneel beside Michael.

'You're gonna need our help,' said Eleanore, with a sidelong glance at the Warrior Archangel.

Michael nodded his silent thanks and the three turned back to Azrael.

Az met his brother's blue-eyed gaze. *Quickly, please*, he pleaded without speaking. *Or I'll lose his trail.*

Michael closed his eyes once more and his hands began to glow. The archesses followed suit. Azrael rested his head against the arm of the sofa and prepared for the pain he knew would come with the healing. He hadn't looked in a mirror since the wraith had attacked him, but he could feel the damage it had caused. There were third-degree burns across his shoulder, his neck, and the right side of his jaw. Those burns continued across his chest and the right side of his abdomen, nearly to his hip. The entire right half of his upper body was virtually unrecognizable.

Vampires naturally withstood healing where burns were concerned. This would be more difficult to undo than a sword wound. In that moment, Azrael was incredibly grateful for the help the archesses were able to give. He wasn't sure that Michael would have been able to handle this one alone.

When the warmth of their combined healing power enveloped the already burned tissue on Azrael's chest, he closed his eyes and focused inward, pulling himself away from the agonizing sensation. In his mind's cyc, hc saw his archess: her golden hair, golden eyes, and bright, beautiful smile. He heard her voice, soft and sweet. He almost smiled when he imagined her laugh. The hidden smile turned wicked when he heard internal thunder and thought of her intense fighting spirit . . . and the delicious punishments it caused her to bring upon herself.

'Done,' came a tired voice beside him.

Azrael opened his eyes. The pain was gone.

He looked down at his destroyed clothes and caught sight of the smooth flesh beneath. No acid burned in his veins; no fire rushed through his arteries toward his waiting heart.

Azrael sat up and the three healers moved back. Eleanore brushed a lock of raven hair from her lovely face. She looked a tad paler than usual. Juliette's wild hair seemed a bit frizzier than normal where it framed her petite, perfect features. She appeared every bit the highland fairy. Michael stood slowly, his tall, strong frame as warrioresque as ever. But Az could sense his weariness. There was a darkness to his eyes . . . as if his blue skies bore clouds.

'Thank you,' Azrael said as he stood. There was no time to waste. He offered his hands to the archesses, one to each of them, and they accepted, allowing him to help them up. Then he moved around them, toward the foyer and its longer shadows.

'If you're goin' ta fight Abraxos, I'm bloody well comin' with you,' said Gabriel.

Azrael glanced at him over his shoulder to find that the archangel was already steadfastly moving in place behindAz. And he wasn't alone. Michael, Uriel, and Max were right behind him. A few feet back, Eleanore and Juliette shot wary, uncertain glances at one another. They clearly wanted to tag along, but were torn about how much they would actually be able to help – and they were worried about their husbands.

Azrael stopped and turned to face them all. He looked them in the eye, one at a time, and the men straightened, coming up short as they felt Azrael's power pour around him. It was a warning. There were forces at work that none of them understood. 'Phantoms, wraiths, leeches,' Azrael said softly. 'At the very least. This Gregori wields immense power. I have come across only one man capable of controlling a phantom.'

'Samael,' Max said.

Azrael nodded, just once.

'Do you think he's involved?' Max asked.

Az had a feeling he was not. In fact, though he had never met Gregori personally, from what he'd heard and felt around Sophie, Gregori and Samael gave the impression of being spiritual polar opposites . . . like the two ends of a battery. But in truth he had no idea. He knew only that he was wasting time. If he waited much longer, the shadows would completely absorb what traces of Abraxos Azrael would have been able to follow. 'I don't know.'

'Wait.' Michael interrupted. 'If Abraxos took Sophie while the phantoms attacked, then *he* and Gregori, at the very least, *are* working together, aren't they?' Michael asked.

It seemed to be the only explanation. But, again, Az had no idea. So he said nothing.

'The sun is coming up here,' said Max. 'It might be coming up where Abraxos and Gregori are as well.'

The thought had already occurred to Azrael. It was all the more reason not to waste any time, which was a point that he effectively communicated with the deadpan look he gave his guardian.

'Okay, okay,' Gabriel said. 'We get it. Consider us fairly warned. Now lead on.'

Azrael took a deep breath and let it out slowly. Clearly, the lot of them wanted him to pull them through the shadows with him. As he had no idea where they were going and whether there would even be any doors there once he arrived, it was logically the only way they would be able to accompany him in his battle against Abraxos — and whatever else awaited him.

'You two please remain here,' he said, looking from Eleanore to Juliette. Their powers were incredibly helpful in tight situations and they were by no means without defensive recourse, but the archesses seemed to be at the center of everything dangerous these days and he didn't need any more people to protect.

Wisely, the women nodded their consent.

'The rest of you stay close,' he instructed calmly. The party moved in almost as one, as if they were a single organism.

Azrael turned toward the shadows and raised his hand, concentrating. If he could form a tunnel before him, mold the very darkness just right, he could create a passage large enough for all of them to move together and there would be no chance of separation. It was taxing and he didn't like the idea of spending energy he might need later, but the alternative was to face the enemy alone.

After a few tense seconds, he could feel his magic slide

into place and the invisible tunnel before him coalesced into its necessary shape. He lowered his arm and stepped through, his archangel family close behind.

# Chapter 34

*We were the first . . .*

The words echoed in her mind as she stared at the man in white, her mind spinning with questions. 'We?' Sophie asked softly, chancing a glance at the others in the room. For some reason, she didn't think Gregori was talking about them. *And, the first what?*

She didn't need to speak her questions out loud, however. Gregori seemed to pull them out of her head as he continued. 'There were hundreds of us,' he told her. 'The Adarians believe they were the first angels ever created, but they couldn't be more wrong. My brethren and I were a veritable army.' He turned from her to face one of the eight windows and, as he looked out over the frozen expanse, the scenery changed.

Sophie's jaw dropped, her eyes widening as the mountains morphed and the valley melted into a dry, cracked landscape. Before her eyes, beings appeared and the sky darkened with the smoke of a thousand fires. There was a battle raging, one unlike anything Sophie could have imagined. Creatures straight out of nightmares fought hand to hand with winged men in armor. It was an apocalyptic vision brought to life.

'We fought the Old Man's battles for him ceaselessly. Tirelessly. And why?' He glanced over his shoulder at

Sophie, his lips curled into a bitter smile. 'Because he told us to.' He turned back to the window and again the scenery changed. Instead of a dry landscape and a red sky, the window revealed a land of lush forests and green valleys. A river wound its way through the valley, and she could almost hear it babbling over its course of smooth rocks and stones.

On the shores of the river sat people in robes. They were a little too far away for her to make out clearly. Sophie found herself a slave to curiosity, inching forward in order to get a better look. The people sitting on the banks of the river possessed long, beautiful hair in various shimmering hues. *Women. They're all women*, she realized. Around them were patches of bright yellow dandelions that they leisurely picked and handed to the men behind them. These were the men Sophie had seen fighting in the previous landscape. Their wings were folded at their backs and they no longer wore armor.

'One day, our battles brought us to Earth,' Gregori told her, though his gaze was still locked on the image before him. 'Here, we were charmed by the human race's fairer sex. Many of us fell in love.' He turned away from the image fully now, and his ice-cold eyes focused on Sophie's, freezing her to the core. 'Including myself.'

Behind him, the image through the window changed. Sophie couldn't help but be drawn to it. She watched as the sky again turned dark, this time with storm clouds. The clouds opened and lightning sliced its way to the ground. The people below ran for cover as the river swelled beneath torrential rains and trees fell in the building gale. There was an ominous cast to the landscape, a hopeless, horrible air that filled Sophie with both sadness and fear.

Gregori hadn't moved. Instead, he watched her as she watched the sky grow darker and darker until the scene lost all color and everyone was gone.

'He punished us that day. We were banished to Earth.' Gregori shrugged. 'Most of us didn't care. This was where our brides were; this was where we preferred to be. However, as part of our punishment, we were no longer allowed to use our healing magic on anyone other than ourselves. And without it, we were forced to watch our loved ones grow old and die.'

Sophie continued to watch as the world beyond the window eventually went completely dark. Then, in that darkness, a candle was lit. And another. As the glow spread, a final image revealed itself. The angels from the previous two scenes were now standing over graves. Various objects decorated the heads of the graves: a wreath, a bouquet of flowers, a basket of fruit. At the head of the closest grave stood Gregori; she recognized his jet-black hair and slightly taller frame. His wings must have been pure black, because they blended with the night and Sophie couldn't make them out. But beneath his feet, and spreading across the grave were the small, multi-pointed bodies of black dandelions.

'I blamed the Old Man, of course. Our misery was primarily his design. However, for a long while, I also blamed Azrael. It would have been easier to fulfill my ultimate plan by killing you. But I wanted the Angel of Death to know the loss I'd known for all of this time. I needed to make certain the two of you met so that he could fall in love with you . . . before I took you from him.'

Sophie took this in, digesting his words and reasoning. She stared at the darkness beyond the window and thought of her life and the fact that she'd managed to get away with murder because of Gregori. It was all his doing. All for revenge.

Because he'd lost the woman he desperately loved.

As she thought of this, the image before her disappeared. The window's picture warped, revealing the frozen, predawn landscape it had originally portrayed.

Sophie found her throat felt tight. She tried to swallow, and almost choked. Her head hurt, and her chest ached.

'Amara was everything to me,' Gregori told her. His pupils seemed larger now – black stars that grew like a dark weed. 'She was everything kind and good that any of us had ever experienced. She and her sisters taught us what the Old Man had kept from us for eons: that there could be more to existence than pain, more than fighting.'

'I'm so . . .' Sophie began, but stopped when her voice cracked. She swallowed again and felt moisture sting her eyes. 'So sorry.' She meant it. What she had witnessed was heartbreaking. She hadn't thought herself capable of hating the Old Man any more than she already did for what he'd done to Azrael and herself. She'd been wrong.

'I know you are,' said Gregori as he turned away from her again and began pacing around the circumference of the octagonal chamber. John Smith and the other three men in the room remained motionless and silent as he moved. 'And so am I, Sophie Bryce. Because I know you are as innocent as was Amara. You were created and then tossed aside. And in seeing the two of you together, Sophie, I've also come to realize that Azrael is no more at fault than you are. He only did what the Old Man's bidding forced him to do. I've forgiven him,' he said softly. 'And yet . . . you've both found yourselves pawns in a war that will not be stopped.'

'What war?' Sophie asked. A part of her dreaded the answer. The rest of her desperately wanted to know more.

'The Old Man is no longer in his realm,' Gregori said. Goose bumps began to inch their way across Sophie's skin. 'In fact, the realm of angels is empty.'

Sophie's ears began to ring. The world felt far away.

'It has been for some time.'

Her heart beat hard against her rib cage and she felt dizzy.

'Outside of his own world, he is weak. He is vulnerable. If there was ever a time to repay him in kind for what he has done to me, it is now. However, there are a thousand realms to search, and I have not been able to locate him. He is smart . . . His presence is shielded from me.'

Sophie couldn't believe what she was hearing. She could barely think over the roar of blood through her veins, but Gregori's voice echoed in her mind, sounding loud and clear over the din.

'He must be stopped,' he said with quiet resolution. 'Of that, I have been certain since my prison sentence here began.' He took a step toward Sophie then, and she took an answering step back. 'My only hope lies in stopping the Culmination.'

*The Culmination?*

He stepped forward. She stepped back to find her retreat blocked by the hard body behind her. She'd forgotten about the blue-eyed man who had taken her from Azrael's side. Sophie's breath hitched and she again tried to swallow with a dry throat.

'You see, the Old Man didn't create four archesses,' Gregori went on. 'He created five.'

*Five?*

Gregori smiled, clearly having read her doubt. 'This fifth, precious woman, he created different from the other four. Within her, he instilled his knowledge so that she would know who and what she was. When this was finished, he secretly sent her to Earth alongside the Four Favored. She has been hidden from the four brothers, but her destiny is tied to them so tightly that they are nearly as one. When the Four Favored mate with their archesses she will be joined by the Old Man. And the Culmination will begin.'

'I can't believe it,' Sophie said. She didn't understand at all. It was all too incredible. Five archesses? The Old Man not in his realm? Missing angels?

'I know,' Gregori said again. 'But it matters little. What is important is that you are an archess, Sophie. If you never mate with your archangel, if you never earn your wings and your place at his side, the Culmination will never occur. And I will have all the time I need to find the Old Man.'

He moved forward, closing the distance between them, and Sophie absolutely froze in her boots, her gaze trapped in the icicles of his pupils.

'I tried going after the Old Man's archess herself, but I underestimated her,' he said. Something dark moved across his features, there one second and gone in the next. 'Should I fail here and be forced to pursue her again, it is a mistake I will not make a second time.'

*Oh God*, Sophie thought. *He's going to kill me. This is it. This is it.*

Gregori raised his hand and Sophie closed her eyes. When she felt a gentle tug on her hair, she opened them again to find him rubbing a golden lock between his thumb and forefinger. He seemed transfixed by the way it shimmered in the light.

'I had hoped that your death would not be necessary. I had hoped that by giving you free will and by showing you what the Old Man had kept from you, you would sway the direction of fate and turn Azrael down on your own.'

Sophie said nothing. There was nothing to say . . . but his previous actions were beginning to make more sense.

'However, the Angel of Death is an incredibly charismatic individual,' he said, smiling to himself. 'So again, I can't blame you. But . . . are you sure, little one?' he asked, now turning his frozen gaze upon her.

Sophie looked into those star-shaped pupils and felt the world tilt. Blood roared deafeningly through her ears. She squared off with a universe of choices in that moment. She knew she was staring her demise in the face. She had only to give the wrong answer, and Gregori would kill her.

And yet . . . she didn't care. It was a strangely liberating feeling to not care, to be so certain about your emotions that you were willing to die to stay true to them.

When she finally answered, her tone was certain. Shoulders rolled back, chin up, Sophie cleared her throat. 'I'm sure,' she said. 'I freely choose Azrael.' She couldn't believe how strong her voice sounded. It was as if she were watching herself, hearing herself say these things, from somewhere far away. 'I love him.'

There was a tingling on her palm then. It buzzed and shocked, and she winced and looked down at it, unfolding her fist to reveal the winged tattoo that shimmered across the inside of her hand. It seemed to warp across her palm, and as it moved, so did the tingling sensation. It spread up her wrist, buzzed up her arm, and raced across her chest to finally move over her shoulders and settle at the center of her upper back.

Sophie gasped and she heard the man behind her take a step back. Her breath came quick and shallow as she looked up into Gregori's eyes – only to find him staring in fascination at something over her shoulders.

*What?* she thought desperately. *What is it?*

She felt dizzy suddenly. And then light. Then there was a weight on her back, as if someone were pulling at her. With deliberate slowness, almost fearing what she knew she would find, Sophie looked over her shoulder.

'Oh my God,' she whispered.

*Wings*, she thought witlessly.

They were beautiful, the color of her hair, shimmery and enormous. *Honest-to-freaking-God* wings!

In front of her, Gregori released the lock of her hair he'd been rubbing and lowered his arm. She turned to watch him as he took in her glorious plumage with hard eyes and an unreadable expression.

'So that's settled then,' he said softly – so softly that she barely heard him.

He took a quick breath and raised his voice a touch. 'I know you desire Uriel's archess, Abraxos,' he said, obviously speaking to the man who had abducted her. She recognized the name. Abraxos was the leader of the Adarians. 'However, I see no reason why you shouldn't practice with this one first.'

With that, Gregori took a step back, turning his broad back to them in an effective show of dismissal. 'She's yours.'

\* \* \*

Azrael hurried through the shadows, his tall form passing the inky darkness of the corridor as if he were a part of it. It pulled at his black clothes and black hair like it didn't want to let him go. The shadows loved him, recognized him as one of their own. But they knew what he wanted and had to give it to him, though it would take him from their realm. He followed the *other* . . . the rogue, the twice dead, the one with a black heart. They knew where that other had gone, so they led Lord Azrael and his entourage through their kingdom, the shades of night pushing and pulling at their sovereign until he was close enough that he could feel Abraxos – just beyond that final wall of black.

And then they recoiled. Someone else was here.

Azrael felt them a beat before he would have stepped through the final shadow and into his destination. The darkness became hot and smelled like poison, the shadows slithered and recoiled, and every fiber of his being went on high alert.

He spun just as the first black dragon attacked, sliding a strong, leather-clad arm around Uriel's neck and jerking him backward with it into the depthless black of a tall shadow. It happened so fast, it would have been untraceable by the human eye. Azrael himself could not react in time – not before Michael, too, was pulled back.

Az was moving, his own body blurring. But there was too much to do at once. There were too many bodies to defend. The infamous dark dragons had known just when and how to attack so that Az was being torn in too many different directions.

He had just enough time to thank his lucky stars that the archesses had remained at the mansion before he was shoving both Max and Gabriel back toward the opening through which they'd originally come. Gabriel's archangel instincts kicked in, his silver eyes widened, and he covered Azrael's hand with his own, trying to pry it off his chest. But Az was determined in this – and he was stronger. Max had no recourse against Azrael and within milliseconds, the two of them were shooting back into the mansion's foyer.

Azrael turned back to the heart of the darkness then as he himself was attacked by a black dragon, and there was no more time for anything but fighting.

# Chapter 35

Michael could hold his own. He was the Warrior Archangel. Uriel had always had a lot of fire in his blood, but forced to choose, Azrael would bet on Michael lasting longer against the dragons.

With that in mind, he took his torn body through the shadows, which now seemed to help him along toward his destination. He followed Uriel's scent, tracking his brother's trace powers until he came to a final shadow and stepped through it into a rain-wet street beyond.

Uriel was up against a building's wall, his left arm burned black from the shoulder down, his right black from the elbow down. The black dragon had him at the neck, and Uriel could not use his arms to pry the creature's grip from him. Azrael could smell that the dragon's fiery poison was spreading.

Dragon venom could be spread through both tooth and claw. Black dragon poison was the most powerful among dragons. A red dragon's poison was a fire that literally burned the flesh and bone it touched. It was so painful that most victims passed out from shock. It was also deadly for a vampire. Green dragons filled their victim's blood with acid. Blue dragons were incredibly dangerous in that they shot air into their opponent's veins, often causing instant death.

But black dragons, also known as dark dragons, were

special in that they could do *all* of these things – and more. These dangerous creatures could move through the shadows. They possessed the ability to change their appearance in order to hide the traits that would otherwise set them apart as inhuman. They could fly without morphing into their dragon forms. And finally, they differed from their colored brethren in that they lacked what the supernatural world had long ago deemed the 'magpie trait.'

Dragons loved shiny things. All valuable material things, they coveted. Over the course of centuries, they collected gems and precious metals and usually they found a way to carry these treasures along wherever they went. When they appeared as humans, this trait often set them apart from the people around them, helping to identify them for what they were.

But black dragons wore only their skin – black leather. And in this, aside from their height and musculature, they looked like so very many ordinary people. They were not evil by any means, but they were loners, extremely territorial and possessive, and as if it wasn't enough that they had resurfaced after two thousand years, it was virtually unheard of that they would be working together in any capacity.

Az shifted into full vampire mode as he tore across the lot between him and the dragon that held Uriel. The creature dropped the archangel and spun to meet Az head-on. Under normal circumstances – whatever those were – a black dragon would have made for more than a worthy opponent. The fight would have gone on for some time. But Azrael could feel time pressing in on him, and these were not normal circumstances. He needed to get to Michael. He needed to get to Sophie.

The black dragon's attack carried horrendous dangers; however, it was as susceptible to a killing bite as any mortal animal.

The black dragon fell dead at Azrael's feet, its powerful blood drained from its magical veins. Az wiped his mouth on the back of his sleeve and watched for a few seconds as the dragon's body warped and seemed to melt into the darkness, becoming a shadow. Because that's what it now was.

'Thanks,' said Uriel, who spoke through gritted teeth. Az turned to study his brother. The dragon's poison had made its way through much of Uriel's body and would soon head for the heart if he wasn't healed.

'Az . . .' Uriel said then, grimacing in pain before he continued. He nodded to something over Azrael's shoulder. 'Nice wings.'

Azrael blinked. A blur of thought rushed his mind, utterly worthless. And then he seemed to fully hear what Uriel had just said. He processed it . . . and felt the added weight at his back that he'd been too busy to notice before.

Slowly, he turned and glanced over his right shoulder. Massive pitch-black wings veined through with honey gold rose from the middle of his back and spread to enormous, glorious lengths.

'Whatever she did,' Uriel hissed, trying to speak through his obvious agony, 'it must have been pretty great.'

Azrael could barely believe it. The appearance of his wings after all this time could mean only one thing. Sophie had proven her love for him. Az thought of how Eleanore and Juliette had done so for Uriel and Gabriel – both nearly dying in the process. The thought left him terrified.

He spun back to face Uriel. 'Use the doorway to get to the

mansion,' he instructed quickly, gesturing to a nearby service door in the side of the warehouse.

Uriel didn't need to be told twice. He moved quickly for one so injured, and raised the portal with his partially burned arm. Az watched long enough to make certain that Uriel stepped through before he turned and once more shot into the shadows from which he'd come.

Almost immediately after pushing through the inky barrier to the shadow dimension, Azrael nearly tripped over something large lying across his path. He glanced down and then was instantly kneeling beside Michael's unconscious form.

On the outside, there seemed to be nothing wrong with the former Warrior Archangel. However, the bluish tint to his lips and to the skin around his eyes told Azrael everything he needed to know. The black dragon had pumped air into Michael's veins. The amount of air the dragon poison created when they attacked was enormous and it spread with incredible speed. It was the one attack Michael would not have had time to heal before it caused an air embolism of massive proportions and took him out.

Az listened in the stillness, straining to catch the faintest hint of sound from his brother's chest.

It wasn't there.

Azrael's mind reeled at the implication, but without giving it more than a furious, passing thought, he lifted his brother's body, bared his fangs, and sank his teeth into Michael's throat.

It was the only thing he knew to do. Samael wanted Azrael to take Michael's blood? He wanted him to take Michael's healing power with it?

*Fine.*

In this case, it was an act that would not only fulfill Azrael's infernal contract with the Fallen One – it might save Michael's life. For if Az could take Michael's healing ability into himself, he would then be able to *use* that ability.

And he would use it on Michael.

Az felt his wings fold in behind him as he drank, a part of him that had always been there, hidden and out of reach, but that felt now as if it never been gone. Michael's blood poured over his tongue, rushed down his throat, and filled his body with a healing warmth. The vampire in him was immune to the otherwise dangerous bubbles of air the dragon had injected into it.

All Azrael noticed was the blood.

Behind his closed lids, he saw the world as it had been two thousand years ago. He recalled the scent of it, the sound of it, the feel of Michael once again trapped beneath his desperate teeth.

He swallowed. But this was different. This time, it wasn't for himself that he drank.

He swallowed again, concentrating.

*Forgive me, Michael,* his mind whispered. And he took his brother's power as his own. Az felt it slide across his muscles, infusing his body on a cellular level. He drank until he felt it click into place, steady and solid and non-refundable.

Then he pulled his fangs from Michael's neck and laid the Warrior Archangel back on the shadowed ground. He pressed his right hand to his brother's chest, closed his glowing golden eyes, and imagined Michael's heart beating once more. He imagined the air removed from his veins. He wished it with all of his being.

Seconds passed. Azrael tried not to despair. He willed the magic he'd stolen back into the form from which it had come. Little by little, the healing power moved from his glowing hand to Michael's chest, to his limbs – and, finally, to his heart.

Azrael heard the first telling beat of Michael's heart and opened his eyes. The second was stronger.

'Michael,' Az whispered, moving his hand to cup his brother's face.

Michael opened his eyes, blue glowing orbs that pierced the darkness like a sapphire promise. 'Az,' he said, and then could say no more. Azrael had taken a lot of his blood; the archangel was weak.

Azrael leaned over, gathered Michael's heavy frame into his arms, and stood in one fluid motion.

In his tight embrace, Michael closed his eyes. *Show-off*, he whispered into Azrael's mind.

Az ignored him, turning at once back to the shadows. *Guide me*, he called out, knowing that without some kind of miracle, he would never be able to catch Sophie's trail again. Too much time had gone by; Abraxos had passed through too long ago. *Take me to her*, he whispered into the darkness. With the command, he sent out tendrils of his power, allowing it to wrap around the shades of night, pour through them, bring them to life. He coaxed the blackness in ways he never had before. He'd never been this desperate.

*This way . . .*

Azrael followed the lead, clinging to the trail of helpful magic as if it were a lifeline. His body blurred in the darkness, moving with impossible speed despite his burden. After a few seconds, the shadows lifted away and Azrael felt them thinning. There was a light beyond the final barrier, indicating that this was where the path ended.

Sophie was on the other side of that shadowy door.

Sophie watched Gregori retreat. As he moved away from them, his form faded into the white of the marble room until it vanished altogether, leaving her alone with John Smith, the two strange men in the gem-encrusted leather jackets, and the man he called Abraxos, the man who had brought her here. She looked at Smith and the two strangers and felt the weight of what Gregori had just said settle in around her shoulders. He'd not only condemned her to death, but had given her away to her captor as if she were no more than a piece of meat.

'You're close,' said the man behind her.

Sophie spun to face him. As she did so, her wings pulled in around her without her having to think about it.

*Too bad I'm about to die*, she thought haplessly. *I could have gotten used to these.*

'You don't have to die, Sophie,' said Abraxos through perfect, long white fangs.

*I was right*, Sophie thought. *He's a vampire.* She glanced at the windows and the ever-threatening sunrise beyond them. Abraxos was a vampire and vampires couldn't take sunlight. *Just rise already!* she thought desperately. Time moved more slowly here. The sunrise seemed to be taking forever. But if the sun did come up, she might stand a chance.

Sophie stood her ground and stared up at him, finally able to get a good look at her abductor now that she was facing him head-on. He was a very handsome man with a strong chin and nose. He was tall and broad, though not as tall as

Gregori. Height seemed to be related somehow to seniority or rank in the paranormal world. It was something Sophie was learning, along with a whole hell of a lot of other things.

Abraxos's eyes were very, very blue and offset the dark blue highlights in his short black hair. At their centers were pupils that glowed an eerie red. Those were the shapes of stars, like Gregori's.

Sophie swallowed hard, and not knowing what to say, she said nothing.

Abraxos smiled a smile both friendly and cruel and shook his head. 'But I doubt you'll choose to forsake Azrael and swear to supply me with your healing blood forever at this point,' he said, almost chuckling. 'So maybe I was wrong. Maybe you do have to die.'

Sophie took an automatic step back, her mind at once going numb and trying to think of a thousand things. There was nothing she could do in this room. Nowhere she could go. And with that thought, she turned, her body instinctively making a dive for the nearest window. But her arm was wrenched in its socket as she was pulled to a rough stop, no closer to the window than before.

Her hair fanned out around her as Abraxos spun her around; she felt her wings expand, catching at the wind to slow her down. And then she was staring up into a red-eyed, fang-filled face and watching it descend toward her with deadly purpose.

She closed her eyes and reached out with her power, frantically grabbing for the only objects in the room – the support columns of marble that stood several feet away. If she was going down, she was going to take everyone in the room with her.

She heard one of them crack, a sick, ominous sound that echoed throughout the chamber like the harbinger of lightning, and then she felt Abraxos's fingers being wrenched from her upper arm.

They clung to her flesh, leaving bruises as they were ripped away, and Sophie's eyes flew open in time to see Abraxos go flying backward across the room. A second later, he slammed into the same support column Sophie had been trying to bring down. Its hairline fracture split wide open and raced up the length of the marble, sending debris skittering to the polished floor.

'Sophie!' Azrael turned toward her, his gold eyes taking her in, the expression on his handsome face melting into one of stark, fierce relief.

Sophie felt breathless; she couldn't believe he was there. His black clothing was torn and in places scorched. Dark liquid stained it here and there; she knew it was blood. At his back folded a massive set of jet-black wings, glorious and beautiful.

They took her breath away.

But there was no time.

Behind him and against the wall, his brother Michael leaned heavily. There were dual puncture wounds in the archangel's neck.

Sophie had no time to ask any questions before Azrael was shoving her none too gently to the side as he was attacked by the man in the emerald-encrusted leather jacket. Sophie hit the wall, but her large golden wings cushioned her impact. Her hair fell into her face and she hurriedly brushed it aside as she tried to keep track of the bodies blurring into motion before her.

The second leather-and-gem-clad man had gone for Michael. With the way the Warrior Archangel had been leaning heavily against the wall, Sophie wouldn't have thought him capable of fighting. But perhaps that was something the Warrior Archangel was *always* prepared to do, for now the two were literally neck and neck, their fingers wrapped around each other's throat.

Michael's eyes glowed a bright, fierce blue. And so did his attacker's.

*Well, there's the supernatural vividness they'd been missing before*, Sophie thought. She wondered what the hell the man was.

And then he gained the upper hand, slamming Michael's body back against one of the marble walls. He smiled, exposing two rows of nothing but sharp teeth and a tongue that whisked out like a snake's sniffing at the air.

Sophie felt her eyes widen. *What the hell?*

She turned back to the blurring bodies that were Azrael and his own opponents. Both the leather-jacket-clad man and Abraxos were struggling with him. She still couldn't make heads or tails of what they were doing; Az simply moved too fast for her to follow. But the figures in black slammed into one wall after another, and at one point, they struck the same already weakened support column, sending more shards of marble and sand to the floor.

Across the room, John Smith stood as still and calm as ever, his blue gaze resting steadily on Sophie. It gave her pause. She straightened, folding her wings in behind her.

*Can you hear me?* She sent the call out through her mind.

Across the room, Smith nodded coolly.

Sophie took a shaky breath. *Why are you still here? What*

*do you want?* Why hadn't Smith left with his employer?

*Someone has to remain behind to make certain that the job is done,* he told her easily.

A hard chill raced up Sophie's spine and down her arms. She had a very distinct feeling that John Smith himself never took part in any of the killing that went on under his employer's rule. So, he had stayed behind as no more than an informant. He would observe, see that either Azrael or Sophie was killed – or both – and then return to report to his employer.

It was a cold and creepy thing to realize. It was apathy at its finest.

Sophie jumped back and gave a short cry of surprise when a heavy body hit the ground in front of her. Her wings ruffled behind her, her hand over her mouth as she looked closely enough to see that it was the man with the emerald-encrusted leather jacket. His throat was torn open.

Up above, two black-clad bodies still whirled in restless motion: Abraxos and Azrael. Sophie's stomach did a flip-flop of both worry and hope. She looked over at where Michael struggled with his own attacker to find that the Warrior Archangel had, against all odds, gained the upper hand. She watched as he delivered a series of incredibly hard punches to his opponent, and then a kick to the chest that sent the man flying across the room to land half in and half out of one of the eight windows.

As his upper body breached the barrier, the window's magic sizzled and flashed, and then went out. The man lay still, obviously either unconscious or dead. At once, a hard chill began to seep into the room, let in by the destruction of the magical shield that had been keeping it at bay.

Beyond the white horizon, the sun's first rays finally crept over the mountains, setting the land awash in a diamond shimmer of light. Sophie was struck with the beauty – and a nagging sense that she was forgetting something important – but was torn from the image by the roar of pain that suddenly sounded above her.

She looked up as Abraxos shoved himself off one end of the dome ceiling above. A beam of sunlight lit up that side of the room, causing the embedded minerals in the marble to glitter like pixie dust. Sophie blinked as she watched him move, now slower than before. He left a trail of smoke as he once more lunged for Azrael, who was still hovering at the darker end of the room as if held there by invisible wires.

Azrael was ready for him. The two strong bodies slammed into one another, spun, and Az once more had him on the defensive. For a moment, their movements again became impossible to track, but she heard the hard thud of flesh on flesh, and then a growl of anger.

It wasn't Azrael's anger; his voice was so distinctive, she would recognize it in any form, at any time. A few more seconds passed, and the two separated, this time as Abraxos went falling toward the ground.

Sophie watched him hit the marble floor, bounce and roll, and land with the left side of his body in another beam of light. At once, he was hissing and pulling away from the damaging ray of sun.

He came to his feet with fluid grace, like a moving body of water – and then turned and pinned Sophie with glowing blue eyes that flickered like fire in their centers. A hard beat passed between them. The room seemed to have frozen.

And then Sophie was thinking fast and stepping into the

beam of light that lit up the space beside her. The sun washed over her, drenching her in its protective warmth.

It was hard to see through that light, but she retained enough of her vision to watch as Azrael gracefully lowered himself to the floor several feet from Abraxos, his gaze steadily on his enemy. Abraxos looked from Sophie to Az to the rising sun beyond the windows.

The silence stretched.

And then finally, Abraxos turned to look at John Smith. Another telling beat passed between them – and Smith nodded.

With that, the enigmatic assistant raised his right hand, revealing on its palm a black dandelion-like star exactly like the one Sophie had possessed on her own hand only hours before. The darkness spread, warped, and before Sophie's eyes, a cord of black magic passed between Smith and Abraxos, growing to envelop them both. Within seconds, they had disappeared into the wrapping cocoons of darkness. Then the darkness itself shrank until its final tendrils of black writhed like the tails of a whip and went out altogether.

Abraxos and Smith were gone.

# Chapter 36

The octagonal marble room was filled with an odd silence. The only sounds were the hard breathing of both Michael and Azrael and the morning wind that whistled through the broken magical window.

Azrael stood frozen to the spot, his wide-eyed gaze glued to Sophie where she stood in the ray of sunshine coming through the window.

She was the most astonishingly beautiful thing he had ever beheld. No painting could have done her justice. Her golden hair shimmered beneath the touch of the morning star, her wings glowed with a soft light, fittingly angelic. Her tall, lithe form stood poised and perfect, and her eyes . . . they settled upon him, open and honest and innocent, and they took his breath away.

The windows all around the oddly shaped room were letting light in now. Dangerous beams began to slide in from all directions, lighting up the dust motes in the air. On the windowpane, the sapphires of the blue dragon's jacket reflected the light a million different ways, refracting blue-tinted rainbows like prisms. On the floor, the emeralds of the green dragon's jacket did the same. Little by little, the room was filling with different forms of brightness.

There were no shadows here. There was no escape outside

the windows; day had broken. There were no doors through which to call up a portal.

Azrael stood at the center of it all, his tall form monopolizing all that was left of the darkness. He knew it wouldn't last. And if he had to die, there was something he wanted to be doing when it happened.

'Sophie,' he breathed.

Against one wall, Michael straightened. Azrael could feel his brother watching him, but would not meet his gaze. Nothing could make him take his eyes off of his archess in that moment.

Across the brightening expanse between them, Sophie came toward him. She glanced at the windows and the small circle of darkness within which he stood, and full comprehension darkened her lovely features.

She passed from sunbeam to sunbeam, and as she did, he caught the shimmer of the single tear on her right cheek.

And then she was in his arms, and Azrael was closing his eyes. She was warm — *so warm*. The sun had heated her body, infused her skin with life. He felt its glow beneath his touch, basked in the waves of sunshine her closeness transferred to him. His hand brushed tenderly, slowly, along her hair to the tops of her glorious wings.

'So soft,' he murmured, his heart aching uncontrollably. 'So warm.'

'Az,' came a male voice from far away. Azrael ignored it. He barely heard it. Sophie was his dream come true; he could feel the sun in her hair, on the down of her satiny feathers. For thousands of years, he had yearned for this. He'd longed for it with every fiber of his being. It was a madness of a dream, so clear and pure, so unattainable – until now. It was a dream worth dying for.

'Az.' The voice again. His subconscious vaguely recognized it as Michael. Again, he ignored it.

Sophie shuddered in his arms, a sob wracking her entire body. Azrael leaned over, his eyes still closed, and placed a kiss upon her head. *Sunshine*, he thought, concentrating hard to make certain she heard it. *My sunshine*.

She was so warm. It was as if she were wrapped in the sun. It was radiating off her now, enveloping him in its heat. In fact, it felt nearly *too* warm, almost hot.

A thrum of terrible warning rushed through him. It hurt. Deep down inside, it hurt almost as much as he knew dying would.

*No*, he thought desperately. It was happening already. The sun must have found him. It would kill him now. He would burn beneath its deadly rays, and if he didn't let Sophie go, he would wind up hurting her in the process.

His hands automatically clutched at her tighter. He would have given anything in that moment to be able to hold her while he lost his life. But it wasn't meant to be. And he loved her too much.

With the first tears he had ever shed leaving his eyes and streaming down his cheeks, Azrael, the Angel of Death, slowly pulled away from his archess and let her go.

'Az!' Sophie cried. Tears strained her voice, but her breathless tone was one of stark shock.

Azrael's eyes flew open at the sound. He looked down at her, the sun glinting off her wet cheeks and the honey in her eyes, the edges of her wings glowing as if they were lit from within, and once again he lost his breath.

But then he noticed that she was looking at him in the same way.

'Az, the *sun* . . .' Sophie breathed, her gaze skirting from his neck to his shoulders and to what he could only imagine were the massive black and gold wings at his back. He looked down at the places her eyes had touched him.

The sun was touching him as well.

Azrael blinked. His chest froze in mid-breath, his eyes widened. The sun had completely taken over the white marble room; not a space of the chamber remained in darkness, including the very spot in which he stood.

Bright yellow-white light wrapped around him, showing him the black of his clothing in a way he'd nearly forgotten it could appear. He turned his hands over and watched in mute fascination as sunbeams illuminated the tiny, thin hairs on the backs of his hands and the undersides of his short fingernails. He watched as it radiated off the multiple jackets he wore and touched lovingly upon the exposed skin of his throat.

And face.

'It isn't hurting you,' Sophie said, her entire body radiating the awe that she expressed with her words. She reached out and took his hands in hers, turning them over herself in fascination. She then dropped his hands and ran her fingers over his chest, then cupped his neck. She leaned into him, running her fingertips through the raven locks of his hair. He could feel the sun's warmth there as well, and he imagined that she did too. The size of her eyes said it all.

'Az . . . How?' she asked.

It took a moment for Azrael to find his breath. And then another for him to find the voice that went with it. He couldn't believe what he was feeling . . . what he was seeing. A part of him wondered if he'd actually died there in that room and this was some sort of reward left for him by the Old Man. The sun, the warmth, Sophie's fingers running through his hair . . .

But the rest of him knew it was real. And that he was very much alive.

'*You*, Sophie,' he whispered, shaking his head in wonder. At the moment, it was all he could manage. 'It's because of *you.*'

He was moving then, cupping her face with his hands and pulling her in for a kiss. Her lips were as soft as the rest of her, warm and yielding and sweet with the taste of promise. Azrael parted them and she melted beneath him, curling into him with abandon. All around him, the sun's heat caressed and welcomed. His heart hammered as if it would break free of his chest and fly with wings of its own.

He was happy.

For the first time in his life, he was happy.

Slowly, Sophie broke their kiss and pulled away. Her smile beamed up at him as brightly as the rays of the sun touching it, and as Azrael gazed down at her, he realized that he was smiling just as brightly.

Movement to his right drew his attention to his brother, who stood several feet away. Michael's cheeks were wet, and when Az tried to meet his gaze, the Warrior Archangel smiled an embarrassed, lopsided smile and briefly looked away to dry his tears on his sleeve.

'Welcome back, man,' he said softly.

And then Michael laughed, and Azrael couldn't help but join him.

\* \* \*

They took the dragons' jackets with them when they left the strange marble chamber in the glaciers of the Arctic. It wasn't as if the archangels needed the gems; it was that the jackets were the dragons' hoards, and they were irreplaceable in that respect.

They returned to the mansion, much to the vast relief of everyone inside. When Max, Gabriel, and Uriel saw Azrael step through the bright, sunlit foyer rather than returning to his chamber belowground, they were understandably stunned into silence.

The celebratory tears and hugs soon followed.

Juliette made a big deal about Sophie's wings, and Sophie could only grin with glee. Eleanore laughed good-naturedly when Sophie accidentally knocked one of the side tables over with them. Both archesses assured her that they took some getting used to and that they'd be happy to help her learn to control them.

That Sophie had turned out to be an archess was mind-blowing enough for her. That she would be able to remain with her best friend and join what she was fast beginning to think of as her family was more good fortune than she felt she deserved.

*You deserve it, Sunshine*. Az's voice caressed her mind. She looked up at him, as always caught in the pull of his beauty. *You earned it*.

There were important things to discuss and the threat of danger was by no means eliminated, but at Gabriel's brogue-thickened insistence, drinks were passed around and welcome toasts were made. No one minded. The 'archangel family,' as Sophie had secretly named them, was worn out, both emotionally and physically. They'd come up against so much in the last few months. So much had happened – so very much had changed. Everyone welcomed the brief respite that their togetherness and a few good beers could bring.

As the hours wore on, the subject of conversation returned to the dangers of what had transpired over the last few days, from the accident on the bridge to the phantoms, dragons, and wraiths to the fact that Az had signed a contract with Samael to the enigmatic Gregori and his dandelion-star eyes.

It was all taken in stride.

Sophie was told by the archangel brothers that they were very lucky neither of the dragons in Gregori's marble room had changed into their true forms during the fights, or Az and Michael might not have gained the upper hand. When she asked why they hadn't done so, Az and Michael smiled.

'Not enough room,' Michael told her. Apparently, a dragon's true size was immense, and the dragons would have been squished inside the marble cage of Gregori's magical chamber.

This, however, made Sophie wonder why Gregori would post dragons there with him rather than phantoms or wraiths or any of the other supernatural baddies that the archangels had come across. When she mentioned it, Max admitted that he had been wondering the same.

'Perhaps he meant to let you go,' he ventured carefully.

Sophie considered that. 'That makes sense, actually,' she said. When Max asked her to explain, she told them about her brief conversation with Gregori, about his lost love, his need for vengeance and, eventually, his willingness to forgive Azrael – but not the Old Man. She told them about what Gregori had called the 'Culmination,' and how he was certain the Old Man was no longer in the angel realm. And finally, she told them about the Old Man's archess.

A long, pregnant silence followed this news. Everyone looked at each other, their eyes wide, their faces somewhat pale.

'The Old Man has an archess of his own?' asked Eleanore softly.

'A *fifth* archess?' echoed Juliette.

Another silence followed that until finally Gabriel sighed heavily, blew a bit of a raspberry, and downed half of his beer. 'This is bloody confusing.'

Juliette patted him on his well-muscled thigh, and he gave her a wink.

Max seemed to mull everything over quietly.

Michael spoke up. 'Sophie's right about Gregori. I think he wanted us to win. Those dragons were not even close to the toughest they had to offer.'

Sophie's brow rose. *They weren't?*

*There is always another who is stronger*, said Azrael, again speaking in her mind. *But these were strong enough. And Michael is angry with himself for not finishing his opponent faster.*

'Even the black dragons were weak compared to most of their kind,' Michael admitted. 'It shouldn't have taken us so long to defeat them.' His words confirmed what Azrael had just told Sophie. He was pissed at himself.

'In the shadows, they surprised us,' said Azrael. There was nothing Michael could have done against an attack of that nature. 'And when you faced the green dragon, you were severely injured.'

Sophie looked at him and then at Michael. Two of the most powerful men on Earth had nearly been taken out in that marble chamber. Michael had been beat to shit by the time he'd arrived in the white room: Michael was the W*arrior* Archangel, and yet he'd barely won. These dragons were scary.

'I thought you were near death when you arrived,' she said out loud, talking to Michael now. He turned his sapphire eyes on her and cocked his head slightly to one side, giving her his full attention. 'But you defeated the dragon anyway.' She was impressed. There was a strength to Michael that she was pretty sure she normally missed because she was too busy being impressed by Azrael.

There was a soft chuckle in her mind, and a shiver rushed down her spine. She glanced at Az, caught his smile, and then went on before he could deter her further.

'Most of the time, tough guys play *up* their opponents after a fight,' she told Michael. 'But not you. You almost get your ass handed to you and then admit that you were fighting a wimp to boot.' She smiled and Michael threw back his head and laughed.

Sophie knew now that Azrael had taken Michael's blood in order to heal him. Michael had gone into the fight already weakened from all the people he'd had to heal over the last few days and from the poison the blue dragon had injected into him. That he had been able to fight at all was proof that he lived up to his reputation as the warrior among archangels.

She also knew that because Az had signed a contract with Samael, the Fallen One's magic had something to do with the fact that Michael's healing powers had yet to return to him.

Sophie looked at Michael now, took in the darkness beneath his blue eyes, and the somewhat tired bent to his tall, strong frame, and she knew in her heart that Michael had mixed feelings about this. The man didn't trust Samael at all and he was clearly disappointed that Az had made a deal with the Fallen One. But he was trying hard not to judge. After all, he probably would have done the same thing in the same situation. Honor was one thing, but nothing was more important than family, and archesses were family. He also knew that if Az hadn't taken his blood and healing power, and turned around and used it on him, he would be dead right now. That made it a hell of a lot easier to forgive Az.

'So this Gregori guy is after the Old Man,' said Eleanore softly, once everyone had stopped chuckling along with Michael. 'And he says that the Old Man is not where he usually is?'

Sophie nodded.

'So where *is* he?' asked Uriel.

'That seems to be the question of the hour,' said Max. His expression was contemplative, his gaze on something in the carpet, his thoughts obviously turned inward. After a few seconds, he looked back up. 'There's also the Adarians to consider. From what you've told me, Azrael, it would seem Abraxos is working without his brothers now, and more surprisingly – and *importantly* – working for Gregori.'

'He had no heartbeat,' Az told them. 'There was a stillness to him that I noticed while we were fighting.' He paused, frowned, and then said, 'I think he's dead. In the truest sense of the word.'

'But he couldn't stand to be in the light,' Sophie said, recalling how Abraxos had been forced to recoil from the sun's rays. 'Like a vampire.'

'*I'm* still a vampire,' said Azrael, smiling to show her his fangs. A warmth coiled low in Sophie's stomach, spreading quickly to her core. She swallowed and looked away to hide her blush. No one was fooled. 'And yet I can walk in the day,' Az went on, doing a much better job at hiding his own smile. 'Thanks to you,' he added meaningfully. 'Things can clearly change in some ways – and yet clearly stay the same in others.'

'So he's a reanimated vampire,' suggested Max. No one said anything to the contrary, so he took a short breath and asked, 'Then who killed him in the first place?'

'Gregori?' Juliette suggested.

'But he was alone,' said Sophie. 'Does that mean Gregori killed all of the Adarians?'

'Either that,' Michael ventured, his face taking on the expression of a seasoned detective, 'or the other Adarians killed Abraxos. And Gregori brought him back.'

That gave everyone pause. It was a possibility, just as everything else was.

'Well, we clearly have a lot to think about,' said Max. 'And in the meantime, *you*,' he said, looking at Azrael, 'have a concert to give.' He turned to Uriel next. 'And you have the last scenes of a movie to film.' He stood up, setting his empty beer mug on the coffee table and running a hand through his brown hair. 'I've got enough to straighten out these days without having to fool hundreds of thousands of people into believing Valley of Shadow isn't on tour and the *Comeuppance* sequel was supposed to come out a month later than it actually was.'

'And I have a criminal to catch,' Michael added, standing up as well.

*Sophie*, came Azrael's voice in Sophie's head. She turned to look at him. His gold eyes were glowing. *Marry me.*

Sophie went still. Her breath hitched, her jaw went slack. The room fell into silence. She could feel everyone's eyes on her and Azrael . . . as if they'd heard what he had just thought. She wasn't even certain *she* had heard it correctly.

But he smiled, again flashing the faintest hint of fang.

*Marry me, Sunshine.*

He slowly stood up, all fluid grace and darkness, and Sophie's heart danced in her chest. Amid the rapt attention of the room and the unmoving universe, Azrael bent over the love seat where she sat, bracing his hands on either side of her to lean in until they were inches apart.

*Marry me and I'll only bite you once.* His eyes glittered intensely, his smile thoroughly promising.

Sophie felt her entire body flush with heat and anticipation. *Liar*, she said.

Azrael's deep, dark chuckle echoed through her mind. *Is that a yes?* he pushed.

Sophie waited a beat. Then another.

*Yes.*

# Chapter 37

'Is it like you imagined?' Sophie asked, leaning over to whisper the words in her lover's ear.

Azrael's gaze remained locked on the spinning carousel, his smile one of peaceful bliss. He shook his head distractedly and gave her hand a squeeze. 'No,' he said. 'It's better.'

He reminded her of a child in that moment, held rapt by the eye candy he'd dreamed about for oh, give or take forty years – as long as the carousel had been open. The carousel on Pier 39 turned and turned, a whirlwind of color and sound as children waved for cameras and mothers held toddlers tightly in their painted saddles. All around them, tourists and shopkeepers traded their services and money, and the smell of sourdough bread and fresh-cooked waffle cones pervaded the air.

Sea-gulls cried overhead, swooping over the crowd. Out on the bay, a tug-boat sounded its horn. A group of teenagers rushed past them, giggling about something one of them had done the night before. A father turned around and pulled his four- or five-year-old son closer and reminded him not to stray.

Sophie and Azrael had walked the circumference of the seaside tourist attraction several times that morning. Az hadn't gotten tired of the morning sounds, the feel of the sun on his face, or the way the seagulls and pigeons acted differently when vying for food in the mornings than they did at night. They were hungrier now. Sophie enjoyed watching Azrael smile as he fed them almost more than she enjoyed watching them eat.

In front of Pier 40, tourists lined up for Blue and Gold Fleet ferry rides out to Alcatraz Island and the Golden Gate Bridge. As the line grew, those waiting shifted their weight from one foot to the other, clearly weary of standing but humming with excitement for what they were about to do. The kite shop nearby buzzed with color as the sea breeze brought its displays to a rainbow of whirling, spinning life.

On the south side of the pier, the sea lions slid heavily off of the wooden rafts set up for them and then expertly climbed back up. They barked at the tourists, slapped their bodies with slick black flippers, and yawned lazily as they squeezed in for a midmorning nap.

It was just past noon and a band was setting up in front of the Hard Rock Cafe at the opening to Pier 39. While Azrael watched the carousel, Sophie watched the lead singer test out the microphone, switching wires and adjusting the stand. She recalled the bands she and her parents had caught here when she was a little girl. Thinking of them now, she turned to look at the man beside her, probably the single best lead singer on the planet. No one knew who he was here. Onstage, he always wore a mask, just as he'd done for the wildly successful concert he and his band mates had given two days earlier.

No one recognized him, though Sophie had to admit to her slightly jealous self that quite a few women – and men – stopped to ogle him when they thought no one was looking.

She couldn't really blame them. He was gorgeous. If she hadn't been who she was and hadn't known *him* for who *he* was, she would have wondered whether the tall, beautiful, and built man watching the carousel was a famous actor on holiday, hiding out from his adoring fans. Or maybe a model.

At the very least.

And because he was out during the day, she would have had to disappointingly toss out any fantasies of him being a vampire.

Which made her laugh. Because that was exactly what he was. At the least.

Azrael turned to look at her then, his smile turning slightly mischievous. 'You have a dizzyingly busy mind, Sunshine,' he told her softly, his deep voice wrapping around her. 'But I like it that you get jealous.' His smile cracked into a grin, and she caught the hint of fangs.

Sophie rolled her eyes and punched him gently in the arm. It was like punching a tree trunk in a leather jacket. She winced and gave her hand a small shake and Azrael took the hand in both of his to lay a tender kiss upon her knuckles.

'What's next?' he asked then.

Sophie's mind must have been in the gutter, because all she could think of for a moment was taking him back to the mansion and ravishing him – and having him ravish her.

But she did actually have things planned for the day. She'd gone out of her way to make up a list of attractions she wanted to show him in the light of the sun. There was so much she wanted him to see . . . Pier 39 was just the beginning.

So she swallowed hard, cleared her throat, and said, 'I was thinking we'd cross that bridge,' pointing in the general direction of the Golden Gate Bridge. Az had only ever seen it at night. It wasn't orange at night. He'd always missed the very best part of it.

'Sounds good,' Az said, smiling broadly. There was a sparkle in his eye that made Sophie both nervous and excited. He leaned in a little. 'Go on.'

Sophie's gaze flicked from his eyes to his mouth, where she knew his fangs were hiding. She licked her lips. 'Um . . . Well, depending on how long it takes us to cross it both ways, I was thinking that we'd go to Golden Gate Park. I mean, I know you've always been able to go through the park whenever you wanted, but it's pretty impressive in the sunlight.'

Azrael's smile deepened, and something dark flashed behind his eyes. 'Okay,' he said, leaning in a little more. 'And after that?'

'We'll probably be starving,' Sophie ventured, her heart rate picking up. 'So we'll need to eat. Or at least I will.' As she said it, she thought of what exactly it was that Azrael would 'eat.' Lately, his diet had consisted mostly of *her*.

'I imagine you're probably right,' he agreed too easily. His gaze slid from her eyes to her lips to her throat and the top button of her long-sleeved Henley shirt. She looked down, as if to see what he was looking at. But then she closed her eyes as he curled his finger beneath her chin to pull it back up and brushed his thumb across her cheekbone.

'Or . . .' she began, but had to stop when his thumb dropped to the pulse in her throat. She took a shaky breath and started again. 'Or we could eat now instead. We could use the energy to get across the bridge,' she finished in a rush. She opened her eyes.

Azrael cracked a grin, exposing the fully lengthened fangs that had been lying in wait behind his lips. 'Now *that* sounds like a plan.'

The name of the boat was the *Sand Dollar Angel*. She was another cutter ketch, with two masts and four sails, and this morning, the pristine sailing ship was outfitted with silk streamers and wedding bells.

Michael adjusted his collar and took in the scene. The sun had yet to come up. Twilight smoothed out the surface of the water, giving it an airbrushed quality. The *Angel*, as Michael called the boat for short, was anchored nowhere near any bridge of any kind, as neither Azrael nor Sophie wished a repeat of what had happened with the *Calliope*.

The ceremony would take place at dawn. Michael and his brothers had always assumed that when Azrael found his archess, the two would be married at night and he would be surrounded not only by his brothers but by the vampires who loved him as well.

But fortune had turned a page on Azrael's life. Because of Sophie's love, not only was the sun no longer a problem for him, it was no longer a problem for *any* of the other vampires who had been turned under his sovereignty.

The members of Azrael's band were there on the boat, each of them wearing dark sunglasses and dressed in varying degrees of dark shades. It was fortunate for them that the area had been blocked off for the private event, or Valley of Shadow fans would have been swarming the docks to get a look at them.

Randall McFarlan now stood in a group on the dock with Terrence Colby and Casper MonteVega. The vampires wore dark suits, as was customary, but was also most likely as they preferred. Michael had noticed that despite Azrael's immunity to the sun and his reduced need to feed, nearly everything else about his vampirism remained the same. He still loved black, he still preferred the night. He possessed all the strengths and powers of a vampire but now he suffered from almost none of the weaknesses. If Azrael had been formidable before, now he was nearly unbeatable.

It was a good thing, not just for him, but for Sophie. The young archess now not only had the *protection* of Azrael's vampires during the day as well as the night, but she also had their *gratitude*. In becoming vampires, they had all lost something very precious, and Sophie Bryce had given it back to them.

There were issues the four brothers had yet to contend with. Gregori was out there and none of them could tell what exactly he had planned for them. The consensus was that Michael's archess would most likely be in great danger, since stopping their mating would stop the 'Culmination.'

There was also a general awakening of the supernatural world to come to grips with. Monsters of all kinds were coming out of hiding. The world was reverting to what it had been thousands of years ago, and the human race was as unsuspecting and ignorant as ever.

These creatures were on the offensive, and controlling them would most likely call for everything the archangels could throw at them. Dragons were not normally dangerous on their own; they were not inherently evil, just as Nightmares were not. However, dragons that worked for fallen angels were another matter. And rogue Nightmares bent on seducing their way across an army of innocent women were no small problem either. Michael and his brothers had their work cut out for them.

And then there was Samael to consider. The Fallen One's deal with Azrael had taken Michael's power – a power that Michael had yet to regain. Michael knew that this wasn't normal. He knew that were it not for Samael's infernal, blood-signed contract, his healing ability would have returned to him days ago. Samael was keeping it from him somehow; it was yet another magical ability belonging to the Fallen One that Michael and his brothers could not comprehend. Sam was just too powerful.

And enigmatic. For instance, what in the world had Samael meant when he'd told Azrael to convey to Michael that if he wanted to find the rapist in New York, he should 'take a walk in the park'?

Michael could only sigh heavily and shake his head. He had no idea. But he imagined he would soon find out.

However, for now . . . At this *very* moment . . . The sun was coming up over San Francisco Bay. Across the vast expanse of blue, the first rays of the massive star began to creep over the water. The priest at the prow of the boat glanced over his shoulder, caught the glint of light on the waves, and turned back to face the bride and groom. The father was smiling; he was another of Azrael's vampire creations. He hadn't acted as a priest for a hundred years, but what he had once been was good enough for Az and Sophie, who smiled back at him now.

The ceremony began.

As the newlyweds exchanged rings and vows and then leaned in for their kiss, Uro pulled a guitar out of a case behind him and began to strum. To the sound of 'Hallelujah,'

Michael and the rest of the wedding party – the priest, Gabriel, Uriel, Max, Eleanore, Juliette, Devran, Mikhail, and Rurik – disembarked, leaving only Uro, Azrael, and Sophie on the boat.

Sophie and Az continued to kiss. Uro continued to play. On the pier, Gabriel unknotted the ropes that moored the *Angel*, and the sails unfurled on their own. The wind caught them, stretched them taut, and those still on the docks waved, though the new husband and wife aboard the boat were unaware, as they were still kissing.

The ship sailed slowly from the dock, heading straight for the rising sun.

Beside Michael on the pier, Randall McFarlan took a deep breath and let it out in a sigh. Michael watched as the retired cop took off his sunglasses, closed his eyes, and turned his face up to the sun. Monte patted him on the shoulder in solidarity, the same knowing smile on his own face.

'Beautiful day,' said Uriel beside Michael.

Michael turned to regard his brother.

Uriel's green eyes were vivid in the morning light.

'Indeed it is,' agreed Michael. 'Indeed it is.'

# Epilogue

Central Park was New York's most obvious park, of course. Sam could have technically been referring to any park in the world, but because Michael lived in New York and because the rapes he had been investigating had occurred here, Michael had a feeling the enigmatic man had meant this one.

It was the first day of May and gardeners were working around the clock to trim hedges, prune trees, and fertilize flowers and grass throughout the park. At this time of the day, late afternoon, there were people everywhere, from families with Frisbees to drunks and drug addicts who were sleeping in the shade and hopefully not dead.

Michael stood on the walkway beside a park bench and slowly scanned the area. A few yards away, a hot-dog stand filled the air with the smell of cooking quasi-meat and mustard. Pigeons pecked at leftover pieces that had been swept off of the main path, and the occasional dog on a leash attempted to chase the birds.

Everything looked normal.

But if the last two thousand years had taught the Warrior Archangel anything, it was that nothing was ever as normal as it looked. And time would always tell.

So it was with well-learned patience and senses on high

alert that the Warrior Archangel and NYPD plainclothes detective sat down on the park bench, reclined against its backrest, and crossed his legs at the ankles.

An hour passed. And another.

A man sat down beside him on the bench and propositioned him. Michael politely declined. A few women smiled at him as they passed by. A group of teenage girls in the green expanse before him tried to get his attention by acting ridiculous. But for the most part, people kept their distance. He gave off a certain vibe – intense, perhaps a bit frightening. Maybe they could tell he was a cop.

Maybe they could sense he was something more.

When night fell on the park, the buzzing overhead lamps popped on one after another, shedding a weak aura onto the walkways beneath them. Bugs swarmed around the bulbs, thickening in numbers as the hours passed. People began clearing out, and the park's 'clientele' changed. Families were nowhere to be seen. Lovers dared to walk closer to one another and some tucked themselves away beneath trees or between bushes.

Bottles of alcohol made their brown-bagged appearances. Lighters flickered in the darkness here and there, and Michael was well aware that not all of them were lighting cigarettes.

The cop in him might have cared – *might* have – but for the fact that walking for generations among humans had given him a very clear understanding of their pain and their need to escape that anguish. It was an intrinsic right of all life to strive to live that life with as little suffering as possible. It was only when the choices that one made brought harm to *another* that his blood heated and he came forward.

Michael frowned as he considered that. It had been countless ages since he'd flown at the head of an angelic army, but the sword he'd once carried had left an imprint in his palm. It was invisible, but it was there, deep and grooved, and it dictated most of the actions he took as a police officer, and as a man. He was a defender – a warrior – that much was true.

But he was also a healer. And at the moment, Azrael was in possession of Michael's magical ability to mend wounds. It hadn't reverted to Michael yet, no doubt as per Samael's underhanded and mysterious machinations. Who knew what the Fallen One was up to? Michael was only painfully aware that a part of him was missing, and he could only pray that he wouldn't need it anytime soon.

Michael took a deep breath, let it out silently, and stood. The path stretched in either direction, more or less the same. He chose a direction and walked, his hands in the pockets of his leather jacket, his eyes and ears open to the world around him.

The night grew darker, the shadows deeper, and the surrounding foliage quieter. Michael's boots beat out a harsh and lonely rhythm in the growing silence. A cool breeze prickled at the back of his neck, and he absentmindedly turned up his collar.

Something beckoned behind him. It was a pull in the air, a shift in sound, and Michael was spinning. But the path was dark and empty. The night breeze gently rocked a branch of an overhanging willow. Nothing else moved.

There was a brief flash of something blue to his right, and again Michael was turning, but once more, nothing out of the ordinary presented itself. The green expanse of lawn that led to a small pond beyond was still. The shadows were stationary and the moon cast a diaphanous glow on a static field.

But something was wrong.

Michael's skin pricked at the rather abrupt change in the night. It was as if it had been waiting to breathe but now inhaled, filling its lungs with the murky electric miasma of magic. He could feel eyes on him. He could almost hear the hiss of released air through sharp teeth. His blood felt as though it bubbled in his veins, reminding him of his battle with the blue dragon two weeks ago.

The wind picked up around him, and out of what had been a clear sky only moments ago, thunder rumbled. Michael looked up to witness the swirling eddies of building clouds, coalescing at their center like a massive cumulus whirlpool. The trees answered the growing wind, bowing in its presence, their leaves quaking and dancing with fervor. A flock of birds erupted from a copse not far away, their black bodies forming a swarm as they left the park and headed for calmer territory.

And then, with such unexpected and violent force that it actually caught the Warrior Archangel off guard, something slammed into him, knocking him to the side. Michael caught a whiff of faint perfume and saw a flash of red as he stumbled slightly, regained his balance, and turned to face what had hit him.

*I was right*, he thought. But it was a fleeting, disturbed, and confused thought. Before him indeed stood a tall man in a black leather jacket that was encrusted with countless sapphires and aquamarines. A blue dragon.

But between the dragon and Michael stood someone else. She was tall and lean, with the build of a woman who trained several hours a day. Her long red hair was filled with waves that made it look as though she'd just come in off the sea. It whipped around her figure in the building gale, the thick carmine locks falling clear to her waist. She was dressed in black jeans, a black T-shirt, and black boots.

He couldn't see her face because her back was turned to him, but her stance was broad and defiant, her arms out at her sides as if she were preparing to cast some sort of sorcery.

Michael was divided among several equally strong and equally distracting reactions. That the woman had shoved him aside as if to protect him from a man she clearly recognized as something *more* than a man was enormously perplexing. How did she know the man in the blue jacket was so dangerous? He wasn't as large as Michael. And Michael was armed – every tall inch of him screamed undercover cop.

And what gave her the impression that she would be more capable of fighting the stranger than Michael would? Who did she think she was?

And that was perhaps the most confounding distraction of all. The issue of who she was.

There was something so fundamentally familiar about the woman, even from behind, that a part of Michael was transfixed by the image of her. It spoke of storms and ancient promises and eons of searching. There was a component of him that *knew* what that thing was – it really did. The knowledge was branded on him. But it would take more time to fully realize that knowledge. And time was something they did not have.

Even as Michael attempted to rush forward, intent on facing off with the dragon himself, the beast struck with the incredible speed of its kind. It was clear at once that the monster's mark had never been Michael; it was the woman all along. The dragon completely ignored the archangel and had yet to even make eye contact with him.

Lightning scorched the ozone nearby, and Michael's progress was roughly halted as he was once more slammed into, this time by a third party. This impact was intended to deal harm, and the brutal force sent the archangel flying back several paces to contact with the pole of a park lamp. The metal bent beneath his body, groaning as it crumpled inward. Overhead, the bulb hissed, flickered, and just before it went out he saw the auburn-haired woman duck beneath an attempted backhand and then jump to kick her dragon opponent squarely in the chest.

The lamp popped and went out, casting the area into darkness as Michael again got to his feet. From this inky black came the sounds of horrible battle, painful impacts, and grunts and hisses of agony. Michael had barely righted himself before whatever hit him before was on him once more.

By the cold of its touch, the sudden frost in the air, and the icy stench of its breath, he labeled it immediately. Phantoms had once been called upon solely by those most powerful in the supernatural community. They were the elite assassins, difficult to come by and almost impossible to pay. Yet they seemed to be coming out of hiding in droves lately, pooling together in impossibly large numbers and working toward a goal as impossibly elusive as the man in charge of them. Gregori.

Was he at the heart of this attack?

As Michael sent the phantom flying with a single strike, he couldn't help but wonder – and if so, were the phantom and dragon working in tandem?

Were they all there for the woman?

A sudden spike of sharp ripping pain in Michael's right shoulder brought his thoughts to an agonizing halt. He looked down to see the claws of a second phantom extending from his chest, the shirt and skin around the open wound crackling to fleshy rime with horrid, unbearable speed. Gritting his teeth with the effort it took not to cry out from the pain, Michael grabbed hold of the appendage and tried to break it clean off. However, the phantom was well ahead of him, switching into incorporeal form before Michael could get a firm grip.

To his left, the night parted and a third phantom made its untimely appearance, creeping ominously closer. As if sensing the coming meal a fourth intruder arrived almost on its tail, skulking near the ground. It slipped from its magic invisibility to a more comfortable, goblin-like appearance. Catlike eyes reflected back at Michael as it slithered toward him. It was an Icaran, a 'leech', no doubt drawn to the scene by all the magic.

If Michael's luck didn't change rapidly, it would get the meal of a lifetime.

Lightning slammed into the ground not fifty yards away, sending a burning, buzzing kind of silence into Michael's ears. His head felt light and puffy in the aftermath of the blast. But the phantom behind him cruelly yanked its claws from his chest, bringing his attention back into sharp focus.

The Icaran in front of him bared his glowing, neon-white teeth, crawling ever hungrily closer as the phantom he'd sent flying picked itself up off the ground and rushed him. The phantom to his left attacked at the same time, and the one behind him grabbed him by the back of the neck, sending a popping, crackling frost down his spine. In the near distance, the woman who had initially attempted to protect him continued to fight her own battle, moving with incredible speed and agility. That she wasn't yet dead was mind-boggling.

And also . . . it wasn't. He understood. Deep down. But if he allowed himself to come to grips with the truth, he would be numb with fear for her – and they would both die.

Instead, Michael allowed his blood to sing an ancient tune. He remembered who he was and where he'd come from. He was the Warrior Archangel. He closed his eyes, allowing this age-old truth to infuse his body like an elixir. When he opened his eyes again, he could feel the heat of their glow. The park spun around him as his body moved of its own accord. He was no longer consciously in charge of his actions, and the world moved out of time and space as it, too, remembered.

Within seconds, two phantoms lay dead, the Icaran had turned invisible in fear once more and had no doubt slunk away, and Michael was facing off against the final phantom as the red-haired woman continued to battle her dragon opponent.

But then the shadows bulged, as if filled to the limit with new inhabitants, and suddenly those inhabitants were pouring into the park, dark shapes closing in with unbelievable malice. Among them were black dragons, at least a handful, sending a rivulet of fear like a hiccup of doubt through the Warrior Archangel's attack.

Michael faltered, missed a block, and felt the return of agony as a second wound was opened in his body, iced at its core, and crackling with a spreading, frozen pain. Yet he tried to keep the dragons in his sights. The dark, dangerous group moved slowly, gauging the scene, their attention clearly focused on the redheaded woman.

He wasted no strength in calling out a warning. Instead he pulled in his power, redirected it once more toward the enemies around him, and let loose with everything he had. Bodies fell at his feet in quick succession. Michael made his way through the opposition like a whirling blade, his movements so fast there could be no conscious thought before them. There wasn't time.

The black dragons had divided and were concentrating on him now, recognizing him for the threat that he was. Michael took them on without pause, without hesitation, and the fearsome beasts went down before him. The night filled with the sounds of combat: bone on flesh, grunts of pain, and the sickening sound of skin tearing. But the noise of the battle had no effect on Michael. Not until he heard the woman scream.

It was a gut-wrenching wail of defeat, hopeless and final. It shattered the night and brought a temporary halt to the turning of Earth. It was the sound a person made before dying.

Electricity split the heavens a final time, striking a nearby tree and rending it in two. Michael didn't know exactly what happened next. Sound left. The world became a buzzing strangeness. Time skipped and life blurred. The woman's attacker stepped from her fallen form and slid back into the shadows, the only remaining enemy yet standing. It escaped, its job done, as Michael made his way with both supernatural speed and horrible, dream-like slowness, to where the woman lay, half on the grass and half on the trail. Her hair spilled across the park walkway like a waterfall of shimmering blood.

Her head was turned away, and for an eternity Michael still couldn't see her face.

And then he was kneeling beside her, taking her chin gently in his hand, and absorbing everything at once.

*Oh God.*

Something had him in its clutches. It was invisible, inaudible, and left no viable trace, but it was as real and as physical as the monsters he'd just battled. It squeezed his chest, crushing his heart in its merciless grip, and sent a torturous frisson of emotion careening through his soul.

She was breathtaking. Her eyes were closed but he knew what they looked like. He knew as if he'd always known. He knew every curve of her delicate features as if he'd drawn them himself. He knew what her voice would sound like should she ever speak his name. And what her touch would do to him.

She looked like an angel.

Because she was one.

She'd been bitten by one of the dragons; there was air in her veins. Her full pink lips darkened to purple before his eyes. Air poisoning was a sensation he was well familiar with. There wasn't much time, and unfortunately the damage of this kind of wound took precious seconds – sometimes minutes – to reverse.

'She needs to be healed.'

Michael tore his eyes from his archess's face to look up. A second woman stood beside him. He hadn't heard her approach and hadn't seen her arrive. But for some reason it wasn't strange that she was there.

She was medium height and had an average build and was dressed in jeans and a Chicago Blackhawks jersey. She had shoulder-length brown hair and brown eyes, and Michael knew at once that it was a disguise. This was not what she really looked like. Something greater, something incredibly different, rested beneath the woman's facade. There was an unseen power wrapped around her that was so great, it actually reminded Michael of Samael.

He didn't ask who she was. At the moment, he barely cared. The entire universe lay at his feet, everything he had ever wanted, dying, and his mind was busy taking in what the stranger had just said. He inwardly recoiled at the word 'heal.' It stabbed through him like an ice lance, sharp and cold.

'I can't,' he whispered. He couldn't heal her. Samael had stolen that ability from him and given it to Azrael. Michael needed a door to transport across vast distances. But he was in the middle of a massive park, nowhere near any doors of any kind. He couldn't reach his brothers or their archesses in time, and even if he phoned them now and any of them picked up, they would still have to travel the same distance. It was too far and time was too short.

What were the chances of that? Why had this happened *here*? Why now, and like this? It was as if he were being punished, as if everything he'd begun to suspect about falling out of the Old Man's favor was true.

'I can't,' he repeated.

'I know,' said the woman. Then she knelt beside him and looked down at Michael's fallen archess. 'But I can.'

Michael froze. Had he heard her right?

She smiled at him. 'Her name is Rhiannon,' she told him.

Then she leaned over, placing her palms on Rhiannon's chest in much the same manner that Michael would have.

Before his eyes, Rhiannon's lips faded to blue.

He didn't have to tell his mysterious companion to hurry. The woman seemed to know the urgency of the situation. The world went still as the stranger closed her eyes and her hands began to glow.

*Rhiannon*, Michael thought. It was a beautiful name, wild and strong and perfect.

He felt the surge of magic leave the woman beside him to enter Rhiannon's form. It was just beginning to repair the damage, doing away with the deadly air in her veins, when suddenly the brown-haired woman stiffened and her eyes flew open.

She dropped her hands, cutting the healing spell short long before it'd had a chance to do its job. Alarm shot through Michael.

'No,' the woman said, shaking her head. Her gaze slid from Rhiannon's still unconscious form to meet Michael's eyes. 'He's coming. He can't find me. I can't stay. I'm so sorry!' She looked desperate, even stricken. And in the next instant, she wavered – and vanished.

Numbly, Michael stared at the space where she'd just been. His body felt as if it wasn't there. Reality was sawing him in half. His very last hope had literally just disappeared. This wasn't happening; agony was filling his world.

He looked down. The blue tint returned to Rhiannon's lips. 'No,' he said, choking on the word. And then, as if to make up for its lack of volume, for its lack of righteous rage, Michael gripped the front of her warm shirt in his fists, threw back his head, and cried out into the night, '*Nooooooo!*'

'Really, Michael,' came a cool, familiar voice from the shadows in front of him. Michael's voice hitched, his body going immobile in trembling disbelief. 'Such drama.'

The Warrior Archangel watched as Samael stepped out of the darkness, tall and calm and dressed as ever in the most exquisitely tailored suit money or magic could buy. His hands were in his pockets, his composure that of a man completely at ease. From behind him stepped Jason, his 'assistant.'

Samael gave him a look that was neither friendly nor un-friendly, and then both he and Jason turned their attention to Rhiannon's prone form.

'You need to heal her soon, Michael, or you'll lose the archess you've been searching centuries for.'

'You son of a bitch,' Michael whispered. 'I will die trying to kill you.'

Sam seemed not to hear him, or perhaps he just didn't care. 'If you hurry, I believe there is a twenty-four-hour X-rated video shop at the end of that walk there. It has a door. I think it's the closest one.' His stormy gaze slid from Rhiannon's face to Michael's and held there. 'At your speed it should only take you a few minutes.'

Beats of silence passed between them. A more pregnant silence had never existed. Michael had never felt more suicidal, and the night had never been so dark.

'Or I could heal her for you,' Sam said.

The shadows perked their ears. The moon turned to listen. The world waited.

Michael straightened, his cheeks wet, his heart bleeding out into his chest. *Please*, he thought wretchedly. 'Do it,' he said, his voice quaking.

Samael's smile was slow and utterly devoid of kindness. He took a step forward, coming to Rhiannon's side, and then gracefully lowered himself to one knee. There were fathomless secrets behind the storm clouds of those eyes. Michael experienced the terrible urge to rip them out of his head and pop them between his teeth like caviar.

But his life was slipping through his fingers – through the fervent, white-knuckled grip he had on his archess's shirt. 'Please,' he added. There was no pride here. Not for him. Not anymore.

Samael held his gaze for a moment longer, and then he cocked his handsome head to one side. The steel of his eyes glinted in the moonlight. 'There's a price, Michael,' he said. 'But you knew that, didn't you?' His smile seemed almost sad now. 'Nothing in life is free.'

Michael's blue eyes went to ice. Fury and helplessness warred within him. Neither he nor Sam was under any illusion. They both knew that Michael's consent to do whatever the Fallen One asked had really been given the moment Sam appeared on the scene.

Samael placed his hand to the archess's chest, and the breath stilled in Michael's lungs. Sam's gaze cut to him again.

'Now then, Warrior Archangel,' Sam said, his words dripping with the triumph the implied vengeance of this long-awaited moment symbolized. 'What is she worth to you?'

# Messenger's Angel

## Heather Killough-Walden

After spending an eternity walking the earth in search of their lost soul mates, four archangels are about to learn that finding their archesses is only the first harrowing step to claiming their souls.

Juliette Anderson has recently begun to fear for her sanity as inexplicable, and apparently supernatural, powers take hold of her life. Offered the opportunity to work in a beautiful country which has always fascinated her, she accepts, desperate for escape.

Gabriel, the Messenger Archangel, has always called Scotland his true home. Nevertheless, he is stunned when his archess suddenly appears, after centuries of searching, in the land closest to his heart.

Juliette's encounter with the gorgeous silver-eyed stranger changes their worlds for ever. But even as they find each other, enemies – old and new – surround them. With danger closing in, they will have one chance to fulfil a destiny written for them in the stars . . .

Praise for *Avenger's Angel*:

'Good story pacing, believable characters and sizzling sex add up to an author and a series to watch!' *Romantic Times*

978 0 7553 8041 1

## headline